Donna Wichelman

pure pleasure. This is a must-read if you are looking for a love story that reminds us that love conquers all. The Author combines history, romance, and adventure in one tightly woven story that is sure to delight.

— JANE M. CHOATE—PUBLISHERS
WEEKLY BEST-SELLERS LIST FOR HER
LOVE INSPIRED SUSPENSE, *SECRETS
FROM THE PAST,* AND *ROCKY MOUNTAIN
VENDETTA.*

In *Song of Deliverance,* Donna Wichelman weaves intrigue and faith to create a touching romance set during a most turbulent time. Her lyrical prose and vivid description transport you to the rugged 1872 mining town of Georgetown, Colorado, where Anna and Stefan navigate the complexities of loss and suspicion over a tragic mining accident. As the mystery of the mine collapse deepens, whispers of accusation grow louder, burying the truth of the disaster with each new revelation. An intriguing blend of history, romance, and mystery, *A Song of Deliverance* demonstrates the enduring power of hope and love in the face of adversity. A truly heartfelt read!

— AUDRA HARDERS, AUTHOR OF *ROCKY
MOUNTAIN HERO,* A LOVE INSPIRED
ROMANCE, AND THE CIRCLE D SERIES
BOOKS 1-3

Intrigue, danger, and loss blend with themes of forgiveness, hope, and love in this charming series starter from the lyrical pen of author Donna Wichelman, who transports readers to the Singing Silver Mine in the rugged Rocky Mountains of Colorado. It's a place where old-world opulence meets wild-west innovation, people from different backgrounds find opportunity, and communities come together after tragedy. The delightful cast of characters and detailed research serve to draw readers further into the story, and I'm confident *A Song of Deliverance* will resonate with fans of the genre.

— CANDEE FICK, EDITOR, WRITING COACH, AND AUTHOR OF THE *WITHIN THE CASTLE GATES* SERIES

A Song of Deliverance weaves together a love story between a man and a woman from two different cultures, antagonists for generations: a poor Irish lass and a rich English mining mogul. The catastrophic aspects of mining and the greed of its mine owners drive this story forward. Bringing lighthearted relief through her characters, the Author shares a unique historical perspective gained through her rich research and travels. Bravo!

— RUTH TRIPPY, AWARD-WINNING AUTHOR OF *THE SOUL OF THE ROSE* AND OTHER HISTORICAL ROMANCE NOVELS

This novel shines from impeccable research. Without needless description, rich historical details transport the reader to life in a Colorado mining town in the 1870s. Vivid characters keep the pages turning fast. It's a sweet romance laced with faith, action, and mystery. A lovely book from start to finish!

— GRETCHEN CARLSON, AUTHOR OF THE
AWARD-WINNING YOUNG ADULT
HISTORICAL NOVEL, *MORE THAN GRIT*

Wichelman delivers a story set in the mining world that is rarely explored with such depth of research. Readers will appreciate Wichelman's attention to detail and story where the hurts of the past meet the tragedy of the present with a heart for community and hope for a better future. Definitely check out this beautiful reflection of God's love and provision during unexpected and difficult times as soon as possible.

— CRYSTAL CAUDILL, AUTHOR OF
COUNTERFEIT LOVE

Most folks say history is boring, but this book will prove them wrong. The Author weaves an intriguing tale set in a mining town in Colorado, combining local details, historical settings, faith, suspense and romance, and weaves a tale you won't want to put down. Highly recommended.

— DONNA SCHLACHTER, HISTORICAL
MYSTERY AUTHOR

a Song of Deliverance

Donna Wichelman

Scrivenings
PRESS
Quench your thirst for story.
www.ScriveningsPress.com

Published by Scrivenings Press LLC
15 Lucky Lane
Morrilton, Arkansas 72110
https://ScriveningsPress.com

Printed in the United States of America

Paperback ISBN 978-1-64917-432-1

eBook ISBN 978-1-64917-433-8

Editors: Amy R. Anguish and Heidi Glick

Cover design by Linda Fulkerson - www.bookmarketinggraphics.com

All scriptures are taken from the KING JAMES VERSION (KJV): KING JAMES VERSION, public domain.

All characters are fictional, and any resemblance to real people, either factual or historical, is purely coincidental.

To anyone who has faced unexpected tragedy and found the courage to trust God even in the most profoundly difficult circumstances:

May the God of Hope fill you with all joy and peace in believing, so that by the power of the Holy Spirit, you may abound in hope. (Romans 15:13 ESV)

One

Georgetown, Colorado
October 1872

Was this to be the day Anna Katherine O'Sullivan would die?

Anna grabbed the handle hanging from the ceiling with one hand and clasped the leather satchel in her lap with the other, closing her eyes against the thunderous stampede of the stagecoach's six horses dashing around another bluff. Ach, the drivers of these western territories certainly lived up to their reputation of the wild west. The reckless haste left her breathless and gasping for air. Who would care for her Uncle Liam's day-to-day affairs if she perished? Her now-deceased aunt had counted on her to arrive in one piece.

"Lord, preserve us," she prayed under her breath.

For six months, Anna had anticipated her new life in America. She didn't fancy her body mangled in the twisted wood and metal of the stagecoach at the bottom of the Clear

Creek Gorge without having had the chance to find the prosperity she'd been offered.

The coach straightened and slowed as it ascended another incline. Anna released the handle, fixing her gaze on the sleeping derelict across from her. He snorted and sputtered like a broken steam engine. Considering the jostling of the stagecoach, it was mystifying how he didn't awaken from his slumber.

Perhaps the man was too intoxicated to notice. His tanned, bearded face, tattered coat, and dark curly hair peeking out from under a bowler reminded her of the poor Irish famine folk like her parents had once been back in Ireland. Was he one of the mining prospectors she'd heard about—the homeless wanderers who tramped about the hillsides hoping to strike a gold or silver lode and make it rich? By all appearances, luck had escaped his grasp.

The stagecoach rounded another bend at breakneck speed, and Anna's satchel flew to the floor, landing near the sleeping giant. The noise should have roused him, but he still slept.

Anna attempted to reach for her bag, but before she could grab the satchel's handle, the coach rounded another curve, knocking her off the seat and propelling her luggage farther under the man's extended legs. How was she to retrieve her satchel without disturbing him?

"Ach, what a nuisance." She blew away a stray amber lock that loosened from under her straw hat. "It's devilment, that's what it is." She would have to employ the stealth of a cat on the prowl to get to the bag.

She maneuvered her body and stretched her arm under the seat, careful not to touch the man's legs.

"What do you think you're doing?" A hand grasped her shoulder.

Anna snatched her hand away, fear rattling her bones at

the sound of the man's stern voice. Well, this was a fine kettle of fish. She couldn't blame him if he suspected her of attempting to steal his wallet and wanted to boil her in the pot.

"My bag has landed under your seat, sir. If you would allow me to fetch it, I—"

Immediately, he released her shoulder and adjusted his legs. Reaching under the seat, he laid hold of her bag and handed it to her. "Madam."

She stared at the man's hand. Why did a poor prospector have a signet ring displaying a coat of arms on his left little finger? Only men of high social standing among the European rich wore such rings.

"Madam?" He surveyed Anna with unabashed amusement around his eyes.

She squirmed under his scrutiny and grabbed the pouch from him. This derelict wasn't drunk at all. His eyes were too bright, his disposition too much in control. But why did he smell as if Irish whiskey oozed from his pores?

"Thank you." Anna tried to be gracious. "Though you might have told me you were awake."

"But then, I wouldn't have had the pleasure of watching you go through all those contortions." He spoke in the Queen's English, smirking.

Anna scrambled back to her seat and placed the satchel on her lap. "And you being the gentlemanly sort, I suppose." She tucked stray curls underneath her hat and squared her shoulders to save her dignity. Of course, the man would have to be an Englishman and an educated one at that.

He shrugged, averting his eyes, which was just as well. Anna wasn't sure she wanted to carry on a long conversation with him, whoever he was.

Opening her leather pouch, Anna rummaged for her gold

pocket watch—the only item of Da's she'd kept—and checked the time. Two-fifty. She snapped the lid shut, thankful it wouldn't be long before the stagecoach pulled into Georgetown.

Though Anna regretted Aunt Caitlin's death, she was eager to reunite with an uncle she hadn't seen since childhood.

She turned her head to peer out the window at the narrow canyon and pressed her lips. These mountains didn't appear at all like the ones on the miniature painting she carried in her satchel. The watercolor her uncle had sent to entice Anna to the Territory of Colorado depicted hillsides covered with forests and a radiant sun shining over grand peaks. But as she strained her neck upwards, the canyon was shrouded in shadows, and scant dark pines struggled for survival on granite walls whose apex was rocky and barren.

A chill coursed through Anna's bones in the thin mountain air. What she wouldn't do for a steaming hot cup of tea and crumpets. She drew her woolen travel cloak tighter about her.

It wasn't that Anna wasn't grateful for the opportunity to live in America. But she missed the undulating hills of her homeland carpeted in emerald grasses and the roaring ocean that crashed against her rugged Irish shoreline. The highest mountain in Ireland was in her own County Kerry, rising thirty-four hundred feet. She'd always believed its green and golden slopes inspired the kind of awe only due to the Creator —a magical, mystical place where rainbows streaked the skies with brilliant color. Seamus used to say the rainbows were God's playful promise the world would persist through the ages, just like their love.

But today, no rainbows brushed the sky. And like the mighty winds that swept across the hills and changed the landscape in County Kerry, she could not alter the forces of change at work in her new world.

4

Seamus was half a world away. Her heart ached for him, and her lips burned for his kisses. But it was no use regretting how things had turned out between them. Hadn't the Irish system of land-holding and the English policies that fueled it favored the moneyed class, making her future in Ireland impossible? She'd made her bed. It was time to focus on what lay ahead in this new land.

"You're Irish."

"Yes, but—"

"It was how you said, 'thank you.'" He pronounced the word *tank* and then added, "And you drop the g on many of your words that end in *ing,*" he said with an offhand wave. It put Anna on edge. He didn't have to be so cheeky.

"And you're an Englishman," she announced, sitting straighter, poking her nose skyward. "Though I can't place the particular region." She pondered the notion without his response. "No matter, you're all alike, you Englishmen—running about like you own the world."

"That's because we do." He stretched his legs again, taking up space.

"Ha! I seem to remember you lost America over a simple thing. Tea, wasn't it?" Anna bit back. "At least the Americans had the good sense to throw you out on your bums rather than give in to a life of poverty on the streets with no opportunity to earn a decent living. I should think you Englishmen—"

"Georgetown." Anna heard the driver's voice through the window and looked out.

The coach slowly turned left, and the horses' hooves clomped across a narrow wooden bridge over the trickling Clear Creek. Her heart hiccupped as if she'd inhaled too fast.

"Are you all right? You look a little piqued."

Anna's gaze shifted back to the Englishman. Was that genuine concern he voiced? The English had only ever fretted about their vast estate holdings in Ireland and made their money on the backs of the people who'd suffered more than their fair share.

"A bit nervous, I should think." She averted her eyes. "I was two the last time I saw my uncle—barely old enough to remember him. Ma used to say my aunt and uncle were as sweet as the sticky toffee pudding we ate for Christmas dinner and as welcoming as a summer breeze."

"Then it seems you should receive a warm welcome."

Anna met his focused gaze. "I understand my uncle makes a good living as a miner. He assured me I would find much to my liking in this growing cosmopolitan community ..." Her voice drifted off as the coach turned onto a dusty road.

Anna's jaw dropped as they drove past a business district with little more than two blocks of rustic clapboard buildings and storefronts—a general store, a bakery, one two-story brick building, and one under construction—not quite the metropolis her aunt and uncle had described.

"I'm afraid your uncle has overstated the case a bit." The Englishman's dry tone suggested he had read her mind.

She surveyed him again. Who was this gentleman who spoke like a proper Englishman but looked and stank like he had stepped out of a bog? "I'm sure there must be hidden treasures here if my aunt loved it so much ..."

The stagecoach made another left, the horses' hooves clopping up a gentle incline past several more clapboard buildings. "Whoa!" the stagecoach driver commanded the horses. "Barton House."

Anna leaned forward, twisting her head and fixing her eyes on the extensive white, two-story inn as the stagecoach rocked, then came to rest. All went silent, and Anna held her breath until the door flung open and banged the coach's exterior. "End of the line." Anna stared at the buckskin-clad driver. Was her month-long journey really at an end?

"Any day now would suffice, madam." The Englishman spoke dryly.

Anna shifted her gaze to the Englishman, suddenly aware of blocking the stagecoach doorway. "Of course." She gathered her leather bag and climbed out the open door, her feet hitting the dusty road.

The Englishman followed behind her. "I hope you find what you're looking for."

Anna turned, expecting a smirk, but was met instead with a grave expression around the man's eyes. She drew back slightly, licking her lips. "I believe I shall."

"I bid you adieu." He lifted his bowler and walked up the hill away from Barton House without retrieving any luggage from the back.

Anna furrowed her brow. Odd. The man had brought nothing with him. Who was he?

"Ma'am." The driver's voice startled her out of her reflections. He set her small trunk on the ground, then tread to the front of the coach, crawled atop the box, and tapped the whip to encourage the horses farther up the incline.

Anna's gaze followed the coach as it continued toward the south end of town, passing houses scattered along the road like dice thrown haphazardly here and there. She inhaled a quivering breath. Time to meet her uncle.

Anna searched north along the narrow thoroughfare of clapboard-constructed businesses. A wood-clad chapel sat on a small hill directly across from the inn. She looked for anyone resembling a short fifty-year-old balding Irishman with a cap walking the inclined road. But only a middle-aged woman with a straw hat carrying a fruit basket went by. The woman smiled, nodded briefly, and continued on her way.

Anna knitted her brow. She had wired Uncle Liam from Cheyenne three days ago with the date and time of her arrival.

A telegraph reply came back the following morning.

Excited for our reunion at last. Will meet the stagecoach at the Barton House on Thursday.

"Can I assist you with your luggage, ma'am?"

Anna jerked her head toward a bellhop, his welcoming smile an oasis from her qualms. "Thank you, no. I won't be staying at your fine hotel." She offered a wan smile. Hadn't he noticed her plain and simple dress, her dull and dingy shoes? She had come to America with little more than the few possessions in her small trunk and leather pouch. "But I am waiting for my uncle. He should be here soon ..." She peered up and down the street, her distress growing.

"We can send for your uncle. What's his name?" The bellhop seemed determined to help.

Anna would have liked to take him up on his offer, but she had so few funds to spare. "If you would be so kind as to direct me to—"

"Young man, I must have your attention." A man rapped his walking stick, his tone insolent, his accent foreign— German, perhaps.

Anna whirled around, only to be suddenly overcome with a compulsion to flee. The man wore the kind of top hat and frock coat given to men of the gentry. She'd encountered men like him in Ireland. Their cold eyes and dismissive posture revealed contempt as if she was no better than a waif on the street. Her gaze shifted to the lady on his arm, who appeared to have just stepped out of *Harper's Bazaar* and eyed Anna from head to toe with a superior gleam. Their kind couldn't bother with the likes of her but tossed a tuppence into a cup as if it exonerated them from responsibility.

She angled herself toward the bellhop, gazing at the couple out of the corner of her eye. She drew herself up. Let them think what they may. She'd come to America to improve her lot in life, and she wouldn't cow to the likes of them.

"A package for my friend should arrive within the hour." The German looked down his nose at the bellhop. "Please bring it to Miss Wagner's room as soon as it arrives." He nodded toward the woman.

"I'll be sure to deliver it myself." The young man's smile didn't reach his eyes. His apologetic gaze shifted back to Anna. "As I was saying—"

"And my associate, Peter Lehmann, will join me later this evening," the German continued, unaffected by the bellhop's dismissive manner. "Would you make sure you settle Mr. Lehmann comfortably in his room before he comes to dinner?"

"Yes, sir." This time, the bellhop's deadpan face could have killed the cat.

Anna twisted away to hide the giggle threatening to bubble to the surface. Once the couple moved on, she breathed a sigh of relief and joined the bellhop, examining the uppity pair as they climbed the three white-washed wooden steps under the portico and through the inn's French doors. "A bit brazen, isn't he?" She hoped never to encounter the German again.

"I'm sorry, ma'am. Some people have no manners." The bellhop's forehead creased.

Anna's eyes softened. The young man couldn't have been more than seventeen—still naïve and full of spunk. Blemishes marked his face. "Not to worry. You did nothing wrong."

"No, ma'am." His countenance hardened. "Still, there's no excuse for surliness, even if you are wealthier than most."

"You're a kind young man, Mr. ..."

"The name's Jake Sieger, ma'am."

"Well, all right, Mr. Sieger. I appreciate you coming to my defense, but ..." She looked down at her modest clothes. "I would be grateful if you could show me the way to Liam O'Hallisey's residence. I can walk from here."

He raised a fisted hand to his lips, his eyebrows furrowing in concentration. After a moment, he waved his hand. "I'm sorry, ma'am. I'm not very good with names. We'll have to ask the innkeeper." He picked up her trunk and indicated the steps.

Anna hesitated. She'd meant to wait outside while the bellhop made inquiries, but he left her no choice. They climbed the steps onto the porch and through the French doors.

The delicious aromas of freshly baked bread and brewed coffee hit Anna at once with a painful awareness of the gnawing in her stomach. She hadn't eaten since breakfast at the coach station in Denver and had been looking forward to tea with her uncle. It seemed she'd have to wait a little longer.

Anna admired the lavish décor of the inn as she walked across the thick carpet to the reception area. The proprietor had spared no expense on fine woods of walnut and curled maple, Victorian wallpapers, and Venetian blinds. Walnut and leather chairs sat in a grouping near the lobby around a table strewn with newspapers. Ten feet away, a wide staircase of lush floral carpeting and white balusters led to the upper floor.

Anna's reluctance to approach the reception area returned, and she halted. Would everyone she met in this grand inn treat her with the same contempt the German had?

"Come on." The bellhop passed her from behind, still holding her trunk. "We don't put on airs here. You'll see. Mr. Tucker will be more than happy to help you."

Anna studied the middle-aged man behind the counter

with his graying hair and bushy sideburns. She inhaled and stood taller. What harm was it to ask a few questions?

The bellhop led the way and approached the desk, introducing them. "This lovely lady just arrived on the stagecoach."

"What can I do for you, ma'am?" Mr. Tucker leaned on one elbow and flashed a disarming smile.

Anna lowered her defenses and reached into her leather bag for the letter. "I'm looking for my Uncle Liam, you see. If you could tell me where I might find—"

"Well, I'll be." Mr. Tucker held up a hand, his face brightening even more. "You must be Caitlin's niece, Miss ..."

"Sullivan," Anna blurted out. She'd decided on the name change when the emigrant boat docked at Castle Garden, New York. Anna supposed her aunt might have disapproved, but she was gone now. The change seemed a way to simplify and get on with her new life. She hoped Uncle Liam would not argue against it. "Anna Sullivan."

"It's wonderful to make your acquaintance, Miss Sullivan." Mr. Tucker nodded his head. "Mr. O'Hallisey has been awaiting your arrival for days—couldn't stop talking about it— preparing like a parent buying gifts for his kids at Christmas time."

"You know my Uncle Liam, then." She leaned in with relief. "I was so afraid he had forgotten about me."

"I'm sure Mr. O'Hallisey will be along soon." Mr. Tucker spoke with a reassuring smile. "It's a fair trek from the mine back to town."

"I must say, I am relieved to hear it." Anna put her shoulders back.

"Can't say I blame Mr. O'Hallisey for being anxious about your arrival, though. He misses your aunt something fierce."

Mr. Tucker's brows furrowed. "It must have come as a shock to you, as well, thinking you'd be helping her with her sewing business."

"Yes, sir." Anna softened her gaze. She could see her aunt's death had made an impression on the clerk.

"Caitlin had a heart of gold—making clothes and not charging folks who couldn't afford them. And she had quite the reputation in these parts for her tailoring skills. Why, she used to make the finest women's clothes in the county."

Anna's spirit perked up. "Mum used to say Aunt Caitlin was the best dressmaker in the West of Ireland."

"It wasn't easy to get an appointment with her—always in high demand."

"That's grand. Perhaps I—"

"It *is* odd your uncle hasn't come for you, Miss Sullivan." Mr. Tucker frowned. He scribbled a message on a notepad, then called to the bellhop from the doorway. "Please dispatch a carriage directly to the mine." He handed the note to the young man.

"Oh, but I'm afraid I can't afford—"

"A pleasure to meet you, ma'am." The bellhop lifted his hat in salutation.

Anna caught her breath, a sudden pang of anxiety in her breast as she watched Jake head out the door. She worried her uncle wouldn't want to carry the expense of a carriage ride, and she had nothing to contribute. Well, there was nothing to do about it now.

"Nice young man." Mr. Tucker crossed his arms on the counter. "I imagine you must be hungry about now, Miss Sullivan. You're welcome to some refreshment in the dining room while you wait." He indicated toward the left.

The delectable smells wafting from the kitchen *did* entice Anna to satisfy her cravings. But how could she take advantage of the man's offer? She looked down at her travel clothes, the lack of refinement evident.

"Look, Miss Sullivan." He leaned in toward her with sympathetic eyes. "I dare say many folks come here in travel clothes as plain as yours. No shame in that. So, you go right on in there and have yourself a cup of coffee and a pastry." He nodded toward the dining room.

"But I—"

"You can leave your luggage here." He cut her off before she could protest. "And vittles are on me."

Anna inhaled, then smiled. "Well, then, I think I shall take you up on your fine offer."

Mr. Tucker emerged from behind the reception area through the side door and took Anna's luggage. She nodded her thanks and then headed toward the dining hall.

Then, as if a wind storm had descended, the inn's front door banged open, and heavy footfalls followed. Anna whipped around.

A gentleman in a bowler and another man in a cap and dusty workman's dungarees trailed him. "I understand Mr. Töpfer is meeting with several German scientists in this hotel. I need to speak with him immediately." He spoke with authority, his accent British like the man she'd met on the stagecoach.

"He's here, Mr. Chelsea." Mr. Tucker's voice registered with reluctance. "But Mr. Töpfer asked not to be disturbed."

"I believe Mr. Töpfer will make an exception when he hears a deadly incident has taken place at the Singing Silver Mine."

A deadly accident at the Singing Silver Mine? Her uncle worked there. Anna swallowed, her hunger fading. What if ...?

Mr. Tucker's eyes bulged. "I'll get him right away, sir." The clerk left the reception area and scurried up the staircase, leaving Mr. Chelsea waiting with hands dug deep in his pockets.

He whispered into the ear of the workman, who nodded and hurried to the main entrance.

A sense of urgency compelled Anna to approach the Englishman. "Mr. Chelsea."

The man spun on his heel, his curious eyes roving her over. "Have we met?" He frowned.

Heat crept up Anna's neck. She didn't mean to be impertinent, but she *had* to know. "Is it true? People have been hurt at your mine?" The words tumbled out.

"I have no information—"

"Please, sir," Anna pleaded. "My uncle is one of your miners."

Mr. Chelsea removed his hands from his pockets and rubbed his anguished eyes. "I didn't want to say—reporters from *The Colorado Miner*, you know. Newspapermen are always looking for the sensational angle." He straightened. "We won't know who or how many until we've assessed the situation, Miss ..." He acknowledged her for the first time.

"Anna Sullivan—just arrived from Ireland. I was to meet my uncle—Liam O'Hallisey." Driven by her distress, Anna acted against her sense of propriety. "Please, sir, I can see you have more than your fair share to deal with in these circumstances. But I must beg a ride to the mine."

Mr. Chelsea crossed his arms. "You understand we don't know yet the extent of what we're looking at, and it could be late into the night or even tomorrow before we learn anything." The gravity in his voice was palpable. He eyed the reception area, fingers drumming an elbow.

"No matter. I must support my uncle, you see."

Mr. Chelsea nodded and drew a breath through his

nostrils. "I'll take you with me as soon as I finish my business here. You'll have to—"

"What is this business about an incident at the Singing Silver Mine, Chelsea?" The same German voice that had interrupted her conversation with Jake Sieger bellowed.

Anna turned and saw the German approach. So, *this* was Mr. Töpfer. Her skin prickled, and she shivered.

"A *deadly* incident." Mr. Chelsea's eyes narrowed.

"What do I have to do with anything at your mine?" Mr. Töpfer scoffed, waving his hand. "The Singing Silver Mine is your providence. If anything sordid happened there, turn to your crew, not mine."

"Did I say sordid?" Mr. Chelsea raised his brows, his eyes steely and penetrating. "Mr. Maier requests your immediate presence."

"Look here, Chelsea. I have a delegation of men here for only a day of meetings. I will not be ordered—"

"I can take you in my carriage."

The two men locked eyes, and Mr. Töpfer's jaw muscles clenched. "That won't be necessary." The German walked away before Mr. Chelsea could respond.

Anna approached the miner, her leather bag dangling from one arm. "I admire your restraint, Mr. Chelsea. If it had been me, I would just as soon slug him as look at him."

Mr. Chelsea eyed her bag, a brief twisted smile appearing on his lips. "You give me more credit than I deserve, Miss Sullivan." His forehead creased. "Where is the rest of your baggage?"

"I've got it right here." Mr. Tucker spoke from behind the reception desk. "But you needn't concern yourself with your luggage, Miss Sullivan. It'll be safe with me behind that door." He indicated a storage room. "I can also take your satchel if you like."

Anna stared at nothing for a long moment. All her possessions were in her small trunk and satchel. What would she do if she lost them? But taking them into a chaotic situation didn't make sense either.

"All right, then, Mr. Tucker. I thank you for caring for my things." Anna handed him her bag, then turned to Mr. Chelsea. "I'm ready to go with you now."

Two

Stefan Maier leaned forward over his horse, his bowler pressed down as firmly as his thick curls would allow. Thankfully, the snow had remained at bay this year, so he didn't have to contend with pushing Sally through insurmountable drifts up to the mine.

He pushed Sally to her limits on the dry, dusty road up the hillside, squeezing hard with his legs against her ruddy, thoroughbred body. Though he carried a whip, Stefan had never slapped his horses with it since he was a boy, observing a merciless merchant in London's chaotic market district using the cruel instrument to control his horse. They had an understanding, Sally and him. Stefan would treat her with the gentleness deserving of a lady if she complied with his commands, and right now, he needed her to give all she could.

"Hah, hah." Desperate, Stefan shouted to Sally as they rounded a corner up an incline above the small mining camp of Silver Plume. "I know you've got it in you, girl." Sally whinnied in response—anguishing, it seemed—as if to say she was doing her best to go at breakneck speed to get him to his destination. "I know, girl. You can catch your breath when we get there."

Getting to the Singing Silver Mine in record time was imperative. Hurting people—the ones trapped inside the mine and those outside waiting for word of their loved ones—needed his and William's assurances that they would do everything humanly possible to rescue the men. No doubt, emotions rode high and were at peak levels. How many men had survived? That any of them should have died made Stefan want to vomit.

He had just arrived from Central City on the stagecoach, hurrying home to rid himself of his wretched clothes, when William Chelsea found him. Only Stefan's encounter with the Irish woman had provided a diversion from his troubles. He'd hoped to have a reprieve when he arrived in Georgetown, but it appeared that much-needed rest would have to wait.

William had given him a brief account of the disaster awaiting them at the mine. At first glance, the cage carrying the men into the belly of the mine broke from the hoist cable and plummeted to the bottom of the shaft. The domino effect was inevitable as timbered columns supporting the tunnel gave way and caved. They wouldn't know the extent of the damage or how many men had survived until they could get access to the bottom of the shaft, and that would take time—time they couldn't afford.

The timing of the disaster roused Stefan's suspicions. He instructed William to find Georg Töpfer and bring him to the mine, then rushed home, changed, and saddled Sally.

What would he find when he arrived? The priority was to rescue the men, but what about the condition of the mine? Men's incomes also depended upon output. How long would it take before he could repair and bring the work back to performance levels?

Though he owned several mines, this one was his baby—the first he had acquired after immigrating to the Territory of Colorado upon leaving England. It was also the one that gave up the most ore. But this crisis could change everything for his British-American Mining Company. Millions of dollars and pounds were at stake.

Stefan nudged Sally through the final hairpin turn, ascending the steepest incline to the more level ridge. At the top, he stopped.

Ahead of him, several dozen people milled about the property with its many clapboard and metal buildings. What concerned him most was the rectangular shaft house and cupola—a dome-like structure with a triangular apex over the headframe—where a cage had shuttled people and equipment up and down the now-damaged shaft.

Stefen set his lower jaw. He owed these people an explanation for why their loved ones were trapped at the bottom of the mine. If someone had mucked with his equipment, he would spend the rest of his days, if he had to, proving who had sent his men to their graves. But first, he had to face the crowd and do whatever it took to rescue those still alive in the belly of the earth.

He gave Sally a final squeeze and sent her barreling toward the shaft house and the people who had every right to question his integrity.

"Whoa." Stefan reined in Sally at the front of the shaft house, where a crowd gathered upon his approach. He leaped off his horse and handed the reins to an assistant.

Stefan turned to the men and women who had assembled. People often called him insensitive, saying his upper-crust wealth kept him removed from the plight of the common folk. But today, walking among them, fingering the signet ring on his right hand, he assessed the melancholy air and knew they looked to him for answers—answers he still didn't have.

"Are you going to get our boys out of there, Mr. Maier?" An elderly, balding man in tattered trousers and suspenders shouted from the crowd.

"I'm going to make every effort to bring our men up, Mr. Stokes," Stefan yelled back, shaking his head. "But I won't insult your intelligence with a lie. I can't promise every man will be brought up alive." Tall as he was, he peered above most heads and addressed them. "Pray—that's what we all must do. If anything will work, it's calling on the Almighty for help in our need. God willing, we'll secure the lives of your loved ones."

He pushed through the murmuring crowd, paying little heed to their remaining questions. It wasn't that he was unwilling. He just had nothing else with which to comfort them. And with that awful dilemma, he entered the shaft house, ready or not to take on the task of bringing up the men, dead or alive.

Anna twisted her head toward Mr. Chelsea. He brooded in a way that forbade discussion as he commanded his two horses to take the carriage up the incline along the Clear Creek. Anna didn't mind the silence. Her heart reached out to the families whose husbands and sons may have died in the mine, and she anxiously awaited the fate of her uncle—a man she had only met as a small child. All that death and sorrow, and what would she do if her uncle was among the dead?

Mr. Chelsea clucked his tongue and reined the horses away from the river and up a slope. Halfway up the hill, a consistent beating of horses' hooves grew increasingly louder. Anna twisted around. Another carriage with four horses came up from behind, gaining ground and overtaking them quickly, nearly running them off the road.

"See you at the top, Chelsea—that is, if your two horses can make it up the mountain." Mr. Töpfer tipped his bowler and spewed a maniacal laugh as he passed.

"Exhibitionist," Mr. Chelsea spit out, taking control of the reins to keep the horses steady. "The man would sell his mother's soul to win an advantage." Mr. Chelsea's sarcasm left Anna in little doubt about his disdain.

She returned a nod. "Ach, I suspected as much during my short encounter with him."

"You've talked to Mr. Töpfer?" Mr. Chelsea gave her a sidelong glance.

"We never exchanged words." Anna shook her head. "But his true colors came through by his abuse of the bellhop at the Barton House."

"I'm not surprised." Mr. Chelsea smiled wryly. "Töpfer turns on the charm when it suits him, but his tactics are brutal. My partner, Stefan Maier, despises him even more than I do."

"Understandable, I should think." If Anna's experience was any measure to go by.

"He has an absentee associate, Mr. Peter Lehmann, who spends most of his time in Denver employed at his father's bank. Mr. Lehmann seems more reasonable, but I couldn't say with certainty since I've had fewer dealings with him. I'd stay far away from the whole lot if you can." Mr. Chelsea clucked his tongue to motivate the horses to pick up their pace.

"I assure you, I have little desire to associate with Mr. Töpfer." Still, Anna couldn't shake the foreboding that she would not escape the man's company in this small community. "What about your partner?"

Mr. Chelsea studied her, then turned his head back to the

road before answering. "You don't become a successful entrepreneur without a competitive spirit. But you won't find anyone with more integrity. He and I will do everything we can to rescue your uncle."

Mr. Chelsea's apparent sincerity comforted Anna about the scruples of the owners of the Singing Silver Mine. She bit her bottom lip. The uncertainty about her uncle's fate still unnerved her.

A short while later, they turned onto a steeper road that traversed the bare hillsides. "What has happened to all the trees on these mountains?"

"Logging, ma'am. These hillsides used to be thick with pine forests." He waved his hand. "But they've been cut down to provide housing for the miners and businesses supporting them."

"A shame." Anna reflected on the watercolor in her satchel back at the Barton House. Indeed, people needed a place to live and fuel to heat their homes, but perhaps a few more trees would make the mountains appear more hospitable.

A sudden burst of burnt-orange sun glowed in the western sky as they climbed higher, but its appearance over the crest couldn't stave off the shiver that crept up her spine as the crisp wind blew across their path. How strange this thin mountain air was.

At the next hairpin turn, the carriage's two horses bucked the steep grade, and Mr. Chelsea had to lash the reins to coax them forward. When they finally reached the top of the ridge, they passed a rare grove of pines to their right, sheltering a two-story log house. The rest of the land had been cleared to make room for the business structures of the Singing Silver Mine.

Several dozen men and women tramped about the property, the distress in their eyes arresting—a telltale sign they feared for the fate of their loved ones. Anna's stomach churned. Would her uncle be among the living or the dead?

"Whoa." Mr. Chelsea brought the carriage to a standstill a small distance from the structures and looked at her. "I pray your uncle is …" He moved his lower jaw, but it seemed he couldn't get out the words he wanted to say. He turned face-forward.

Anna placed a hand on his arm. "Thank you, Mr. Chelsea. I will never forget your kindness."

She rose and jumped out of the carriage to join the throng milling about the mining camp. What would she find waiting for her here amid the people whose names and faces were unknown to her but whose lives hung just as much in the balance as hers? She dreaded what the next hours or even days would bring.

Three

Anxiety hovered over the Singing Silver Mine's property as Anna strolled the grounds and searched the sea of worried faces. She brushed loose locks under her straw hat, feeling out of place—a stranger and alone among the families huddled together.

Anna desperately prayed her uncle would be among the survivors. Though she didn't really know her aunt and uncle, except for the letters from America and stories her Ma had shared of their childhood exploits, Anna had been wholly surprised and significantly moved they'd provided an opportunity to come here.

"Pardon me, miss. Can I be of help?" A gentle feminine voice spoke from behind.

Anna whirled to find a woman who appeared to be in her mid-fifties, her graying chestnut hair swept into a chignon. The woman wore a black cloak trimmed with fur the color of pewter over a bustled dress. The cloak's hood hung down her back.

"I …" Anna fumbled. Not usually given to lack of words, how did she begin explaining how the woman could help?

"I'm Laurel Thomas." The woman smiled kindly, her brown eyes crinkling with crow's feet. "My husband and I want to help if we can. That's my husband over there." She pointed.

Anna twisted toward a middle-aged man with long sideburns, wearing a long, dark frock coat and trousers. He held a Bible in one hand while speaking to a mother and two school-age children near a megalithic pile of rocks. "You're a preacher's wife."

"Indeed." Mrs. Thomas waved a hand. "And you are …?"

Anna turned back to Mrs. Thomas's searching gaze. "Anna Sullivan, ma'am. Liam and Caitlin O'Hallisey are—that is, *were* my aunt and uncle."

"Of course." Mrs. Thomas's eyes glowed. "I see the resemblance."

A spark of hope ignited in Anna's chest. "You knew my aunt, then."

"Caitlin and I were the best of friends." Mrs. Thomas's words hummed with warmth and cordiality. "You look just like her with your fair Irish complexion and amber curls—a rare beauty—inside and out."

Anna's chin dipped, then up again. "Thank you, ma'am."

"Your aunt couldn't stop talking about you—so thrilled that you'd decided to join them here in Georgetown."

"And I was just as eager." Though nothing had turned out how as it was supposed to.

"It must have been difficult to receive news Caitlin had died."

"I almost didn't come." Anna averted her eyes.

Anna recalled the day the letter arrived. She had argued with Seamus—a row that had played in her mind a thousand times since. *"We both know your parents won't approve of a marriage between us."*

"I'll tell them—"

"Tell them what? That you love a poor peasant girl with no dowry, nothing to offer to enhance your financial holdings? They'd put you out to pasture with the sheep until you got some sense about you." If only she hadn't allowed pride to get in the way of love.

Anna shifted her gaze back to Mrs. Thomas. "But there was nothing left for me in Dingle after Da died, and Uncle Liam implored me to come."

"Liam was relieved. He thought you might back out, not wanting to care for a poor widower you didn't know or take on Caitlin's sewing business—" Mrs. Thomas stopped mid-sentence. "But how did you come to be here at the mine?"

"I was waiting for my uncle when the news came to Barton House just after I arrived." Anna glanced past Mrs. Thomas at Mr. Chelsea near the shaft house, distracted by the men gathered near the entrance door on the short side of the shaft house. "I begged a ride to get here."

One man headed away from the others, leaving Mr. Chelsea with Mr. Töpfer holding a piece of timber. A fourth man, taller than the others with dark hair curling under his soft-brimmed hat, appeared angry, pointing at Mr. Töpfer, then at the shaft house. In sudden wild abandon, Töpfer hurled the timber and stomped away, rounding the corner of the building and out of sight. The two remaining men leered after him, the taller one with hands on his hips.

"That didn't go well, did it?" Anna's arms encircled her waist, disquiet settling over her soul. "How can any of it spell good for the miners?"

Mrs. Thomas placed a hand on Anna's arm. "Take heart, my dear. You must believe that God will work out all things for the good. And who knows? Your uncle may still be alive, and all this," she waved her hand, "will have been a minor detour on your journey."

Anna stared vacantly for an overlong moment, struggling to hold on to hope. She needed to prepare for the worst if her uncle was dead. "It's hard to keep one's faith when all looks bleak, Mrs. Thomas."

Tender eyes met Anna's. "I understand. But I promise God hasn't abandoned you." Mrs. Thomas removed her hand.

Anna's cheeks burned. She hadn't meant to respond so tersely to the minister's wife. She cast Mrs. Thomas a wan smile. "You and your husband do a good thing here."

Mrs. Thomas averted her eyes briefly, then returned a compassionate gaze to Anna. "I should talk to the other families, but I'll be back to check on you later." Anna nodded, and Mrs. Thomas moved away to counsel another wife and her son nearby.

As twilight descended, the stars came out, and the temperatures plunged. Torches were lit across the property and along the canyon road.

Someone started a campfire, and Anna joined the sedate circle of people clustered together. Another good soul distributed tin bowls of soup provided by a local saloon in Georgetown. Anna welcomed the nourishment to fill her hungry belly, even if its temperature had gone tepid long before she'd had an opportunity to drink the broth.

Silence overshadowed the dismal mood for a time. Then, one man's voice broke out in mournful song. Anna recognized the Irish folk tune as one she'd heard among the working men of her village. The lyrics reflected the dangerous life of a miner. Memories of her homeland tugged the melody from her lips, and soon, others joined them. How could such sorrow and hope commingle?

Low voices rumbled around the circle after the song died

away. "How is it I hear such a song in this place?" Anna marveled aloud, the song igniting camaraderie with her kinsmen.

"There are plenty Irish in Georgetown, though not everyone appreciates the likes of us." A middle-aged gent leaned in next to her. "But we're good workers, and no one complains when the ale's flowin' and the fiddles are playin'. Then they'll be dancin' and frolickin' till midnight."

The Irishman dropped his g's as the man on the stagecoach had accused her of doing, and it suddenly struck Anna with how she and her kinfolk stood out. "That many?"

"Nigh to enough to establish a chapter of the Fenian Brothers in Georgetown." The Irishman tilted his head.

"It must be—"

"Mind if I join you?"

Anna peered up at the sound of Mrs. Thomas's voice above her. Her presence was a welcome surprise. "Please." Anna indicated a seat.

"Hello, Jim. How are you holding up?" Mrs. Thomas peered around Anna.

"I can't help fearing the worst. But it's what we signed up for in these mines, 'tisn't it?" He averted his eyes, stating the matter as a fact, then fixed his gaze on the preacher's wife.

Mrs. Thomas pressed her lips with a sympathetic nod, the silence settling between them like a sledgehammer, hitting them with the hard truth of a miner's life. She turned to Anna. "I saw you singing with the miners a little while ago. You have the voice of an angel like your Aunt Caitlin." Her eyes sparkled in the firelight.

"Music's in the Irish blood. It's a way of giving voice to our troubled hearts." She licked her lips, then twisted her body toward the woman. "I owe you an apology for being in a snit a while ago. I'm truly grateful for what you're trying to do."

Mrs. Thomas offered her a fading smile. "You wouldn't be human if you weren't emotionally overwrought, my dear. I've endured many a rankled spirit much worse than yours."

Relief flooded Anna's spirit. "I'm so glad you don't hold it against me. I couldn't bear it if—" She grabbed sudden hold of Mrs. Thomas's arm, mystified by the man approaching. He stopped only a few feet away. "Who is that man?"

Craning her neck, Mrs. Thomas looked to where Anna pointed. "That's Stefan Maier, one of the two men who own the Singing Silver Mine. The other is Mr. Chelsea, whom you've met. My husband has very high regard for Mr. Maier." Mrs. Thomas's bit her lip. "Though he must be beside himself."

Anna focused on Mr. Maier. In the dim light of the surrounding torches, he resembled the man from the stagecoach. But how could that be?

She *had,* at first, mistaken the man in the stagecoach as a derelict. She leaned forward. This man appeared refined, tall, and handsome, his strong bearded jaw jutting out—in charge. But then, hadn't that also been true of the man on the stagecoach if she looked past his disheveled appearance?

"Ladies and Gentlemen. Mr. Chelsea and I can't express enough of our sincerest sorrows for what has occurred at the Singing Silver Mine today." Anna listened to the strong voice that rang out across the valley. No doubt she'd heard it earlier in the day—a perfect English accent, not German as his name implied it should be. Another surprise. Though it seemed impossible, the man on the stagecoach, the tall man arguing near the shaft house, and this man speaking were all one and the same person. "We would like to tell you that all the men are safe and alive, but this would be wishful thinking."

A low rumble coursed through the crowd, and Mr. Maier waved his hands for quiet. "Shortly before nine this morning, the hoist cable attached to the cage in the shaft house failed."

He pointed toward the building where Anna had seen him arguing with Mr. Töpfer. "This caused the cage to crash to the bottom of the shaft with four men aboard."

"No, please, no." A frantic woman's voice reached Anna.

"As the cage fell, it picked up momentum and triggered the timbers undergirding the shaft to give way. We aren't entirely sure how much damage we'll find at the bottom nor how many additional men were trapped by the falling timbers.

"We will work through the night to secure a safe method to retrieve the men. We understand you're anxious to know if your loved one is alive. We simply cannot answer that question at this time. All we can do is ask for your patience and earnest prayers."

Another grumble chased through the assembly.

"I can tell you from experience," Mr. Maier spoke above the voices, "temperatures will continue to fall sharply on this mountain, and you will be in danger of frostbite if you remain. Bett's Boarding House is between those trees." He pointed to the stand of trees Anna had noticed when she'd arrived. "Bett can still take a few of the women. However, I encourage the rest of you to return home for the night."

"What if it were your son whose life was on the line, Mr. Maier?" One man shouted. "Would you abandon him to the mountain?"

Mr. Maier directed pain-ridden eyes at the man, then lumbered off toward the shaft house, his shoulders bent as if he carried so great a load of bricks they might crush him.

Anna had difficulty reconciling this Stefan Maier with the derelict she'd met on the stagecoach. That man had been abrupt and rude—someone who appeared down on his luck. This man seemed grieved—a person depleted by tragedy. Still, they were the same man, and both versions resembled a man broken and bruised. Anna furrowed her brow, her heart reaching out to him. Perhaps she had misjudged him.

"*Fräulein.*"

Anna peered up into the kindly face of a stocky woman with wisps of gray hair falling out of a bun at the top of her head.

"Anna, this is Mrs. Mueller, owner of the boarding house." Mrs. Thomas stood, and Anna followed.

"*Bitte,* call me Bett. Everyone does." The German woman offered. "Mr. Maier has asked me to take good care of you for the night."

"Mr. Maier?" Anna blurted. "B-but why me?" After all, didn't he have more immediate families to worry about?

"Go on." Mrs. Thomas coaxed. "I'm sure Mr. Maier had good reason. You'll be warmer in Mrs. Mueller's little cabin than out in the open."

"He seemed very insistent." The German woman acquiesced with uplifted brows.

"Well, all right, then." Anna turned to Mrs. Thomas. She hesitated, then hugged her at the last moment. "Thanks for everything."

"Try to get some sleep." Mrs. Thomas released her. "You'll need it for tomorrow."

Anna nodded and followed Bett through a stand of trees to the log cabin. They stepped through a threshold into a rustic room, and Bett pointed to the cramped area near a young mother and toddler son, both in ragged clothes. "Nina, this is Anna. She's joining us tonight, waiting for news about her uncle."

"Please to meet you, Nina. And who is this sweet boy?" Anna softened her words.

Nina's frightened eyes angled up at Anna from bare planks. She placed a protective arm around her child, her body curling and taking up less space, if that was possible. Anna had seen homeless folk like her in the streets of Dingle. Many poor in Ireland preferred to stay invisible, anonymous, and undercover. But Anna couldn't judge them. It kept them safe.

"As I said, it's not much." Bett handed Anna a bedroll.

"Ach, but 'tis a fair more than I thought I'd have just a while ago." Anna smiled, grateful for the small comfort, and accepted the woolen tartan blanket. "Though I still don't understand why Mr. Maier should single me out among the other families here."

"Perhaps you should not question it." Bett's countenance became thoughtful. "Just accept his generosity at face value."

Anna nodded, inhaling deeply. "I think I shall rest better now."

"*Gut.* There'll be coffee and bread for you in the morning." Bett headed away.

Anna unrolled and covered herself with the blanket. She was grateful for a place to lay her head, but a dullness of heart overcame her, and a tear rolled down her cheek. Truth be known, she wished she was anywhere but here in this barren place, carrying a burden too heavy to bear. What would tomorrow bring? And what would become of her if Uncle Liam was dead?

The smell of burning wood and brewing coffee woke Anna from a fitful slumber. Between the hard plank floor of the boarding house and the single blanket Bett had given her, she couldn't stop shivering through the night.

Anna poked her nose above the wool blanket and noticed the warmth in the air—most likely from the fireplace ablaze in the next room. The sun also streaked through the windows, throwing shadows from the outside lodgepole pines. She hoped the sun's rays bode well for a day that would be better than yesterday.

She disentangled herself from the bedroll and scrambled to her feet, surveying the primitive space. Curious. Where were Nina and her child? She heard a mixture of male and female voices coming from somewhere else in the boarding house. Perhaps they had gone in search of coffee.

"Morgan." Bett nearly bumped into Anna as she entered. The German woman carried a metal tray with a tin cup of black coffee and two slices of buttered white bread piled on a plate. She set the tray on a nearby table. "Now, I know you want news of Mr. O'Hallisey, but it will do you no good if you faint from hunger." She handed the cup to Anna.

Anna sipped the acrid brew and winced. The penchant for coffee in this country—especially black-like-mud coffee—eluded her. Ach, but she must be thankful for how it warmed her insides. "Have you seen Nina and her child?"

"Nein. They were already gone when I peeked in on you earlier."

Anna sipped her coffee, wishing she could have bridged the silence between the woman and herself. "Have you heard anything?" She ventured the question with hope in her voice.

A sorrowful expression crossed Bett's face. "I'm sorry, dear. Nothing." Anna nodded, a heaviness in her chest. "It's in the Lord's hands now." Bett left to finish her breakfast rounds.

Anna's heart pounded. How much longer would they have to wait? She set the plate of uneaten bread and the half-drunk cup of coffee on a nearby table and donned her cloak. It was time to head back to the camp.

Pushing the door open into the crisp mountain air, Anna buttoned her cloak and set off. The trek through the trees seemed onerous, like taking steps toward a guillotine. As she came into the open, she peered around. Neither the preacher nor Mrs. Thomas was in view. They likely had gone home and hadn't returned yet.

Men and women roamed about or sat dazed on logs around the smoldering embers of last night's campfire. Most looked haggard and worn. Anna didn't want to think about how she might appear in her days' old clothes. She probably stank like a skunk as well.

Had Mr. Maier and Mr. Chelsea made progress rescuing the men below the earth? Could any of them have survived the night trapped in their dank tomb?

Feeling chilled, Anna looked about the campfire for kindling and found some small logs nearby to lay on the smoldering embers. She fanned the embers, but the fire wouldn't light. "Ohhhh." She brushed unruly strands of her hair from her face.

"Perhaps you should give the job to someone who knows how to start a fire." The wry tone Anna heard before irritated her like a mosquito bite.

Anna spun around. "What are you doing here?"

Mr. Maier stood before her in dark, dirtied trousers, a shadow crossing his face. "I needed to take a break for a few minutes." He rubbed his forehead.

Anna shrank back, immediately sorry for sounding so harsh. What was it about this man that seemed to get her dander up? "Well, if someone had been tending the fire, I wouldn't have had to take matters into my own hands."

"Touché, Miss Sullivan." Mr. Maier reached into his pocket for a small metal box with a screw attached at the end. He squatted, opened the hinged part of the lighter, and popped the screw with his thumb. A stench of rotten eggs permeated the air before the fire sparked in the small hole.

Mr. Maier's focused attention gave Anna a chance to study

him. Dark circles rimmed his eyes, and his face looked gaunt. A lump formed at the back of Anna's throat. She shouldn't have been so hard on him. A bit of compassion would have been better than a slick tongue.

The wood burst into flame a moment later, and Mr. Maier rose. "That should provide enough warmth until the sun rises higher in the sky." He walked away, then turned. "By the way, you have a lovely voice, Miss Sullivan."

Anna stared and blinked as he paraded away. So, Mr. Maier had heard her singing with the Irishmen. She shifted her stance, off-balanced by the knowledge he'd been in their midst, watching her. The man was full of surprises.

"Mr. Maier." She sprinted after him.

He halted in his tracks and turned.

"I ..." The pain behind his eyes arrested her. She hadn't expected to see the raw emotion. Guilt reared up inside. She needed to apologize for a second time in less than twenty-four hours. "About what I said—"

"We're all under a lot of strain, Miss Sullivan."

"I've been so anxious, you see ... I wonder ... how close ...?"

He put a hand out to steady her. "Close, very close—perhaps this morning." His touch had an unanticipated comforting effect on her despite the uncertainty of his words. "We're doing all we can." A fleeting smile crossed his face, and then he released her and retreated again.

"Mr. Maier." She called out, stopping him a third time. "Why did you keep your identity from me when we met on the stagecoach yesterday?"

"I never hid my identity from you, Miss Sullivan." His lips curved into a crooked smile, making his already-handsome appearance more appealing, even rakish. "You had already assumed my character. I just didn't correct it." He didn't wait for her response, leaving her mouth gaping, and hustled toward the shaft house.

Anna shook her head. It wouldn't do to waste time looking after the man just because he showed her a little compassion. She spun on her heel and walked back to the fire. On a whim, she twisted back in time to see him meet up with Mr. Chelsea at the shaft house and disappear inside.

"You've got gall. I'll say that for you." A woman no more than a few years older than Anna had inched closer to the fire. Wisps of sandy brown hair had loosened from her chignon.

"What do you mean?" The heat crawled up Anna's neck.

"Talking to that Mr. Maier."

"Ach, he's just a man."

"Mm-hmm. Just a man, but a rich one. I wouldn't get any ideas about him." The woman narrowed her eyes, making Anna squirm.

"Let me assure you I have no *ideas* about Mr. Maier." Anna leaned in.

"Just as well."

Anna wouldn't own up that perhaps she might fancy him too much, which would be a mistake. She'd allowed his momentary compassion to turn her gaze toward him. But the rich weren't to be trusted. She'd learned that from Seamus's family over the years. They'd never seen her as anything more than a dalliance for Seamus's amusement. But when it came to marriage, she hadn't been good enough for their son.

"Look." A boy of thirteen in overalls ran by her shouting.

Anna turned. The preacher and Mrs. Thomas were making their way up the road in a buggy followed by a canvas-covered wagon drawn by two horses. "What do you suppose they're up to?"

The boy ran toward the wagon, then turned, running

alongside to where it halted near their campfire. "Bread!" he shouted, and people crowded around.

"The Delmonico Bakery wagon." The woman next to her stood and followed the others.

Anna rose and walked to the wagon, aware of the gnaw of hunger and an empty stomach, and took her place in line. It seemed she'd done this all her life, begging on the streets of Dingle, waiting in queue for a bite of bread and a bowl of broth when she was barely old enough to understand a thing or two.

Those were the famine days her father had recounted to her many times—especially during his drunken stupors when he blamed the world for his lot in life. He'd claimed he had hunted for work, though the jobs were few and the pay even less while the wealthiest ate and drank and made merry in their comfortable homes. The rich couldn't be concerned about the men, women, and children dying on the streets just outside their windows or down the road in the workhouses. Why should they care? Their lives were not dependent upon the blighted potato.

Anna stepped forward and stretched out her hand.

"*Signorina.*" The middle-aged baker bent down to give her a bun. "There is water around back if you want it. And remember, we're praying for you."

"Thank you." Anna accepted the bun and choked, confused by the overwhelming kindness she'd received, even as a poor stranger. It stood in contrast to her father's bitter experience.

"You're welcome, *signorina.*" The baker gave her a sympathetic smile, and Anna slogged to the back of the wagon for the treasured water.

Anna trekked back toward the campfire with her cache but became distracted by the rare sound of laughter in their midst. She halted, sloshing water out of her cup, and spied three younger men near a lone pine, one sitting on a large boulder.

She recognized the man with disheveled, sandy blond hair who had run off from the shaft house the day before. He took a swig from a wine bottle and continued blathering on to his friends as if they hadn't a care in the world. Anna frowned. How could those men be so glib when everyone else around camp worried whether their son or husband was still alive? She moved on and found her place by the campfire, still dismayed by the brazen display.

"How do you fair this morning, Miss Sullivan?" Mrs. Thomas wore the same black cloak with pewter fur trim she'd worn the previous day.

Anna waved her bun toward the men and women around the campfire. "I suppose not much different than the rest of them."

Mrs. Thomas sat next to her. "What do you think of the bun?"

Anna nodded. "It's a fine thing they do, bringing food up to the folks this way."

"Good Christian people from Northern Italy—Piedmont region in the Italian Alps." Mrs. Thomas appeared to know them well. "It's what we do in Georgetown when there's a need."

Anna finished her bun, then slapped her hands together to remove the crumbs. "So different from—"

"They're bringing up the men." Multiple shouts seemed to come from everywhere across the property.

Anna perked up, her blood pulsing in her ears. Fear froze her where she sat. Was Uncle Liam alive or dead? She supposed it was better to know than not. But what would she do if he had succumbed in the mine?

A stampede of people headed for the shaft house, and Mrs. Thomas slid an arm through Anna's. "Come on." They shuffled with the rest.

The mob crowded the doorway. Heads wagged, trying to get a look inside the building. Anna stood in the middle of the pack, shoulder-to-shoulder with the rest.

"Please, everyone. Quiet." Mr. Chelsea's voice bellowed above the boisterous crowd.

The people went silent. Anna rose on her toes to see around them.

"Please move away from the door. We must have room to work." Mr. Chelsea's hands waved people back. A low rumble coursed through the gathering, but he forced them backward until he was outside the shaft house. "I know you're all anxious about your loved ones. You've had more patience than any man should expect. But we must ask for your patience a little longer. It may be hours before we have rescued all the men."

"But we've already waited so long." A woman called out in distraught.

"Yes, ma'am." Mr. Chelsea directed his gaze at her. "It's too dangerous inside the shaft to hurry the process." He addressed the assembly. "We'll bring up the men one by one until they're all accounted for. But please, for the safety of everyone present, stay your distance. We don't want to see anyone else get hurt. You may come to the door of the shaft house when you hear your loved one's name."

"But who are the survivors?" A man close to Anna shouted.

"We don't have enough information at this time to give you a proper report." Mr. Chelsea stared at his empty hands, then peered up at them again, the pain in his eyes palpable. They would have to bring up the dead as well as the living. "We'll let you know as we can." He went back into the building, leaving a mass of unhappy folk.

"Will you be all right for a bit?" Mrs. Thomas placed a hand on Anna's arm.

"Of course." Anna nodded, peering around. "They need you too."

"I'll be back as soon as I can." Mrs. Thomas squeezed her arm.

Anna dispersed with the rest and returned to her place near the fire. Others sat where they could—on logs, rocks, the ground. A few meandered about like people without a compass.

They waited for the next hour and a half, the tense atmosphere thick as fog.

"Claude Blaise!" someone shouted.

Despite Mr. Chelsea's warning, everyone rushed toward the shaft house. Anna joined them but kept her distance.

Mr. Chelsea appeared at the door, holding up one of the miners. Though dirtied and bruised, the man was nonetheless alive. "Glory be!" His wife gushed tears as she and her son rushed to the man, leading him away.

Mr. Chelsea turned to re-enter the building.

"You said you'd tell us who was still alive down there." Anger emanated from the man who had first questioned him earlier about the survivors. Anna scanned the assembly. Many called out and nodded their agreement.

Mr. Chelsea whirled. "I'm being as straight with you as I can. Unfortunately, Mr. Blaise couldn't tell us anything. He was separated from the others by the cave-in. I promise you'll be the first to know when we have better information." He walked back inside.

Anna studied the disgruntled men and women. It would be a long day.

By half-past one, three more miners had been retrieved alive. Calvin James had been the most recent to be led away by his family while the rest waited for word.

"Mr. Maier's come out to talk to us." The call came to

assemble for the fifth time that day, and everyone gathered *en masse* near the shaft house door.

Each of the other four times, Mr. Chelsea had brought out the surviving miner. Why did Mr. Maier appear this time unless ...? Anna swallowed, feeling the potato-size lump in her throat, her hopes fading for the first time since Mr. Blaise had come out. If Uncle Liam was alive, wouldn't they have known by now? Her spirits dwindled like the dying campfire.

"Ladies and Gentlemen ... I must inform you ... that is, we have been able to ascertain ..." Mr. Maier choked. His jaw clenched. In the end, he simply shook his head and cupped his mouth.

Tears stung Anna's eyes. Not another living soul would be forthcoming from the bowels of the earth. Uncle Liam was dead as sure as she drew breath.

A fracture formed like a gaping wound, renting her soul as horrifying howls and bloodcurdling shrieks from the families left behind ascended heavenward and echoed against the close mountains. The dark shadows of grief snuffed out the daylight like a candle snuffer extinguished a flame, and in the wake of the terror, Anna Sullivan was alone in the world once more.

Four

Anna drifted among the people still roaming the property. The dead lay lined up outside the shaft house, the nine white-linen-covered bodies appearing like ghosts, waiting to inhabit this desolate land.

An eerie, chilling silence had supplanted the shrieks of despair, giving Anna the impression she had joined the procession of the walking dead. A watery memory rose to the surface, haunting her past—recollections of the poor souls, like her parents, left behind after the famine took their kin.

"Miss Sullivan." A male voice startled Anna. She peered into the hollow eyes of Mr. Chelsea, telling the story of one who had been to Hades and back. "Please accept my sincere condolences. Your uncle's life was extinguished much too soon."

"Thank you, sir." She lowered her eyes, words failing her. Truth be told, Anna hadn't known either her aunt or uncle. She'd only had her dead ma's reflections to remember, but now even her ma's connection to the past was gone.

Mr. Chelsea nodded, his lips compressed. "Mr. Maier has

asked me to bring you to his office." He led her to a small outbuilding constructed of rustic timber and a slanted roof, where she entered a meager waiting area, sparsely furnished with two rickety wooden chairs. A shaft of light shone through a tiny window. Muffled voices came from a room down a short hallway.

Mr. Chelsea indicated a chair on the outside wall. "Please wait here." He walked down the corridor and entered an office. The voices grew louder, then muted as the door closed.

Anna sat on the edge of the chair, retreating into mental numbness as if she, too, had died. Occasionally, angry voices boom from the back. Peering around the room, she found a plat of the Singing Silver Mine property hanging on one wall and a card portrait of Georgetown hanging opposite.

She rose to get a closer view. She'd had no idea how immense the property was with its many outbuildings. But now, studying the plat, she gasped. A hundred and sixty acres. That was more than thirty times the land her father had once farmed in Ireland. Near the edge of the plat, a boundary line marked another property called the Mother Lode Mine.

A door opened, and Mr. Töpfer bellowed. "You know what you can do with your accusations, Maier."

Anna jumped and scurried back into the chair as the German bolted past. He threw open the outside door and slammed it behind him.

What had just happened? Anna bowed her head, eyes searching, vainly attempting to understand the climate she was walking into. Would she be the next one to receive the wrath of Stefan Maier? Surely not. After all, Mr. Töpfer had already proven himself to be a despicable man. What could Mr. Maier have against *her*?

"Miss Sullivan, please come with me?" Mr. Chelsea towered above her.

Anna leaped up and followed him down the hallway past a rack of keys and three modest offices until they came to the last one and entered. She stopped before a simple wood desk where Mr. Maier held a fountain pen, his eyes focused on a document. She stood with hands folded before him as plain as day, but he didn't acknowledge her presence.

The longer Mr. Maier kept her waiting, the more irritable Anna became. What had happened to the compassion he'd shown her yesterday? Her muscles quivered, but she would not be intimidated. Instead, she studied the stack of folders on one side of his desk and read the titles of the books piled on the other side. The books appeared to be academic texts about geology and mining. But it was the singular rock placed on the center of the desk that captured her attention most. She wanted to examine the shiny silver vein running through it more carefully.

"Please sit." He pointed to the two chairs before his desk without looking up. "I'll be with you in a moment."

"I prefer to stand if you don't mind." She wanted to leave with dignity if he intended to pack her off like a scullery maid to a grand house. Mr. Chelsea had begun to take a chair but remained standing after her response.

Mr. Maier looked up, his gaze roving over her. "Do what you will." He resumed writing, leaving Anna to observe the signet ring on the little finger of his left hand. Now that she knew who he was, she assumed the coat of arms represented his family heritage—most likely wealthy, aristocratic, and well beyond her means.

At last, Mr. Maier put aside his pen and rose. "I'll come straight to the point, Miss Sullivan. Your uncle has been leasing a house on the north side of Georgetown managed by the S & M Banking and Leasing Corporation. According to the lease agreement, if the paying tenant dies, the landlord has the right to terminate the contract at the time of death. You are, of course, entitled to his belongings but not to the rental property."

"But I ..." Anna shuddered, her shoulders drooping. She had no idea what personal belongings Liam and Caitlin had, nor did she understand what Mr. Maier expected of her if she knew. Penniless with no prospects for a job, where would she go?

"Mr. Chelsea spoke with Mr. Sieger earlier today." He pointed in his partner's direction, but his gaze avoided hers. "I suggested he might speak to you himself, but Mr. Sieger requested the Singing Silver Mine take care of initial business to set your expectations."

"Mr. Sieger?" The bellhop's father? "But ..." She straightened. A sudden dose of reality left a bitter taste like taking a teaspoon of ipecac soured her stomach. Of course. S stood for Sieger and M for Maier. "What sort of business?" Anna could only imagine, knowing what wealthy proprietors did to people in Ireland who couldn't pay the rent. Eviction without an ounce of compassion, regardless of their situation —that's what they did.

"I will be blunt, Miss Sullivan." Mr. Maier tapped the tips of his fingers on the desk. "While your uncle was alive, you had secure living arrangements as long as he worked for the Singing Silver Mine and could pay the rent. I might add that Mr. O'Hallisey did quite well on three dollars per day—a good wage for a miner. He told me recently that he'd saved enough to stake a claim on some property and planned to build after your arrival."

Anna looked at him wide-eyed. "My aunt and uncle didn't mention property in their letters—only that I had a home with them for as long as I wanted to stay."

"I see." He cleared his throat. "You'll want to look into the land. Meanwhile, you are entitled to their belongings but not their housing unless you have the means to pay for it."

Anna's mouth gaped. In one day, she had gone from having a family and a home to being orphaned and tossed onto the streets—no better than the beggar she had been in Ireland. Perhaps she hadn't misjudged Stefan Maier after all.

Anna brushed loose curls away from her face and bolstered herself. She might be homeless and destitute, but she had her pride. "I have no need of such things if I have no place to put them. And an empty plot of land is still an empty plot of land, Mr. Maier."

The man glanced at Mr. Chelsea before shifting his eyes back to Anna. "Should you refuse to claim your relatives' personal effects, the rental's owners have the right to put the estate up for auction and retain the collected balance."

"Then I am pressed to the wall, Mr. Maier. As you are aware, I only just arrived in Georgetown. Everything I own sits in a storage room at the Barton House."

"Not everything, Miss Sullivan." Mr. Maier spoke wryly.

"Until the S & M Banking and Leasing Corporation decides to auction my inheritance." She raised her eyebrows.

Mr. Maier exchanged glances with Mr. Chelsea a second time, and though slight, she detected a minute softening. "Mr. Chelsea and I understand these are tragic circumstances over which you had no control. Perhaps we can come up with a temporary solution."

"I'm listening."

"The Singing Silver Mine will uphold the contract through the end of the month. It's the least we can do for your uncle's loyalty to the company. That should give you time to make alternative arrangements."

Anna stewed. Her uncle had just died, and now it seemed she was indebted to Mr. Maier—a situation she would have preferred to avoid at all costs. She wanted to refuse his offer, even if it meant she would have to sleep on the road. But the prudent course was to accept his apparent generosity and enjoy some comfort before the inevitable occurred.

"It seems I have no options, Mr. Maier. I accept your offer."

"Very good." He turned over a sheet of paper. "Mr. Chelsea has a master key and will take you back to town to retrieve your belongings and settle you at your uncle's house."

The sun dipped low in the sky when Mr. Chelsea pulled his carriage in front of the Barton House. He helped her out of the buggy, and the bellhop flashed her a fleeting look of compassion before returning his attention to the current guest. Did he know about his father's part in evicting her from her aunt's home? Doubtful.

Anna and Mr. Chelsea followed a couple into the inn and waited as Mr. Tucker greeted them with the same winsome smile he'd given her the day before. Oh, to be one of those guests, oblivious to the hardships suffered in the cold, stark reality of the tragedy she'd endured. Like them, she'd had so much future to look forward to, but even with the lingering aroma of rosehips that followed the lady, Anna could not hide the smokey odor of the campfire on her dress.

After the couple moved away, she stepped forward, but Mr. Tucker scurried around the desk, mournful and misty-eyed, before she had a chance to speak. "You poor, dear girl. My condolences on your loss."

"Thank you, Mr. Tucker. But how—"

"The news spread like wildfire around town as soon as the survivors started coming down the mountain." He clasped his hands together. "It'll be front-page news in *The Colorado Miner* tomorrow." He glanced at Mr. Chelsea, then returned to his place behind the desk. "Will you need a place to stay for the night? It'll be on the house."

"You're very kind, Mr. Tucker, but no." She pressed her lips together. "If I may retrieve my belongings, sir."

"Of course." Mr. Tucker turned toward the storage room around the corner.

"Thank you for taking such good care of my things." Anna met him at the door, took her leather satchel, and allowed Mr. Chelsea to hold her trunk.

"Just glad I could oblige, Miss Sullivan." His compassion-filled eyes said everything. "Your aunt's passing left a big hole in this town. And now your uncle ... I suppose it's too soon to know what you'll be doing." He rubbed his bottom lip.

Anna twisted around to look at Mr. Chelsea. Dark shadows around his eyes made him appear weary and disengaged. She turned back. "I'll stay at my uncle's house temporarily until I can make other arrangements."

"Well, now, just let me know if there's anything I can do for you."

"Thank you, sir." Anna followed Mr. Chelsea out the door to his carriage.

By the time the carriage halted in front of a small white cottage, twilight had fallen. "It's not much to look at, but at least you'll have a bed," Mr. Chelsea spoke flatly.

"For a few weeks anyway." Even to her ears, Anna's voice sounded forlorn. She fixed her eyes on the plain white-washed exterior with its two long windows on either side of a solid white front door. A recessed section equal in width with another long window sat on the eastern side of the house.

"Shall we?" Mr. Chelsea held out a key. She eyed it for a moment. "Yes, of course." She took the key, grabbed her leather bag, and accepted his help down.

"I'll grab your trunk." He went around to the back of the carriage.

Anna trudged to the front door and slid the key into the lock. After hearing the tumblers fall into place, she opened the door and walked two paces over a short rug, then onto primitive pine floorboards into a dimly lit space. It was an empty shell without anyone in it.

She twisted her head at the sound of footfalls entering the small room. Mr. Chelsea crossed the space with her trunk. "Shall I take this to the bedroom?"

"Yes, please." Anna rubbed the back of her neck. He skirted around her as she removed her bonnet and peered around the snug interior and white-washed walls.

When he returned a minute later, he lit an oil lamp on a small table between two cushioned chairs. "I'll light a fire."

Anna moved into the living area as Mr. Chelsea squatted and kindled the fire on the far wall. She spied a framed tintype of her aunt and uncle on the mantel above the fireplace and went closer to study their faces. She didn't remember them but would have recognized her aunt anywhere as she looked at the spitting image of her dear ma. Tears ran down her cheeks. Now, she had lost both of them. She brushed the tears away and scanned the rest of the room.

A divan sat across from cushioned chairs, making a homey setting in front of the fireplace. Anna touched a folded newspaper—*The Colorado Miner.* It lay on the divan as if Uncle Liam had still planned to read it.

Anna walked across the small space to the tiny kitchen and dining area. It harbored a woodburning stove against the wall next to a waist-high icebox and a rudimentary counter in the corner that held a washbasin, pitcher, and tub. Three open shelves contained cookware, food items, and plain white dishes.

She shifted her gaze to the sewing materials on a farm table—a pin cushion holding needles and pins, a spool of thread, measuring tape, fabric, and two hand-drawn patterns. She examined the patterns—one for a suitcoat and another for a waistcoat. Aunt Caitlin must have been working on the project before she died. But why hadn't Uncle Liam put it aside for a time?

Anna placed her bonnet and satchel on the table and walked through a narrow entryway between the living room and kitchen. The short hallway led to another scant corridor where two angled doors on the left and right gave access to small rooms, each with a bed and nightstand and one with a narrow wardrobe. A pair of her uncle's shoes still lay on the floor of the latter room.

Anna quickly closed the door, spun on her heels, leaving the other bedroom door open, and retreated to the front of the house. Who was she to intrude on her uncle's privacy anyway?

"That should warm the place for a while." Mr. Chelsea rose, clapping his hands of dust and appearing gaunt in the firelight. "I left logs for the morning." He pointed to the short stack.

"Thank you, Mr. Chelsea. Once more, you've come to my rescue."

An awkward silence followed until Mr. Chelsea brushed back his dark locks. "Miss Sullivan, I beg you not to judge Mr. Maier too harshly. There are circumstances—"

"I think I'd like to be alone for now." Anna bolstered herself, unable to bear his pity or his explanations. "Besides, you look as exhausted as I feel."

He nodded, then trekked to the door and turned. "Don't forget to lock the door after me. Most folks in Georgetown are friendly enough, but you can't be sure about the transients."

"All right, then." Her voice sounded flat, even to her own ears. "Perhaps I shall see you around."

"Not for a while, madam." He met her gaze. "I'm traveling to London to answer questions and forestall further disaster at the home office. It's uncertain when I shall return."

"I didn't realize there was a home office."

"Investors." He wore an ironic smile. "People who have a stake in the operation and want assurances their money is being put to good use."

Anna had little knowledge of such things, but she supposed in times like these, severe consequences could follow. "Then I wish you good travels, Mr. Chelsea."

He lifted his bowler, opened the door, and strode to the carriage. Anna watched him long enough to see him hop aboard, then she closed the door, switched off the oil lamp, and slogged to the bedroom where she had left the door open.

Anna found the bronze oil lamp on the nightstand inside the darkened space and lit the wick. The light shone on the cozy room. She looked down and suddenly desired release from the filthy travel clothes she had been wearing for three days. She wanted a bath and a new dress, but more than that, she needed sleep. She opened her trunk and took out a flannel nightgown. After removing her day dress, she slid it over her head.

Dread settled in. What would the morrow bring? How could she bear the days ahead?

She glimpsed a violet-colored velvet box half-buried under a linen towel in her trunk. Seamus. At times, during her month-long travels, she'd been driven by her obsessions, missing him, wanting him, beset over the finality of their last words, wishing she had the chance to do it over again. But she'd made her choice, and nothing could change that.

Tentatively, Anna reached for the velvet box and then sat

on the bed. Slowly, she opened the lid to view a shiny gold Claddagh ring that held a tiny heart-shaped diamond in the middle of two hands joined around the heart and topped by a crown.

Seamus had given her the Claddagh ring a year ago on a warm, sunny day in October. They'd strolled hand-in-hand along a grassy knoll to the Dingle Lighthouse as if they hadn't a care in the world. Then, overlooking the harbor, Seamus bent on one knee and spoke the words she had longed to hear. "Anna Katherine O'Sullivan, I can't remember a time when I didn't love you. I can't imagine my life without you in it. So, I'm asking you now to marry me. And if you say yes, I pledge my love, loyalty, and friendship for the rest of our lives."

Utter joy had filled her heart so full she'd believed she would burst with laughter.

Seamus had leaped up and twirled her around until she had become dizzy in love. No two people had ever been happier until two days later. Seamus's parents forbade the marriage and threatened to take away Seamus's inheritance. Endless days of arguing ensued, tormenting Anna with the responsibility of tearing apart the family.

"You were so brave to stand up to them, saying you would give it all up for me." Anna held a fist to her chest. But she'd feared he would hate her forever when poverty came knocking at their door.

Anna had tried to give him the Claddagh ring back, but he'd closed her hand around it. "As a symbol of what we meant to each other." The next day, Anna wrote her uncle.

Anna wrapped her arms around her middle, agony welling in her soul like giant storm waves pounding her rugged Irish coastline and spilling over the rocks. Her shoulders quaked. Tears cascaded down her cheeks.

Was it too much to ask for a life of love and joy and

contentment? Would she always be relegated to this lonely, utter despair? Mrs. Thomas said God works all things together for good. Anna didn't mean to blame God for her misfortunes, but she couldn't see any good in her situation, no matter how hard she tried.

"So, if you don't mind, I need a bit of help understanding what you're planning to do with me here in this strange place." Anna tipped her head heavenward. "Because nothing is how it's supposed to be, and I don't know where to go from here."

Anna fell onto the bed, weeping. After a while, her fervent cries became a whimper, and then a quiet tear descended her cheek. Finally exhausted, she doused the light, crawled under the duvet, and closed her eyes.

Five

Anna stirred from a sound sleep and squinted against the sun, peeking through white lace curtains at the eastern window. Where was she?

Her eyes popped wide open, and the nightmarish events of the day before seized her. She cast off her blankets and ran to the front room. But her aunt and uncle were not waiting for her. No welcoming aromas of baked bread emanated from the kitchen. She was alone.

A sudden chill crept up her spine, the gooseflesh rising on her arms even in her long-sleeved flannel nightdress. Anna wrapped her arms around her shoulders and returned to the bedroom where she'd slept. She couldn't call it *her* room because the cottage had always been a rental. Now, it had become a temporary abode. At least she could be grateful for a few weeks' reprieve before she needed to leave the premises.

But ach, it was cold in the house, as icy as her soul, which had frosted over in the last twenty-four hours. A fire would help thaw her bones. But her heart? She didn't know how to stop the keen ache in her chest.

After slipping on one of four dresses she'd packed in her trunk, she walked out front to light a fire, grateful Mr. Chelsea had added a few logs into the holder.

Her thoughts rambled as she rubbed her hands together and stared into the flames. How would she fend for herself without her uncle's support? Not only did she need alternative living arrangements, but she also needed a way to pay for food.

Food? The last time she'd eaten had been Delmonico's bread nearly twenty-four hours ago. No wonder her stomach gnawed with hunger.

Anna abandoned the fire and walked to the kitchen. Perhaps a nice cup of hot tea would warm her spirits.

Viewing the kitchen in daylight, Anna marveled. Various pots and pans hung over the icebox. Atop the appliance, glass jars held different herbs, spices, and, thanks be to God, a jar with black tea leaves. Perhaps a rich American or wealthy Englishman would scoff at the small space. But to a poor peasant girl from Ireland, it was far more outfitted than the one she'd ever had in her tiny cottage in Dingle.

Opening the metal-hinged side chamber to the woodburning stove, Anna found fresh kindling wood. Uncle Liam must have thought ahead to prepare for the evening meal night before last—a meal neither of them had had the chance to eat.

Anna's fist flew to her chest with a sudden intake of breath. Her pulse raced. She closed her eyes, released a slow exhale, and reopened them. "Ach, Anna, you can't change what is." Hadn't she learned that lesson her last year in Ireland?

She grabbed the flint on top of the stove, opened the compartment, struck a matchstick, and lit the kindling. Now, she could heat water for tea.

Only, the water pitcher was empty. She'd have to brave the outside elements, after all.

Anna picked up the pitcher, opened the side door, and hastened to the water pump a few feet from the house. Priming the pump, she shivered in the nippy air. "Saints preserve us." She chattered as ice-cold water came tumbling into the pitcher. "And to think it's only October." She hurried back toward the house, passing a bed of dying red and purple verbena and opening the door into a warm kitchen.

Anna filled the tea kettle with water, set it on a burner to heat, then packed a tea ball with leaves and left it in the teapot.

While she waited for the water to boil, Anna searched the kitchen for food. Opening the icebox, she found a scant jug of milk, a plate of butter, and two eggs. Several potatoes and onions sat in a three-tiered bin. Praise be, she could make herself a small breakfast.

A sharp rap sounded at the door.

"Now, who can that be?"

Who would call on her unless Mr. Maier had come to remind her of her circumstances? She dipped her head and peeked through the window on her way to the door.

"Well, I'll be."

Mr. Tucker and Mrs. Thomas stood on her doorstep.

Anna opened the door and looked from one to the other. Mr. Tucker held a basket in one hand, and Mrs. Thomas looked refreshed with her hair swept up under a straw hat and wearing a simple bustled dress.

"Good morning." Anna greeted them.

"Good morning, Miss Sullivan." Mr. Tucker smiled pleasantly. "I hope we're not intruding."

She ran long fingers through unkempt curls, the heat rising in her cheeks. She hadn't taken time to wash off the dirt from yesterday. "Well, I—"

"I couldn't sleep, thinking about your situation—seeing as you don't know anyone here in Georgetown—and it just didn't seem right. The missus prepared a basket of cinnamon buns," he held out the wicker container, "and said to bring Mrs. Thomas along—"

"But I already had left the house to call on you when Mr. Tucker and I met in the street, so we came together."

Tears pricked Anna's eyes. It was a kind gesture of Mr. Tucker's wife, it was.

Anna accepted the offered buns. "Where are my manners? Won't you come in?" She indicated for them to enter just as the kettle whistled. "Would you care for some tea?" She hurried to the kitchen, laid the basket on a counter, and poured water into the teapot.

"That would be lovely." Mrs. Thomas' warm voice wafted across the room.

"None for me." Mr. Tucker said. Anna twisted her head to protest, but though he'd removed his bowler and held it between his hands, he shook his head. "I need to get to the Barton House in pretty quick order. But please, if you need anything, Georgia—Mrs. Tucker—and I are at your service."

"Then it seems I'm in your debt once again, Mr. Tucker." Anna followed him to the door, hating to see him leave. He'd been most charitable and a godsend.

"Not at all, Miss Sullivan. Glad to oblige." He replaced his bowler.

Anna closed the door, then turned with an arm around her waist. Eyeing the sewing materials scattered across the table, she hurriedly gathered them into a heap and moved them onto the divan in the living area. "I wasn't expecting company."

"Of course, you weren't." Laurel removed two white ceramic cups off a shelf and set them on the table. "If I were you, I would be at a terrible loss to know what was expected of me at all."

Anna brought the teapot and basket of buns to the table.

"Won't you sit, Mrs. Thomas?" Anna indicated one of the chairs. After sitting, she poured tea into each cup, her emotions guarded. "You knew my aunt well, then?"

"Oh, yes. Bosom buddies, as they say." Laurel brought the cup of tea to her mouth and sipped. "We both moved to Georgetown in 1868—my husband to pastor a church and your uncle to work for the mine."

"It must have been difficult—coming here, I mean." Anna took a bite of the bun, savoring the sweet cinnamon flavor.

"I didn't want to come at first." Mrs. Thomas gazed at Anna in thoughtful repose. "But my husband believed God had called him from a flourishing flock in Ohio to establish a church where there was none. 'It was the Lord's work,' he said. Even if we had an adequate home and grown children in Ohio, we would be like Abraham, who left his family in Ur of the Chaldees to establish a nation in the promised land."

"And you didn't try to stop him?"

"It wouldn't have made a difference." Laurel shook her head. "There's one thing I've known about Clinton Thomas from our early courtship days: his devotion to God rules his heart, which is why I married him in the first place. If he believes God is moving him across the universe, then he will move heaven and earth to make it happen."

"Even so, you must have felt the pangs of leaving family and friends behind." Anna bit her lips, envying the woman's loyalty to the man she loved.

Mrs. Thomas's lips curved into a whimsical smile. "That's why Caitlin and I became fast friends. She knew what it meant to be homesick and heartbroken away from the family she loved, and we bonded immediately."

"Coming here has been the hardest thing I've ever done, and now ..." Anna looked away.

Mrs. Thomas lowered her cup to the table, her eyes

glowing. "You should have seen Caitlin. She nearly danced a jig when she received your letter. 'My dear niece has decided to come to America, Laurel. Won't it be grand?'" Laurel affected an Irish brogue. "Your aunt saw you as God's gift of a daughter she'd never had."

Anna fidgeted under Laurel's scrutiny, fingering the bread crumbs on her plate. She didn't like to complain, but neither did she care for how God had handled her affairs thus far. "But if that's true, how could God be so cruel? How could He bring me here just to take away my only living relatives, leaving me alone with no way to earn a living?"

Mrs. Thomas's eyes softened. She leaned in. "I know it feels that way now, only just arriving and circumstances not what you had expected. But you're not alone. You've already got a champion in Mr. Tucker, and I'm delighted to make your acquaintance after all of Caitlin's remembrances about her family."

Anna dipped her chin. Was this woman the Lord's provision in her need? "I can see why my aunt felt drawn to you and the Tuckers."

"And she was a blessing to us." Laurel smiled. "If she could, she'd encourage us to support one another in our sorrows and seek God's counsel to get us through these tough times."

"That's all I've been doing for months, seeking God's counsel."

Mrs. Thomas studied her. "Most of us make our plans, and we think we've got everything under control. Then something gets tossed at us—something we didn't expect, like a potato famine or a mine disaster—and we're left to figure out what to do with a circumstance we would never have chosen for ourselves. That's where God's providential plan comes in."

"Ach, but it's a poor plan from where I sit." Anna tapped

the table with her finger. "I surely would have stayed in Ireland had I known what fate would befall me here."

"Would you have?" Laurel tilted her head. "Perhaps that's why God doesn't show us the future, so we don't make faulty decisions that take us down all the wrong paths."

"Can anything be worse than what I'm facing now?" Anna blurted. "According to Mr. Maier, I have three weeks to find alternative arrangements, or he'll toss me out like a beggar on the street."

Laurel gasped. "I know Mr. Maier. He can be a ruthless businessman, but—"

"He made it perfectly clear, Mrs. Thomas."

"But I've never known Mr. Maier to—"

A knock sounded at the door. "I wonder who that can be." Anna rose and looked out the window, then turned to Mrs. Thomas. "Well, if it isn't the devil himself." She opened the door and ushered him in. "Mr. Maier."

"Good morning, Miss Sullivan." The man removed his top hat as he entered.

Mr. Maier's attire—a black wool frock coat, vest, and cravat tie—gave him a distinguished air. Cleaned-up and clean-shaven, he could even be called dapper—a far cry from the man Anna met on the stagecoach or yesterday when he'd been exhausted and aggrieved.

She perked her nose. "Mrs. Thomas and I were just talking about you."

His gaze roved over the small space before addressing Anna. "Miss Sullivan, forgive my intrusion. Mrs. Thomas." He focused past Anna. "I wasn't aware you knew each other."

"We met during the rescue efforts." Mrs. Thomas joined them. "My husband and I were consoling the families."

"Yes, of course." Mr. Maier nodded absently.

"How are you getting along, Mr. Maier?" Mrs. Thomas

stood tall, her shoulders squared and hands folded at waist level.

"Awful business, I can assure you. But I won't consume your time with my concerns." He turned back to Anna. "Miss Sullivan, before we speak about other matters, I must seek your forgiveness for my lack of decorum yesterday. I was under extreme stress, but that is no excuse for bad manners. Please accept my condolences." He bowed.

Anna gave him an appreciative nod. Though by his perfunctory manner, she suspected he wasn't used to apologizing.

"I've also come on a matter of a delicate nature."

"I can't imagine ..." Anna's wariness grew once more.

"As you know, your uncle owns a piece of property. However, though he carried no debt, he had little to provide for funeral and burial expenses. As next of kin—"

"And, of course, you would know this because the S & M Banking and Leasing Corporation holds his accounts."

"Yes." He lowered his head, then looked up, his eyes aggrieved. "But as next of kin, you have the right to make decisions on behalf of your uncle. It's my intention—"

"You made your intentions quite clear yesterday." Anna's tea and cinnamon roll turned sour in her stomach. What could he possibly say that would make her feel better? "Well, you can keep your intentions. I've had quite enough of them."

"You misunderstand, I—"

"My husband has already offered to conduct a graveside service at the Old Town Cemetery for Mr. O'Hallisey, Mr. Maier." Mrs. Thomas extended a palm up.

"You would do that for Uncle Liam?" Anna's mouth fell open.

"Well, we couldn't let your uncle go without a proper burial next to his wife, could we?" Laurel directed her soft gaze at Anna. "And as you don't have nearly enough room here, you must use our parlor for the wake."

"I-I don't know what to say." Tears sprang to Anna's eyes.

"Say nothing. It's the least we can do." Mrs. Thomas linked arms with Anna as she faced Mr. Maier again, her jaw set.

A slow but crooked smile grew on Mr. Maier's lips. "I'm greatly relieved and grateful for Pastor Thomas's generosity. I also want to ensure a proper burial and thus have authorized a payment to Owen McCabe to provide a simple coffin for Mr. O'Hallisey."

Anna's hand flew to her chest. "Why would you make such an overture?" Had she misjudged Mr. Maier's intentions yet again?

"Out of respect for my employee and benevolence toward his next of kin, Miss Sullivan."

Anna unlinked her arm from Laurel's and stepped forward. "I don't know how to thank you. I assure you my uncle would be in your debt." Tears pricked her eyes.

"There is no debt, Miss Sullivan." His gaze remained fixed on hers for a moment longer than was necessary.

Anna had a compulsion to flee, her thoughts muddied by the mercurial nature of the man's moods and uncertain what he expected of her. She turned away. "I don't know how to make you out, Mr. Maier." She whirled back around. "But I'm grateful nonetheless."

"Perhaps you should not try." Mr. Maier popped his hat back atop his head. "If it's all right with you,"—his eyes shifted to Mrs. Thomas—"Mr. McCabe will deliver the casket to your parsonage later today."

"That will be acceptable." Mrs. Thomas nodded her head.

"I'll be on my way, then." He headed for the entrance. "Good day, Miss Sullivan, Mrs. Thomas." He opened the door and departed.

"Well, of all the—" Anna stared at the door. "That man is the most mystifying person I have ever met."

"It is a puzzle ..." Mrs. Thomas's voice drifted off, her knitted brow and lowered countenance suggesting she was also baffled. Then she peered up, her eyes gleaming. "And a *wonderful* miracle, in fact."

Anna frowned. "I don't see what cause there is for celebration. Mr. Maier hasn't reneged on an eviction, even if he has paid for Uncle Liam's casket."

"Anna, may I call you that?" Mrs. Thomas seemed light-footed as she rounded the divan and grabbed hold of the material her Aunt Caitlin had been working on. "Caitlin told me she had planned to expand her business once you arrived. Is that right?"

"True enough. My aunt knew I'd been earning my living sewing in Dingle. But I tell you, my skills don't nearly compare to hers. I'd hoped to learn from her."

"Well, there's no time like the present to learn, my dear girl. Stefan Maier may not have expected you to pay a debt, but you will do that and much more."

"Mrs. Thomas, I—"

"Laurel, please. I insist we should be on a first-name basis, especially if we're going to be in cahoots together."

"Cahoots?" Anna was at a loss for words.

Laurel handed the material to Anna. "Caitlin was making this piece for Mr. Maier."

Anna looked at the material in her hand. "I had no idea it was Mr. Maier's. I couldn't even fathom why my uncle had left the material untouched." She met Laurel's gaze. "I should think it's a wonder Mr. Maier has remembered the frock coat at all, especially now with the mine disaster taking up his time."

"Then you must finish it."

"Fill my aunt's shoes? Her work was unrivaled in Dingle *and* here in Georgetown."

"Do you remember what we discussed before Mr. Maier came by?"

"You mean about making faulty decisions?"

"I mean finding yourself in circumstances you would never have chosen for yourself." Laurel's gaze roamed the room, her hand waving toward the ceiling. "Perhaps the situation isn't ideal. You had hoped Caitlin would teach you everything she knew. Oddly enough, she has left you with an opportunity. You must have the faith to snatch it up."

"I don't know—"

"Trust God's guidance to show you the way despite not knowing."

"You would say that because you're a minister's wife."

"I say it because I know it's true. Do you think I knew anything about how our lives would take shape when Clinton brought us to Georgetown?" Laurel half-shrugged. "As far as I knew, coming here might have been the worst mistake we could have ever made. But it's turned out well. Not perfect— my children and grandchildren aren't here—but I've met good friends like your Aunt Caitlin and learned a thing or two about living in these Rocky Mountains."

Anna couldn't deny the generosity she'd received despite being a stranger to the community. Only Mr. Maier had been ready to give her the boot, and he at least had found some measure of humanity.

"If there's one thing I've learned about Stefan Maier," Laurel continued, "it's that he thrives on innovation and creativity and admires others who do the same. You'd do well to finish his frock coat and deliver it to him according to his specifications."

Anna held up the material. Could she fashion it into a work

of art as intricate in detail, as nigh to perfection as Aunt Caitlin could? "Can God miraculously make the same coat Aunt Caitlin would have made?"

"Perhaps not," Laurel shook her head. "But maybe you'll make an even better coat than your aunt would have."

Anna considered Laurel's proposition. "You make a good argument." She drew herself upright. "All right, I accept your challenge, though I still haven't concluded what I think about the man. But if it's a stepping stone to earning a living, perhaps I can bend a little."

Laurel placed a hand on Anna's arm. "I believe God will answer all our prayers and more before He's through." She sat Anna down next to her on the divan. "Now, shall we talk about arrangements for tonight's wake? I'm happy to lend you a black mourning gown ..."

Six

Stefan stomped up the walk on the side of his house, yanked open the side-entry door, then jammed his hat and coat onto the hall tree. "Miss O'Donnell," he called. When his housemaid didn't come, he marched into the dining hall and placed hands on his hips. "Where is that girl?" He tilted his head upwards and bellowed, "Miss O'Donnell."

Hurried footsteps sounded from the back hall. His housemaid appeared in the dining room, red-faced and flustered. "You wanted me, sir?"

Hearing her Irish brogue—similar to Miss Sullivan's—and observing her gasp for breath, he regretted his petulance. Tempering his response, he softened his tone: "Yes. A pot of tea, please. In the parlor, if you would, Miss O'Donnell."

"Of course. Right away, sir." She scampered off toward the back of the house to the kitchen.

Remorse assailed him—something to which he rarely succumbed. Stefan wanted to rescind the peevish spirit that had pummeled poor young Sarah O'Donnell. After all, she hadn't done anything to deserve his ire. More than that, he wished he could travel back in time to save the men who died in his mine. They had paid the consequences for his stubborn refusal to heed the warning bells. But then again, he hadn't believed anyone would go so far as sabotage.

So many lives, so much misery, and one young Irish lady whose hopes and dreams had been destroyed in a deadly game of cat and mouse.

It pained him to think Miss Sullivan had arrived so buoyant and yet so oblivious to the nefarious forces beyond her control —forces that had begun their treachery long before she'd stepped foot on her emigrant boat. Stefan wrung his hands. No, he hadn't caused the cage to snap. But he should have taken the threats more seriously—found a way to assuage the lion in his den.

He walked to the parlor with all its lavish Victorian décor and paced until he spied the day's *Colorado Miner* sitting atop an oblong marble-top table. He lit the ceramic globe lamp, picked up the newspaper, and read:

Nine Dead, Four Wounded in Singing Silver Mine Collapse— Mournful Tunes Heard Across Clear Creek County

While nine families mourn the deaths of their dearly beloved, others are asking whether Mr. Stefan Maier and his partner, Mr. William Chelsea, will ever hear the sound of silver singing again in one of the most prolific mines of Clear Creek County. It's a tune that will continue to play out as rumors float around about who or what caused the hoist cable to break ...

Stefan crushed the newspaper and threw it across the room. He wanted to march to the newspaper building and demolish the reporter who wrote the damaging words. He suspected the journalist cared more about how sensationalism would sell newspapers than he did about telling the truth.

Of course, the newspaperman was only doing his job. But didn't he see how this kind of half-baked journalism, with its half-truths and innuendos, could hurt innocent people? Didn't he care how it could affect the entire community's well-being by implicating an innocent man?

Stefan owed it to his employees and their families to find the truth. He owed it to his investors. He owed it to his and William's reputations. He owed it to ...

Stefan glanced up at the black and white tintype on the rosewood credenza against the wall. He and his wife Charity had attended one of the grand balls hosted by the Prince and Princess of Wales at Marlborough House, and Charity had never looked more stunning in a ruffled and bustled white and blue taffeta gown with its long train flowing behind her. She'd piled her luscious blonde hair on top and let it fall in ringlets down her back. A hat of ribbons and lace set the entire effect.

Stefan's heart squeezed tight in his chest. If only ...

"Sir, I've brought your tea." His housemaid set a silver tray on the marble-top table and removed the fine bone china. "Shall I pour, sir?"

"Please."

Miss O'Donnell poured the tea into the cup and added the cream and two lumps of sugar with the rose-gold tongs. "Your tea, sir." She handed him the cup on a saucer. "If that will be all, sir?" She picked up the silver tray and turned to leave.

"Wait." Desperation surged through Stefan's veins. Usually, his housemaid would have completed the service, and Stefan would dismiss her. But he didn't feel like being alone, nagging regret plaguing his thoughts. And though this slip of a girl was only a servant whose station in life was below his, he suddenly realized he knew nothing about her. "Where do you hail from?"

Miss O'Donnell riveted, her mouth falling open. "I ... County Cork, sir, a few miles north of the city near the River Lee."

"Ah." He absently stirred his tea with a small spoon. "You must miss your family. How long has it been?"

"Oh, yes, sir." Her eyes took on a faraway look. "Three years since I left my da and ma and two brothers to make a life on my own."

"I imagine it hasn't been easy." It had been four years since Stefan had arrived in Clear Creek County—four years he and William had spent building their mining empire.

"It was nigh to impossible at first, feeling the hard looks of the folks in New York when I was trying to find work. Their blunt stares told me more than the signs on their windows— 'No Irish Need Apply.'" She lifted her chin. "Then one day, I overheard a black man in the market square say he was heading west where people were less inclined toward prejudice, and I mustered the coins to buy a ticket that very day."

"Fortunate for me." Stefan sipped his tea.

"No, sir, fortunate for me," Miss O'Donnell insisted. "Instead of treating me with disdain, you hired me on the spot despite my being an immigrant. I've heard it said we're an ill-mannered and unruly bunch, and that may be true for some. But most of us only want to live peacefully, earning a decent wage."

Stefan let out a puff of air through his nostrils. He hadn't known that offering Miss O'Donnell a position had meant so much to her. For most of his life, rejection had not been a factor, having come from the high echelons of society. Only now, since the disaster, did he endure the biting remarks spoken behind his back and the pain of their disgust.

"Scorn is a hard thing to bear." He set down his cup and saucer on the table. "People make assumptions based on rumor without checking on the facts."

"You get used to it. Eventually, you just let the reviling roll down your back."

Stefan looked into her softened features and nodded. "Mr. Chelsea and I had such high hopes in the summer of 1867 when we first entertained the notion of coming to Colorado."

Stefan and Charity had been guests of a high-society family in Surrey, who'd welcomed them back to England after a two-year mining apprenticeship in Peru. William had just finished his master of science degree, and their hosts believed he and Stefan would get along famously. They both had mining interests in common, so it was only natural they would form a fast friendship.

They met multiple times after that, their discussions sometimes spirited. They debated into the late hours, arguing whether the lodes in America could render enough supplies of ores to fill their coffers for years to come. But they could only know with certainty if they explored the land in person.

"And look at you now, sir, you and Mr. Chelsea being some of the wealthiest men in Clear Creek County." Adoration shone in Miss O'Donnell's bright eyes. She held the tray flat against the front of her skirt, one wrist over the other. Her words were true enough.

When Stefan and William set sail for America and the Territory of Colorado, leaving Charity waving them off at the Thames River docks, they had no idea what they would find. But a month later, after they rode into Clear Creek County, Stefan was convinced the landscape safeguarded treasures beyond imagining. Instinct borne of studies at Germany's

Freiberg University in mine engineering and a two-year apprenticeship in Peru had taught Stefan to recognize the value of the land by its unique physical and electrical properties.

Still, wealth hadn't stopped his men from dying. "I only wish—"

A knock sounded at the door. Stefan started toward the door, but Miss O'Donnell rushed ahead. "I'll get that, Mr. Maier."

"Yes, of course." Stefan cleared his throat. He'd almost forgotten it was his housemaid's place to answer the door. What had he been thinking to confide in her? It just wasn't done.

"Pastor Clinton Thomas for you, Mr. Maier," his maid announced.

Stefan turned. His friend and mentor approached him from the threshold, wearing his minister's frock coat and collar. "How are you doing, my friend?"

"To be honest with you, I've had better days."

"That's what I thought." Clinton cast him a wry smile.

Behind Clinton, his housemaid began to retreat, but Stefan stepped forward. "Miss O'Donnell, I ..."

"Sir?" She raised her brows, her voice expectant.

Stefan pulled back, suddenly aware he was acting foolishly. Though grateful for her ear earlier, engaging her had been a mistake. More than likely, his behavior had something to do with his sympathies for Miss Sullivan. "Another pot of tea, if you would."

"Yes, sir." She walked past Stefan, replaced the tea service on the tray, and headed out of the room.

"Please take a seat, Clinton." Stefan used the pastor's given name out of earshot of his housemaid. He indicated a red velvet-cushioned chair that was part of a furniture grouping. A settee and burr walnut coffee table also sat in front of an intricately carved walnut wood surrounding the fireplace. The mirror inset above the mantel made the room appear more extensive than it was, and a porcelain and gold ornamented clock at the center of the mantel gave it an air of elegance.

Stefan sat opposite. "I suppose you saw this morning's *Colorado Miner*."

"A scathing report." Clinton's voice was devoid of emotion, though he wore a grave expression. "Not your finest hour."

"You certainly know how to hit a man when he's down."

"That wasn't my intention." Clinton steepled his fingers. "But you have to admit it doesn't look good."

"None of it's true. It's a vicious attack without substance."

"Do you have any idea what caused the cable to break?"

"I wish I knew." Stefan leaned forward, rubbing his hands between his knees. "This couldn't have happened at a worse time."

"You're talking about the smelting works you and William want to build."

"We've been negotiating with a candidate and waiting for him to return to Georgetown from overseas. William and I hoped to settle the issue before Thanksgiving, but ..." He felt a knot in his stomach. "I fear our efforts may dwindle to naught with this unfortunate incident."

"Surely you're being a little melodramatic." Clinton leaned back.

"Have you ever known me to be overly emotional?" Stefan directed a caustic glance at his friend.

Clinton opened his mouth to speak but closed his lips again, glancing past Stefan.

"Excuse me, Mr. Maier. Your tea."

Stefan rose and walked toward his housemaid. "Thank you, Miss O'Donnell." He softened his voice. "You can leave the tray on the table." She nodded with a shy smile and headed toward the door.

Stefan picked up the teapot and poured a cup of the hot liquid for Clinton and a second cup for himself, then added the cream and sugar as Clinton joined him, taking the offered cup. "I sincerely hope what I just witnessed didn't suggest something more indiscreet."

"Don't be ridiculous." Stefan met Clinton's gaze with a hard stare, but he squeezed his eyes shut with a silent sigh, the heaviness in his chest overwhelming. "Nothing happened, I assure you. She caught me at a difficult moment after I'd seen today's newspaper and lent a sympathetic ear."

"I see." Clinton nodded, stirring his tea. "Perhaps a prudent word would correct any misunderstandings."

"If it weren't for this awful business ..." Stefan shook his head.

"One doesn't have to live long in a mining town to know that accidents happen. They're always tragic, but—" Clinton laid his spoon on the tray. "Thank God, they've been few and far between in Georgetown. Given time, this will blow over."

"I'm not so sure." Stefan sipped his tea. "I may have overplayed my hand this time."

"What have you done now, Stefan?" A wary tone escaped Clinton's lips.

"You don't want to know."

"I'm sure I don't." Clinton blew a quick puff of air through his nostrils. "As your friend, I sympathize with your pain. But as a man of God, I cannot stand by and watch you continue to sling mud at God's law."

"It's not as if I've done anything wrong. I—"

"Don't even go there with me, Stefan." Clinton held up a hand. "I've seen your handiwork. You keep a mine owner embroiled in legal troubles until you've convinced him it's wiser to sell his property and reap the current market value than to watch his wealth diminished by lawyers' fees."

"Can I help it if—"

"You've cajoled at least three unsuspecting men out of their claims in the same way." Clinton set his tea on the table. "You cannot expect God will grant you peace of mind as long as your heart in this matter is corrupted by greed."

"Now, just wait a minute." Stefan tensed. He slammed his teacup and saucer onto the table. "Maybe what you call greed, I call shrewd. Doesn't the Scripture say, 'Behold, I send you forth as sheep in the midst of wolves: be ye therefore wise as serpents?'"

"Yes, but you're forgetting the second half of the verse." Clinton stood his ground. "It also says, 'and be harmless as doves.'"

"That's not always how business works, Clinton. Sometimes men get hurt in the spirit of competition." Betting on the Singing Silver Mine's ability to produce ore had made him one of the wealthiest men in Georgetown, even if he wasn't always well-liked. Besides, his business prowess had benefitted everyone in town by helping to develop the central business district and renovating a ramshackle building or two. Such was the price of being an astute businessman. Sometimes, it begot staunch competitors.

By playing his hand right, Stefan had accrued more profits for his British-American Mining Company in a year than any other man in Clear Creek County except William Hamill. Last spring, when they'd shipped one hundred tons of ore to Swansea, Wales, investors on both sides of the Atlantic Ocean had counted windfall profits. "But competition often means more investment in the community, more jobs, and more growth. It's a win-win for everyone involved. The smelting works would have expedited ore production and improved profits even more."

"Yes, but at what cost to those who've lost out?" Clinton insisted. "You may view your practices as wise in your own estimation, but if your cunning hurts others, it will come back to haunt you in ways you never imagined and perhaps already has."

Stefan averted his gaze, and silence descended between the two friends. Stefan didn't want to admit it, but his outlook had turned bleak, and it was all because he hadn't taken his competition seriously enough.

At last, he met his friend's gaze once more. "I'm not as heartless as you may think, Clinton. Regardless of who or what caused the incident—and I have a pretty good idea who—I still claim responsibility for ignoring the inevitable. So perhaps your prediction of my demise is not so unwarranted."

"I'm glad to hear it." Clinton reached out a hand to Stefan's shoulder. "Go carefully, my friend. These days may not go easily for you. But consider this: God disciplines those whom He loves, and He is not finished with you yet."

Stefan chewed his cheek before seeing Clinton to the door, then returned to the parlor, his gaze first falling upon the tintype on the credenza. Why had he kept it displayed all these years? It wasn't as if he could roll back time. Yet, acknowledging the twisted sense of guilt that had gnawed at his gut all these years, the photograph reminded him why he had exchanged one life for another and persisted in the fight. This time, he battled a foe who would and did go to hideous lengths to get what he wanted, and more people could get hurt before it was all over.

While he'd never resorted to causing physical injury or death to force a business owner's hand—one could argue that his shrewd business tactics and legal threats had harmed, if not significantly diminished, the welfare of a man and his family. This time, he was on the other side of the court's bench and knew the full weight of what it meant.

He kicked the crumpled newspaper he'd carelessly tossed earlier, and it landed near the Steinway petite grand piano across the room. Stefan eyed the beautiful instrument made from the finest of rosewood. He couldn't remember the last time he'd played it. As a boy, playing the piano had always provided comfort for what ailed him. Yet, as a man, Stefan rarely indulged in self-pity. But today, he needed to find calm for his restless soul.

Stefan sat at the Steinway and stretched his fingers, testing the smooth ivory keys. Tentatively at first and then with vitality, his fingers flew across the keyboard, exploring the tempestuous themes in Beethoven's Piano Sonata No. 23 in F minor—the *Appassionata*—written at a dark time when the composer had struggled with the certainty of going deaf.

When, at last, he played the final full F minor cadence at the bottom of the lowest octave, Stefan leaned on it one moment longer, his body trembling from the toil. Though sweat beaded on his forehead and exhaustion had left him lethargic, he experienced a renewed determination to fight for the mine and his reputation. "With God's help," he declared, "I will not let that man win, even if it is at the expense of my dying breath." More importantly, Clinton was right to have confronted him. It was high time Stefan assessed how he conducted his business affairs.

Stefan rose from the piano bench to find Miss O'Donnell and gently but firmly correct any confusion arising from their discourse earlier. His interests leaned toward another Irish woman who had made an indelible impression on him with her feisty ways since he'd first encountered her on the stagecoach.

Seven

Anna dipped teacups into a washtub of hot water. How had she received such unexpected kindness from Laurel and Mr. Tucker—people she barely knew? All she could give back was a tribute at tonight's wake and a brave face at tomorrow's graveside service.

Laurel's suggestion to finish Mr. Maier's frock coat gave Anna pause. She had done many simple sewing projects in her time, but they were nothing like the frock coat. Anna wetted her lips as she dried the teacups. The proof was always in the details, and Aunt Caitlin had proved her skill in Ireland and America. Could Anna measure up to the task, and her first attempt being Mr. Maier's coat, no less? She threw the linen drying towel onto the wash table and walked to the divan, where the unfinished material and pattern lay folded.

Anna held the material in her hands—a soft, supple fabric the shade of dark sable—and admired the expensive brushed cotton. She laid the fabric on the farm table and spread the pattern over the material. They matched perfectly.

The pattern consisted of a three-quarter length cut for the coat that fell to the knees, an interior breast pocket, a four-button front, a notched lapel, and intricate detailing on the back two panels with their two triangular darts and four buttons—all finished off with gold satin lining. It was one of the finest coats Anna had ever seen. She picked up the fabric, folded it against her torso, and returned to the divan to assess the fabric and pattern for the waistcoat.

A knock sounded on the door for the third time that day. Still holding the fabric, Anna went to the door, her mouth falling open. What was *he* doing here? "Mr. Maier, I wasn't—"

"I'm sorry to bother you a second time today." His gaze shifted to the fabric in Anna's hand, and he knitted his brow. "Isn't that the material for the frock coat your aunt was to make for me?"

"I ... yes, it is." Anna tightened her clutch on the fabric, a self-conscious flush creeping across her cheeks as if she'd been caught doing something naughty.

"I'd forgotten." He seemed to marvel. "But what are you doing with it?"

A cool breeze kicked fall leaves around the exterior of the cottage, giving Anna a chill. It wasn't proper to invite a man in, but what else could she do without seeming rude? She scanned the street. "Won't you come in, Mr. Maier?"

A brief smile curved on his lips, and then he stepped inside. "I won't take up much of your time." He removed his top hat and faced Anna.

Once more, Anna became aware of the man's magnetic pull, but feigning indifference, she lifted her chin. "My uncle had the material the whole time. I want to finish the work my aunt never had time to complete." She hadn't actually decided she could do the coat justice, but there they were, the words tumbling out without hesitation as if she'd planned it all along.

"I didn't realize you were a seamstress, Miss Sullivan."

"How could you?" She softened her tone. "You were preoccupied with other concerns."

"Yes, that." He donned a thoughtful expression, then gazed up. "You're obviously a woman of many talents. You sing. You sew. What other gifts lie in wait to be discovered?"

"Well, I ..."

"No need to be coy, Miss Sullivan." He stood taller with his feet wide apart. "You finish the work as well as your aunt would have, and I will pay you handsomely for it."

Anna's mouth gaped. The man was full of surprises. "All right, Mr. Maier. I accept your offer."

"Good. Then I shall be off." Mr. Maier returned his hat to his head and put his hand on the doorknob.

"But you never told me the reason for your call," Anna said before he could open the door. He must have had a purpose for his visit, after all. Had he intended to reinforce her need to pay the rent or find different accommodation?

"Oh, yes." He turned to her with a steady eye. "I've spoken with Mr. Sieger. He's agreed to allow you to stay in the cottage for as long as it's necessary to get established in Georgetown."

"But you said—"

"I know what I said, Miss Sullivan. Despite Mr. Sieger's misgivings, I've changed my mind."

"But I—"

"Would you like me to change it back?" A whimsical smile curved on his lips, and Anna shook her head. "Good." He opened the door and walked out, leaving Anna staring after him.

"Will wonders never cease?" Anna absently closed the

door, then fixed her gaze on the fabric in her hand. What had she just committed to? Panic set in.

What if she made a mistake cutting or sewing either of the projects? An expensive error she could not afford. What had Laurel said? It took faith and prayer. That was God's way.

Anna laid the material on the back of the divan. But did she have *enough* faith?

If you have faith as small as a mustard seed …

She lifted her gaze to the ceiling. "Well, now, You have my attention, putting that Scripture passage into mind. So, I'm asking You to give me the faith of a pretty large mustard seed, and I'll be counting on Your guidance to help me make a frock coat so fine that Mr. Maier will not throw me out on the street like a beggar."

Anna exhaled through her nostrils. It was time she headed out the door for Laurel's house on the east side of town. She reached for her cloak on the nearby wall peg.

"Your uncle was the best of men, Miss Sullivan." The wife of a middle-aged couple dabbed her eyes. "He sure missed your aunt something fierce. We all did. Your coming was the one bright spot in his life." The woman sniffled into her handkerchief. "It isn't right they died before their time."

"It comforts me to know they had folks like you who cared so much for them." Anna took the woman's hands into her own. The woman acknowledged Anna with a tearful nod, and her husband moved them away from the pine coffin to make room for others.

While an undertone of sadness prevailed, occasional laughter wafted from the back of the house, one of the attendees in the parlor shared several anecdotes, suggesting her uncle had been well-liked and her aunt well-appreciated. Their many remembrances warmed Anna's heart with gratitude.

Her eyes swept across the Thomas parlor with its ornate fireplace, lace window curtains overlaid by green velvet draperies, American Empire furnishings of mahogany, and a Rococo sofa with scrollwork and gold cushions. A square piano sat against one wall. How could she thank Laurel and her husband for their kindness?

Anna adjusted the black bonnet and veil hiding her piled-up hair, then pressed a hand to her stomach and smoothed the black bustled mourning dress Laurel had loaned her. Though convention called for wearing the dress, she felt oddly out of place among people who knew Uncle Liam better than she did.

"I left Clinton to handle the food for a few minutes." Laurel came around the corner and put a hand on Anna's arm. "Are you doing all right? Need anything?"

Anna shook her head. "The people are grand, and you and Pastor Thomas have done so much." Anna offered her a whimsical smile. "I don't know how I shall ever repay it."

"Now, don't you worry." Laurel bent close to her ear. "My husband has always said the Lord's work has its own rewards. He wouldn't take a penny even if you offered it."

"Well, okay, then."

She turned to the next couple—a miner and his wife—who'd come to pay their respects. Anna accepted their condolences and then urged them toward the kitchen. "You'll not want to miss Mrs. Thomas's lovely spread of breads, pies, and fried chicken."

"Thank you, Miss Sullivan." The miner's wife placed a hand on her chest. "You're just like your aunt—always thinking of other people before yourself."

Anna accepted the compliment with a wan smile. Seamus

had once made a similar observation. "'Tis a mighty fine thing you do, Anna, my girl, making strangers feel at ease—as if you feel their hurts and concerns. I know you'd just as soon while away the hours contemplating the stars, but you seem to know their hearts nonetheless." He'd taken her hands into his then and looked deeply into her soul. "Can you see into mine?"

"Good evening, Miss Sullivan." A soft Southern drawl distracted Anna from a long-ago painful memory and jarred her with the tall woman's dark skin and hair ribboned with silver. She wore a black dress and carried a black reticule. "Please accept my condolences."

On her way west, Anna had seen a few black people roaming homeless or living in scrubby shacks near weed-packed railroad beds. She'd been told they were not welcome to join white wagon trains and were relegated to ride in their own unkempt train cars. So, who was this woman who seemed perfectly comfortable inside Laurel's home?

"I done think I scared you." The woman chuckled. Her gaze shifted to Uncle Liam in the casket and became sullen. "Your aunt and uncle always treated me real well. 'Ventually, we became good friends. Caitlin and I even studied the Bible together a time or two. It's a sad thing to have lost your uncle now too."

Anna swallowed, not meaning to stare. "You must think me ungracious. I hope you'll forgive me." She curled her hand about her waist.

"You don't have to apologize, chile. I'm Cecilia Richards." The woman folded her hands, the black reticule she carried dangling from her wrist. "The good Lord knows I don't mind people's reactions anymore. It comes with the territory. I figure they gots to get to know me, or they can go their own way."

"Being Irish has its moments too." Anna lowered her guard.

The woman's unreserved speech seemed to have that effect on her. "I'm grateful to meet you." Her throat choked up again. How would she get through this evening if she could barely talk?

"The good Lord knows your sorrow, dear chile." Cecelia leaned forward, her voice rich and soothing. "Oh, I know the future seems dim right now, but don't think for one moment He didn't know you'd be standing here tonight, greeting people you never met before and trying to keep it together. Yous got to trust He's going to lead you through it."

Anna nodded, remembering Laurel's similar words earlier. Tears that had threatened a moment ago spilled over. She wanted to believe. Oh, she really did. But nothing about being here made any sense to her. She tried to brush the tears away.

"Now, don't you worry about those tears none." Cecelia's consoling words stroked her need for a calming voice. "Tears have a way of cleansing our hearts and bringing things into focus. You'll see. It'll all become clear in time." The woman stayed with her a few moments longer, then walked on after Anna assured her she had recovered.

Mid-evening, a hush fell across the house, and the air grew thick as fog over a marshland when Mr. Maier entered the parlor, parting the crowd as if he were the crowned prince.

Anna's body went rigid. Her pulse raced.

Mr. Maier removed his hat. "Please accept my condolences, Miss Sullivan. Your uncle was a fine man and a good worker. We will miss him at the Singing Silver Mine."

"Thank you, Mr. Maier." Anna nodded. "You've confirmed the many kindnesses spoken of him."

The man lingered longer than was necessary over the coffin, his fingers fidgeting with the brim of his hat. Anna believed he wished to say more. But in the end, he only lifted his glassy-eyed gaze to hers, speaking the silent words of sorrow that no one else could hear.

When at last Mr. Maier departed, she heard him say a quiet good evening to Laurel, and the door gently closed. Immediately, the atmosphere gained fluidity again as if the house waved a sigh of relief. The experience left her breathless and confused.

During a lull near the end of the evening, Anna's stomach growled, making her aware she hadn't eaten in hours. She drifted across the rug-lined hall to the dining room, catching whispered words that made her stop short and hide behind a large grandfather clock.

"It's a fact. People are saying it was no accident. That maybe men like Liam O'Hallisey didn't have to die."

Not an accident? Anna clamped a hand over her mouth to keep from gasping and being discovered. Had that been the reason everyone became tense when Mr. Maier arrived? Were the mine's owners to blame for negligence?

She'd observed the sorrow in Mr. Maier's eyes, the weary slump of his shoulders at the mine, and how he had tried to make amends for her uncle's death. But was it guilt or sorrow or both that had provoked him? And what about the words of anger and accusations he and Töpfer had exchanged in his office? So many questions and no answers.

Anna had a sudden need to make her presence known. She gathered her skirts and went around the grandfather clock in the hall to enter the dining room. Two men holding cups of coffee lingered near the buffet on the other side of the wall. "Good evening, gentlemen. I didn't know anyone was still here."

"Miss Sullivan." The man in less formal brown Herringbone trousers and waistcoat jumped, spilling coffee over his cup. Anna recognized him as the man with the devil-may-care attitude who had set her teeth to grinding at the mine. But now he seemed nervous as a mouse looking for a rat hole, which made her secretly smug. "We were just on our way out." He lay his half-drunk cup of coffee on the buffet.

"Thank you for coming to pay your respects, Mr. ..."

"Jones, Elias Jones. I was a surface hoist man for the Singing Silver Mine. My condolences, ma'am."

She eyed the other gentleman accompanying him. He appeared more refined with his thick mustache, frock coat, and top hat between his hands, yet he was much bulkier in build than Mr. Jones, perhaps a man of sport or a former military man. "And you are ...?"

"Sigmund Dreher," he answered in bland indifference.

Anna fixed her eyes on the German and attempted cordiality. "Nice to meet another immigrant, Mr. Dreher." She offered a polite smile.

"I am not an immigrant, Miss Sullivan." His tone suggested he had taken offense. "I have business here in Georgetown and hail from Westfalia."

"I see. But you knew my uncle, then?"

"I never had the pleasure." He laid his coffee cup on the buffet. "I am afraid I must be on my way. Goodbye, Miss Sullivan." He hastened away, and Mr. Jones scuttled after him.

"*Ara!*" Anna grunted and stared at the front door after it closed.

"What's this?" Laurel had come up behind her, looking after the two men.

"I have not met a more insufferable man."

"I thought that was how you felt about Stefan Maier." Laurel brandished a wry smile.

Anna eyed her with a sidelong glance. "Even Mr. Maier is preferable to this bloke."

"What did he say?"

"Nothing, nothing at all." She didn't want to repeat what the men had been talking about—at least not until she verified the rumors. "I don't even know why he was here. He said he didn't know my uncle. I don't think he knew anyone here except for Mr. Jones, who I must say doesn't impress either."

"Who did you say he was?" Laurel knitted her eyebrows.

"A Mr. Sigmund Dreher." Anna frowned. "In Georgetown on business, he said."

"German. They're common enough around here." Laurel's eyebrows rose. "He and Mr. Jones must have come in while I was cleaning."

"Ach, you didn't miss anything except his appalling rudeness." Anna returned to the dining room. "He didn't even offer condolences."

"Then I'm gratified I didn't have the misfortune." Laurel followed her. "And you shouldn't concern yourself with him either. You're not likely to run into him again."

Anna picked up a ham sandwich from a plate at the buffet and bit into it, but she found herself no longer hungry and laid it back on the plate. "I think I shall turn in for the night. Do you mind, Laurel?"

"Of course not, dear." Laurel linked arms with Anna and led her up to the second floor.

Outside the bedroom door, Anna turned to Laurel. "Thank you for letting me stay the night. I could have returned to my uncle's cottage, but it would have been a cold and lonely place on the night before the graveside service."

Laurel lifted Anna's chin. "You're not alone, my dear. The Lord is with you wherever you go, and don't forget you've also got Clinton and me standing beside you too."

Anna hugged Laurel. "I don't know what I would do without you."

"Get some rest." Laurel released her. "You have a long day tomorrow."

Anna entered the already-lit room and eased herself onto the bed. The day had been entirely befuddling, but she had no energy to think about it now. Without turning back the coverlet, she lay her head on a feather pillow and closed her eyes.

Eight

A moderate breeze swept away the remnants of golden leaves from the nearby quaking Aspen. They fluttered and fell at Anna's feet as she waited with the Thomases next to the farm wagon that would haul her uncle's coffin to the cemetery. Once more, she had the Thomases to thank for finding the transport.

She remained unmoving as the six pallbearers exited the Thomas's home and slowly marched toward them. Not until they had advanced upon the wagon did she notice Mr. Maier was one of two who held up the coffin at the front. Clyde Tucker was the other.

Anna did a double-take. Why had Mr. Maier volunteered to assist? After overhearing talk of his negligence at the mine the night before, she hoped he had acted because Uncle Liam had been an esteemed employee and not to give the appearance of goodwill. He'd also shown her a sympathetic heart when he conceded to her living arrangements in the cottage instead of evicting her at the end of the month. But did he have an ulterior motive there as well?

A niggling doubt dogged Anna as the farmer led the procession through town with his two horses clomping steadily down the lane, and she walked Main Street to the Old Town Cemetery behind him. How was she to resolve her conflicting emotions?

After the graveside service, Anna remained behind as people dispersed. She set a flower on top of the piled-up packed dirt covering the coffin and then placed one on her aunt's grave.

"Are you ready to return to the parsonage?" Laurel asked softly from behind.

"I can't seem to cry." Anna stared at the dirt. "I'm certain people in this town must believe my heart is as cold as my uncle's body in the grave."

"Let them think what they will," Laurel said with resolve. "I've learned not everyone grieves in the same way. It doesn't mean you're hard-hearted, Anna."

"I do mourn." Anna's spirit hurt as if a great hole had opened in her heart, and she couldn't bandage the wound.

Laurel's hand touched her shoulder, and Anna turned to look into her understanding gaze. "Maybe it's not your aunt and uncle you grieve. After all, you never got the chance to know them. Perhaps the promise of a life you had hoped for seems no longer possible."

"I gave up everything to come here. My life, my home, the man I loved—all with the hope of a better life with relatives who wanted me. And now ..." Her voice cracked, remembering Seamus's words before she left Ireland. *Contrary to what you've heard, the streets are not paved with gold in America.* She had scoffed at him then—all high and mighty about her grand plans to make good in America. But now his words rang with profound truth.

"Now, you must dig deep down to find the courage to

create a life without them." The sting of Laurel's scrutiny pricked deep as she searched Anna's face. "No one said it would be easy, Anna. But I know you have it within you. You got on the boat in Cork, didn't you?"

Perhaps Laurel was right, but the anguish tore at Anna's soul. "Thank you for all you've done for me, Laurel. I'll stay here a while longer, and then I'll return to my uncle's cottage."

"Of course, I understand." Laurel gave her a reassuring hug and a tender smile. "I'll check on you later."

Anna watched her walk as far as the cemetery's iron gate, then turned to her aunt and uncle's graves. "Oh, Auntie, don't be thinking I'm blaming you for dying. You didn't know you'd be lying in this grave when you asked me to come. Still, here I am, and now Uncle Liam is dead, too, and I haven't got a notion about what I'm doing here.

"Part of me wants to be very angry with you. Laurel says God's providence always seeks our ultimate good. But I tell you, I don't see the good in being left behind." Anna hung her head, the tears she hadn't been able to shed now cascading down her cheeks. She swiped at them as if she could stop them, but they kept coming—softly, swiftly, uncontrollably.

"Don't misunderstand me. I *am* grateful for the generosity of the fine folk here. They've been so kind—Laurel and Pastor Thomas, Mr. Tucker, and the others who came to pay their respects. But if you must know, I miss Dingle more than ever, and I can't help regretting how things have turned out. What would you do if you were me—a woman destitute with only strangers for her comfort?" Anna fell to the ground, pouring out her angst for some time, waiting for answers that never came.

The approach of clomping horses' hooves and swell of loud, heartrending laments reminded her that another funeral had commenced. She rose from the ground and dabbed her eyes with a handkerchief. Ach, what was the use of crying anymore? It didn't change a thing.

After brushing the dirt from her hands and skirt, Anna headed toward the cemetery gate and pushed it open. But as soon as the gate closed with a clang, Anna came face to face with the one man she didn't want to see. "Mr. Maier." Her hand flew to her chest. "I didn't know you were still here."

"I didn't mean to startle you, Miss Sullivan. I ..." Mr. Maier's Adam's apple bobbed. "Are you all right?" His gaze bore into hers.

"I just lost the last living relative I had, Mr. Maier. How would you feel?" Anna uttered her acerbic retort before she could take it back.

She perceived an almost imperceptible light flare in his eyes, but then he looked away. "Confused. Betrayed. Bitter, even." His gaze met hers once again.

"Then you can imagine this has not been a good day for me." She sidestepped him, hoping to discourage further inquiry, but he came alongside her anyway.

"No, I suppose not. May I walk you to the house?"

Anna didn't want the man's company but decided on decorum. "This is a free country, as I understand it. Do as you see fit."

They had only gone a short distance on Rose Street before Mr. Maier halted their progress. "I wish to express my sincerest sorrow for what you're going through—what *all* the families of this community are going through." He seemed troubled, his eyes appearing crazed with anxiety. "If I could, I would set the clock back and save your uncle and all of them from their fate."

"And if Eve hadn't taken a bite of the apple ..."

"Touché, Miss Sullivan." The wry tone of Stefan's voice

bewildered Anna since she still couldn't decide what to believe about his guilt or innocence. "What I meant to say is that I regret you've had to endure the untimely death of your uncle."

"We all regret many things, Mr. Maier." Anna walked on, her eyes fixed in the distance.

"I should have taken the threat to the safety of my men seriously before the incident."

Anna knit her brow. "They say the accident didn't have to happen. That your negligence caused the hoist to fail."

"Do you believe everything you hear, Miss Sullivan?"

Anna cast him a sidelong glance. He wore a pained expression. Was that remorse she saw? She knew better than to believe the newsmongers and busybodies. She'd been the subject of their slander enough times by the upper classes in Ireland to vow she'd never do it herself. "Not everything."

Mr. Maier's hand halted her once more. She peered up into earnest eyes—eyes that seemed to pierce her soul. "Appearances can be deceiving. I implore you to remain open-minded and consider there may be two sides to this story—that perhaps innocence is on my side."

"I would like to believe you, Mr. Maier." She returned with equal sincerity. "If you are innocent, as you say, the evidence should bear the examination."

"I appreciate your candor, Miss Sullivan. I only ask you to stay impartial long enough to allow the facts to come to light."

"And the facts are …?"

Mr. Maier drifted forward again, his hands linked behind him, his words well-considered. "I prefer not to elaborate at this time. Some would use my words against me."

"And you think I would say something to give you away?"

"Intentionally, no. But I cannot afford to tip my hand just yet."

They walked on in silence along a trail, following Clear

Creek. The afternoon sun streamed through the pines and mostly dormant Aspen along the rippling river. Anna still couldn't decide whether to believe this man or not. "Why did you offer to be one of my uncle's pallbearers?"

"What?" Mr. Maier halted. She slowed and turned. He stared at her with a dazed look.

"Did you offer to be a pallbearer as a ruse to put me off the truth?"

A dispirited expression asserted itself again. "Your uncle was a valued employee. I offered to be a pallbearer out of respect for him and you. I promise you I had no other motive."

Anna shrank back. "Thank you for your honesty. I can see my question unsettled you."

He led them forward once more. "I don't blame you for your distrust. Some claim me to be callous because I have a competitive nature. I have no devious design. I can only defend my position by asserting that in competition, sometimes new ideas are formed."

"That is not wholly bad."

"But, I have learned, not wholly good as well," he voiced with gravity. "I can only assure you that Mr. Chelsea and I wanted nothing more than to make our mark on Colorado history and to provide the means to benefit the citizens of this county. Intentionally putting my men in harm's way would defeat that purpose."

Anna stopped at the north end of town where the first cottage appeared on Rose Street and turned to him. "Whether you are innocent or guilty, I cannot say, Mr. Maier. Only the Almighty knows. But the truth always bears out in the end. If you are innocent, then you can be assured of my loyalty. But if you are responsible for the deaths of all those men, then may God have mercy on your soul."

Anna continued down the lane, aware Mr. Maier hadn't

budged from his spot and sensing his focus drilled into her back. Did he perceive her as a woman to be pitied?

No matter. Even if Anna could blame someone else for her circumstances, she was still alone with an uncertain future and had no idea how to navigate these tumultuous waters. She hurried her step, seeking refuge in the tiny cottage.

Nine

Stefan hastened down the dusty lane lined with Victorian homes. They increased in size and stature as he advanced farther south on Rose Street toward the other end of Georgetown.

"Stefan." A female voice halted his tracks. "What keeps you on this end of town?"

Stefan turned. Laurel came down the Tuckers' walkway, still in her black hat and dress. He lifted his hat in greeting.

"I had business on this side of town." He didn't want to disclose with whom or that the encounter with Miss Sullivan had unsettled him. Observing the torrent of tears she'd poured out on her aunt and uncle's graves had compelled him to allay her fears and dispel her doubts about his part in the mining disaster. He could only pray that he'd made his case well enough to convince her. "And you?"

"Georgia and I had church business to discuss. But I wanted to call on Miss Sullivan before I headed home."

"Ah, yes. I'm sure Miss Sullivan will welcome your visit." Stefan dug his hands into his pockets. He'd known to approach her carried personal risk, but he'd never been a man to avoid a difficult task. Face the crisis head-on. That was Stefan's motto.

"What about you?" Laurel's brow furrowed. "Clinton hasn't said much, but I sense he's concerned."

"Your husband is a fine man of God." A smile curved his lips. "I appreciate his and your friendship—more than you know."

Though Stefan had never viewed his business practices as reprehensible, discourse in the last two days had led him to take stock of his life. Clinton didn't know how close he'd come to the truth. And Miss Sullivan … In the short time he'd known her, she had touched him as no woman had in a very long time. He couldn't stomach how this mine disaster had upturned not only his life but hers as well—and left her alone and bereaved.

"I haven't had the chance to thank you for coming by Miss Sullivan's yesterday." Mrs. Thomas measured her words. "Your generosity made an impact despite earlier misconceptions."

"You mean, instead of contempt, Miss Sullivan now at least tolerates me."

Laurel's mouth slackened. "I'm not sure I'd put it that way."

"I'm a realist, Laurel." He flashed a grin. "Don't think I'm unaware of how others view me upon first impressions. Miss Sullivan wouldn't be the first to accuse me of being an insensitive boor."

From the time Stefan happened upon Miss Sullivan on the stagecoach, attempting to retrieve her bag from under his legs, he'd found her captivating. She had a physical allure that would turn any man's head with her amber curls, fair skin, and comely figure.

But more than her physical beauty, he found her feisty disposition enchanting. Perhaps other men had no patience for an opinionated woman, preferring a docile, namby-pamby they could order about. But Miss Sullivan's enthusiasm only ignited his desire to engage her more. He admired her integrity, fighting for truth, even at her own expense. It made him long to prove his innocence of the gross negligence others had accused him of committing.

"I know you like to believe you're hardhearted." Laurel's eyes glistened. "But yesterday, I saw a man whose heart had grown a little more tender with the tragedies that have shaken one young Irish woman's life. Perhaps it's not as cold as you think."

"Be careful, Laurel." Stefan chuckled. "You may ruin my reputation as a formidable man to be reckoned with."

"Would that be so terribly bad?" Mrs. Thomas raised her brow.

Stefan crossed an arm and rubbed his forehead. "I suppose that depends on the situation." He dropped his hand to his side, clenching and unclenching it, anger suddenly scorching his soul like a hot iron. How dare that pompous German think he could get away with murder?

"Stefan." She grabbed his arm. "You look flushed. We should find a place to rest." She looked around.

"No, no. I'm perfectly all right," Stefan insisted, disentangling himself from her. The last thing he needed were rumors accusing him of an affair with his pastor's wife. "You and Clinton must believe me. I did not neglect my duty to inspect the mine's equipment and safeguard my property."

"I never thought you did." Laurel shook her head. "You are many things, but a laggard you are not."

Stefan inhaled deeply, then exhaled slowly. "Thank you. I appreciate your and Clinton's support more than you know."

"Of course, Stefan." Laurel's eyes softened again. "Just remember, you're always welcome to drop by the parsonage. Let's plan to have you over for dinner very soon," she offered.

"But now, I must visit Miss Sullivan before the day gets away from me."

Stefan indicated a hand for them to move on together. At the corner of Ninth Street, he lifted his hat once more in salutation. "Please give my regards to Miss Sullivan."

Stefan hurried past the business district, then turned the corner down the street past William Hamill's lavish estate. Another worthy competitor on Brown Mountain, Hamill and he both hailed from the English gentry. They also conducted their business enterprises similarly. But neither of them would murder nine men to wrangle a competitor's property.

"I *must* find the evidence I need to prove my innocence." Stefan's vehemence compelled him forward. He barged through the white-washed gate of the wooden fence surrounding his house, bolted up the porch stairs, blasted through the front door, and tore up the stairs to his bed chamber to change into his riding breeches. It was time he returned to his Singing Silver Mine to investigate what happened to thrust his life and the entire community into turmoil.

Stefan crossed his expansive yard to the timber-built carriage house on the side of the property. He unlatched the massive sliding barn doors and pulled one of them open. Within minutes, he saddled Sally, ready to dash toward the Clear Creek trail.

"Hello, Stefan. Where are you off to in such a hurry?"

"Paul Rutherford." Stefan dropped the lead and rushed forward to reach the friend he hadn't seen for months but had known since their days in Peru. They shook hands, and then he pulled Paul into a hug. "Good to see you, old friend, and none too soon! When did you get into town?"

"Only just. Ian wanted to get home straight away, so I sent him on with the luggage." Paul's voice was light and bubbly, his brown eyes sparkling in the sunshine. "I couldn't wait to share what I've learned in Swansea. My hunch paid off, Stefan. I've found a way to extract ores from hard rock more efficiently than the Bruckner furnaces. We can start building the smelting works tomorrow."

Stefan tensed. Paul Rutherford was a decade his senior, an affable gentleman most women fawned over for his tall and handsome features. He'd attended the Royal School of Mines and studied how to perfect smelting processes a half dozen years before Stefan entered the University of Freiburg. Several years later, Paul joined Stefan in Peru. Two years after Stefan moved to Georgetown, Paul followed him to take a job with a smelting works plant in town. How did Stefan tell his friend all they had hoped for —including funding for Paul's smelting works—was on hold?

"You haven't heard, then?"

"Heard what?" Paul's smile faded. "What's the matter, Stefan? You look as if your dog just ate your lunch."

"I wish that's all it was." Stefan scratched his head. "Look, Paul, some things have happened since you left. I'm heading to the mine now to take care of business."

"Okay. I'll come with you." Paul appeared unbothered.

"You may not want to after you hear the gruesome details."

"Try me." Paul crossed his arms.

Stefan related the details. "Georg Töpfer is the only competitor devious and disgruntled enough to destroy me. He made several attempts to buy the mine. Each time, he became more belligerent and threatening."

"Threatening how?" Paul frowned.

"Last Saturday, I went to Central City to meet with the district judge for dinner. Töpfer filed a claim disputing the land between the Singing Silver Mine and his Mother Lode Mine adjacent to my property. Despite my latest legal win, Töpfer vowed more litigation. I wanted to know if I had recourse to end his efforts. The judge's answer gave me little satisfaction.

"On Monday, before leaving, I stepped into a saloon for a meal before catching the stagecoach. I'd only ordered when two men ambushed me. I tell you, it was a real Wild West brawl rivaling Jessie James. By the time the bartender broke up the fight and tossed all three of us onto the street, I looked like I had stepped out of the pages of Dickens' *Oliver Twist*."

"I'd like to have been there to see that." Paul flashed a sardonic smile. "The always well-kept man of breeding turned rogue."

"Yes, well, after warning me to give up my land, the two men dashed off down a side street, leaving me to brush myself off and looking like I'd just spent a night on London's Saffron Hill. No wonder Miss Sullivan mistook me for a bum sleeping off my liquor when I caught the stagecoach."

"Miss Sullivan?" Paul's voice rose.

"An Irish woman new in town. Her uncle was one of the men killed in the disaster."

"I see." Paul studied him, then uncrossed his arm. "Meet me at my house in fifteen minutes." He headed down South Street toward his house.

True to Paul's word, they were on their horses fifteen minutes later, dashing alongside Clear Creek through thick pines and dormant aspens, ascending the mountain toward the Singing Silver Mine. Twenty minutes later, they reigned in their horses near the mine office.

"Wait here." Stefan jumped off Sally and hitched her to the rail by the entrance. After locating his key on the rack in the hallway, Stefan strode back to the exit and paused with his hand still holding onto the doorknob.

How could the air surrounding the Singing Silver Mine be so quiet? Not even the few pines still on the property rustled like they so often did in these mountains as if they swayed to the music of a wild square dance. But today, it seemed as if the musicians had packed up their instruments and left, and all that remained was a hollow music hall filled with ghosts whirling to the music of a silent orchestra.

He shut the door and walked several paces forward, then stopped and scanned the vast, empty hillside. Standing in the center of a deforested hollow, Stefan became profoundly aware of being alone on the mountain for the first time in more than three years, and it made him feel like an ant in the middle of a rock garden.

"So quiet." Paul joined him.

Well, almost alone. Stefan glanced at his friend. He'd told Paul the gist of the story, but he hadn't spilled the details of what he was planning to do.

"Do you ever regret your decision to move here?" Paul peered at the grand mountain vista in front of them.

Regret? Oh, Stefan had had many regrets over the years— most of them concerning Charity. "In the beginning, regret was all I had. I knew it wouldn't be easy to persuade Charity to come to America, but I never guessed how much her affinity for the Prince and Princess of Wales would engage her displeasure at the idea of leaving them behind."

"I remember Charity talking about the royal parties even in Peru," Paul said. "She put up a good front, but I sensed she was never happy there and couldn't wait to return to England."

"You were a might more in touch about that than I was." Stefan gave Paul a sidelong glance. "Once William and I had settled on emigrating to Georgetown, it would be no exaggeration to say Charity threw a fit rivaling the eruption of Mount Vesuvius."

Paul laughed. "I can believe that. I caught her once scolding one of the servants. She was embarrassed when she saw me but feigned indifference."

"Yes, well …" Stefan dipped his chin. It never served him well to conjure the memories. He laid a hand on Paul's back. "Time we move on to what we came here for." He didn't want to collect more regrets.

Stefan led Paul west past the ore sorting house to the long, rectangular clapboard shaft house with its blacksmith shop at one end and the front door at the other. Going around the building in the looming shadow of the cupola on the shorter side, he inserted his key into the front door, turned it, and entered.

He allowed his eyes to adjust to the dim light, then led Paul across a large room to a foundation where a hoist system sat acutely silent.

A massive drum with a heavy, twisted wire cord wrapped around it like a giant spool sat on a concrete foundation across from a boiler. The cord led from the drum at a forty-five-degree angle to the top of the two-post timber headframe, then over a pulley and straight down at a ninety-degree angle to the shaft below it. Before the disaster, a metal cage had been attached to the cable to transport men and equipment from the ground floor to various levels below. At present, a hook and harness system dangled at the end of the cord—a makeshift device his foreman Horace and their blacksmith engineered to secure a way to retrieve the men from the bottom of the shaft.

"So what have you got in mind?" Paul placed a hand on his hip, and the other held onto a timber post, peering into the dark tunnel.

Stefan scuffed his feet through the dirt that had billowed

out of the opening when the cage plunged, reliving the horror of those lengthy and treacherous hours after Georg Töpfer stomped away in indignant denial of the disaster. "You're not going to like it."

"I didn't think I would." Paul looked up, smirking.

Stefan straightened. "When the cage catapulted down the shaft, the end of the cable still attached to the cage wrapped around the timber columns undergirding the mineshaft, bringing the timbers down." He gestured with his hands.

Paul whistled, looking into the shaft once more. "You mean you've got a cave-in down there."

"We knew sending anyone down the shaft to rescue the men would be dangerous. No matter what we did, the rescue team would descend at significant risk. Horace devised a plan to send two men down at a time, using the remaining three-quarters of the cable still wound on the drum. Then, using a signaling system—a combination of whistles and cable pulls —we communicated with the men every step to ease them through the fallen timbers."

"Sounds slow and arduous." Paul moved away from the shaft and studied the hoist.

"With every man I watched descend into that shaft, I feared a wrong move could result in another cave-in and another man's death." Stefan could still taste the bile he'd swallowed that day. "The first time we received a signal to halt, I prayed a rush of wind and tumult would not reach the surface. We heard the call six times, but thank God nothing ever happened."

"And you have no idea how the cable broke."

"None." Stefan waved his hand. "Those cables are supposed to last two years, and we installed the new line only a few months ago. I also inspect it every Friday except this last Friday, when I made a trip to Central City."

"So by all standards, the cable should not have severed."

"Which is why I need to get down there—"

"Have you lost your mind, man?" Paul's eyes bulged. "There's no telling how unstable the tunnel or equipment has become in the last several days."

"There is no other way." Stefan waved his hand. "And when have I ever played it safe?"

"That's what I like about you, Stefan." A voice responded from behind. "You've always loved a challenge, haven't you?"

Stefan spun around. Georg Töpfer. "What are *you* doing here?" He marched toward the entrance, his fury growing with each step. Of all the untimely—

"I suppose the same as you and Mr. Rutherford." Töpfer sauntered forward, his feet shuffling across the plank floor until they stood face to face.

"I doubt that." Stefan glared.

"Easy, Stefan."

Paul's warning only served to provoke Stefan's fury. "Did you come to gloat? Or have you come for some other deranged reason?"

Töpfer craned his head over the vertical tunnel, his hands digging deep into his pockets. "Shame about all those men dying in the belly of the earth."

"As if you care one speck of dirt about those men." Stefan nodded toward the hoist, knowing full well Töpfer would have just as soon sent them all to their graves if it meant he'd get hold of Stefan's property in the end. "Come to think of it," he waved a hand, "I didn't see you at the wake or the graveside service."

"Come now, Stefan. We used to be friends." Töpfer met his gaze, his voice scoffing.

Stefan laughed in mirthless humor. "We haven't been friends for a long time."

Paul laid a hand on Stefan's arm. "You're only egging the man on. Let's get out of here."

"You still haven't answered my question." Stefan ignored Paul's plea. "What are you doing on my property? Or have you forgotten I still own the rights to my land and what's underneath?"

Töpfer lowered his gaze as if he were examining the damaged drum and promenaded past Stefan. "Miss Sullivan is a rare beauty, even in black." The German's suggestive tone sickened Stefan.

Stefan whirled around to face him, wanting to wipe the secretive smile off the man's face. "Leave Miss Sullivan alone." He pointed straight at him. "If you harm her in any way—"

"Oh, I see." He drew up a knowing grin. "Relax, Stefan. I have no designs on the likes of a scullery maid. She's all yours."

The disdain in the braggart's voice was the last straw. Stefan clenched and unclenched his fists. "Get out."

"But you still don't know why I'm here. Surely, your curiosity is still piqued."

"That's where you're wrong. I no longer care why you're here or what you came for. I want you out of my sight and off my property."

Töpfer shrugged. "Have it your way." He paraded to the entrance of the shaft house, brushing past Stefan. A moment later, the footsteps halted. "This *was* a courtesy call." Stefan turned, observing Töpfer's hand on the doorknob. "Now it's a warning. Take from *your* property whatever you can. It may not be yours much longer once my lawyers get through with you." Töpfer twisted the knob and walked out, leaving the door wide open.

Stefan stalked Töpfer until the man mounted his horse and galloped down the dirt road out of sight. If Töpfer believed he could steal the Singing Silver Mine from Stefan, he was very much mistaken.

"Töpfer's not a foe I'd want to cultivate." Paul came up next to Stefan.

"He's tangled with the wrong man. I will not let Töpfer get away with murder."

"Come on, Stefan." Paul placed a hand on Stefan's back. "Twilight will descend soon. We can't do anything more here today."

Stefan looked back through the open door of the shaft house with regret and nodded. He chewed his cheek. Töpfer's warning meant easing investors' concerns about the future of the mine preceded anything else, and Stefan had a Businessman's Association banquet three days hence in Denver. He had much to prepare for to secure his claim.

Stefan closed and locked the door behind him, then pocketed the key. He wanted no chance of anyone else having access. In the meantime, he would post a guard at the entrance gate to keep the riffraff out. Stefan jumped on his horse and headed down the mountain with Paul galloping alongside him. Soon—very soon—he would prove Georg Töpfer's guilt, whatever it took. *Whatever* it took.

Ten

Anna woke to the sound of an axe splitting logs behind the cottage. She lay nestled under the blankets in a lethargic half-sleep, not wanting to brave the chill until another whack made her give way to the inevitable. She sighed. Ach, it appeared devilment would deny her another moment's rest.

Propping herself on one elbow, Anna grabbed her da's pocket watch on the night table. Eight-fifteen. Had she really slept for more than twelve hours? Oh, but the air in the house was as nippy as an Irish winter.

Anna rose and dressed and lit a fire in the front room. After standing by the flames to warm herself, she threw on a shawl, grabbed the water pitcher, and headed out.

As she pumped water, the man from the larger house across the way stacked wood next to the house's back exterior. Laurel had told her the infamous Mr. Sieger lived in the house behind her. So, *he* was the devil who had disturbed her sleep— the devil who would also turn her out of her home if Stefan Maier hadn't stepped in to give her a reprieve.

Mr. Sieger appeared to be forty, his light brown hair parted in the middle and with a longish beard. His brown breeches made his legs look long and lanky. He didn't resemble a demon —if one believed William Makepeace Thackery's depiction of one in his now-famous sketch of 1866. But then again, she'd read in the Scriptures that Satan could appear as an angel of light.

Mr. Sieger glanced her way and gave her a brief nod. "Fine day." He pointed to the sun in the cloudless sky.

"It is that." Anna continued pumping water. He couldn't blame her for being on her guard. After all, he was the S in the S & M Banking and Leasing Corporation.

The pitcher now full, Anna dropped the lever and would have retreated into the house when a familiar figure rounded the corner of the large house. A smile sprang to her lips. She might not have cared for the father, but the son was a good fellow.

"Hello, Mr. Sieger."

"Well, if it isn't Miss Sullivan!" The young man sprinted toward her. "I wished I'd known the people who lived here, them being your relatives and all. I could have—"

"Jake." Her landlord reprimanded his son.

The boy twisted around. "I won't be but a minute, Pa." A tinge of belligerence had entered his tone.

"Better be."

Jake drew closer. "I'm awfully sorry about your loss, Miss Sullivan. I can't imagine how you must be feeling."

"You're very kind. Thank you." She eyed his father. "But it seems you'd better get to your chores. We'll talk again soon."

"Sure thing, Miss Sullivan. If you need anything, you just give a holler." He waved and took off across the grass.

Anna thought she had stopped envying others long ago, but as Jake stacked the cut wood, the curse of covetousness slammed her with its ugly and unholy compulsions. She might not care for the man who could turn her out of her uncle's cottage, but Jake was fortunate to have a da who provided for him instead of one who drank away even the bit his daughter scraped together. An unbidden tear moistened her cheek.

Da had tried. Oh, how he had tried. But bitter about his lot in life, he didn't have it in him.

Anna brushed the tear away, threw open the door, and stepped inside the warmed house. She would not become the likes of her da, wasting her days in antipathy with the world. It was time to shed her self-pity and get on with making something of her life.

She placed the pitcher onto the counter and crossed the short space to the divan, where she picked up the dark sable material, holding the soft brushed cotton against her chest. Yes, she had everything to gain from finishing the frock coat. If she had any hope of making a living in this foreign land, she would have to prove her worth to Mr. Maier and the rest of the community.

Anna studied the pattern her aunt had made of Mr. Maier's measurements. He was a tall man with broad shoulders and a long waist—handsome. She hadn't thought so in the stagecoach. But even then, he had teased her with the same mischievous smile he'd displayed at the campfire. She supposed most women found him dashing—perhaps even a man of wit and charm.

After the graveside service, his blue eyes—not changeable like Seamus's—had been pained and sympathetic. His concern for the mourning families had seemed genuine. He appeared in earnest to gain her trust as well. But why entreat her, a poor Irish immigrant of no consequence? She couldn't fathom.

After a small breakfast and a pot of tea, Anna prepared the space at the kitchen table with the sewing materials and sable fabric. She had just stuck a needle into the cut material when a knock sounded at the door.

"Ach, who could that be?" She set aside the project and answered the door. "Laurel." Anna beamed. "What brings you by so early?"

"I've come to see how you're fairing after yesterday." Laurel folded her gloved hands atop her brown bustled skirt and beige tartan bodice. A reticule swung from her wrist. "And to ask if you'd like some company."

Anna opened the door wider and ushered Laurel in. "There's nothing I'd like better, but to be honest, I'm determined to complete Mr. Maier's frock coat." She pointed to the fabric.

"That's wonderful." Laurel's eyes danced with delight. "You will not regret it."

"Well, yes, but if I'm going to finish it by tonight—"

"Tonight?" Laurel's eyes widened.

"As an old friend in Ireland used to say about his crops, 'Whoever watches the wind will not plant; whoever looks at the cloud will not reap.'"

"Ecclesiastes—yes, I know the verse."

"Then you'll understand the enormity of the task I've set myself if I want to get it done." Anna eyed the material.

"I completely understand." Laurel grinned, then just as quickly, her smile faded. "You've heard the rumors, I suppose."

"About Mr. Maier's negligence at the mine?" A wave of disgust passed over her. "That's what those men were talking about in your dining room and what I couldn't bear to repeat."

"It's not true." Laurel leaned in, her tone adamant. "I've never met anyone, except my husband, with higher integrity. People like to criticize Mr. Maier because he's successful and rich. But they don't know the man underneath—the man who'd rather put his own life on the line than put his men in peril."

"Why are you telling me this?" Anna had already come to the same conclusion.

"Because if you're going to sew his frock coat, I don't want you to think it's his fault your uncle is dead. Events in Stefan's past would prevent him from being anything but good to the people under him. There must be another explanation."

"You don't have to be concerned, Laurel. If you say it, I believe you."

"Good." Laurel seemed to lower her guard. "Then I will leave you to your task, but I promise to pray heartily for your work and return this evening to check on you."

"I would like that very much. I may need your shoulder to cry on."

"Somehow, I don't think you'll need that shoulder." A whimsical smile slowly curved on Laurel's lips.

After Laurel had gone, Anna poured herself another cup of tea and returned to her sewing. She had no idea what events in Mr. Maier's past influenced how he treated his employees. But if what Laurel said was true, then perhaps Anna needed to give him the benefit of the doubt—which gave her an even greater impetus to have the frock coat done by the end of the day and see Mr. Maier wearing it to church on Sunday.

Eleven

A sudden shadow settled over the room. Anna glanced up from her sewing and peered out the window. Her work on the coat had so absorbed her she hadn't noticed the fire go out or the sun set far enough over the western mountains to darken the world. Would she ever get used to these early evenings in Georgetown in this close mountain valley? Anna put her sewing aside and rose to put a log on the dying embers in the fireplace and light candles around the room.

Of course, winter in Dingle wasn't that much different. Though they hadn't the tall peaks to hide the sun, they had the low-lying wintry clouds that hung for months. She rather fancied the blue skies here in Colorado.

Anna blew out the starter candle and reseated herself. Taking up the garment, she marveled at her remarkable accomplishment, her hand gliding over the supple sable fabric. Indeed, its warmth would be enough for the cold months ahead.

She had finished the front with its interior breast pocket

and sewn the side panels to the front section. She'd also easily attached the four buttons and cut the buttonholes. The collar and notch in the lapel had been painless as well, though it still needed to be connected to the body of the coat, and she couldn't do that until she did the intricate detailing on the back two panels with their triangular darts and four buttons.

Her breath hitched as an uninvited memory rushed upon her. Seamus and his parents had been invited to a dinner party at an estate outside Dingle. She'd only found out about it by chance, on the road going out of town—they, driving in their fine carriage, and she, walking in her worn-out shoes. The carriage halted, and Seamus jumped down to greet her.

On most occasions when they had been together since childhood, they'd had an easy camaraderie. But this time, Seamus had appeared so dapper in his evening coat that she'd felt self-conscious in her drab dress. But then he smiled at her, giving her a dim hope that their differing stations in life had little effect on their relationship.

"Come, Seamus. We don't want the Johnstons to think we're discourteous by arriving late." Ina O'Connor spoke with an assuming air, then directed her words to Anna. "The Johnstons are entertaining the Herberts of Muckross House at Killarney, you see. It will be a good connection for Seamus."

"Ma," Seamus warned her before turning his admiring gaze on Anna. "We'll talk when I return." He leaned forward and whispered into her ear, his lapel brushing her nose. "Don't worry, *mo ghrá*. I still have eyes only for you." He climbed back into the carriage, and Patrick O'Connor clucked his tongue for the horses to move on.

Anna had wanted to believe Seamus with all her heart, especially when he had said "my love" in Irish. Still, remaining planted in her spot, she'd looked after the carriage, the diminishing echo of the horse's hooves clopping away from her and repeatedly plodding the same rhythmic tune. *He will never be yours. He will never be yours. He will never be yours.* And she'd known then that his parents would never consent to a marriage despite his protestations.

"Ach, I'm wasting precious time thinking about things that don't matter anymore." Anna brushed away the unwanted tear and shook herself out of her reflections. "I'm in America now and ..."

Anna blinked. In a flash of memory, she saw the detail around the buttonholes of Seamus's frock coat. "That's it—a personal signature." Anna would create a distinguishing mark for every project she did going forward.

Her eyes shifted heavenward. "Let's just hope it impresses Mr. Maier." She inhaled deeply, smelling the pungent tallow the candles burnt off, and set her nimble fingers back to fashioning the coat.

A knock at the door sounded sometime later, and Anna looked up. How had the candles burned a third of the way already? She put aside her work and rose to open the door.

"Laurel. Please come in." Anna smiled at her friend, now dressed in evening attire. How much she relished this friendship in such a short time since her arrival in Georgetown.

Anna grabbed her arm. "You must tell me what you think."

"That's why I've come. I couldn't wait another moment to know how you were getting along." Laurel swooped in and dropped her reticule on the small table.

Anna picked up the nearly finished coat and held it against her chest. "You must tell me the truth, and you mustn't flatter me if it isn't deserved."

Laurel stepped forward, reaching for the coat to take a closer look. "May I?"

Anna gave her the coat and allowed her friend to study it.

While Anna gnawed on her knuckle, Laurel's eyes searched

each inch of the fabric for the tiniest flaw. Her face seemed to go through various contortions, her eyebrows knitting then lifting as if she had been surprised by something she'd seen.

At last, Laurel looked up. Her eyes sparkled like the radiance of a thousand candles. "Truly remarkable—a work of art every bit as finely executed as your dear Aunt Caitlin."

"You think so?" Anna's jitters subsided, though a remnant of doubt lingered.

"I like how you've chosen interesting places to use specialty stitches, like the featherstitches around the lapel notch. It's a detail not found on similar coats."

"You like it, then? I wasn't sure, but I wanted a signature stitch I could call my own."

"It is different, but well done."

"But will Mr. Maier like it?" Anna bit her lip.

Laurel's grin deepened the crows' feet around her eyes. "I don't think you have anything to worry about, my dear. You've surely demonstrated a unique style demanded in this situation."

"Well, if that's true, I have only you to thank." Anna took the frock coat back. "And the Almighty for directing my hands."

Laurel placed an arm around her shoulder. "Now, don't forget. It would be best if you approached Mr. Maier with confidence in your stride. He will admire and respect you for it."

Anna hugged her. "And I'll be counting on your prayers in the morning to see me through it."

"You've got it." Laurel drew away and peered into Anna's eyes. "Never doubt the blessed Lord will be with you every step of the way."

Despite the brave front, an apprehensive twitch still fluttered in Anna's stomach. She felt like a deer whose ears flicked when it sensed danger nearby. Would she survive Mr. Maier's scrutiny? Anna prayed it would be so, for tomorrow would be the test.

~

"You've exceeded my expectations and more, Herr Dreher." Georg grinned. He counted out the bills he owed on his desk in the office of the Mother Lode Mine. A picture of the mine site and a map of his homeland hung on the wood plank walls. He also proudly displayed his German crest over the door. Two chairs, a desk, and a cabinet furnished the room. "You've proven your reputation to be well deserved—but then again, I am not surprised." He handed Dreher the stack of bills.

"Of course. That is why I come at a premium." Dreher tucked the bills inside his frock coat pocket. "And why I pay men well to betray their closest friends."

"Yes ... the rumors are making the rounds." Georg reached into the bottom drawer of his desk and found a bottle and two glasses, then poured drinks for them. "Your favorite brand of French Cognac." He raised his glass.

Dreher sipped the cognac, then studied the amber color. "Mr. Jones has been instrumental. But then, that is what I look for when I pick out those who serve my purposes—men and women whose greed motivates their loyalty."

"What did you promise him?" Georg sat back, savoring the liquid in his glass.

"A foreman's position at the Singing Silver Mine when you have acquired it."

"You had no right ..." Georg sprang forward in his chair. He didn't like other people controlling his operation.

"Come now." Dreher's silky-smooth voice reminded Georg

of a slithering snake. "All jobs come with a cost, and yours is to compensate men like Jones for the risk."

"You've compensated him with cash. Isn't that enough?"

"If you want him to remain quiet and under your thumb, you must motivate him."

"Listen to me, Dreher. You work for me, not the other way around. I suggest you remember that in future dealings."

The German's lips curved into an ironic smile. He downed the cognac in one swallow, then set the glass on Georg's desk. "I will stay in Idaho Springs overnight, then Denver for the duration." He rose and opened the office door. "You know how to get in touch with me when you are ready for the next phase of the operation." Dreher banged the door shut on his way out, rattling the thin walls and knocking over the tintype of Georg's graduation from the Strasbourg School of Law.

He set the photograph upright and then studied the picture. His degree had served him well over the years, giving him an edge in gathering all the right resources, and Dreher had been a good resource. He stroked his mustache. On the other hand, Dreher was indeed menacing—a man Georg needed to stay ahead of at all times in the game of chess they both played. Perhaps a bit like himself, he smirked. No matter. He could live with the man's personality as long it got him the Singing Silver Mine in the end.

Twelve

～～

O n Saturday morning, Anna stood on the northeast corner of South and Argentine with her brown-paper-wrapped package for Mr. Maier in one arm. Behind her, a short distance on the other side of the street, guests sat drinking tea on the balcony of a brick mansion turned into the prominent Phelps House Hotel. Another estate opposite the inn belonged to William Hamill.

She rotated around with the morning sun at her back and gawked at what the fortunes of the mining industry could afford. Mr. Maier's considerable property nestled against the hillside rivaled Hamill's. Both homes consisted of wood-framed, three-story houses with numerous gables, decorated windows, and a turret. Scalloped wood cornices ran the roofline. But whereas Mr. Hamill's carriage house and stables were constructed of granite, Mr. Maier's sat off to the side and were built of timber. A white picket fence surrounded the entire property.

Though not nearly as grand as Muckross House, this one

outshone every Victorian she had passed except Hamill's House. Anna shifted her stance. Her chest constricted. Who was she—a poor Irish immigrant—to barge an entrance into such a distinguished home? She closed her eyes. *Dear Lord, calm my anxious heart.*

"Miss Sullivan? What are you doing here at this time of the morning?"

Anna jumped. She'd been so distracted by her reflections that she hadn't noticed Mr. Maier coming through the gate of the picket fence. His eyes bored into hers, his mouth agape.

Once again, his presence and stature rendered her speechless. He looked every bit the proper Victorian gentleman attired in a striped frock coat, streamlined and suitable for daytime business. The cane and bowler added an air of dignity. Though she was not a short woman at her own five feet seven inches, he towered above her.

She bolstered herself. "I've come to deliver the frock coat."

He stared at the package under her arm, then perused her face. "So soon?"

"I've finished it."

"In one day?" His head jerked back, eyes widening, and she nodded. "A wonder, Miss Sullivan." He cleared his throat. "I'm afraid—"

Horses' hooves clopped behind them on the street, and Mr. Maier twisted his head. Anna followed his gaze, taking in the lavish Victorian carriage with a groomsman at the helm stopping next to them.

"Whoa." The driver commanded the two lovely horses with chestnut and flaxen manes.

Anna stroked the white blaze on the mare's face closest to her. The horse was smaller than many breeds but muscular and sturdy. "Beautiful creature." Anna had always wanted a horse in Dingle, but her family was too poor. Her father had kept a plow horse during Anna's early years but sold him to pay a debt.

"Haflingers." Stefan's eyes beamed as he stroked the horse. "A new breed developed in Europe known to give a smooth and energetic gait. I had the mares shipped from Austria. So far, these have lived up to their reputation."

Anna stepped away from the horse. The man had enough money to have the horses shipped from Europe. More proof that his superior station in life far acceded her own. "I see you're going out."

"I am ..." He checked his pocket watch. "I'm due at a nine o'clock appointment with my lawyer in ten minutes."

"I see." Anna lowered her head. She should have considered an important man like Mr. Maier might have other pressing concerns. "Perhaps tomorrow would be better, then." She offered him a fading smile, then turned away.

"Please, I'd like to see how you've got on." Mr. Maier caught her elbow. "I should be back within an hour. Meanwhile, my housekeeper can fix you up with a cup of tea and scones from breakfast." He swept her through the gate toward three stone steps leading up to the side entrance.

"Are you sure?" Anna halted at the bottom of the steps. "I can return when it's more convenient."

"I wouldn't want your effort to be for naught." Mr. Maier glanced at the package encased in her arm. "Besides, I'm anxious to try on my frock coat." He indicated the way up to the entrance, hastening up the steps behind her and opening the ornamented wood door.

They entered a small hallway that led into a conservatory, which looked out at the mountains. "Wait here," Mr. Maier ordered. He darted across the wood-plank floor through half-closed pocket doors of a wide-arched passage, leaving her to look after him.

Anna rambled in the same direction and peeked through the doorway. "Well, now, what am I to do?" She pulled back when Mr. Maier's footfalls approached. "Mr. Maier, I think I should return—"

"Miss O'Donnell will be with you shortly. In the meantime, there's a lovely view through those windows." He pointed, placed the bowler on his head, and hurried out the door.

Anna stepped closer to the windows, finding a spot between two tall ferns, and watched him jump into the carriage before it proceeded left and out of view. "I suppose one can be officious when one is a mining mogul."

She looked up and around at the mountains, which loomed large and impressive. Across the street, several lovely Victorians stood in the foreground before the rising peaks. What would it be like to be the mistress of such a home in this setting?

Her eyes grew wide. Now, what could have possibly made her think of such a notion? The man was too pompous and proud for her liking. Besides, she doubted he would ever consider her—the penniless daughter of a drunkard.

"Your tea is ready in the parlor, Miss Sullivan."

Surprised by the Irish brogue, Anna straightened and turned. A young girl wore a black bustled servant's dress and a white apron, her dark hair piled under a white cap. It would take little imagination for Anna to see herself donning an apron over her mourning gown if Mr. Maier was unhappy with her sewing.

Anna drew closer to the girl. "Thank you ... Miss O'Donnell, isn't it? From Ireland?"

"Yes, ma'am. County Cork."

"Ah, yes. Three days from my village of Dingle, in County

Kerry." Anna smiled, remembering her bittersweet travels across the country to catch the immigrant boat at Cobh Harbor. "And how long have you been in America?"

"Three years, ma'am. Left my da and ma and two brothers to make a life on my own."

"Brave girl, you are." Anna wanted to get to know her better. "I think I will take that tea now." She hefted her package and followed Miss O'Donnell into the central part of the house.

They entered a room several times the size of her cottage's little sitting area illuminated by an oil-lit chandelier and wall sconces. She stared in awe at the exquisite accouterments. Rarely had she had the opportunity to spend time in such a fine parlor. It reflected the grace and elegance belonging to the upper class.

Anna moved farther into the room and laid her package on a red velvet settee, which made part of a furniture grouping in front of the wood surround fireplace. She imagined it made for a cozy setting in front of a blazing fire on a cold winter's night.

As she continued to study the room, her gaze fell on a tintype displayed on a Rosewood credenza. Anna drew nearer, her interest piqued by the fair-haired woman in a ball gown next to a younger version of Mr. Maier in evening attire. They made a handsome couple in their fineries. But who was the woman? A wife? A sister? Laurel hadn't mentioned that Mr. Maier had a wife. But then again, neither had she indicated that he didn't. Was this a woman of Stefan's past that Laurel had alluded to?

Footfalls across the carpeting jarred Anna's attention, and she forgot the tintype as Mr. Maier's housemaid entered the room with a silver tea service and a basket of scones. She set them down on an oblong marble-top table across the room.

"It's so good of you to make tea." Anna flashed a grateful

smile, taking her place at the table and allowing the maid to pour. A ceramic globe oil lamp shone on the porcelain china of delicate roses and a gold leaf edge. Anna couldn't think of a time she'd taken tea at such a fine table. She assumed one place setting was for her and the other for Mr. Maier when he returned.

"Will that be all, ma'am?" Miss O'Donnell folded her hands.

A sudden desperation to stop the girl from leaving arose deep within Anna's soul. It all seemed wrong for her to sit at such a fine table with this slip of a girl serving her when she could likely end up in the same position. "Will you not join me?" Anna reached for the teapot.

"It wouldn't be right, ma'am." A horrified expression crossed the girl's face.

"And why not?" Anna's eyes widened. As soon as the words were out, she knew very well why not. Servants never presumed upon their employers or guests a right to sit with them anytime. Their place was in the background and the servants' quarters. But Miss O'Donnell didn't know that Anna's station in life matched hers in every way that counted.

"If Mr. Maier should return to see me hobnobbing with a guest, I should be sacked as sure as my name is Sarah O'Donnell."

Anna sympathized with her predicament, knowing the girl had every reason to fear banishment if she crossed the line. Perhaps Anna's behavior would cause his wrath, as well. "I promise I shall vouch for you."

Sarah clutched her stomach, biting her lip. "I-I don't know, ma'am."

"Please ... Sarah, isn't it?" Anna indicated the other chair, refusing to remain formal with the girl. "I'm missing home so very much, you see. I'll tell Mr. Maier I demanded your company and put you in the chair."

Sarah donned a brief smile and removed her arm from around her waist. "All right, then, ma'am—if you insist. But only a half cup." The girl sat on the edge of her seat, her eyes darting between Anna and the entrance to the room.

Anna poured tea, giving Sarah slightly more than the half cup she'd requested. Then Anna offered the basket of scones.

"Oh, I couldn't eat a bite, Miss Sullivan." Sarah shook her head.

Anna conceded, accepting that Sarah had come as far as she could. "Cork's a fine place, isn't it?" She sipped her tea.

"You know it, then?" Sarah widened her eyes.

Anna replaced her cup. "Only a little, I'm afraid. I passed through on my way to Cobh. But people say it's become quite the industrial town."

"Yes, ma'am. My brother Michael works in the shipping industry. My mum's last letter said he'd recently made foreman." Anna noted the proud tilt to her perk nose.

"Ah, good man, huh?"

"The finest brother." Her voice had turned wistful.

"You were close to him, then?"

"Michael always watched out for me, would have paid a dowry for me if he could ..."

The girl's blue eyes took on a faraway sheen, provoking Anna's regret that her own brother Ryan had died of dysentery when he was twelve, unable to see his sister grow up. Nor had he had the chance to take on responsibility for the family where their father had failed.

Sarah met Anna's gaze. "But I'm here now, and I must look out for myself."

Anna nodded, understanding well Sarah's position. In

many ways, she and Sarah were two of a kind. "Tell me about Cork ..."

～

"Forgive me for my long absence, Miss Sullivan. The meeting lasted much longer than I anticipated and ..." Mr. Maier's voice trailed off. Anna peered up as he came across the lushly carpeted room, disapproval written on his furrowed brow. "Miss O'Donnell, care to explain?"

The girl jumped out of her seat. "I-I'm sorry, Mr. Maier. I-I ..."

"You mustn't blame Sarah." Anna rose, the bustled mourning gown swishing around the table legs. "I insisted she must sit and tell me all about her home in Ireland. You *did* know she is from Ireland—Cork—isn't that right, Sarah?

"Yes, I did know. But the fact remains—"

"That you left me completely on my own with not even so much as a book to read, you know. Out of utter boredom, I practically dragged her into that chair, and having been trained by you to take care of your guests with the utmost care, she had no choice but to comply."

Mr. Maier rocked back on his heel. "I suppose under the circumstances, I can forgive—"

"That is very good of you. Now, Sarah—" Anna spoke to her and winked. "—I want to thank you for indulging my desire for company. Your kindness is well noted."

Sarah bowed and bolted through the threshold.

Anna turned back to Mr. Maier. A hand covered his mouth as if he held something back. She lifted a quizzical eyebrow, and he burst out in laughter. "Very cunning of you, Miss Sullivan. I don't think I've ever seen a more ingenious design to put me off guard."

She puffed out her cheeks, pretending she had no idea what he meant, then couldn't stop herself from giggling. "It was quite clever if I say so myself. Someone has to bring the grand Mr. Maier down a notch or two from time to time."

His laughter transformed into a mere muse. "Mm-hmm. I'm afraid you must stand in line for that, Miss Sullivan. Talk around town is I need bringing down."

Anna grimaced. A twinge of guilt assailed her for the ill-timed joke, and she adjusted her temperament to match his. "I'm sorry for your ordeal, Mr. Maier. It cannot be easy."

"A shrewd businessman expects to take his lumps occasionally." He dug his hands into his trouser pockets. "You don't get to where I am without making a few enemies along the way."

Though he smiled, the sentiment didn't reach his eyes.

Despite his affectation of casual indifference, Anna suspected Mr. Maier cared more than he let on. She stepped forward, sympathetic to his plight. "Well, you know more about these things than I do, but I can see the stress is taking its toll. Perhaps you need an advocate—"

"I have a competent lawyer, Miss Sullivan, and can stand on my own two feet." His voice dripped with sarcasm. He skirted around her, stopping near the fireplace, his frown reflected in the inset mirror above it.

"I'm sure you can." Anna folded her hands in front of her. "I'm only suggesting—"

"I've had my share of opposition over the years." He rubbed his hands together. "Competitors who would just as soon annihilate me for breathing, people who despise me because I have more material wealth at my disposal."

"Of course, criticism comes with the territory, but—"

"They've forgotten their bread is buttered because I run a successful mining operation."

"If you'd only listen to reason—"

"You brought a frock coat you've made for me." He ceased grinding his hands and stood taller, peering at her with expectation.

Anna met his steely gaze. She'd only wanted to encourage him. But he seemed determined to thwart her every effort. She didn't care if he was piqued. She wouldn't force her charity on anyone.

"Well, I can see you're in a mood." Anna moved to the settee where she'd placed the brown paper-wrapped package, picked it up, and practically shoved it into his hands. "Your coat, Mr. Maier."

He fumbled for the package, his lips curving into a crooked smile. "Thank you, Miss Sullivan." He tugged the ends of the string to release the bow, and the wrapping unfolded to reveal the coat.

Clutching the sleeves, Mr. Maier held the coat up for inspection. "Well done, Miss Sullivan." His disgruntled attitude dissipated into animated delight. "You've made a coat as fine as anything your Aunt Caitlin could have tailored for me. And the stitching around the buttonhole, what do you call that?" He pointed.

"You mean the feather stitch?" Anna feigned nonchalance. "I designed it myself. But perhaps you should try it on just to be sure the fit is also satisfactory."

A brief smile touched his lips. "Of course." He removed his coat and placed it on the chair, then slipped his arms through the sleeves of the new jacket. After rotating his shoulders, he declared, "Quite suitable, Miss Sullivan—fit for a king." He peered into her eyes.

Anna bounced on her toes, the exhilaration flooding her heart. "Ah, 'tis grand you be liking the coat." She could barely contain the grin that spread across her face.

"And the waistcoat ..." He folded the frock coat over his arm.

Anna stiffened, the smile freezing on her face. "To be honest, there just wasn't time. I would be glad to—"

"Oh, no need to look so stricken, Miss Sullivan." He peered at her. "I will speak at a Businessman's Association banquet in Denver on Tuesday. Do you think you can have the waistcoat ready by the end of the day on Monday?"

"It would be my pleasure, Mr. Maier." Anna threw her shoulders back.

"Very good." Mr. Maier tossed the coat over the settee, then turned back, his frown well pronounced. "It seems I owe you another apology, Miss Sullivan."

"Oh?" Anna raised her brow.

"I'm afraid I was rather impertinent a moment ago." Mr. Maier pocketed his hands. "It's a habit I've developed over the years. I suppose I've become a regular old Scrooge—crotchety and—"

"Understandable, I should think." Anna let down her defenses. At least the man was making an effort.

"But it's no excuse for bad manners." His steady gaze met hers. "You deserve better."

Anna drew in a quick breath, a floating sensation sending her hopes sailing that perhaps Mr. Maier would allow her to give him some comfort to ease the pain.

He crossed his arms. "This unfortunate business has done more damage than anyone can imagine. We forfeit tens of thousands of dollars every day the mine is closed."

"Tens of thousands?" Anna's eyes grew large. She couldn't fathom that amount of money even if she tried. "Couldn't you stay open, even at a minimal level?"

"I cabled the hoist company for parts yesterday." He unfolded his arms and paced away from her, then spun around. "It could be days or even weeks before we're fully functional again. Lost time we can't afford."

"Ach, what a business."

"Yes." He brooded. "But the disaster was no accident, nor was I negligent."

"No accident?" Anna peered into his troubled eyes, stunned by the revelation. If not, then that meant someone had purposely caused it. "'Tis what you were alluding to after the funeral, wasn't it?"

"Oh, the cable broke." Mr. Maier spoke through his teeth, eyes squinting. "But someone tampered with it."

Outrage surged through Anna's soul. "Who would commit such an evil?"

"That is the quintessential question, Miss Sullivan. Who, indeed?"

Silence permeated the air with emotional electricity.

Anna stepped forward. "That's why you asked me to keep an open mind."

He gave her a sullen nod.

"But if what you're saying is true, then it seems high time we search for the person who killed my uncle, don't you think?"

Mr. Maier's stony gaze softened, and his shoulders relaxed. "Though it gives me some small comfort, I am relieved at least one person harbors no ill will against me, Miss Sullivan. Though, by all means, you have a right to it. As for who committed the heinous crime, I'm convinced I will be hard-pressed to uncover the culprit."

"Have you any idea who could have done such a thing?"

He nodded, the expression in his eyes grave. "But proving it will not be easy."

"Perhaps not. But I believe the truth always bears out in the end." Anna pressed her lips.

"I hope you're right, Miss Sullivan." Mr. Maier clenched his jaw. "Too many people have been hurt and will continue to suffer the consequences for the man to escape punishment."

She stepped forward, finding an acute sense of purpose she hadn't known for a long time. "Mark my words, Mr. Maier. The murderer may mask his face in the dark for a time, but he will make a mistake along the way, and his face shall come to light." She tightened her fists. It just had to, for everyone's sake.

Thirteen

On Monday morning, Anna made a cup of tea and set it on the kitchen table, then picked up a pair of scissors to cut out the pinned-up fabric for Stefan's waistcoat. She'd just completed the job to her satisfaction and taken hold of a needle and thread when a knock came at the door. She glanced at the clock on the wall. Nine o'clock. She returned the needle to the pincushion and rose to answer the door.

Anna's mouth gaped at the mother and daughter who stood before her. "Can I help you?"

"I very much hope so. I'm Georgia Tucker, and this is our sixteen-year-old daughter, Prudence."

"Mrs. Tucker, I'm so glad to meet you at last." Anna smiled. "I was just—"

"It's about time, don't you think?" Mrs. Tucker rushed on. "Clyde has spoken so highly of you. And now we've come because news is all over town that you're a seamstress just like your Aunt Caitlin," Mrs. Tucker announced. "There's to be a Harvest Ball at the Barton House the Saturday before

Thanksgiving, and Prudence would like you to make her a gown."

Anna stared at the expectant face of the woman whose ash-blonde hair was piled under a straw hat. How had the news spread so quickly? Had Laurel fanned the flames of the rumor mill?

"Won't you please come in, Mrs. Tucker?" Anna finally found her voice.

"We're so obliged, Miss Sullivan." The woman pushed her daughter inside the door ahead of her. "I hope we're not intruding."

Anna didn't want to begrudge her fortune, but eyeing Mr. Maier's waistcoat, she felt a strong urge to rush the conversation with Mrs. Tucker and her daughter.

"Of course, we would gladly pay you Caitlin's going rate."

Anna glanced at Prudence. The girl had clasped her hands behind her back, fidgeting, her eyes looking everywhere except at Anna. "That's more than acceptable." Anna readjusted her stance and studied the girl's frame, wishing she could put her at ease.

An inch shorter than her five feet seven inches, Miss Tucker was a tad overweight. But her piercing blue eyes and comely face made up for her lack of figure. Depending on the style and color of her gown, Anna believed she could do Prudence justice.

"I can come by tomorrow at nine to discuss what you might fancy for a gown if that's all right with you, Prudence? We'll take measurements, and you can tell me the kind of material you'd like—sateen, something with lace and ribbons and bows—whatever you prefer."

"Is that all right, Mother?" The girl grinned.

"Oh, Miss Sullivan, you are a lifesaver." Mrs. Tucker waved

her hand in dramatic flair, reminding Anna of an actress on stage.

"Well, we'll wait and see if she likes the dress before we determine that, shall we?" Anna smiled and folded her hands in front of her. "Where shall I come?"

"We have our house on Rose Street. You'll know it by the lavender trim." Mrs. Tucker pointed northeast of the cottage. "Clyde thought about changing the name of the inn when we first purchased it—"

"You're the *owners* of the Barton House, then?" Here, she had thought Clyde was the clerk.

"That, my dear, is a very long story." She leaned in. "It all started—"

Anna glanced at her sewing project. She didn't want to be rude, but time was getting on.

"You probably have things to do," Mrs. Tucker scoffed. "But I promise to tell you the whole story another time."

"I shall look forward to it." Anna cast her an appreciative smile.

"Tomorrow, then, at nine o'clock." Mrs. Tucker whisked Prudence out the door with a satisfied saunter in her step, leaving Anna to wonder what had just happened.

Four more sets of mothers and daughters came by afterward, including the mayor's wife and daughter, Virginia and Elizabeth Henley, all with the same request. It seemed all of Georgetown regarded the Harvest Ball as *the* event of the fall season, providing an opportunity for a single young lady to catch the beau of her dreams. And for her parents, it meant espying the right young man for their daughter to marry. As for the rest of the town, the social extravaganza allowed them to enjoy a respite from their labors.

Anna waved the last of her patrons out the door and stared after them, exhausted and spellbound by the whirlwind of activity throughout the morning. Her sewing business had grown overnight, and her worries about rent and wood for the winter vanished before her.

She looked toward the ceiling. "Lord, I'm thankful for all the work, but perhaps you've overdone it a wee bit. Could you give me some breathing room to finish the waistcoat for Mr. Maier?" She picked up the coat and resumed her sewing.

At half past one, Laurel came by.

"Would you mind if I keep working while you're here?" Anna pleaded, spilling her story of the five women who'd come by to commission her to make their gowns for the Harvest Ball. "I promised Mr. Maier I'd have the project ready by evening, and I feel determined to do it."

"Of course, you must." She set her reticule on the nearby table. "I'll make us some tea, then we can chat while you work, and I can tell you all about the Harvest Ball."

Anna sat and drew another stitch through the waistcoat while Laurel went to work making tea.

After the tea had steeped, Laurel brought their cups into the sitting room and sat across from Anna. "Now, let me tell you all the scoop on our ball." She spent the next several minutes talking about the annual event.

"It sounds delightful, Laurel, but it's all so daunting." Anna laid the waistcoat on her lap and looked at Laurel. "I've got six weeks to complete five ball gowns. I'll be working my fingers to the bone to get it all accomplished."

"I must say, I'm not surprised after seeing your work." Laurel sipped her tea. "But how did everyone find out so quickly?"

Anna stared at Laurel. "I thought you had spread the word."

"Oh, no, my dear. I wish I could tell you I had." Laurel gazed at her in return.

"But who then?"

"Can't you guess?" Laurel placed her tea on the table, her eyes beaming.

"No." Anna couldn't believe it. "Mr. Maier?"

"Just as I'd hoped." Laurel clapped her hands. "I suspected he might throw business your way if he liked your work."

"But I saw him at church yesterday. He wasn't even wearing the frock coat, which discouraged me. I thought he hadn't cared for it after all." She inserted her needle into the fabric.

"Mr. Maier is a fashionable man. Perhaps he was waiting for his waistcoat." Laurel picked up her tea again. "No matter. If he said the word, people would listen, especially Mrs. Henley. And word spreads like wildfire in this small community."

"Ach, I've noticed." Anna's eyes grew wide. In many ways, this environment wasn't much different from the one she'd grown up in. "I doubt one can hide much in this town."

"It's a blessing and a curse." Laurel's voice hummed with humor. "But it's a wonderful problem to have, don't you think? You'll have no end of work to ensure your living."

"It seems I already have more than I believed was possible, and I've got you to thank for insisting I take on the unfinished project." Anna resumed sewing the buttons on Mr. Maier's waistcoat.

"Don't forget Mr. Maier and the good Lord himself." Laurel sipped her tea.

"I just hope I can do justice to all those ball gowns, or I might still find myself tossed out on my bum."

"I doubt you have anything to worry about, my dear." Laurel gave her a reassuring smile. "I believe God has His plans all laid out for you."

"Then, I must be thanking Him for it. But I sure hope He knows what He's doing."

~

"Well done, Miss Sullivan!" Stefan flashed a wide grin, standing before a mirror in the vestibule of his home. Indeed, the waistcoat complemented the frock coat well and gave him a sophisticated flair. He turned to face her. "Once again, you've come up with a unique design."

"I'm glad you approve." Miss Sullivan's voice bubbled with joy, giving Stefan a sensation of weightlessness despite the burden he carried on his back.

"I heard you will make a ball gown for Mayor Henley's daughter." Stefan had spoken highly of Miss Sullivan's talents to the mayor's wife at the end of an unpleasant conversation with the mayor after dinner on Saturday night.

"But how did you know?" Anna's eyes widened. "She only came by this morning."

"I saw Mrs. Henley this afternoon outside the Opera House." Warmth radiated throughout Stefan's body. He could barely contain the satisfaction of his efforts. "She seemed quite taken with you—said a number of the ladies in town have contracted your services."

"And I wonder who told the ladies of Georgetown about my tailoring skills?"

"Perhaps since you and Mrs. Thomas have become well-acquainted," Stefan bounced lightly, "she put in a good word for you."

"Funny, that." Anna lifted her chin. "Mrs. Thomas protested only two hours ago that she had not and made the same suggestion about you."

"Well ... I ..." Stefan didn't want her to feel she owed him anything, especially after they had started on the wrong footing.

"I'm sincerely grateful for your vote of confidence in me. You've kept your word. And where I come from, that means a lot."

Stefan's shoulders relaxed. "Then I am equally pleased."

His gaze lingered on Anna's softened eyes. He had a sudden desire to run his fingers through her long amber curls and imagined removing the black teardrop mourning hat to unpin them. He reached up, but Miss Sullivan turned, and he dropped his hand.

"I should be getting back." Anna retrieved her reticule from a nearby entrance table. "My first appointment tomorrow is with Prudence Tucker at nine o'clock sharp, and you will be traveling to Denver in the morning."

"I'll walk you to the cottage. I insist," Stefan said when Anna would have protested. He donned his top hat and coat, then draped Anna's cloak over her shoulders. "You never know what animals might cross your path." He couldn't keep the sarcasm from escaping his lips.

Anna offered a diminutive smile as he opened the front door for her to step into the crisp night air.

They walked the first block down Rose Street in silence, Stefan's thoughts returning to Saturday night's dinner. Though he boasted a close relationship with Charles and Virginia Henley, Charles had invited him into the parlor for a digestif to warn him that he could not shelter Stefan if the law went against him.

"You understand. It's not personal."

It never was when political aspirations were involved. Still, the declaration felt like a betrayal by a friend, and Stefan had left the stiff brandy untouched on the expensive mahogany table in the foyer.

"You're concerned about the banquet." Anna broke into Stefan's thoughts.

He shrugged. "Best case, I convince investors I'm not guilty of what I have been accused of and am worthy of their trust. Worst case, no one will touch me with a ten-foot pole, and I walk away without a speck of credit to my name." His tone was light, but the burden was heavy on his shoulders.

"Surely the investors won't deny you a loan." Anna halted near Alpine Street and searched his face in the moonlight.

The enticement of concern in Anna's gaze precipitated a yearning so intense, so deeply hidden and forgotten since the drought of loneliness and despair had taken hold of Stefan's life years ago that he desperately desired to quench the thirst. Oh, how he wanted to draw fresh water from the cistern before him, allowing her sweet taste to satiate his need. Stefan swallowed, resolve asserting itself before he let his passions rule. Anna Sullivan deserved better than his self-indulgent cravings.

He cupped her elbow and led her forward. "I am sincerely grateful for your regard of my troubles, Miss Sullivan. I shall leave for Denver in the morning, knowing I now have three people in Georgetown who believe I'm innocent."

God willing, he would also convince several investors at tomorrow's banquet to count him trustworthy. Otherwise, everything he had invested to create a productive life in Georgetown would come to ruin.

Fourteen

Stefan put the final touches on his apparel, buttoning a pair of gold cuff links given to him by his father and brooding about the journey he embarked on. A little more than a week ago, he would have looked forward to the Businessman's Association banquet, satisfied with the empire he had built out of the profits from the Singing Silver Mine. Now, getting ready on this chilly Tuesday morning, it seemed his fortune had taken a detour. He desperately needed to persuade investors to continue banking on the mine.

He slipped on the waistcoat Miss Sullivan had tailored, running a hand over the fine stitching. Who would have guessed she would be the brightest spot in the shadows of his life at present?

His thoughts returned to the night before when he desperately wanted to kiss her, acknowledging her concern for him had awakened a desire for a relationship that had been missing in his life for a very long time. Had he only imagined she cared for him? Or was her concern merely guided by her compassionate nature? Either way, he was drawn to her in a way he hadn't been drawn to anyone since Charity. He would put her out of his mind if he had any sense, for he could not imagine what his aristocratic parents would say about an Irish girl of no breeding.

"Preposterous!" he could hear his mum express as if she performed in a melodrama. He twisted his lips. Dear Mum. Her years at the Royal Opera had made her more, not less, pompous. Still, he loved her, and she would forever be immortalized by his Singing Silver Mine if, indeed, he could find the ongoing financial backing. But she could not dictate who Stefan wanted for a companion.

He donned the matching frock coat Miss Sullivan had tailored, picked up his small travel trunk, and hastened to the lower floor. In the library, he found the papers he had prepared and assembled on his desk, then placed them in a leather pouch, latched the clasp, and put the strap over his shoulder. He grasped his trunk and strode to the back door where Sarah waited.

"Your hat, sir." She handed him his bowler.

"Thank you, Sarah." Stefan popped the hat on his head, then gazed at the umbrella stand. "Do you think it will rain while I'm away?" He'd never consulted his housemaid on anything before—always ordering her about, according to his whims. But today, her opinion on the weather mattered to him.

"I don't …" Sarah hesitated.

"It's all right, Sarah. I want your honest opinion."

"Well, sir … it never hurts to be prepared."

"Quite right." He grabbed an umbrella and gave her a wisp of a smile, then pushed the door open for a five-minute walk to the Barton House to catch the nine o'clock stagecoach.

The morning sky belied the need for the umbrella he carried since there wasn't a cloud in the sky, but one never knew the state of the weather from one hour to the next in this Territory of Colorado. Typically, William would have accompanied him, but his partner was halfway to England by now. Stefan had to face the Businessman's Association alone, and one never knew the climate he might encounter there, either.

At Barton House, Stefan handed his trunk to the stagecoach driver for storage in the baggage boot, then poked his head into the stagecoach.

"Wait! Mr. Maier!"

Stefan backed himself out of the stagecoach. There before him, the visage of his dreams gasped for breath. "Miss Sullivan, are you all right?" He grabbed Anna's arm.

"Yes, I'm perfectly fine." She inhaled deeply. "I wanted to give you something I found among my uncle's things." She handed him a sterling silver Celtic cross to wear around his neck. "I'm sure he would have wanted you to have it—to remind you you're not alone. Keep your heart close to God, and He will grant you the desires of your heart."

"I don't know what to say." Warmth radiated through Stefan's body as he studied the simple design. He gazed at her with softened eyes. "I will treasure it with my life."

"All aboard the stagecoach bound for Idaho Springs."

Stefan listened to the driver's announcement. "That's my call." He gazed at her again. "This means a tremendous amount." He closed his fingers around the cross, then entered the stagecoach, sitting at the back. The coach jerked, and they were off. He waved, smiling at her as they passed, rejuvenated by Anna's gift. Perhaps all would work out as he hoped at this evening's banquet, and he would secure the loan he sought.

~

Anna dug into her tote bag for her father's pocket watch. Thankfully, she still had five minutes to reach her nine o'clock appointment at the Tucker House. The brisk October air energized her pace. Was it only yesterday her life seemed to have changed overnight? She had more work than she could have ever imagined, thanks to Mr. Maier and the good Lord's doing.

Mr. Maier seemed well-pleased by her gift—her uncle's Celtic cross. She hoped it would give him peace and comfort during his trying time at the banquet. God knew enough enemies surrounded him.

She said a small prayer for his safety in travel and successful engagements with the investors who held his financial future in their hands. But even if they decided against him, Anna believed God would be faithful to work it out. Hadn't He done so for her living in Georgetown?

Considering her discourse with Mr. Maier the night before, Anna's heart raced. Had she only imagined he wanted to kiss her? She didn't think so. But if she was honest, she had wanted him to kiss her too. But what could the future hold for them? He was still a wealthy man of noble birth, and she, a poor Irish peasant from Dingle.

She shook her head. For now, she wouldn't think about the consequences of an entanglement with Mr. Maier as she approached the lovely, white two-story Victorian with lavender trim next to the south branch of Clear Creek. She walked to the door with its bouquet of dried flowers and reached for the knocker.

Mrs. Tucker opened the door, looking fresh in her bustled beige skirt, and pulled Anna into the confined foyer. "We're so thankful you've agreed to help us, Miss Sullivan. Prudence has been waiting on pins and needles all morning." The woman snorted. "Oh, my, did I just make a pun?"

Anna let out a soft laugh. "Quite appropriate in this case. But please, call me Anna. I dare say, after the way you and Mr. Tucker have welcomed me, I feel most obliged. Besides, if Prudence believes we're on good terms, it will ease her nerves about working with a new seamstress."

"I'd like nothing better than to be on a first-name basis." The woman leaned in. "The name's Georgia, but I'll still require Prudence to call you by the proper address. Sometimes, the girl's head is so high in the clouds she forgets her manners." Georgia pointed her head up the steep stairway in front of them with its wallpaper of blush and pink roses. "Prudence, Miss Sullivan is here."

Footsteps scurried across the floor above them, bounding down the stairs. Then, they halted. Anna walked to the stairway and found Prudence hesitating on the third step. She wore a brown gingham dress and had plaited her thick, chestnut hair. Yet it was her eyes, the color of an azure sky, that impressed Anna most.

"I promise not to bite." Anna hoped humor would put the girl at ease.

Prudence sauntered the rest of the way down, perking her nose upward and affecting a casual indifference.

Anna stifled a laugh and folded her hands in front of her. "I hope you're as excited as I am about the gown we're going to make for you. Shall we get started?"

"I sure am ... I mean, yes, Miss Sullivan."

"Wonderful." Anna grinned.

"You can use the front room over here." Georgia walked past Anna, leading them into a living area where the sun shone through the windows.

"What a lovely room." Anna compared the warm and

inviting interior to her sparse space. A gold velvet divan and two chairs surrounded a center table before the fireplace, and a pianoforte sat against an inside wall. Next to it was a bookshelf with books of every kind. She put her tote on the floor next to the divan and removed her hat. "This will do quite nicely. But why did your family never move into the Barton House?"

"Oh, that's a long story." Georgia waved her hand.

"We have a little time." Anna encouraged her. "I'd love to hear it."

Georgia clasped her hands. "William Barton was an upstanding man from Boston who came west for a change of pace. When he built Barton House in '69, everyone in town raved about the two-story inn on Taos Street for business travelers. But a fire destroyed the house two years later."

"How terrible. But a house stands there now."

"Mr. Barton was not one to waste time." Georgia shook her head. "He set out immediately to rebuild and made it an even finer house than the first one, which was why everyone was surprised when he put the inn up for sale a short while later."

"It is odd, isn't it?" Anna frowned. "But 'tis a grand house, I'll give him that much."

"I think he ran out of steam running the place and missed his hometown. We'd already purchased this house on Clyde's wages as a lawyer. But Clyde thought he might enjoy hospitality for a change—'the ability to dispense generosity rather than greed,' he said.

"From my experience, you both do that very well, indeed."

"I'm delighted you think so." Georgia beamed, then looked at her daughter. "Living here also gives Prudence a normal life, and we can employ other staff to fill in."

"Sometimes I feel like we live in two houses." Prudence rolled her eyes.

"Surliness is not becoming of a girl, young lady." Georgia

scolded her daughter, then addressed Anna. "I should let the two of you get on with your task. I'll be in the kitchen if you need me." She headed to the back of the house.

Anna turned to Prudence. The girl fingered a necklace, her eyes flitting back and forth. It seemed wise to put her at ease.

"Let's get to know each other a little before we start, shall we." Anna chose a nearby armchair while Prudence gingerly sat on the edge of a divan cushion. "Tell me what you enjoy for your leisure activities."

"I like to read." Prudence bounced her leg beneath her fluttering skirt.

Anna smiled enthusiastically, happy she'd found something in common with the girl. "Ah, very good. What are some of your favorite books and authors?"

"I've become enamored by Jane Austen's books. I've read every one of them. *Pride and Prejudice* is my favorite. And everything by Charlotte and Emily Brontë."

"I suppose you're like my good friend in Ireland. Clare adores Heathcliff in *Wuthering Heights*—says he's wickedly dark and daring, a man that sweeps a woman off her feet."

"That's what makes him all the more attractive," Prudence announced, her chin bearing up again. "Heathcliff so desperately loves Catherine that he wants her in spite of despising her love of money and status."

"Em, the plight and plague of many a girl." Anna had known some in Ireland. "What else tickles your fancy?"

"Music. I love to sing and play piano—maybe sing in the opera someday." Prudence became animated, but then her countenance fell. "Only ..."

"Only what?" Anna prodded, tilting her head.

"Studying music is just another reason I get left out of the social circles."

"How so?" Anna frowned.

"Surely you've noticed?" The girl seemed desperate. "I'm not very pretty and maybe a bit pudgy. The girls call me 'Goody Two-Shoes' and say I'm too moralistic and always have my head in a book. They're always flirting with the boys and acting all coy-like." She straightened, tilting her chin up. "They giggle and sap about what it would be like to be married to this one or that one, all the while saying none of the boys would ever want me."

"I'm sure that isn't true." Anna wanted to encourage her.

"Oh, but it is." Prudence leaned in with an insistent voice. "The boys say I'm hoity-toity. I overheard one talking behind my back the other day. 'No one wants to make love to a brain.'" She swiped the tears away from her cheeks. "They don't know how much what they say pierces me to the bone."

Perhaps the girl had a penchant for the overly dramatic, but Anna knew how much their remarks hurt and understood Prudence's anguish. "It's not easy being on the receiving end of ridicule, is it?" Anna looked away, remembering her schoolmates' intimidation.

"But you're so pretty and kind and full of wit. Why would anyone treat you with such disdain?"

"Now there's a tale for the telling." Anna peered back at Prudence. Perhaps telling the girl what her life had been like growing up in Dingle would give her some perspective.

"Though I studied alongside girls from the upper-class gentry, I didn't share in their wealth. We moved in very different social spheres. Theirs aroused my envy, while mine spawned their contempt. You see, my parents came from peasantry, and ..." Anna poured out her story.

Ma had worked as a domestic for the O'Connor family and left her sister Caitlin to care for Anna. But when Aunt Caitlin and Uncle Liam emigrated to America, the O'Connors allowed

Anna to tag along with her mother, stipulating Anna must not interfere with Ma's duties.

Anna played with the three O'Connor children, including the eldest, Seamus, as if they were family under Ma's care. Seamus and Anna's bond grew over the years going to school and becoming best friends with Clare Doherty and Ryan O'Neill. "We became as impenetrable as a thicket of trees."

However, the relationship didn't mean Anna was impervious to heckles from the wealthier girls. Maeve Kelly tormented her so severely about her shabby clothes that Anna came home from school one afternoon with her dress torn and bruises on her arms and legs.

Despite her attempts to hide her injuries, the evidence was apparent to Seamus. Anna had been assaulted as sure as the rain gave birth to the rainbow. He dragged the whole story out of her and vowed no one would treat her that way again. And none had.

Not long afterward, Anna had reached the age where she could no longer attend secondary school at the state's expense. Instead, she aided Ma at the O'Connor farm, corralling the younger children and helping with their schoolwork. "Sometimes, after Seamus came home from school, I joined him in the pasture, tending the sheep and devouring everything he had learned that day." Over time, their mutual passion for literature and the land blossomed into a love for each other that seemed to take root like the sweet yellow buttercups in the field.

Meanwhile, Ma taught Anna tatting and sewing in the evenings to give her work skills. The prospect held little appeal for Anna since she had greater aspirations to marry Seamus. But having observed her daughter's affections, Ma reminded Anna often that a future with Seamus was impossible. Her employers would never allow Anna to marry him. She had no dowry, nothing material to offer the family. Ma advised her to join her aunt and uncle in Colorado. "Go to America. Forget about Seamus. Forget about me. It's the only way you'll ever do better than egg and butter money."

Six months into her training, Anna came in through the back of the O'Connor house and overheard Seamus and his ma having words in the kitchen.

"I don't know why you insist on carrying on with that girl." Mrs. O'Connor seemed loathed. "It can come to nothing."

"Why do you call her 'that girl' as if she were no better than a scullery maid, Ma?" Seamus sounded irritated. "You've always treated her like one of us."

"Perhaps that was my first mistake. Anna has never been 'one of us.' She has no pedigree, no dowry, nothing that can recommend her."

"I love her. That should count for something."

"What does love have to do with it? Desirable, yes, but not necessary. You'll get over her in time. Men always do."

"I will not stand for your insults, Ma. I love Anna, and I want us to be married."

"Then you listen to this. If you persist in this nonsense, you will lose everything—this farm and your inheritance. Better to cut Anna out of your life now."

Anna brushed the moisture from her face. "That's when I ran out of the house, sobbing so hard, I couldn't see the road in front of me for the tears.

"Ma became sick soon afterward. She appealed to me once more on her deathbed to join my aunt and uncle in America. 'Your da is too consumed with drink to provide for you, and a future with Seamus will never be forthcoming.' She grabbed my hand. 'Promise me you'll go to America, my child. It's the only way you'll do better than butter and egg money.'"

"Is that when you came here?" Prudence asked.

Anna shook her head. "No. I remained another five years in Ireland, taking care of Da. But I never forgot Mrs. O'Connor's tone or the humiliation that ripped my heart to shreds."

"What happened to Seamus?" Prudence furrowed her brow.

"He tried to convince me love would always prevail." Anna averted her eyes. "But I knew in my heart his parents would never allow it." She peered into Prudence's eyes once more. "After Da died, I set sail for America to make my living and help Uncle Liam."

"Oh, Miss Sullivan, it is a dismal fate to be a victim of unrequited love. I hope to be as brave as you if I'm ever in similar circumstances."

Anna quelled the smile at Prudence's melodramatic outburst. "I hope you never will, Prudence. But more importantly, you mustn't ever allow another person's petty behavior to rob you of your self-worth. You have the most penetrating blue eyes I have ever seen and a natural beauty that Da Vinci himself would have admired." Anna grabbed hold of Prudence's hand. "Don't let the other girls and boys shame you into believing anything else. All right, so you're a little chubby. That's easily taken care of with a small change in diet. As for your brain, a mature man admires a woman who can keep his interest with her intellect."

"You really think so, Miss Sullivan?" Prudence dabbed her eyes with a handkerchief.

"Mark my words. It will be a man worth keeping who uncovers the precious gem in you."

"You've made me feel so much better, Miss Sullivan." Prudence brightened. "I think I'm ready for you to measure me now. And make the waist size a little smaller. I intend to lose five pounds before the Harvest Ball."

"Excellent," Anna declared with bravado. "Now, I can't promise the dry goods store will have it, but what do you think of sapphire blue for the gown to go with your stunning eyes? And if we can't find it, we'll come up with a color equally as complimentary ..."

Fifteen

Two hours after the stagecoach left Barton House, Stefan pocketed the Celtic cross in his frock coat for safekeeping and exited the stagecoach at the Idaho Springs station for a temporary stopover. On his forty-minute break at the L & L Roadhouse, he ate an early lunch at a rustic table, drinking coffee—dark as mud and thick as tar—and savored every last bite of hearty beef stew.

Stefan set the bowl aside, his thoughts turning to Anna. He removed the cross from his pocket and smiled. She couldn't know what it meant to him.

Stefan repocketed the cross and searched his leather pouch for a pen and notebook. He needed a ready response to every objection investors might have about his cash-flow problem.

"*Bist du wegen des Banketts des Wirtschaftsverbandes hier, Stefan?*" An officious voice interrupted in German, breaking Stefan's concentration.

Stefan went rigid. The monster in a black cutaway morning coat and pinstripe pants had just commandeered his perfect day. The wire-rimmed, bespectacled Georg Töpfer towered above him, obviously enjoying the advantage. Using their mother tongue added to the man's attitude of self-importance.

"You know very well I'm attending the banquet," Stefan responded in English.

"I thought you might skip out on an event that could cause embarrassment. After all, your reputation has been sullied by the, shall we say, *unfortunate* incident at the mine. What are you losing? Ten? Twenty thousand a day?"

Stefan's irritation burned like bile in his throat, but he kept his temper in check. "The Singing Silver Mine will prevail and come back even stronger after the truth comes to light." He waved away the man's accusations like a pesky fly.

Töpfer peered over his wire-rimmed glasses at Stefan. "You've got nerve. But I wonder what you will say when the hoist remains at the bottom of the shaft, and you discover the last song has been sung at your singing mine. Better to sell now while you still can."

"And I suppose you're the one to buy it."

"I'll give you a fair price."

"You speak as if you believe it's a *fait accompli*."

"Come now, Stefan. Isn't it time to cut your losses?"

Stefan wanted to wipe the smug smile off the braggart's face. But before he could comment, the stagecoach driver's siren call boomed through the dining hall. "Stagecoach to Denver leaving in five minutes."

Stefan threw the pen onto his notebook and rose, standing several inches taller than the German. "I'll take my chances. You can keep your money and your priggish attitude, Töpfer. Now, if you don't mind, I have a stagecoach to catch."

Stefan slid the pen and notebook into his pouch, sensing the German staring after him as he headed to the exit. Let him. Stefan had more critical fires to tend.

Sigmund Dreher relished the hot mineral bath at Idaho Springs. It reduced his stress and worked wonders for his circulation. Of course, the small wooden structure that housed the Ocean Bath House was minuscule compared to the lavish Roman-style bathhouse he was accustomed to at Baden-Baden in his native Germany.

Sigmund laid his head back against the hard rock of the hot springs bath. He missed the scenic village set between the idyllic green rolling hills and valleys of the Black Forest to the north, the Rhine River Valley to the west, and the Swabian Alps to the south. The spa's thermal waters were a prime destination for relaxing and enjoying a summer holiday and catered to Europe's elite. Even Queen Victoria had once enjoyed its august ambiance and medicinal benefits.

Sigmund couldn't imagine any of Europe's wealthy class dipping their toes into these waters, let alone bathing in them, even if it did advertise itself as the "Saratoga of the Rocky Mountains." He snorted. He'd been to Saratoga Springs, New York, and this place didn't come close to the beauty of the bathhouse gardens nor the elegance of the Grand Hotel that served its charming guests. The Ute and Arapahoe nations may have held these hot springs sacred, but this house sat in the middle of an open, dusty field along a pathetic creek. That it boasted the outlaw Jesse James had visited once didn't seem something of which to be proud.

Still, the Ocean Bath House did him well in a pinch and provided a clandestine meeting spot for his purposes. He smirked. Perhaps he did have something in common with Jesse James.

A short while later, the hireling Sigmund had prearranged to meet came through the door and placed himself inside the nearby gazebo. The man removed his hat, displaying the mat and dirt of his long, sandy blond hair. Dried mud clung to the bottom of his sack suit jacket.

Sigmund groaned, his blood boiling and bubbling, and he hadn't yet had a chance to talk to the obtuse little man. Couldn't the dolt have washed his hair before appearing at a public spa? Sigmund liked neatness. It demonstrated healthy self-respect and consideration of others.

Hopping out of the hot springs, Sigmund dried himself with the plush towel, then threw it around his shoulders and headed to the pavilion in his swimming attire—a hip-length top and trunks that ended at the knee. He scanned the pool area, grateful they had no one to observe them. "Must you show up like a worm that crawled out of the mud? It draws needless attention."

"If you'd lay aside that arrogant attitude of yours for just a second," Elias Jones narrowed his eyes, "you just might ascertain that I got into a scrape with one of the local natives."

"Indeed." Sigmund crossed his arms.

"He ambushed me, pushed me into the river, and stole my food before I chased him off."

Sigmund chewed the inside of his cheek, skeptical of the scene Elias had painted. Natives were known to be hostile but rarely traveled alone. They didn't like to for fear of spiritual forces they thought roamed the woods. "You say one lone native attacked you?"

"He was young—twelve maybe—and scruffy." Elias directed a menacing gaze at Sigmund. "Come to think of it," Elias placed his hands on his hips, "he seemed more scared of me than I was of him. I think he saw my rifle and took off."

Sigmund didn't believe a word of it. Where had the rifle been while Jones was in the river? He'd probably been sleeping off an overindulgence in alcohol after gambling away most of his earnings. However, Sigmund didn't intend to tangle with the imbecile. He needed Elias to dispose of business he preferred not to handle himself.

"Perhaps that good aim of yours will come in handy for what I have in mind since my skills aren't so ... dexterous."

"Yes, sir." He swiped his nose. "So long as it means I get my fair share."

Sigmund grabbed onto his towel with both hands and pulled. The tension between his shoulder blades had returned in full force. "Oh, you'll get your fair share. Don't you worry about that. Just do the job you're hired to do."

"Well, now, what did you have in mind?"

Sixteen

Anna floated on air as she strolled to the upper side of town for her second measuring appointment. Helping Prudence gain a more positive perspective on herself gave new meaning to her job.

Though one had to sew material together to fit a person, the real art happened before a stitch was ever sewn—connecting with their thoughts and feelings and understanding what made them feel most confident. She would do her job well if she could make a difference in how people viewed themselves.

Still, the farther Anna walked into the Henleys' neighborhood, the more her misgivings crept up, like when she'd first come to this side of town to deliver Mr. Maier's coat. She knew why the south side was called the upper side. Not only was it uphill from the north side of town, but the houses were more prominent and the façades more elaborate. She knocked on Mayor Henley's door with a tad more trepidation than she had experienced at the Tuckers'.

"Good morning, Miss Sullivan. So good of you to be on time." Mrs. Henley met Anna with pinched lips and an upturned chin. Her bustled skirt and ruffled bodice bespoke elegance, and her blonde curls piled atop her head and adorned with jeweled pins were equally stylish. By all worldly standards, Mrs. Henley appeared to be an attractive and accomplished woman of regal bearing. She ushered Anna into the foyer, folding her hands and blatantly taking inventory of Anna's person. Anna felt compelled to check her hair and dust-covered shoes but fought the urge.

"I always say you can judge a person's character by the time they keep."

"I shall always do my best, Mrs. Henley." Anna squared her shoulders and spoke with more assurance than she felt. She would need to keep some rules if she wanted to remain employed by the Henleys. Rule number one: be as wise as a serpent and innocent as a dove. Rule number two: mind your time.

"Please follow me." Mrs. Henley led Anna into a parlor as luxurious as the woman herself. "I'll go in search of Elizabeth. Now there's one who's rarely on time." The woman waved a finger. Anna wasn't sure what that said about Elizabeth Henley, but the daughter obviously hadn't met the mother's high expectations of her.

After Mrs. Henley retreated, Anna examined the room while the porcelain mantle clock ticked off the minutes. Like the ambiance in Mr. Maier's parlor, the Henleys' contained opulent carpeting, wallpapers, and furnishings, including a pianoforte and a lavish wood-surround fireplace. But the room also held a more feminine touch—a proper place to entertain, especially for a husband with political aspirations and social connections. Anna expected she wouldn't receive an invitation here for any other purpose than to provide sewing services.

She dared not sit on the red and gold velvet designer divan for fear of presuming upon her proper place.

"Here we are." Mrs. Henley walked in at last with the younger Miss Henley trailing her. "I'm sorry we've kept you waiting."

"Not at all." Anna turned to the sixteen-year-old, who appeared as comely as her mother with her blonde hair, blue eyes, and fair complexion. Yet Anna immediately recognized the air of entitlement the girl bore. It was in the way she sauntered in sneering, her head rolling and eyes hard as granite. The girl would not be easily pleased or care if her behavior offended another.

Anna stood a little taller. Despite Miss Henley's prideful attitude, Anna couldn't let the girl's contempt disarm her as it would have done in years past. Instead, she'd manage her approach to make a good impression on both mother and daughter.

"You've given me the time to think about what sort of gown would work well for a young woman of Miss Henley's stature." Anna attacked the subject with an air of deep contemplation. "It has to be sophisticated but tasteful, unique but in keeping with the current styles, elegant but befitting Miss Henley's age. What do you think, Miss Henley?" She peered into her eyes.

The girl tilted her head away, her downturned mouth indicating she might spit out some contemptible remark. Anna braced herself. But a sudden sparkle entered Miss Henley's eyes, and she wore a wide grin. "Why, Miss Sullivan, you've expressed exactly the kind of dress I hoped to wear. What do you think, Mother?"

"Sounds absolutely perfect, my dear." Mrs. Henley seemed pleased. "Miss Sullivan, you impress me, and that's not easy to do."

Anna bowed her head, acknowledging the compliment. "Well, then, shall we get on with the measurements?"

Thirty minutes later, Anna left the Henleys, grateful to have won over the mayor's wife and daughter and her prospects for the future brighter than ever. Strolling down Taos Street, she passed the Barton house on her way to Alpine Street, where Laurel had assured her she'd find Margaret Cody's well-stocked dry goods store.

A block before the intersection, Anna observed a woman carrying a child in her arms, scurrying around the corner. She wore a ragged coat, like the one Nina had worn at Bett's place. It must be her, but how had she been living?

Anna ran after her, turning the corner in the same direction. "Nina ... Nina, wait." But the woman had disappeared like a phantom in the forest from her Irish folklore.

Anna wandered the dirt road, passing the three-story Italianate-style McClellan Hall and Opera House, and tried the locked door to no avail. Next, she entered the Delmonico Bakery, the aromas of sweet bread making her mouth water. But still, there was no sign of the girl inside. Finally, she walked to Griffith Street, where the road curved to the left. Still, no trace of Nina. Ach, how was that possible? Her shoulders fell, and Anna gave up, heading back in search of the dry goods store to complete her business.

Once inside, Anna discovered that Cody's Dry Goods Store was a gold mine, as Laurel had suggested. It stocked plenty of materials and sewing supplies to offer the most avid seamstress her choicest selections.

"May I help you?" A kind feminine voice spoke next to her.

Anna fingered a shiny fabric, admiring the color of translucent sapphire. "This taffeta is exactly what I hoped to find. It will do very nicely for the girl I'm thinking about."

"A piquant shade, isn't it?" The woman touched the fabric. "What will you use it for?"

Anna twisted her head to look into the face of an older, statuesque woman with graying dark hair. She surmised her to be Margaret Cody, the widowed woman Laurel had described as the owner. "The Harvest Ball."

"A lucky lady." Margaret's face shone with delight.

"I hope she will feel like a princess in this dress."

"And you would be her fairy godmother, I think."

"Well, we'll see if her dreams come true." Anna bit her bottom lip. "The proof is always in the pudding, as they say."

"You must be Miss Sullivan."

"Oh, but—"

"Your Irish brogue gave you away, and the fact you are as lovely as Mr. Maier described you." Mrs. Cody smiled.

Anna rubbed her neck. "Ach, my goodness. Mr. Maier is a chatty sort, isn't he?"

"Don't take offense. Mr. Maier doesn't dole out compliments easily. But somehow, you've managed to bring out a kindlier spirit in him."

Anna's heart skipped a beat, surprised by the store owner's observation. "I didn't know."

"Didn't you?" Mrs. Cody raised her brow. "Then, whatever you've done, he wears it well." Anna hadn't a clue how to respond to her comment and let it slide with a brief smile.

Mrs. Cody helped Anna select the same fabric and lace in ivory and apricot. It was just the right color for Elizabeth Henley's complexion. But after measuring the material left on the bolt, the woman frowned. "I'm afraid there isn't enough here for the gown. Perhaps another color will do just as well."

Anna expelled a heavy sigh, her shoulders dropping. "Normally, I'd consider a different fabric, but we're discussing Mrs. Henley's daughter."

"Ah, I see." Mrs. Cody raised a knowing brow. "I can send a wire to the warehouse in Denver and O'Flahtery's Dry Goods Store in Idaho Springs—see if either one has the material."

"That would be grand." Anna's day suddenly grew brighter.

"I'll send the wire immediately." Mrs. Cody led Anna to the register and folded the pieces of fabric and lace for Prudence's dress. "I was so terribly sorry about Caitlin, you know." She looked up from her task, her voice holding regret. "She was always in here, choosing fabrics and ordering what she thought would appeal to her customers. Everyone loved her."

The stories about her aunt always produced a slight ache in Anna's chest, but she was glad to hear them. "I don't know if I'll be able to fill her shoes, but I plan to do my best."

Anna signed the ledger, and Mrs. Cody handed over the brown paper-packaged material. "I'm sure I'll be seeing you often, then."

A wistful smile touched Anna's lips, and she walked out of the dry goods store, stupefied by Mrs. Cody's last comment. The woman's words echoed Laurel's previous admonitions and left Anna confused. Had the Almighty intended all her apparent misfortunes for a different purpose altogether?

"Anna." An insistent voice called her name.

Laurel waved from where she engaged with a young couple and their three children in front of the Delmonico Bakery.

"Oh, hello, Laurel." She deviated toward the group.

"You must have been deep in thought." Laurel linked arms with her, enfolding her into the circle. "I called your name several times before you heard me."

"Oh, dear. I'm sorry. I was preoccupied. I just bought material from Mrs. Cody's Dry Goods Store, you see."

"Well, let me introduce you to Mr. and Mrs. McKinley, their children, Aiden, Logan, and their four-month-old daughter,

Rachel. They attend our church, and Mr. McKinley is one of two foremen at the Singing Silver Mine."

"These must be hard times for your family." Anna gazed at the child in Rebecca's arms. "Hello, little one." She broke into a smile and caressed the child's cheek.

"To be honest with you, Miss Sullivan, we've got five mouths to feed." The wife's Scottish brogue carried clear and plaintive. "Unless Mr. Maier gets the mine in operation soon, I don't know how we shall live, isn't that right, Horace?"

"We're getting by." Mr. McKinley's tone became gruff. He took Rachel from her mother's arms and moved her out of Anna's reach. "We're a hardy lot, we Scots."

"Miss Sullivan arrived the day of the disaster and lost her uncle, Liam O'Hallisey." Laurel pushed her shoulders back. "I'm sure you can appreciate her situation."

"Can't say as I can." Mr. McKinley squinted, his voice rough.

"Horace." Rebecca rebuked her husband. She appeared apologetic and addressed Anna. "Of course, being alone in a foreign country would be a heavy burden, especially if you'd expected kin to support you."

"We've all suffered a tragedy." Anna remained judicious with her words. "Like you, I'm trying to make the best of a difficult situation."

"Come on, Rebecca, I think it's time we were going." Mr. McKinley tipped his hat at Laurel but refused to acknowledge Anna as he dragged his wife and children away.

"Of all the hypocrisy ..."

"No matter, Laurel." Anna dismissed the man's aversion to her. "Do you think this is the first time I've experienced someone's animosity?"

"Well, it makes my blood boil." Laurel blurted out. "Mr.

McKinley claims to be a God-fearing Christian yet treats you like dirt just because you're Irish. It makes me sick unto death."

"Truly, Laurel, I'm all right." Anna placed a hand on her arm. "I can handle one man's hostility. But it does bring to mind a thought."

"I see the mischief twinkling in those big blue eyes of yours, Miss Anna Sullivan. You're just like your aunt." Laurel wagged a finger. "What have you got cooking?"

"I believe I may have an idea to help the McKinleys and others like them." Excitement swelled in her chest. "Can you gather a group of Georgetown's prominent ladies for tea—say, by day after next?"

"It's awfully short notice." Laurel bit her lip. "But I think I could manage it—especially if they think it's for something of utmost importance."

"Wonderful. I hope you'll all be dancing an Irish jig after I've presented my proposal."

Anna said her goodbyes to Laurel and headed away, her thoughts turning to Stefan Maier. The idea of a fundraiser had fomented during her encounter with the McKinleys. If Mr. Maier and the community were to survive this crisis, they needed to unify their resources. Despite Mr. Maier's efforts at his association banquet, she feared investors might still go against him.

Anna recalled how she had awakened early that morning while it was still dark, feeling an urgent need to find Mr. Maier before his stagecoach left for Denver. She'd bolted out of bed with a heightened sense she must encourage him somehow.

She had nothing of hers to offer, but perhaps something of intrinsic value was among her aunt and uncle's effects. Anna hadn't entered their bedroom since the day she'd first stepped into the cottage for fear of disturbing the sanctity of their private domain. A silly notion, she knew, but wanted to avoid nonetheless.

Compelled by a greater purpose, Anna entered the bedroom. That's when she discovered the Celtic cross lying in a tray on her aunt and uncle's dresser. Its beauty and simplicity struck her immediately, and she knew it would serve well for her purposes.

She'd quickly dressed and headed for the Barton House on the other side of town, catching Mr. Maier just as he boarded the coach. He seemed astonished to see her at first, but his eyes beamed when she placed the silver cross into his hand. "I will treasure it with my life." His tender words stayed with her long after the stagecoach had disappeared around the corner.

"Miss Sullivan." Anna heard an insistent voice calling her. She whirled around as Mrs. Cody caught up with her, gasping for air. "I thought you'd gone all deaf on me." The woman gulped, pressing her hand against her chest.

"Mrs. Cody." A flush crept up Anna's neck. She dared not reveal what occupied her thoughts.

"No matter." Mrs. Cody waved a piece of paper in front of her. "I have good news for you. The O'Flahterys wired back. They have your fabric."

"Isn't that grand?" Joy bubbled up inside Anna. "I shall head straight away to Idaho Springs in the morning."

"You've got a good heart, Anna Sullivan, that I will say for you." She tilted her head. "I hope Miss Henley appreciates your efforts."

"Well, we'll see how the dress turns out." That would be the real test to determine whether Anna could make a living in this community. Despite Mr. Maier's recommendations, she knew Miss Henley would have the last word.

Stefan peered out the stagecoach window to view Denver as the horses clopped across the Cherry Creek Bridge and down Larimer Street. The bustling metropolis that had been merely a camp on the prairie a decade ago had grown into one of the Rocky Mountains' most prominent cities since then. It had grown by leaps and bounds even since William and he had made Colorado their home in 1868.

This time, Denver seemed more vibrant with activity than ever—multi-story brick buildings had popped up, and a horse-drawn streetcar shuttled people on the main thoroughfares. Talk of the railroad expanding beyond Denver spawned hope for future industry. The population would undoubtedly grow exponentially in the years to come. And no wonder. With gold and silver mining booming in the mountains, people had flocked to the territory to cash in on the resources. Many hailed as Easterners in polished suits who had made their way to the western territory. A few were Ute or other native nations dressed in beaded hides. Some immigrated from Europe with Irish, German, and Italian accents—all in search of their cherished dreams—like Anna Sullivan, hoping to find a place beyond the rainbow for a better life.

Stefan frowned. He'd been one of those people who'd come to make his mark and earn his fortune to help build this "City on the Plains." But it could all be for naught if investors failed to believe in him now.

He removed the Celtic cross from his coat pocket. Dearest Anna. Like his foreman Horace McKinley and many others in Georgetown, her life depended on making a living from the profits of the Singing Silver Mine. But instead of bearing reproach on his rumored negligence, she had chosen to believe in his innocence.

"You're not alone," she'd said, placing the cross into his hand.

Stefan closed his eyes. How long had it been since a woman had shown such selfless regard for his well-being? His heart warmed, and he felt a sense of calm. Töpfer may have meant his actions for evil, but perhaps God meant them for good, bringing Anna into his life.

The stagecoach halted, and Stefan opened his eyes. They'd arrived. He shouldered the strap of his satchel, stepped out to retrieve his travel trunk from the back, and hurried to catch a passing streetcar heading to Cherry Creek, where the Tremont House had been in business since 1858 when it was a small boardinghouse. Now, the hotel boasted a reputation as one of the finest in Denver, known for its exquisite dining, entertainment, and accommodations. It hosted governors, entrepreneurs, and European dignitaries alike.

Striding onto the white-washed, colonnaded front porch and into the three-story brick hotel, a sense of familiarity enveloped Stefan. The Tremont House had a certain charm with its upgraded Victorian décor, a conference room, and a refurbished dining room. He would regret never enjoying its graces again.

"Good afternoon, Mr. Maier." A blond gentleman who appeared to be in his mid-thirties, wearing a red, white, and black brocade waistcoat and black ascot, greeted Stefan from behind a check-in desk. He flashed a welcoming smile. "A pleasure to see you back, sir."

"Likewise, Thomas." Stefan returned a capricious smile.

"Father reserved your usual room. He's in Kansas caring for my ailing grandmother, but he wishes you well." Thomas turned the register toward Stefan and handed him a fountain pen.

"I'm sorry to hear your grandmother is ill." Stefan frowned, taking the pen in hand. "Please give your father my wishes for her health."

"Thank you, sir." The owner's son seemed subdued.

Stefan signed the register, then dropped the pen into the book's crease. "I'd like a maid sent to my room to press my clothes for the evening's event."

"Of course, sir. Right away." Thomas waved a hand at the bellhop, who immediately left his post and scurried down a corridor. "Will there be anything else, sir?"

"If anyone asks for me, I don't want to be disturbed until the men meet for *aperitifs*."

"Yes, Mr. Maier." He handed Stefan his room key.

Stefan picked up his trunk and satchel, then climbed the stairway to the second floor. After finding his bed chamber at the end of the hall, he turned the key and opened the door into a room with all the accouterments he expected, including a sink in the corner with running water.

He placed his trunk on the quilt-covered bed, then walked to the table near the window and laid down his satchel. Parting the lace sheers, he looked east toward the city's center and the newly built Union Station, where trains made daily arrivals from Cheyenne and Colorado Springs. Investors interested in Colorado's mining industry would have already arrived on those trains—some with political aspirations—aspirations that could propel his career in the future.

Stefan let the sheer drop from his grasp. He needed to assure them he could deliver on the income he had promised them. After lighting the oil lamp, he sat at the table and went to work on his proposals.

Seventeen

◦⟡◦

Stefan stepped before the mirror and adjusted the white ascot around his neck. The well-groomed, bearded image looking back at him appeared robust, tenacious, prepared in his evening attire of black tails and a waistcoat with the shawl opening low, a second under-shawl mimicked by a fold of white silk, and a pair of black cashmere trousers.

The men who wanted to ruin him would be at the banquet, ready to do their best to destroy him. They believed they had the upper hand, but not one of them knew who he tampered with—not even Töpfer.

Stefan gave himself one final inspection. How would Anna view him? He stopped for a moment. Anna—yes, he had begun to call Anna by her given name as if it was sacred. She may seem a common Irish immigrant to others, but she was anything but ordinary. Would she admire his appearance, or would its social implications put her off? He hoped the former but believed the latter. Anna was not a woman to put on airs or be overly concerned with material wealth. Oh, she was a beauty, to be sure. Yet, her character and genuine concern for others attracted him the most.

Stefan shook his head. Now was not the time to think about such things. There were other more pressing affairs, like the private cocktail party in the gentleman's bar on the ground floor. He picked up the Celtic cross, slid it into his inside breast pocket, and opened the door.

He tramped down the corridor to the stairway and hastened downstairs to a room outfitted with rich wood and crystal chandeliers. The room was filled with well-dressed businessmen engaged in conversation, most holding drinks in their hands. On the other side of a lit fireplace, a chamber orchestra played classical pieces.

Affecting a relaxed pose, Stefan immediately came across one of his compatriots.

"Good to see you, old boy." William Burleigh reached out a hand, leaning in as if he wanted to share a secret with him. "Though I wouldn't have blamed you if you hadn't shown."

Burleigh had invented a drill on the East Coast that saved two-thirds the expense of hand-cutting through hard rock. Then he made his way West, bought a mine above Silver Plume, and brought the technology to Clear Creek County, making his fortune selling drills and mining ores. Stefan owned thirty of Burleigh's drills and believed they had saved him hundreds of thousands of dollars in less than a year.

Stefan flashed an easy smile, giving Burleigh a firm handshake while, on the inside, he seethed. Did Burleigh really think Stefan would slink away as if he were guilty? "Contrary to rumor, I plan to have the mine back up and in operation within the month."

"Glad to hear it." A wisp of a smile appeared around Burleigh's lips as he released Stefan's hand. "I didn't think you'd be waterlogged for long." He rubbed his ample belly.

"But, uh … I just want you to know if you need a buyer for those drills … perhaps William Hamill would be interested—"

"I don't believe that's likely." He cut the man off with a false smile and a steely eye. He would not give Burleigh the satisfaction of knowing the mine's future was in doubt. And without the men to operate the drills, they were as good as wasted resources.

"Good, good." Burleigh rocked on his heels. "It would be a shame if they went unused."

"I wouldn't worry about it."

Burleigh patted him on the shoulder. "I'll hold you to that." Burleigh moved off to greet another colleague.

"Pariah," Stefan spoke under his breath. He wouldn't put it past the man to stoke the rumors to pad his coffers. No doubt Stefan would have to brace himself for an onslaught of opinions like Burleigh's, coming from all corners of the room.

Stefan stepped up to the bar and ordered a drink, then turned to face the room, his elbow resting on the bar. Observing men greeting one another, he had little interest in speaking to most until he spotted Paul Rutherford.

"Your drink, sir."

Stefan turned to accept the glass from the bartender's outstretched hand, then thanked him and hastened to join his Cornish friend.

Paul Rutherford offered a hand. "You're looking dapper as ever, Stefan, recent events notwithstanding."

Stefan knew the slight jab held no malice. Still, a good tit-for-tat was in order. "You've been reading that rubbish in the newspaper, I see. Perhaps we must find a new candidate for our smelting works plant."

"Ouch." The man feigned hurt. "A little below the belt."

Stefan chuckled. "Serves you right, and you know it."

"I suppose it does." Paul's laugh lines showed, his voice light and airy.

"How does Ian fair these days? Glad to be back in Georgetown, I hope."

Paul snorted a mirthless laugh. "I'd ship him back off to my sister's place in Cornwall if I didn't think he'd get into more trouble before getting there."

"That bad?"

"Oh, you know boys his age. They think they own the world, and before you know it, they've caught a tiger by the tail." Paul indicated with his glass. "Seems like he's not the only one getting mauled."

Stefan scanned the room. How many of these men believed he was guilty of a crime? How many would just as soon lock him up and throw away the key? "I intend to beat the tiger at his game."

"Töpfer will not give up easily." Paul sipped his drink, his gaze averted, scanning the room. "Men were killed in your shaft, and in anyone's book, such a catastrophic event deserves an investigation."

"Let us not fool ourselves." Stefan waved his glass. "Töpfer is taking advantage of the situation. You and I know there are risks associated with our industry, much of it out of our control."

"That's not what they're saying, Stefan." Paul directed a blunt gaze at him.

Stefan returned a steady eye. "I thought you were on my side."

"I am." Paul stepped closer, keeping his voice low. "But this thing isn't going away anytime soon. People are going after your neck."

Stefan ground his teeth, nagging regret undermining his achievements and stealing his second chance at love. "It's so blasted unfair, Paul. Until now, I was perfectly content to immerse myself into building my mining empire, entombing Charity in the recesses of my mind. But now, it seems my sins are coming back to haunt me."

"Charity?" Paul frowned. "What does she have to do with any of this?"

Stefan rubbed his forehead. "You remember I said Charity threw a fit before we set sail for America. But I've never told anyone, not even you, about the most agonizing part of it ..." Stefan averted his eyes, clenching his jaw.

"I know she became ill—"

"It was more than that."

"What do you mean?" Paul appeared confused.

"In the end, Charity resigned herself to coming to America under duress from me. But the rift left a fracture in our marriage so wide that on the morning we boarded the ship for America, I didn't know whether it could ever heal. The disparity pained and angered me."

"I can see how that would have been very difficult for both of you." Paul studied him with a sympathetic gaze. "All marriages run aground at some time or another."

"Ours came to a screeching halt when she died of typhus halfway across the Atlantic."

"But you couldn't have known—"

"She also carried our child." Stefan looked past his friend.

"I'm so sorry." Paul narrowed his eyes and shook his head. "But you weren't to blame."

"No?" Stefan met Paul's gaze again. "I could have stayed in England. Instead, I quelled my remorse and buried my emotions at sea with Charity and our unborn child."

"Perhaps appropriate. What else could you have done?"

"I threw myself headlong into building my mining empire. William and I were soliciting mining interests on both sides of the Atlantic. We only needed a productive mine to persuade our fellow Englishmen to invest."

"The Singing Silver Mine," Paul said.

"I never questioned the purchase because I believed it would perform as exquisitely. And I've been proven right. It's never disappointed—"

"Always the unflappable braggart, aren't you, Maier?"

Stefan spun around. Töpfer's sudden presence fanned Stefan's flames of wrath once more. He needed to cool the embers before the sparks flared out of control, and he lost his reputation for remaining rational, relentless, and reposed in a heated exchange.

"I'm still prepared to offer you a tidy sum for your mine—what's left of it." Töpfer continued. "But I would advise you to act soon before my offer dwindles to nothing."

Stefan's jaw muscles went taut, and he sent a quick, steady glance in Paul's direction. "I believe I've already given you my answer. I will not be selling the Silver Singing Mine now or ever."

Töpfer clucked his tongue. "Too bad. After all, what will you do when investors no longer have faith in your integrity and they call in your loans across Clear Creek County? Hmm? Then, that little mining empire you've built will crash in on your world like the cave-in buried your men. Oh, what will you do then?"

Stefan studied his drink to restrain his response. If he endured the German's haughty grin one minute longer, he'd take a swing at him in the most vulgar American fashion.

Regaining his composure, Stefan tilted his head again, narrowing his eyes and meeting Töpfer's gaze. "We'll see who pays the piper in the end."

Their eyes met in a contest of wills. Töpfer's face sobered. The edges of his eyes twitched. The boorish man's lips twisted into a smirk reminiscent of a court jester. "You think you can beat me at my own game. But it's I who will have the last laugh." He slammed his empty glass so hard onto a table that Stefan cringed. The man stalked out, leaving a murmur across the room.

"Phew." Paul exhaled loudly, his eyes growing wide. "The German's got it in for you."

Stefan glanced at his colleague. He hated to admit it, but his confidence was waning. "There's much more at stake than you realize."

A bell clanged, silencing any further discussion. "Gentleman, dinner is ready." From the threshold, a *maître 'd* motioned a hand toward the dining hall, and Stefan and Paul joined the gathering of men at the back of the queue.

Night had descended black as ink in Denver when Georg set out along the gaslit streets to the address Dreher directed him, downriver from the Tremont Hotel. Lights flickered through two vertical windows and a transom over the front door of the redbrick Italianate house. He strolled the walkway onto the porch with its scalloped overhang and knocked.

The door opened, revealing Sigmund Dreher in a white shirt unbuttoned to his chest and brown woolen trousers held up by suspenders. His brown hair, parted in the middle, appeared unruly as if he'd been in a windstorm. Without a word, the man indicated Georg's entry.

Georg stepped into a lavish foyer, hung his hat on a coat tree, then followed Dreher into an elegant parlor. He glanced around the splendid interior while Sigmund walked to an ornate bar cabinet and poured sherry into two glasses.

"You've done well, Sigmund—you don't mind if we're on a

first-name basis, do you?" He spoke in their native tongue as he accepted the Roemer ruby etched glass made in Germany.

"As much as I would like to claim ownership," Sigmund waved his glass in the air, "the house belongs to the father of a mutual friend of ours—someone who will be useful to us."

"Really? I can't imagine." Georg found his countryman's indulgent desire to be deliberately vague an annoyance.

"Friedrich Lehmann."

"Peter's father?" Now Sigmund had Georg's attention. Friedrich Lehmann's firm in Denver was a top investor in Stefan Maier's mining enterprise. "How did that come about?"

"Friedrich and my father went to military academy together." Herr Dreher studied his glass. "My father chose to remain in Baden after the March Revolution failed in the late eighteen forties and kept his position. The elder Lehmann was more liberal-minded and emigrated here." Sigmund peered at Georg. "He's currently at your association event."

"Opportune. The association explains your proclivity for physical training."

"Our father demanded no less than he expected of himself," Sigmund spoke dismissively. He moved to the fireplace, then whirled around, wearing a macabre sneer that sent shivers through Georg's spine. "As we speak, an operative is planting information that will undermine investor interests in certain mining concerns. By tomorrow, Stefan Maier will not find one loan to keep his Singing Silver Mine in operation."

"Very good." Georg couldn't have been more pleased despite feeling repelled by Sigmund's demeanor moments earlier. "Within several months, you and I will be holding stakes in a number of mines and, within two years, will claim to be the richest men in Clear Creek County." Georg stepped closer and raised his glass. "A toast to the future."

The man kept his glass close to his chest. "A bit early to

celebrate, don't you think? I prefer to wait out the game a little longer and assess our options before we show our hand."

Georg drank his sherry bottoms up and put it down on a nearby table. "There are no other options. We're already too deep into this scheme to fail."

"It is a shame you never had military training." Sigmund's countenance became circumspect once more. "To guarantee victory in the campaign, you must first plan your long-term strategy and employ it with great patience while keeping your enemy off-guard. If he discovers your plan at any point, it would be prudent to retreat and regroup."

Georg's fury overcame his better judgment. Who did this underling think he was telling *him*—the mastermind of the plan—how to take care of business?

"There will be no retreat, understand? You had better hope your man does his job well, or there will be a price on his head." Georg hastened to the foyer, where he swiped his hat off the hook and opened the door. He'd had enough of the priggish man.

Eighteen

The Tremont's dining hall resounded with conversation as Stefan and Paul joined their friend and associate, Jerome Chaffee. The territorial delegate to the United States Senate was an excellent ally, especially at this point in Stefan's career. As founder of the First National Bank in Denver, his name carried authority. Though Stefan had taken on substantial business competition with Chaffee at times, their mutual political posture remained strong.

Stefan fixed his eyes on the last remaining table with seats and loathed his lack of choice. Could he stomach the father-son duo of Friedrich and Peter Lehmann? He didn't know about the father, but as an absentee associate of Töpfer's, the younger Lehmann also had much to gain from toppling Stefan's mining empire.

"Might as well bite the bullet," Paul spoke into Stefan's ear.

Stefan shot a sarcastic glance at Paul, then headed to the table with his two companions.

"Please, gentlemen." Peter's smile did not reach his eyes. It seemed Töpfer's partner was as unenthused to have Stefan sit at his table as Stefan was to pull out a chair.

Despite the tense moments, Stefan enjoyed a sumptuous meal of steak, roasted potatoes, green beans, cranberry relish, two kinds of bread, and apple pie with vanilla ice cream. Iced tea and wine flowed heartily, making for amiable conversation despite the competition for mining properties and mineral rights.

"Can you believe how our lives have changed in just a few years?" Paul studied a fork full of apple pie. "A little more than two years ago, we wouldn't have had the luxury of this wonderful meal. Now, we have apples from Ohio due to the railroad coming to Denver and ice cream from the hotel's icebox. Soon, we'll discuss innovations far beyond the steam engine, making our industry even more efficient than Burleigh's drill."

"I've heard of a machine that'll give us the ability to talk across the United States and beyond. They're calling it a telephone. Seems like a good investment for your money, men."

Chaffee sat back after taking his last bite of pie and played with the stem of his wine glass.

"I've told my son Ian he'd do well to pay attention to such things. There's a future in our industrial times." Paul shoved his plate away. "I'm not sure he cares much these days, though." A trace of regret lingered in his last words.

"He's still young. Give him time." Stefan leaned forward. "But I would welcome such a machine. It would greatly improve our ability to communicate with suppliers without wasting multiple days on the post."

"And get the word out about the interests of political

candidates more easily." Chaffee grinned, eliciting chuckles around the table.

"I see the infamous Mr. Hamill didn't make it here this year?" Friedrich Lehmann fiddled with his spoon. "I understand he's tied up with litigation—a property on Brown Mountain."

"He's not the only one." Stefan rued the day Töpfer ever rode into town.

"Yes." Lehmann drew out the word. "Rumor says you may not have the money to invest in a rabbit hole." He spoke his German-intoned words with deliberation.

Paul slammed his fork on the plate. "Look here—"

"Let the man say his piece." Stefan held up his hand. He would not allow his friend to get involved in a debate Stefan believed was only his to bear.

He had been waiting for the gauntlet to fall—had anticipated its acerbic subversion into the table talk like spicy food soured the stomach. His gaze went to the fifty-year-old man whose physique was as fit as a man ten years his junior. "I have nothing to hide. What's on your mind, Mr. Lehmann?" He leaned back in repose, his fingers steepled.

"Word is going around you're not to be trusted handling the day-to-day operations of your mines—that you cut corners and jeopardize men's lives." The elder Lehmann's accusation hurt, though Stefan knew the banker only responded to his son's lies. "Nine men are dead. Others are idle, waiting for parts that may never come. In the meantime, they have mouths to feed, families to provide for, and houses needing firewood for the winter."

Stefan went stiff. He had ordered the cable days ago, but there were reasons to keep the hoist idle. Still, he needed to answer the charges levied against him, and he would respond with patent honesty. He sat up straight and met the banker's gaze. "I cannot refute anything you've said about the desperate situation for families. They should not have had to endure the devastating pain and hardship. Nor can I deny a hoist cable failed. I *am* guilty, but not of what I am accused."

"You're talking in riddles, Mr. Maier. Explain yourself." Mr. Lehmann waved a hand.

"The evidence against me is circumstantial." Stefan glanced at the man's son. Peter Lehmann had gone rigid as a marble statue, staring vacantly into space. Did he know or suspect what his partner had done? Either way, his silence made him complicit in Töpfer's treachery. "My accusers lay unscrupulous motives at my feet as if I have no concern for moral integrity whatsoever. If what they say about me is true, I am no better than a murderer or a thief. But I can assure you that I have always acted with strict moral regard for the well-being of my men."

"Here, here." Paul raised his glass.

Stefan nodded appreciatively, then returned his gaze to the banker. "I have not only been meticulous about regular checks on my equipment, but I pay well for good work."

"Then what has brought on this allegation against you?" Peter Lehmann crossed his arms.

Stefan averted his eyes, then elevated them again to meet his foe. "I have been unjustly impeached for a crime I did not commit."

"So, you're saying your equipment was in good working order the day those men stepped onto the platform?" A touch of skepticism entered the elder Lehmann's tone.

Stefan examined the expectant faces around the table. "I'm saying the fault does not lie with my lack of due diligence on my equipment."

"Do you know what you're implying?" Jerome Chaffee

demanded. Stefan only twisted his lips. "Sabotage is a strong accusation," he warned. "Do you have corroboration?"

"I have no evidence to back up my claim ... yet."

Chaffee's fingers drummed on the base of his stemware. Its repetitive clinking seemed to toll out the death knell to any funds Stefan had hoped to secure to tide him over until he could get the Singing Silver Mine back in operation.

The elder Lehmann scraped back his chair. "May I have a word, Mr. Maier?"

Stefan jumped up and followed the German. He sensed the men's gazes around the dining hall, trailing them to the room's threshold. He didn't like making a conspicuous spectacle, but he was powerless to do anything about it.

"I'm inclined to believe you," Mr. Lehmann said once he and Stefan had stepped into the hallway. "You're capable of many calculated business moves, but you have too much integrity to ignore basic equipment checks—"

"Then you must see—"

Lehmann held up a hand. Stefan compressed his lips, standing at stiff attention, waiting for the man to say his piece. "I am, what shall I say, aware of some unscrupulous practices by parties of which I cannot divulge—"

"Friedrich." Stefan used the man's given name to appeal to their friendship. "You must hear me out. I can withstand the heat—"

"No." Friedrich's harsh response quieted Stefan. The man pocketed a hand. "I'm also aware of a lawsuit—a complaint of trespass—"

"What?" Stefan snapped, his voice a decibel higher than he had intended. He put a fisted hand to his lips.

"A complaint of trespass from the Mother Lode property by the owners of the Singing Silver Mine is to be filed and an injunction placed on mining along with the claim." Friedrich stood his ground, riding roughshod over Stefan.

"This isn't right. You *know* this isn't right." Stefan wagged his head in earnest. "I've done everything by the book, everything the law demands." Or had he?

Friedrich stared at his feet, then tilted his head, squinting. "Whether right or wrong, I am also obligated to shareholders and my board of directors to consider how this scandal—true or not—compounded by a lawsuit will affect your ability to repay your debts." He straightened, his chin jutting out. "For now, I'm denying your loan application, subject to review once all the facts come to light."

"I see." Stefan swallowed hard. His chest tightened.

What he had dreaded most had come to pass. There would be no money to bridge the gap, no way to return his men to work. Of course, the banker had to follow ethical business protocols to satisfy his stakeholders, but it would hurt the ordinary workers first. Töpfer's greed was unconscionable.

Stefan inhaled, hitching his shoulders. "I *will* uncover the evidence I need to prove my innocence. I promise you that. And I *will* secure the funds to keep the Singing Silver Mine and my other properties in operation. Mark my words." He cut the air with his hand, then pulled back. "I just hope this travesty does not hurt the wrong people."

Stefan tramped back toward the table but didn't go far when his stomach seized in knots. He detoured to a back exit.

Outside, Stefan heaved in the chilly night air, his breath steaming in the moonlight. His colleagues couldn't know his circumstance had just become more critical or that he feared the imminent loss of the mine without a loan to keep it afloat. A prudent businessman always kept up appearances, never disclosing certain calamities if he hoped to stay in business. And Stefan intended to remain in business, though he eschewed the idea of taking down Lehmann's son for aiding and abetting Töpfer's illegal activities.

For the first time since Stefan started using litigation to get what he wanted, his chest exploded with a wrenching pain as if a knife had stabbed his heart. He'd never viewed his practices as scandalous or despicable, rationalizing away the bad with the "good" he was doing for Georgetown. In recent days, he'd made an effort to display a gentler side. But in Anna's words, the truth always bore out in the end.

But what is truth? Weren't those the words Pontius Pilate asked the night Judas betrayed Jesus before His crucifixion? Pilate had the power of life and death in his hands and still sent an innocent man to the cross.

Yes, Stefan was innocent of trespassing on the Mother Lode in this case, but he had been guilty of so many past sins. Clinton's words resounded in his soul. "You cannot expect God will grant you peace of mind as long as your heart in this matter is corrupted by greed."

Stefan reached into his breast pocket for the Celtic cross Anna had given him. He had chosen to keep it safe in a place close to his heart. At the time, he'd been thinking of Anna. But now, setting his gaze on the symbol of Christ's sacrifice for sin and death, it occurred to him it was no accident Anna had given him her uncle's cross. Anna had said if he kept God close to his heart, God would grant him the desires of his heart. But perhaps the motives of his heart hadn't been pure for a long time.

How many lives had he trampled upon? How many others had squirmed while he swindled away their livelihoods in litigation? How many families had paid the price for his self-serving ends? Though he gallivanted about the world as a gentleman of high-class breeding, he was, in fact, a fake, a phony, a fraud—a scoundrel of the worst kind.

It was time he owned up to the man he had been, beginning with talking to his lawyer about the lawsuit and proving his inculpability for the Singing Silver Mine's disaster. Then, he would make reparations for all his past mistakes and become the man worthy of receiving the honor that someone like Miss Anna Sullivan would bestow.

Nineteen

Anna stepped off the Wells Fargo stagecoach at a roadhouse station near the top of a main road leading into Idaho Springs. When she'd passed through the town eleven days ago, she'd held onto her seat for dear life without noticing its character. This time, Anna studied her surroundings. As rudimentary as she'd thought Georgetown appeared, it was the thriving metropolis she'd expected compared to the Idaho Springs business district.

Anna laughed aloud. How different one's perspective when seen in the right light. She was surprised the town had a dry goods store at all but couldn't help but be grateful. They had the apricot taffeta material she needed for Elizabeth Henley's Harvest Ball gown.

Leaving behind the four others she'd ridden with on the stagecoach, Anna slipped the handle of a canvas bag over her arm, walked past the roadhouse bustling with patrons, and commenced toward a two-block business district on the dusty road. Clapboard buildings and a two-story brick building lined both sides. At the second intersection, Anna blocked the overhead sun from her eyes, reading a sign on the brick building—O'Flahtery's Dry Goods Store. She pushed open the door, activating a tinkling bell.

Footsteps clomped on the wooden floor planks from the back of the store. "Oh, hello there." A pleasant woman, no more than forty, greeted Anna. "You must be Miss Sullivan, come all this way from Georgetown."

"Indeed, I am," Anna declared with an easy smile, admiring the lady's dress with its caramel and pecan-colored tiered ruffles. "And you are ...?"

"Mary O'Flahtery. My husband and I own this establishment." She walked behind the counter. "We were expecting you." She brought out a bolt of fabric that perfectly matched the apricot and white lace of the other in Georgetown.

Anna clapped her hands in a prayerful pose. "God be praised."

"It is a lovely color, isn't it?" Mrs. O'Flahtery announced in her Irish brogue as she measured the material.

"How long have you been on this side of the world?"

"Oh, 'tis nigh on to twenty-six years since my husband and I sailed from Dublin to escape the famine." Mrs. O'Flahtery paused her scissors, gazing up with a contemplative eye. "We were some of the lucky ones."

"My aunt and uncle, as well."

"Came west a few years back when we'd heard there was gold in these mountains. We haven't made our millions yet, but John's prospecting gets us enough to put food in our stomachs and clothes on our backs. So I'm not complaining." Mrs. O'Flahtery folded the fabric, wrapped it in brown paper and string, and handed it to Anna.

"I'm much obliged." Anna slid the package into her canvas bag and gave Mrs. O'Flahtery the balance she owed.

"You're Caitlin O'Hallisey's niece." Mrs. O'Flahtery declared when their gazes met. "I should have seen it right away."

"I've been told I'm the spitting image."

"It's tragic, both of them gone, eh?" She leaned in with kind eyes. "Caitlin stopped by on occasion when Margaret's supplies got low. People around here loved her."

"I know I've got some big shoes to fill, but I'm determined to do my best." Anna leaned toward the woman.

"Ah, that's the spirit. Caitlin would be proud."

Anna nodded, her footing in the matter still on tenterhooks. She shouldered the canvas bag. "Is there a place you recommend for a bite to eat before I catch the stagecoach?"

Mrs. O'Flahtery knitted her brow. "There is the local saloon, but I wouldn't suggest it for a woman alone. Your best eatery is the L & L Roadhouse you passed when you came into town. Louise cooks up some pretty good grub."

"All right, then. Thanks for all your help." The register rang as she went out the door.

Anna checked her watch. Noon—an hour before the stagecoach arrived. She snapped the watch shut and headed back toward the clapboard and brick roadhouse at the top end of the road.

"Can I help you?" An older woman with wisps of gray hair sprouting from her bun and a pot of coffee in her hand addressed Anna as she entered through a door into a simple room. A handful of people sat at rustic tables and chairs, eating.

"Yes, ma'am. I'd like a meal before I catch the stagecoach to Georgetown."

"Seat yourself anywhere you like." She indicated with the pot in her hand. "It's beef stew or antelope steaks with fried potatoes today. What's your pleasure?"

Anna sat near the potbelly stove to warm herself. Both food items sounded tasty to her growling stomach, but she chose the antelope steaks, never having had them before.

"You can't go wrong." The woman poured her a cup of coffee. "I'll be back in a few minutes with your steaks."

Forty minutes later, Anna left the L & L Roadhouse, thoroughly satisfied with her meal. She'd also discovered the L & L stood for Lou and Louise, the roadhouse proprietors. They told her she was welcome anytime.

The stagecoach approached the designated spot along the road and came to a rocking stop just as Anna walked away from the eatery. Ah! Perfect timing. The stagecoach would take a fifteen-minute break to switch horses, and then they'd be off to Georgetown.

The door opened, and several men and women climbed out, most staying close by to take a break, she assumed, from the uncomfortable seats and harrowing journey. And then she saw him—the last person to hop down from the coach.

Anna's eyes bulged. Stefan Maier here, wearing her frock coat? He wasn't due back in Georgetown for another day. Something must have gone terribly wrong.

"What are you doing in Idaho Springs?" Anna stared at Mr. Maier. "I didn't expect to see you until the weekend."

Stefan had hoped to have had more time to recuperate from the wounding he received during the Businessman's Association banquet. Instead, he'd encountered Anna at one of his lowest moments. "I'm just as stunned."

A moment of awkward silence descended on their meeting. "I—" They both started at the same time.

"You first," Stefan insisted.

"All right, then. It's all because of you, really." Her eyes sparkled.

"Me?" Stefan raised his brow.

"If you hadn't championed my sewing business, I don't know where I'd be. And now I'm making a gown for the mayor's daughter and coming to Idaho Springs for the material I needed." She patted the canvas bag over her arm. "It's more than I could have ever believed."

"If I've done anything, Miss Sullivan, then I'm gratified." Stefan grinned, pleased Anna had found her footing in Georgetown. If only he could regain his.

"What's wrong, Mr. Maier?" She stepped toward him. "I can see it in your eyes and the way your smile faded like the setting sun."

Stefan fingered the Celtic cross in his trouser pocket. Anna had expressed such high hopes for him yesterday morning, yet regrets filled his mind with self-loathing. How did he tell her he'd been a cad for so long he didn't deserve her sympathies? "I've been labeled a financial risk." He slowly shook his head. "No loans will be forthcoming."

"Oh, I see." Anna dipped her chin, then peered up at him. "But surely not all is lost."

"Unless I can prove I'm not culpable." Stefan set his jaw. He knew full well who was to blame. If only he could get into the damaged shaft ...

"Then it's high time we find a way to convince them, show them you're a man of the highest integrity and could never forsake your employees to derelict equipment."

Stefan peered into her determined face and immediately adopted a languid pose, his lips slowly curving into a smile. "How do you do that?"

"Do what?"

"Remain so sanguine when the world around you is crashing before your eyes."

"Ach, you give me more credit than I deserve, Mr. Maier. As you know, life has not always doled out circumstances in my favor." Anna peered off to the western mountain denuded of trees. "The last year has tested the strength of my mettle, and there have been plenty of times I would have given in to despair, or worse, to have become a bitter soul."

"But you didn't." He was amazed she hadn't, considering how he had initially treated her, evicting her from the cottage without mercy.

"Only by the grace of God." A soft glow entered Anna's eyes as she gazed at him again. "If you had told me a month ago I would have to face life here alone without an uncle to support me and only strangers to comfort me, I would have run to the Irish hills. But God didn't afford me the luxury of knowing. And so, here I am, weak as my faith is, having to trust God's grace is sufficient for my daily needs and catching glimmers of hope in the journey whose end is still unknown."

"All aboard for the stagecoach to Georgetown."

Stefan twisted his head toward the driver. People were gathering around the coach. When he'd first seen Anna, he had preferred not to face her. Now, there was nothing he wanted more—more time to talk, more time to gaze into eyes that spoke light and truth into his heart, and at once, he was struck by how, in such a short time, she had utterly changed his life.

He turned back, fixing his gaze on Anna's lovely countenance. She was, without a doubt, one of the most beautiful women he'd ever had the privilege to know. He searched her eyes, and a spark seemed to ignite a connection between them as intense as the night before the banquet. Did she feel it as strongly as he did? He longed to touch her, hesitated, then reached out to caress her cheek. Anna's breath hitched, her lips parting, inviting him to taste their honey-sweet goodness. He bent his head until—

"Last call for the stagecoach to Georgetown." The driver called, breaking the spell, and Anna stepped back, swallowing hard.

Stefan dipped his chin, ruing the lost moment. "Come on." He placed a hand under Anna's elbow and led her to the queue. It was time to go home and face whatever music awaited him.

Twenty

Anna arranged the last of six place settings with floral china plates and tea cups on top of a white brocade tablecloth around Laurel's dining room table. She drew back to assess her work. Would Mr. Maier approve? Somehow, that question had become vitally important over the last several days. Her thoughts never wandered far from him. She touched her lips.

"Here we are." Laurel whisked in and set a basket of scones and a platter of tea cakes in the center of the table. "You think Her Majesty the Queen would approve?"

"'Tis a table fit even for Queen Victoria, I would wager."

"Excellent." Laurel beamed. "Now, all we need are the guests."

Anna wrapped an arm around her waist, touching the crepe of the bustled black mourning dress. She'd come a long way since her first days in Georgetown. With Laurel's encouragement and the faith of a tiny mustard seed, Anna had found the courage to embark on a new chapter in her life.

"Dear Anna, what's wrong?" Laurel knitted her brow.

"A little anxious, I suppose. All these ladies—sophisticated and socially connected, and me a newcomer. What if they think I'm asserting my place—stepping on their toes, as it were?"

"I don't think you have anything to worry about." Laurel gave her a reassuring smile. "These women want to see Georgetown thrive as much as you do. Show them you care about the well-being of this town, and they'll enfold you into their circle and applaud your clever ideas."

"Even the mayor's wife?"

Laurel linked arms with Anna and led her toward the parlor with its beautiful furnishings. "Oh, Mrs. Henley sometimes puts on airs, but don't let her fool you. She can be very charitable, especially when you appreciate her efforts. And remember, she also cares about this community."

The door knocker sounded, and Anna gazed steadily into Laurel's eyes. It was time.

Laurel unlinked their arms and gave her a reassuring smile before they went to the door. "Miss Richards, please come in." Laurel's delighted voice welcomed the black woman, and Anna immediately warmed to her arrival.

"Good afternoon, Mrs. Thomas." The familiar soft-spoken, southern drawl sang like a sweet melody. "I'd a been here earlier if I hadn't had to finish up my laundering. Then, Mr. Jedidiah showed up with a new drill he said was popular with the miners. I told him he should order them if he believed they were a good idea."

"You needn't worry about a thing." Laurel ushered the woman in, her voice humming. "You're the first to arrive."

"A pleasure seeing you again, Miss Sullivan." Miss Richards donned a toothy grin as she entered the foyer. She folded her hands, bearing the same black beaded reticule she'd worn at the wake. But this time, she wore a plain white-collared, green button-up dress.

"The pleasure is all mine, I assure you." Anna smiled, genuinely glad once more to meet this black woman of modest temperament who seemed entirely at ease in their company.

"I've been hearing things about you around town."

"Oh, dear." Anna placed a hand on her chest.

"Now, why would you think they weren't good things, chile?" Miss Richards inclined her head. "Remember I told you God had a plan. You just need to trust He's going guide you through the storm."

"I remember, though I'm still not entirely sure where He's taking me."

"Do you think any of us do?" The woman chuckled. "I think it's the good Lord's way of reminding us He's in control and not us—like me, once an enslaved woman, winding up here a mine owner more than a thousand miles from where I grew up."

"But surely people don't treat you poorly in Georgetown?" Anna couldn't believe anyone would hold such a kindly woman with contempt.

"I would hope not." Laurel's mouth fell open. "Miss Richards has been a part of this community for so long I've never questioned her presence."

"Truth be told, it ain't so for everybody, though." Miss Richards shook her head. "But many of these good folk accepted me a long time ago, and for that, I be grateful."

Anna relaxed in her company. They weren't very different —both of them outcasts in some segments of society. "I'd very much like to hear your story." Anna led Miss Richards to the parlor as the door knocker sounded again, and Laurel opened the door.

Within minutes, the room had filled with the other women

Laurel had invited—Margaret Cody, Georgia Tucker, and Virginia Henley. Mrs. Tucker's voice boomed the loudest among the women. "Our new waiter fumbled a tray of food onto a visiting German scientist's lap. Even got into the poor man's shoes." She giggled.

"No," Mrs. Henley voiced astonishment. "That must have set off those Germans' ire."

"You can imagine." Mrs. Tucker's eyes bulged. "All put out by the poor boy's mistake. Granted, he should have had better control of his tray. But we sure had a good laugh mimicking those high and mighty Germans, not that any of them would have seen the humor in it."

"In my day," Miss Richards' soft voice broke in, "a boy would have had a good whipping if he'd dropped even a morsel of food on his owner. Your boy got away all right, I'd say."

"All in perspective—right, Miss Richards?" Mrs. Tucker rolled her head.

"You got that right."

"Well, let's hope I don't fumble any trays this afternoon." Laurel laughed. "Shall we move into the dining room?" She guided the women forward and appointed their seats, sitting Anna next to Miss Richards.

"Mrs. Thomas, your table is simply lovely. You prove the perfect minister's wife time after time." Mrs. Henley spoke with conviction.

"You're very nice to say so. But I assure you, I'm far from perfect." Laurel shrugged it off. "My children, if they were here, could attest to my shortcomings."

"I believe we're all in process if I may be so bold." Miss Richards lifted her chin.

"Even so," Mrs. Henley leaned in, "I compliment Mrs. Thomas on her gracious hospitality."

"I must give credit where credit is due." Laurel nodded toward Anna before leaving the room. "Anna set the table and made the scones and tea cakes."

"Really?" Mrs. Cody turned inquiring eyes on Anna.

"It's become such the fashionable event in Great Britain since mid-century, you see."

"I love the British grand teas." Mrs. Tucker waved a hand. "Americans may have fought the Revolution, but we still import England's tea habits. I've thought about adding Saturday afternoon teas to our schedule."

"A very nice addition, I would say." Laurel strode into the room, carrying a teapot. She poured around the table, then took her seat. "Shall we?" She prayed before passing the tea cakes.

Anna's proximity to Miss Richards provided an opportunity to study her more. Her face held a certain kindliness, softening her years so Anna couldn't guess her age.

"Chile, I suspect you have a question you want to ask me." Miss Richards tilted her head toward Anna, and Anna almost choked. "It's okay. I'm used to people thinking I be a novelty."

"All right, then." Anna slowly relaxed her shoulders. "I was speculating on your age."

"I see." Miss Richards appeared to ponder the question before answering. "Near 'bouts what I can gather, I be sixty-six years old."

"But how can you live without knowing how old you are?" Anna marveled.

"You have to remember, in those days, they only cared about your worth. You just 'cepted it as if it was normal. As long as you were young and capable and could do the work."

"Slavery's a peculiar institution if you ask me." Mrs. Henley frowned. "I've never understood how those plantation owners could sleep at night."

"Most of us wondered the same thing." Miss Richards shook her head. "But they seemed to do it just fine."

"Didn't you want to escape?" Anna suspected she would have found a way, given a chance. Hadn't she already fled one life for this one?

"There were days …" The woman answered with a resigned nod, then bit into a tea cake.

Laurel peered around the table, her eyes silently asking for consent from Anna and the other ladies. "Why don't you tell us about them?"

"I don't want to bore nobody." Miss Richards hesitated with a tea cake-laden hand.

"It would do us all good to understand what you went through," Mrs. Cody said.

"Well, all right, then." Miss Richards swallowed her tea cake and leaned in. "My earliest years are pretty cloudy. But from the time I can remember, I was sold several times to the highest bidder as if I were some pack mule. 'Bout the time I was near twenty, I married a gorgeous man, golden with muscles like he'd worked the fields all his life." She slid her hands up and down her arms, her face shining with the warmth of the sun. "We had three children, beautiful children.

"Then one terrible day," she scrunched up her nose, "my kids and husband got sold off away from me just 'cause they worth more by selling 'em than keeping 'em. My world fell apart, and I didn't care none if I lived or died. Didn't matter to my owner, though. He got what he wanted."

"That's dreadful!" Anna's indignation flared. How could one human being inflict such cruelty on another human being? No one, no matter their station in life, should be treated with the barbarism the enslaved had been.

Anna's experience growing up in Ireland seemed to echo a similar refrain—the lives of the poor subject to the whims of their wealthy landlords. Both of them had endured the kind of degradation reserved for the dregs.

"After a while, I just got numb to the pain and did my chores as I was 'sposed to. Couple of years later, I was sold to a man with a good heart. I guess he saw something in me and bought me to serve as a domestic in his house. Told me about how the Lord would save me from my sins and wipe every tear away. Before his death, I guess he reckoned it was time to do the right thing by me and changed his will—granted me my freedom and a small purse of money."

"My, my." Mrs. Tucker's eyes widened.

"I just about lost my teeth when his daughter told me. I didn't want to believe it at first. But it was as true as the sun coming up every morning. Seemed like God showed me favor the same way he showed Joseph in Egypt. That ray of sunshine cast its light on me, and I danced around singing *Sweet Canaan's Happy Land.*"

"Is that when you came west?" Mrs. Cody finished off her scone.

"Can't say as I did." A faraway look shone in her eyes, and she blinked tears away. "I tried to hunt down my kids first, hiding out in the fields or behind some cow shed when it wasn't safe to be seen for being caught again. But every lead came to a dead-end, and I ran out of money. People taking advantage, I guess. I knew I had to make some more. Figured I'd ask a foreman where they were building a railroad if he'd let me do their cooking. I could tell he really didn't want to 'cause they already had enslaved people working the line—some of them women."

"Women?" Mrs. Cody flinched. "Those men should have been shot."

"Maybe. But you got to remember this was before the war, and an enslaved woman didn't get any special treatment. She still no better than an animal. I counted it lucky no one roped me in the same way."

Anna wanted to vomit. She covered her mouth with her napkin.

"It took me a long time to figure out the foreman was just doing what he was told. But at the time, I couldn't believe those young girls were digging like workhorses, their faces smudged and blacker than normal. But he finally agreed to let me do the cooking. Made my heart sink to my toes every time those ladies looked at me with them doleful eyes. I left as soon as I gathered the money. All I could do was thank the good Lord for my freedom."

"It must have taken some real courage." Anna's eyes fastened on a pot of jam, thinking about her journey to America and those she had left behind, like Clare.

"I discovered some prospectors heading west on a wagon train and convinced them I could do their cooking for a small penny if they'd take me with them. They agreed, and I came to Georgetown just 'bout the time they were finding ores. I asked the good Lord if this be the place where I should hang my clothes, and He seemed to think it'd be a good idea."

"The Lord knows what he's doing." Mrs. Tucker interrupted.

"I do appreciate your sympathies." Tears brimmed Miss Richard's eyes, and she swiped at them. "I didn't know when I rented my small cottage—similar to the one you're living in, Miss Sullivan—whether I'd have a place here or not. I just picked up odd jobs. Word got around I helped birth a lady's chile, and all the ladies started asking me to attend their birthings. I just kept putting money in the bank, saving out enough to live, giving tithe to the church, and helping people out when they needed it.

"Lo and behold, just 'bout the time the War Between the

States was over and black people were getting their freedom, the good Lord had accumulated more money than I could ever have imagined. I invested in mining and real estate, and well, the rest is history, I guess."

"Not *just* history, Miss Richards." Laurel leaned in. "Your presence in Georgetown continues to bless us all."

"And if anyone has ever had a right to be bitter, you have. But I've never heard a harsh word, not even against those who've shown hostility toward you." Mrs. Henley added.

"She's even been known to take in a person or two down on their luck until they can get back on their feet again." Mrs. Tucker pointed with her fork.

"Well, if that be the case, I be glad for it." Miss Richards's humble spirit impressed Anna as rare. "I don't look down on anyone as if they don't deserve a kindness. I reckon we all got shackles we need to get freed from to get by in this life."

Anna jerked. The woman's simple but modest proclamation startled her. Was it true what she said? Maybe for the oppressed and downtrodden. But everyone, even wealthy people like Mrs. Henley and Mr. Maier or Seamus and his parents? And what about ordinary people like the Thomases and the Tuckers? And what about herself? Anna's chest tightened.

"For some of us stiff-necked ones, it be harder than others," Miss Richards finished, leaving a reflective lull in the conversation.

"It seems now would be the appropriate time to discuss why Anna and I have asked you all here." Laurel's bright smile lit up the room, bringing the ladies back to attention.

"Do tell." Georgia waggled her eyebrows as if she were about to hear some juicy gossip.

"Nothing quite so shocking." Laurel scolded in good

humor. "Anna has devised a plan to help the people in town affected by the shut-down of the Singing Silver Mine."

"Terrible business, isn't it?" Mrs. Henley tsked. "Charles says the economy will suffer."

"All the more reason we should hear Anna out." Laurel gave Anna a reassuring smile. "I suggest we adjourn to the parlor and allow her to tell us what she has in mind."

While Anna sat on the gold-cushioned sofa in the parlor, waiting for the women to refill their cups, she overheard a mention of the rumors plaguing Mr. Maier. She frowned, loathing the rumor mill. He deserved better from them.

"Remember," Laurel whispered in Anna's ear on the way to her seat. "You're among friends."

Anna gave her a brilliant smile. She folded her hands and inhaled, gazing at the ladies before her. "Most of you don't know me yet, but I hear you knew my Aunt Caitlin quite well. You're also aware of the tragedy that has affected me and numerous families in this town—perhaps all of us to one degree or another.

"My aunt and uncle came to this country during the Great Hunger—you know it as the potato famine. Millions starved to death." She hung her head, recalling the meals she received in the O'Connor kitchen—more food than many of the villagers in the famine cottages had eaten for years.

"I'm thankful most of you have never had to experience that kind of poverty here," Anna spoke wistfully, knowing there was one who had, but Miss Richards had risen above it. "But right now, families in Georgetown are hurting, and some wonder where they will find the funds to feed their children. It seems only fitting if we band together to help them."

"A fascinating idea, I must admit." Mrs. Henley leaned in. "But what about the church benevolence fund?"

"I thought about that." Laurel bit her lip. "We've got some

monies, but not enough to cover everyone over an extended period. My husband has met with several clergymen in town to organize meals, and Delmonico's has agreed to provide soup and bread for lunch Monday through Saturday with the help of donations. But these are only temporary measures until more funds can be raised."

"Which is why I suggest a Christmas Festival similar to the German Christmas Markets," Anna broke in once more. "Only this would be more than a holiday festival. It would also be an opportunity to feed and clothe the less fortunate in our community for the winter."

"Surely, the mine will be open for business before the Harvest Festival, don't you think?" Mrs. Henley flapped her hand.

"I don't like to stoke the fires of the rumor mill." Mrs. Tucker shifted positions. "But talk around town says Mr. Maier's financial troubles may not resolve anytime soon. Some of his other properties are also in jeopardy."

Anna had been privy to Stefan's concerns, but hearing Georgia speak them aloud made it all the more painful. "I'm inclined not to pass judgment on Mr. Maier too soon. But we should prepare to offer some long-term alternatives in financial aid." Renewed vigor rose in her chest, convinced more than ever they had a duty to provide for the widows and the orphans.

"Tell us more." Mrs. Cody leaned back against her chair.

Anna smiled briefly, her shoulders back, encouraged by the ladies' attentive faces. "While Christmas markets aren't common in Ireland, we have other traditions passed down through the centuries. We can create a festival, building on all our collective traditions. And we'll invite people from all around—Denver, Central City, Idaho Springs—to celebrate with us."

"I'm certain *The Colorado Miner* would give us free advertising." Laurel held her cup between her hands. "And they'd write an editorial or two, as well."

"That'd be grand." Anna liked the direction they were going. "And I'm sure there must be ladies in town who are good at cooking or crafting—ladies who can sell their wares and give the net proceeds to help the families."

"The dry goods store can give discounts on materials as incentives." Mrs. Cody offered.

"And the local eateries could also contribute. Delmonico's Bakery is already providing breads and pastries. We could also offer traditional Christmas specialties at the Barton House." Mrs. Tucker joined in, bounding with excitement. "And music. We must have music. I'm sure my Prudence would form a madrigal choir in a heartbeat."

"You may tell her I'll be the first to join up." Anna clapped her hands, her excitement growing. "And a Christmas band. Or a boys' choir."

"I can teach folks some good ole spirituals." Miss Richards cast her toothy smile.

"Wouldn't that be grand, as well?" Anna dropped to a chair, relishing how the plan had gained momentum. "The ideas are endless, as long as we remember our main purpose is to raise funds for the families. Whatever we do, we must ensure everybody knows who benefits."

"I'm certain my husband will be on board, and I don't think it will take much to persuade the rest of the council." Mrs. Henley placed her teacup on the coffee table and rose. "Anna— may I call you Anna? This was a brilliant idea—so brilliant, in fact, that a Christmas Festival or Market, or whatever you want to call it, just might become a Georgetown tradition."

Anna's heart swelled. Not only had the idea of the Christmas Festival excited these influential women of the community, but they had embraced her, even suggesting they refer to each other by their given names. More importantly, the hurting people of Georgetown could rest assured the community had come together to keep them afloat in their time of distress.

Now, it was time to do the actual work of planning the event and enticing others to get involved. Last but not least, they needed to develop a list of those who needed the most help, and the first person that came to mind was Nina—that was, if she could ever find her. Where could the girl and her toddler son have gone? The mystery still plagued Anna's heart.

Twenty-One

First thing Monday morning, Stefan headed to the law office of Edwin Willard, Esq. His stomach churned as he approached the Cushman Building on Alpine and Taos Streets. The injunction he'd received on Friday against the Singing Silver Mine property disallowed his miners to work the mine until further notice. He hoped Edwin would have good news to report, because he needed it now more than ever.

Stefan entered the building, climbed the stairs two-by-two, and headed to the law office on the second floor. He rapped on the office door with the anger of a wounded cougar.

A cough came from the other side, then a voice. "Come in."

Stefan pushed the door open into a room that was approximately thirteen square feet. It contained several bookshelves against the wall filled with law books and the bespectacled lawyer sitting at his mahogany desk, surrounded by files and penning a letter. "I'll be with you in a minute, Stefan." The man didn't look up.

Stefan removed his hat and sat in a chair in front of the desk, waiting while Edwin concentrated on the document he wrote, dipping his pen in the ink and writing again. When the lawyer dipped his pen a third time, Stefan uncrossed and re-crossed his legs. "I don't have all day, Edwin. Can we get on with this?"

Edwin eyed Stefan over his spectacles. "I understand you're all out of sorts, Stefan. Wrangling with me will not get this letter done any sooner." He went back to his writing.

Stefan poked his tongue into his cheek. Lawyers were a tricky lot—not as interested in truth as they were in making money. And though Edwin was a good friend, Stefan was under no illusion. The man was just as suspect as any other lawyer. With a stroke of a pen, he could wipe out a man's hard-earned, honest work without regard for the ethical or moral consequences of his actions against those who were the most innocent.

And the innocents, in Stefan's view, were the miners under his employment who could not work because of a man's evil deeds. And now this. It wasn't right or—

"All right, Stefan, I'm ready." Edwin tossed his pen and folded his hands on the desk.

"You've got to get this injunction removed, Edwin. Point of fact, men are out of work and need income."

"Which is why I'm writing this letter of redress." Edwin pointed at the penned document on his desk. "But even if we get the injunction repealed, you still have your ruined shaft to fix. Have you done anything about the cable yet?"

Stefan looked down, clenching the brim of his hat. He still needed to descend into the shaft without destroying the evidence to prove sabotage, but he'd put that on hold with this ridiculous legal squabbling. "I'm working on it. Until then, I had planned to put my miners back to work by drilling new slopes into the mountain. But this absurd injunction ..." His hand pointed at the paperwork. "If I don't get a jump on a new entry by next week, who knows how long the weather will hold?"

"I'll see what I can do, Stefan." Edwin sighed. "I'll add the information to the letter and have it to the judge and a copy to Töpfer's lawyers in the morning." The lawyer picked up his pen. "But a word of warning, Stefan. Töpfer's an ambitious man and determined to win. He could drag this out for years."

"I sincerely hope not." Stefan couldn't imagine paying Edwin the exorbitant lawyer's fees he'd been charging without seeing an end in sight. Besides, the miners were growing restless, and some had already moved on.

Stefan rose and donned his hat at the door. "Töpfer must not win, Edwin. Do whatever it takes."

Stefan thrust the exit door with the strength of Samson, banging it against the side of the Cushman building. He could not allow Töpfer to get away with endless years of litigation. It would destroy the town and the people in it. Stefan rounded the corner.

"Whoa." Clinton nearly careened into Stefan.

"My apologies, Preacher." Stefan grimaced. "I was lost in thought."

"I can see that." Pastor Thomas studied Stefan with a slow smile. "Anything you want to talk about?"

"I ..." Stefan swallowed. He'd been uncharitable the last time they'd talked. But given how the truth had stared him in the face on the night of the Businessmen's Association banquet, he wanted—no needed—to confess his sins. "I would very much like to talk." Stefan lowered his head, his eyes looking up at his friend.

"I'll have Mrs. Thomas make us some coffee." The preacher touched Stefan's shoulder and led him to the parsonage.

After a brief conversation with Laurel, Stefan and Clinton settled into two wingback chairs in front of the fireplace in the library. Their cups of coffee sat on a small round table between them as Stefan unburdened his soul. He unloaded about how he'd used litigation to get what he wanted, rationalizing away trampling on so many men and swindling away their livelihoods by the "good" he was doing.

"I may be innocent of the wrong-doing that Töpfer and the citizens of this community accuse me of." Stefan rubbed his hands between his knees, his eyes focused on the fire. "But my past sins have caught up with me, Clinton. I could hear your words echoing in my soul, and I saw with so much clarity how greed had polluted my motives." He lifted mournful eyes. "I had to be honest with myself. I am no better than the wretch people say I am."

"How do you think we come to that understanding of ourselves?" Clinton leaned forward. "The Apostle Paul recognized how sin enslaves us all and declared, 'Wretched man that I am! Who will deliver me from this body of death?' Elsewhere, he answers that question. 'But God demonstrates His own love toward us, in that while we were still sinners, Christ died for us.' It's not until we see ourselves for who we truly are and recognize our need of a Savior, Stefan, that God can transform us into the people we ought to be."

Stefan sat back. "But it's one thing to discover the error of your ways. It's another repairing the damage you've done."

"A place where the hymn-writer John Newton found himself. He led a dark and troubled life as a youth and later became a trader of enslaved Africans. But he didn't denounce the despicable practice until years after his conversion."

"I thought he wrote 'Amazing Grace' because of his conversion."

"A common presumption." Clinton spread his hands. "But Newton first saw no conflict between his faith and vocation. Only gradually, as his faith grew and illness forced him into a different profession, did he change. He met William Wilberforce, an advocate for the abolition of the slave trade, and together they fought to remove the scourge of enslaving African peoples."

"I know of Wilberforce. Britain abolished slavery a half-century before America."

"To our country's shame." Clinton hung his head, then quickly breathed through his nostrils. "And shame eventually caused Newton to write, 'I thought surely the Scripture proved there never was, nor could be, such a sinner as myself.' You see, his heart had finally glimpsed the depravity of his sin and the depth of the Savior's love for him, and he broke away from all that had enslaved his soul to the world's system. Now, God could use him to aid Wilberforce in transforming the entire British nation. A tremendous legacy to follow, no?"

Indeed. Stefan fingered his signet ring. But could he follow in Newton's great footsteps?

Anna walked up to the Thomases' house in high spirits, admiring the ornamented Gothic Revival architecture with its gables and dormers. The house sat against the backdrop of the mountains, the back garden butting up against a rise. Two ash trees had already lost their leaves in the front, and a blue spruce grew on the side. She climbed five steps to a covered porch and knocked on the green front door, looking forward to dinner with Laurel and Pastor Thomas.

The door opened, and Anna's heart raced. "Mr. Maier. I didn't expect ..." She poked her nose into the house.

"Mrs. Thomas had an emergency in the kitchen, and I happened to have hands free." A relaxed smile curved on his lips. "Please come in."

Anna stepped into the rug-lined hallway, stopping near a small, round marble-top table, where sat a silver five-petal flower card receiver. "If this is an inconvenient time—"

"Oh, stuff and nonsense." Laurel ambled the hallway in her white apron, a spatula in hand. "Mr. Maier had things to discuss with Clinton, and I invited him to stay for dinner."

"Well, if it's okay with Mr. Maier ..." Anna swallowed, heat crawling up her neck, wishing she could slow the rapid heartbeat inside her chest. She'd anticipated their encounter since their moments together in Idaho Springs. But now it was here, she had to suppress the desire to flee.

"No need to worry, Miss Sullivan." Mr. Maier seemed felicitous. "Pastor Thomas and I have completed our business."

"That we have." The preacher joined his wife.

"Why don't the two of you enjoy conversation in the parlor while Clinton and I put the finishing touches on the meal?" Laurel pointed with the spatula.

"I'm happy to assist—"

"No, no." Laurel cut Anna off. "We've got it handled." She nudged Clinton back to the kitchen.

"Shall we?" Mr. Maier indicated the parlor.

Anna put on a polite smile, passing him to enter the parlor, her stomach quivering. She set her reticule on an end table, then perched on the edge of the Rococo sofa.

When they'd last stumbled upon one another, Mr. Maier had received a terrible blow from investors the night before. The wound was still raw, and she had poured a soothing salve on it to ease the pain. For his part, Mr. Maier had championed her sewing business. She was riding high on its success. It would only have been natural for them to confuse gratefulness for attraction.

But the almost kiss would have been a mistake. Anna had known early on when she'd stroked the mane of Mr. Maier's beautiful Haflinger that their stations in life prevented a close association. Hadn't her relationship with Seamus proven a connection wasn't possible between two people from such different social spheres? They could be friends, even good friends, but pursuing an attachment would only cause a world of hurt for them both.

"So it's going to be like this, is it?" Mr. Maier said from the gold-cushioned chair catty-corner to her. He crossed his legs. "I thought we were friends—comrades in arms against an evil foe. You said as much in Idaho Springs. Has something happened to change your mind?"

The weight of his words pressed on Anna—the disappointment in his bitter smile. Did he think she had decided against him like everyone else who had abandoned him? Didn't friends help each other when they were in trouble? Anna inhaled a calming breath, and her muscles relaxed. "Ach, of course, I want to see the truth bear out and the people responsible discredited."

Mr. Maier exhaled through his nostrils. "For a moment, I thought certain ... sensibilities had changed your mind." Mr. Maier uncrossed his legs in a fluid motion, his eyes shining.

So Mr. Maier *had* been thinking about their last meeting. She swallowed. Oh, but how the man's magnetic pull made her resolve come unglued. "Well, I can't very well go back on my word, now, can I? Besides, the well-being of this town depends on the principled people in it."

"Thank you, Miss Sullivan." He flashed a disarming smile. "You have just paid me the greatest compliment."

"Mr. Maier, we must—"

"Isn't it about time you called me Stefan?" He rose and held out a hand. "I mean, if we are to be friends united in the fight against Töpfer, it would be so much simpler if we called each other by our given names."

Simpler, yes. But dangerous. Anna still grappled with the social implications of a closer relationship. Yet, she couldn't deny they'd formed a bond through difficult circumstances.

Anna peered up at Stefan. Mesmerized by eyes beaming at her in rapt attention, she took the proffered hand despite her most earnest efforts to maintain a reasonable distance. Slowly, gently, he drew her up and closer, their gazes locked in an intensity that spoke of longing, yearning, needing until he brought her into the circle of his embrace.

Anna had no resistance—didn't want to resist. Her heart had been starved for far too long. She closed her eyes, savoring the delightful sensations of this wanting and being wanted.

"My dears." Laurel's voice intruded on the moment, and Anna disentangled herself from Stefan just in time to escape her friend's purview of the situation—not that it wasn't evident by the flush rising in her cheeks. What had she been thinking to behave in such a manner in her friend's home and her husband being a respected minister of the Word? It just wasn't done.

"I'm sorry, Laurel." Anna grabbed her reticule from the table, ignoring Stefan's look of dismay. "I've got so much sewing to complete before the Harvest Ball that I must beg your pardon. Please give my apologies to Pastor Thomas." Anna ran out the door despite Laurel's attempts to convince her to stay and have a meal.

Twenty-Two

Anna spent the next two weeks sewing and fitting ball gowns for the Harvest Ball and doing her part to plan a Christmas Festival. In that time, she'd managed to avoid Stefan while he dealt with his legal affairs. Two days before the Harvest Ball, she had completed all the gowns to every lady's satisfaction except one.

No matter how hard she worked, Anna couldn't make the ivory lace and apricot taffeta dress satisfy the likes of Miss Elizabeth Henley. Taking leave of the latest fitting, Anna rehearsed all the various problems the girl had encountered with the dress, including a waistline that was too loose, according to the mademoiselle's vain expectations.

Anna stopped by the dry goods store to buy another spool of thread and paused by the display board. How could the gown have gone so wrong?

"Anna?" Margaret Cody's disturbed voice spoke from behind. "Are you all right?"

"Wh-what?" Anna twisted around.

"You've been muttering to yourself and ... My dear." She lay a hand on Anna's arm and frowned. "You look as if you haven't slept a wink."

"Ach, it's devilment, it is." Anna squeezed her eyes shut. "I have been able to make every ball gown to all the ladies' contentment but one. If I don't get it right this time 'round," she opened her eyes again, "I shall surely be packing my bags."

"I can't believe it will come to that, my dear." Margaret removed her hand.

"Oh, yes, yes, it might. Virginia may have given her enthusiastic approval to the Christmas Festival, but her daughter's dress may be the last one I make in this town."

"You shouldn't be so hard on yourself." Margaret pressed her lips together. "The girl can be demanding—gave your aunt a run for her money a time or two. Besides, Virginia is well aware of her daughter's shortcomings. She might surprise you with her sympathies."

Anna blew air through her nostrils. "I shall persevere through the next two days, even if it kills me."

"Perhaps if you eat a hearty dinner and get a good night's sleep, it'll all look fresher in the morning." Margaret gave her a reassuring smile and led her to the cash register.

Anna paid the bill and headed back to her cottage. Perhaps a good night's sleep would give her a different perspective.

On Saturday morning, Anna refinished the entire length of ruffle on Miss Henley's gown and let out a slow breath. The seams hadn't puckered, and the waist looked more fitted.

A sharp rap came at the door. "Coming." Anna extracted the gown from her lap and went to the door.

"I've come to drag you away—" Laurel stopped dead. "But you look entirely frazzled."

"That's because I am." Anna brushed back a stray strand of hair off her face. "I've agonized nonstop over Miss Henley's gown—all tied up in knots about finishing it."

"Oh, dear." Laurel frowned. "And have you?"

"Just." She bit her lip. "Oh, Laurel, what if I've failed to do right by the girl's dress and for the mayor's daughter, no less? Margaret says I shouldn't fret. But truth be told, I'm at wit's end."

Laurel led Anna to the divan. "May I see the dress?"

Anna held up the gown and waited while Laurel examined the ruffles and ruching, the lacing and bows.

"A most astonishing gown, I must say." Laurel's eyes sparkled. "The color will suit Miss Henley well, but I'm afraid you won't know the fitting until she tries it on."

"'Tis so." Anna lay the dress across the divan once more. "I should not waste another moment." She reached for the white linen to wrap the gown, but Laurel intercepted it.

"You may want to splash your face and fix your hair before you go. I'll prepare the dress. Then, we'll go together, shall we?" Laurel gave her an encouraging push.

Grateful for Laurel's friendship, Anna returned, her appearance more acceptable. At least Laurel would be there to pick up the pieces of her failed career if the gown failed to meet Miss Henley's expectations.

Twenty minutes later, Anna clasped her hands, trying to hide the bundle of nerves threatening to undo her if Miss Henley shunned the dress again.

Elizabeth Henley turned this way and that before the cheval mirror in the Henley's parlor. Attempting to get every point of view of the ivory lace and apricot-bustled gown, the girl swished around in an ecru pair of button-up shoes. She'd also donned ivory lace gloves drawn up to her elbows. Her eyes shone.

This time, the gown fit Miss Henley's figure perfectly, giving her the grace and elegance Anna had hoped for. She was a beauty, to be sure, with her hair drawn up into a bun on top and a waterfall of curls flowing down her back.

"Isn't this the most gorgeous gown I've ever owned?" She swirled about in the dress, her countenance all smiles.

"And you are simply stunning in it." Virginia Henley held her fisted hands against her chest. "You will be the belle of the ball."

Anna closed her eyes in silent prayer, moisture stinging her eyes, relief flooding her heart. She unfolded her hands and smiled.

"I believe you will have every young man at the ball vying for your attention and asking you for a dance." Laurel grinned.

"And I will not miss even one twirl, though I may have to disappoint one or two of the young men." The girl perked her nose.

Virginia handed her daughter a fan and a reticule made in the same color as the dress and trimmed with white lace. "This should finish the look wonderfully, my dear." She whirled around to face Anna. "Congratulations. You've accomplished something few people other than your aunt could have done."

"Thank you, Mrs. Henley. I hope you and Miss Henley will have a grand time at your ball." Anna bowed her head.

"I believe we shall. It is the event of the season, you know," Virginia boasted. "Everyone will be there with their best hats on. And thanks to you, Elizabeth's gown will be the loveliest of the evening. I assure you we will call on you again when we need another."

"Then we shall leave you to it." Anna smiled and made her way out the door with Laurel.

Still, Anna couldn't shake the melancholy that assailed her as they walked Taos Street. She *was* happy Elizabeth Henley's gown had made an impression. Yet the girl also reminded her of girls she'd gone to school with in Ireland—always posturing as if they deserved the royal treatment—the privileged class who attended the grandiose balls and had all the dashing boys trailing after them.

"I've seen that face before. You should be rejoicing about having Virginia Henley as a benefactor, but here you are, grim-faced as ever. What's in that head of yours?" Laurel gathered her shawl around her arms against the breeze that had come up.

Conflicted by her emotions, Anna walked a little farther before answering. She didn't want to appear ungrateful for her good fortune. "You're right, I should, and I am pleased as punch."

"But ...?" Laurel coaxed.

How could Anna explain her turmoil?

Ahead, Barton House was abuzz with people carrying loads of food and decorations into the inn, a sign that preparations for the festivities were underway. Georgia appeared at the door, ushering in musicians.

But while everyone anticipated the event of the season, Anna had been relegated to remain outside—just as she had always been an outsider—on the school playground when the society girls taunted and teased her, left to fend for herself on the doorstep of Da's drunken bouts, and betrayed by Seamus when his family rejected her for lack of a dowry. Would she be forever on the outside looking in?

"I—"

Georgia Tucker re-emerged from the door of the inn, waving them over.

Laurel waved and smiled back. "If I know Georgia, she'll want to show the inn arrayed in all its splendor." She diverted them toward the house. "And don't forget to ooh and ahh no matter how gaudy or tasteless it appears."

Anna complied, dragging her feet, a deep groan coming from her throat. How could she bear the humiliation?

"It's fortuitous you came by." Georgia linked arms with each of them in an animated walk. "You must tell me what you think."

Despite her initial reluctance, Anna admired the décor as she approached the front porch steps. Off to the sides of the portico, squashes of every size—green, yellow, orange—and baskets of chrysanthemums in burgundy, rust, and bumblebee sat strategically placed on bales of hay stacked at varying heights. Ivy had been hung along the scalloped cornice of the portico and strung around the two supporting columns on either side. Similar squashes and baskets of chrysanthemums lined the sides of the steps leading up to the small porch.

"Wait until you see the inside." Georgia pushed the French doors with a flair. "With all the new upgrades after last year's fire, it feels like a hotel in New York City."

Anna walked a few paces inside, gasping and gawking. She didn't know how the hotels in New York City might dazzle, but the interior had been transformed into a sunburst of harvest colors, reaching every corner of the establishment. Not that anything about the decoration was tasteless, as Laurel had predicted. It delighted the eyes, like an Irish autumn countryside—only this was Georgetown, and it shone with its tawny radiance.

"You must see the ladies' parlor." Georgia floated through the corridor, her high spirits evident in her gait.

Once Anna entered the parlor, she understood why Georgia was so excited to show it. Like the other parts of the inn, the ladies' parlor exuded a warm and welcoming atmosphere and made it a place where any lady would want to take refreshment.

She could picture the room in winter, a roaring fire in the

marble-mantled fireplace, and dignified ladies carrying on discourse, sipping tea. Some would sit at groupings of red-cushioned Victorian chairs while others would amuse themselves playing games of Whist at a center oval mahogany table. All the while, they'd enjoy the background music of Chopin or Schubert played by their accomplished musicians at the grand piano on the other side of the room. And tying the entire room together were the rich Victorian colors of the wallpaper and carpeting.

"Georgia, the room is simply outstanding." Laurel beamed. "You must be pleased."

"I am, if I may say so myself." Georgia bowed in appreciation. She led them back to the check-in desk. "When this place went up in flames last year," she twisted to address Anna, "everyone in Georgetown shuddered. People feared it was gone for good. But, thankfully, a few people like Mr. Maier stepped up to help rebuild it."

"I just hope people remember that when they blame Mr. Maier for their troubles." Laurel pressed her lips. "He doesn't deserve to be treated like an outcast."

A sudden pang of guilt settled in Anna's chest. Had she treated Stefan like an outcast, evading him as if he were a demon in man's clothes? She hadn't meant to. It was the impending heartbreak of a social mismatch that had kept her away.

"Still, it's been a sheer joy to see this place blossom again under your ownership, Georgia." Laurel's eager enthusiasm brought Anna out of her reverie.

Georgia opened the door for them. "Until tonight, then."

"I wish you great success." Anna forced a smile.

Georgia's mouth gaped. "Won't you be joining us this evening, Anna?"

"Well, I ..." She bit her lip. "I have no invitation."

Laurel stepped forward, her brows knitted. "So that's why you've been glum all afternoon, isn't it? You didn't think you were invited to the ball."

Anna shrugged. "It's not like I have any rights to your society event, my being new in town and—"

"Oh, balderdash." Georgia waved a hand. "Of course, you're invited, dear girl. Everyone in town can attend the Harvest Ball—no invitation needed."

"Really?" Anna's spirits soared. Then, as quickly, her shoulders slumped again. "But all I have is this mourning gown Laurel loaned me." Anna's hands spread wide in front of her. "And my shabby travel clothes."

"Well, isn't that something?" Georgia's mouth fell open. "The dressmaker has made everyone else's ballgown, but she has nothing for herself. Maybe you could—"

"No, wait." Laurel grabbed Anna's arm. "How long has it been since your uncle died?"

"A wee bit over a month—not the requisite two months to abandon the gown, I fear."

"Why should that matter?" This time, Georgia waved away with both hands.

"Convention has its place, but you've worn that gown long enough. High time to put it away and start living your life again."

Anna stared at Laurel, her lips parted. How could she just dispense with the decorum expected of her? What would people say?

"Normally, I don't suggest such things." Laurel knitted her brow. "But in this case, I'm inclined to agree."

"Laurel, I—"

"Sometimes God's children heap too many burdens upon each other." Laurel shook her head. "The letter of the law instead of the spirit of the law."

"Ach, but the town gossip ..." Anna pressed her hand against her chest.

"Never mind," Laurel spoke definitively. "Knowing your uncle, he would have appreciated your sincere heart, but he would have also wanted you to get on with your life."

Anna met Laurel's tender gaze. Her eyes misted over, and she sucked in a breath. These women had befriended her and had adopted her as family. "But I still have no dress to wear."

"You leave that to me." Laurel linked arms with Anna's and walked her out the door. She stopped and turned at the bottom of the stairs. "Thank you for giving us the tour, Georgia. We're off to find the perfect gown for Anna, and I think I know where it is."

"I can't wait." Georgia clapped her fists together. "I believe this is going to be a night to remember."

Giddy as a bird chirping away in a tree, Anna didn't care if anyone stopped and stared at her and Laurel staggering on Taos Street. She was Cinderella, and her very own fairy godmother had come to dress her for the ball.

Laurel's laughter joined hers, and they frolicked as if they were two youthful girls skipping down the lane without a care in the world.

During the past two weeks, Stefan had been embroiled in Töpfer's vicious lawsuit against the Singing Silver Mine. There had been a firestorm of complaints and counter-complaints between them—Töpfer relentlessly launching savage attacks and Stefan reacting with gloves off to defend the truth. The litigation resulted in a mounting pile of paperwork, not to mention lawyers' bills, court appearances, conflicting testimony, disputed property lines, and accusations of deliberate stealing on both sides. With all the nonsense, Stefan still hadn't descended the shaft.

Today, Stefan had experienced another dissatisfying meeting with his lawyer. It chagrinned him to the bone, ending with Edwin's cryptic advice. "Attend the Harvest Ball, Stefan. Dance with the ladies and forget about the business of the mine for an evening. It might make you easier to live with." Edwin's wry smile had hit its mark.

"*Pfff.*" Stefan glowered at his friend, unappreciative of his so-called advice, then turned the doorknob, dashed down the stairs, and thrust the door into the open air. The weather had turned colder since he'd stepped into the building, and he propped up the collar on his frock coat.

Stefan tramped along Taos Street, still scowling. How could he go to the Harvest Ball when he couldn't drum up the celebratory mood? He had little reason to attend. The deplorable state of his finances left him bereft of doing anything for his employees, and the distance Anna had forged had created a vast fissure between them as wide as Silver Gulch. Perhaps he should avoid the Barton House and turn onto Mary Street, so he didn't have to encounter Georgia Tucker. Stefan liked the woman but didn't want to be strong-armed into attending her ball.

He started to make the turn but froze, transfixed by Laurel and Anna coming toward him. He crossed his arms, bemused by the rare sight of these two usually dignified ladies, skipping and dancing about like two court jesters—and Anna Sullivan in her mourning gown, no less.

"Good afternoon." He lifted his hat when they reached the corner. "You ladies appear to need an escort." He fell into line with them, heading north and away from the Barton House.

"What gave you that impression?" He caught the furtive smile Mrs. Thomas sent Anna's way.

"Oh, I don't know. How much have you ladies had to drink?"

"Why, what could *possibly* give you the idea we've been imbibing the drink?" Anna's fingers touched her parted lips, trying to stop a giggle, her big blue eyes positively incredulous, making them seem more luscious than ever.

"Skipping like schoolgirls in the middle of the street, perhaps?" A smile played about Stefan's lips. "Though I must say it surprises me, Mrs. Thomas. What would *Pastor* Thomas say?"

Both ladies dissolved into fits of laughter, holding onto each other as if to keep from falling into heaps on the ground. Stefan remained fixed, crossing his arms, scanning the environs to see if anyone else was watching them. "I can see you ladies believe this all very amusing, but you might consider how small this town is, and people talk."

"I suppose we ought to behave ourselves, Laurel." Anna straightened, inhaling and pressing her lips together as if she attempted to keep from smiling. However, the light in her eyes betrayed her emotions. "After all, Mr. Maier is right. You don't want to sully yours or the preacher's good name."

"Yes, you're quite right." Mrs. Thomas held a hand to her chest and inhaled deeply. "It might cause quite a stir."

"But you must know I haven't laughed like this since ... well ... since I can't remember when. At least not since I left Ireland, anyway." Anna's demeanor lost some of its luster.

Stefan wished he could rejuvenate it. He rather liked this playful side of her.

He waited until they got their bearings again, then joined them, falling into step next to Anna. She still had a spring in her step and a secretive smile on her lips. He hadn't destroyed her good spirits after all.

He relaxed. "May I ask what has caused this show?"

"I'm going to the ball," Anna announced with bravado. "Oh, I know such a thing might not seem so extraordinary to you, being a man of the world. But I've never been to a ball, and I'm quite bursting with the notion of it."

"I see." Stefan's eyes widened. It would never have occurred to him. Hadn't everyone attended at least one ball? "Then you've not even danced before?"

"Well, yes." She seemed to shrink away. "But only a bit among my school chums did I learn a few steps. Nothing so grand as I'm sure you're used to."

"No need to apologize. I'm surprised, that's all." Most people in Stefan's social circles on both sides of the ocean had attended numerous balls. Charity had craved the society balls, but he'd come to resent them—enduring them as opportunities to conduct business and forge partnerships under the guise of a social gathering. "Perhaps I've lost your appreciation for enjoying what has become commonplace among many of my friends."

"Will you be going to the ball, Stefan?" Mrs. Thomas poked her head out to look at him.

He opened his mouth, then snapped it shut. The question had surprised him. Though he had been set to spend the night alone in his rambling house, obsessing over his latest mine woes, he now wanted more than anything to be present at Anna's first ball.

"Of course, isn't most everyone in Georgetown?"

"I wouldn't have except for Laurel and Georgia." Anna fingered her black gown.

Of course, Anna's obligation to wait out the mourning period would have kept her away. But her minor impropriety stirred something deliciously delightful in Stefan's heart.

"I'm pleased they've convinced you otherwise." He slowed.

If he was going to attend the ball, he needed to get ready. "I hope you will save the first dance for me, Miss Sullivan."

She stared at him, swallowing, her conflicted emotions flitting across her face. Would she decide against him?

"That is if you're not—"

"It would be my pleasure, Mr. Maier." Anna tilted her head in an appreciative bow.

"Very good." He bowed in return. "Until tonight, ladies."

Stefan wheeled around, heat radiating through his chest, and hastened back up Taos Street as if he were running on air. Never had he looked forward to a ball more—even the ones he'd attended at the duke's court in Marlborough.

Twenty-Three

Anna studied her image in Laurel's cheval mirror, her eyes dazzled by the seafoam and ivory lace gown Laurel had rendered from her trunks. She'd never had the opportunity to attend a society ball—never worn such an elegant gown with its ruffled bustle trailing behind her and a ruched front panel that showed off her curves. Nor had she styled her hair with so many twists and beads.

Laurel came up behind her, laying hands on her shoulders. She wore a gown of deep purple and black lace, her brown eyes glowing. "Absolutely splendid, Anna. The dress appears tailored with you in mind."

"But how did you—"

"Our daughter Cassie wore this gown to her first ball. Her coloring and fair complexion are similar to yours, so I hoped it might complement you in the same way."

"But I thought Cassie lived in Ohio." Anna tilted her head.

"Clinton and I mistakenly packed the gown with our belongings when we moved to Georgetown." A faraway look entered her eyes. Then, a smile sprung on her lips. "But I'm certain Cassie would be pleased the dress found a new home."

Anna turned to face her straight on. "I don't know how to thank you—not only for the dress but for styling my hair and ... everything."

"Say nothing of it, my dear." Laurel's sincere gaze met hers. "God has gifted you with beauty *and* talent, hmm?"

Anna nodded her misty-eyed appreciation. No one had ever been so kind to her, except perhaps her dear ma before she'd fallen ill.

"It seems Mr. Maier has also noticed your attributes." Laurel slowly rubbed her hands together. "It's quite an honor for him to have asked you for the first dance."

"Or having mercy on a poor peasant girl in want of a partner."

"I think not." Laurel met her eyes in the mirror. "Mr. Maier would not have paid you so great a compliment if he did not hold you in high regard."

"Perhaps." Anna felt the flush rising in her cheeks.

"No perhaps about it. Just enjoy the evening, my dear." Laurel turned. "Now, I must check on Clinton. I can't think what's keeping him." She left Anna to ponder her reflection.

Anna slid her hands down the sides of her gown. In Ireland, she had always been banned from the privileges of the upper echelons of society. Even as a young girl, romping with Seamus and his siblings on the farm, Mrs. O'Connor demanded she make herself scarce when other strong farmers' families came to call.

Oh, there had been a time or two in later years when Seamus had taken her into his arms—dressed as she was in her shabby skirts—and twirled her to the tune of a waltz he hummed. But she had never been privy to the fancy events his sisters had attended when they were older, nor had she accompanied Seamus to the balls where his parents had arranged for him to consort with women of his social standing. Therein was the rub. Seamus had said Anna would regret coming to America, and in the beginning, she nearly had. Yet, here, in this western Territory of Colorado, Laurel had dressed her as if she were the belle of the ball. How could she not be grateful for how her life had turned out?

Stefan Maier's face welled before her. Their last encounter at Laurel's house conjured the emotions that had rendered her weak-kneed and pliable in his arms.

"Oh, be done with it." Anna chided herself. Laurel was right. She should accept things as they were—no more, no less.

Anna slipped on the ivory shawl and gloves Laurel had given her and descended the steps to the foyer, where her friends waited for her. "Why, Pastor Thomas, don't you look the grand sight? Laurel is a lucky lady."

She noted the twinkle in his eyes as he opened the door for them. "And upon my soul, the Lord has blessed me to escort the two loveliest ladies in Clear Creek County." He ushered them through the threshold.

"You are a dear." Laurel turned to her husband beside the carriage and pressed a gloved palm to his cheek. "Didn't I tell you Cassie's dress would suit Anna?"

"That you did, my dear." Pastor Thomas helped his wife and then Anna into the conveyance.

Though Anna could see her breath in the nippy night air, a warm, tingling sensation chased her spine. She wet her lips and closed her eyes to savor the moment. She knew without a doubt that no matter what happened afterward, she would never forget this as the night she'd been granted two wishes— to go to the ball in a beautiful carriage and dance with a prince.

Clinton coaxed the horses forward, and a jolt brought Anna

back to the present. She laughed and grabbed Laurel's arm. "Pinch me. I think I must be dreaming."

"It's no dream, Anna. We are underway to the Harvest Ball."

❧

Anna feasted her eyes on the Barton House, the outside décor she had seen earlier in the day now illuminated by lantern light. Pastor Thomas reigned in the horses as they waited in the queue to disembark and allow the valets to park the carriage. When it was their turn, Anna stepped out with her two companions and followed the lanterns up the steps to the door.

"Glad you could join us this evening, Miss Sullivan." The younger Mr. Sieger took their overcoats and shawls and handed each a claim ticket.

"Will you be dancing tonight, Mr. Sieger?" Anna hoped Georgia wouldn't expect him to remain at his post all night while the rest of his chums enjoyed the festivities.

"Yes, ma'am." He grinned. "Mrs. Tucker says I can get away once most folks have arrived." He turned to the next couple, and Anna moved forward with Laurel and Pastor Thomas, taking in the aromas of cinnamon and spice permeating the inn. The footman gave them each a glass of punch as they passed.

All aglow in harvest gold, the inn appeared even more spectacular at night, with people milling about in merriment and a string orchestra playing music that filtered down the stairway from an upper room. She sipped from her glass and cringed. "A bit potent, isn't it?"

"Made to enhance conviviality, I'm sure." Pastor Thomas winced. "I think I'll hunt for something a little less spiced." He walked off to find the food and drinks table, leaving Anna and Laurel to search the crowd.

"There you are." Georgia rushed on them as if she was on a mission. Her gown, made in rusty brocade, seemed to fit with the general décor of the season. "You are a vision of loveliness, my dear." She bubbled in effervescent joy.

"It's all Laurel's doing." Anna swiveled toward Laurel.

"I'm sure that's not true," Georgia assured her. "She had a fine subject to work with."

"You see, Anna," Laurel said, "I'm not the only one who thinks so."

"And you're not the only ones who are glowing. Come with me." Georgia turned, picked up her skirts, and whisked them up the stairs to a ballroom where the orchestra played a waltz.

While Georgia peered about the room, Anna spotted Cecelia playing violin with the orchestra on the main stage. Would wonders never cease? The woman seemed to have more talents than three people put together. Cecelia looked up just then and flashed a wide smile. Anna waved back.

"There's my Prudence." Georgia gleefully indicated a young couple.

Anna followed her gaze. Ah, Prudence was one of the prettiest girls on the floor in her sapphire gown, and the small amount of weight she'd lost had only allowed the style to emphasize her figure in all the right places. The girl's eyes beamed in the candlelight. "Who's the young man?"

"Paul Rutherford's son, Ian. Isn't he quite the catch?"

"Ian Rutherford." Laurel fingered her lip. "I seem to recall something ..."

"Well?" Georgia glared at her.

"Thing is, I can't remember." Laurel bit her lip. "But I must say he's grown into a handsome young man."

"Prudence seems pleased." Anna reflected on her

conversation with Prudence and hoped she had played a small part in making this night more memorable for her.

"It was all so unexpected." Georgia's eyes glowed. "She never thought someone so plucky would want her, especially since he was Elizabeth Henley's beau first."

"Where is Elizabeth Henley tonight?" Anna got up on tiptoes to hunt for the other girl on the dance floor and found her laughing in the arms of a handsome young man.

"Good evening, ladies."

Anna had been too busy watching Miss Henley to notice Mr. Maier's approach. Her stomach fluttered, her heart skipping a beat as he bowed in proper evening attire. What was wrong with her? How could the man, who had nearly thrown her out of her cottage weeks ago, cause these reactions?

"You look quite the dashing gentleman this evening, Mr. Maier." Georgia swept appreciative eyes over him.

Yes, perhaps that was it. Anna couldn't deny the attraction.

The man exuded self-confidence, and his broad shoulders and narrow waist filled out the black coattail, white silk shirt, and ascot in perfect form. His dark, trimmed beard and roguish expression gave the impression of a man in control of his destiny, though one couldn't say, at present, that his life cruised an even course.

"You've outdone yourself, Mrs. Tucker. Everyone seems to be in fine spirits." Stefan waved the hand that held a glass of punch between longish, nimble fingers—fingers Anna yearned to feel running through her hair.

Good heavens! What was she thinking?

"Quite a compliment coming from you, Mr. Maier," Georgia responded. "But you should know if these two ladies hadn't come along when they did, I might still be trying to decide where all the decorations belong."

Stefan turned curious eyes on Anna. "And are you always so quick to lend your moral support, Miss Sullivan?"

Heat rose to Anna's cheeks. "Georgia had it all done by the time we arrived. She just needed a little affirmation."

"Here we are jabbering on about the décor when there's a dance proceeding in front of us." Laurel pressed in. "Anna, didn't you promise Mr. Maier the first dance?"

A quiver chased through Anna's stomach at the thought of their bodies so close together. "Mr. Maier needn't feel obliged—"

"I feel no obligation." He grinned, took Anna's punch from her, and handed Laurel both glasses. "If you don't mind …"

He pulled Anna onto the dance floor, and she couldn't deny the ease with which he led her in a waltz to Strauss' *Tales from the Vienna Woods* despite her lack of skill.

Though Anna had dreaded dancing with Stefan, now she inhaled the musky aroma of his cologne, intoxicated by his body next to hers—how it disoriented her senses and made her thrill to his touch. After a few moments on the dance floor, Anna couldn't endure it any longer. She had to speak, or she would lose herself in his arms.

She turned her face up to his. "You needn't have felt indebted to dance with me. Laurel meant well—"

"Here you go again." He twirled her and pulled her closer. "Is it so surprising I wanted to dance with the most astonishing woman I've ever known?"

She hesitated, his assessment of her hard to accept. "We come from two such different worlds, Mr. Maier—"

"Stefan, remember?" He spun her away, then caught her back into his arms. "Does it matter to you that much?"

"I …" Anna had been ready to reference her substandard breeding. Yet, as she beheld the unmistakable admiration he so gallantly granted her in his gaze, she lost all grasp of her senses. "No, not at all."

Stefan's eyes warmed even more, firmly grasping her waist and dancing with an elegance that seemed to give wings to her feet. She gave in to the exhilarating momentum, reveling in the moment—a moment in which no one existed but the two of them together, taking flight across the dance hall as if they were one entity abroad the span of eternity.

All too soon, the piece ended on a crescendo, and Stefan brought them to a standstill. She couldn't move, her gaze locked with his, their bodies still entwined, his breathing labored.

Anna expected Stefan to release her, but he only slightly slackened his hold. "Would you do me the honor of a second dance, Anna?" She thrilled to the sound of her name spoken like a soft caress. But before she could respond, the orchestra played the opening of *The Blue Danube,* and Stefan caught her up again.

A sudden cacophony of commotion interrupted the harmony of their movements, and Anna stumbled as she observed someone dash across the dance floor out of the corner of her eye. Her gaze followed the shadow crossing the room.

"Stop that varmint."

"You, there. Stop."

"Grab that little thief."

More than one voice issued the commands.

The music faded away, and Anna and Stefan turned with the other leering guests toward Elias Jones and Clyde Tucker—both in chase of the runner.

Mr. Jones grabbed the boy by the scruff of the neck. "Got you, you little no-account savage. I should have beaten you to a pulp when I had a chance a month ago."

Anna's mouth gaped. He was no more than a boy, and by the looks of his dirty face, hair, and unkempt clothes, he was a vagrant from one of the local indigenous tribes. Who was he?

"Well, glory be. What is that boy up to now?" Cecelia said from behind her.

Startled, Anna twisted around, suddenly aware they'd halted before the main stage. "You know him?"

"I know him. That boy's in a heap of trouble. Tried to help him change his ways once, but he ran away. Somebody's got to stop him before he lands himself in jail, and they throw away the key." She clucked her tongue and shook her head.

Anna turned back and studied the boy. He looked emaciated, his gaunt face and sunken eyes giving way to remembrances of her poverty-stricken past in Ireland. She imagined he felt the way she always had—alone, outside, unwelcome.

Mr. Jones dragged the boy past her. "You got a nerve coming into a place where you don't belong."

Anna's heart immediately went out to the boy. Someone had to fight for him, and that someone would be her.

Twenty-Four

Anna's outrage grew as Elias Jones towed the resistant vagrant by his neck. No one deserved that kind of treatment—not her and not a poor boy from one of the native tribes.

"Let me go." The boy dug in his feet, and a murmur coursed through the hall.

"You'll answer to the marshal before I'm through with you." The man yanked him.

"Stefan, we have to do something. That savage, as Mr. Jones called him, is probably no more than thirteen years old. By the looks of him, he's been on his own for a while."

"He does look a bit of a tramp, doesn't he?" Stefan crossed his arms. "I wonder why he's separated from his people?"

"I'm going to find out what this is all about." She started for the ballroom door, but Stefan's hand on her arm prevented her from taking another step.

"I don't think we should get involved, Anna. Leave it to the marshal to sort out."

Anna glared at Stefan's hand, then directed a hard stare into his eyes.

Stefan let go as if she'd scorched him. "It's not our place to get between a marauder and the law."

"Ach, if he *is* a marauder. Doesn't the law in this country assume a person is innocent until proven guilty? You, of all people, should understand that."

Stefan put a fist on his hip and looked away.

She'd hit the bullseye, though she slightly winced at stabbing him while he was down. "Besides, we know nothing about him other than Elias Jones has accused him of stealing."

"The boy ran away, Anna." Stefan rubbed his forehead. "That proves his guilt."

"Maybe he's scared out of his wits. Have you considered that? He might be running for any number of reasons." Disquieted eyes stared at the door, her opportunity to discover the answers slipping away. She didn't want to argue with Stefan, but if Cecelia was right, the boy needed an advocate. "For all we know, Mr. Jones could be lying to protect himself."

"Ladies and gentlemen, may I have your attention." Georgia climbed onto the main stage and spoke above the assembly. "We apologize for the interruption of our entertainment. Marshal Jacobs has taken the ruffian into custody. It's time to get on with the festivities." As Georgia stepped away, a palpable relief filled the room.

"It seems the whole matter is out of our hands." Stefan stepped up to Anna with open arms. "Perhaps we should do as Georgia proposed and get on with the festivities."

"I will not." Anna stepped backward. "From what people say, the Marshal hasn't been a friend to the Plains Indians since his early days in the Calvary. I don't intend to stand by and let him harm another." She spun on her heel and strode away.

Stefan cupped her elbow, keeping pace as they stepped through the threshold. "I'm not saying the boy is innocent, but I feel duty-bound to ensure his accusers don't feed you to the wolves."

Anna looked askance at Stefan and almost smiled—almost, because the gravity of the situation warranted little to be happy about. Still, perhaps his desire to lend moral support suggested he shared her concerns after all. She stalked straight ahead with her head held high.

Outside the ballroom, they found Elias Jones, Clyde Tucker, Marshal Jacobs, and the boy traipsing the hallway. Marshal Jacobs had already handcuffed the poor soul and pushed him forward.

"Marshal, wait." Anna picked up her skirts and scurried to where the men halted at the top of the stairs.

He turned. "What is it, Miss Sullivan? I don't have all night."

"I'm aware of that, Marshal." Anna studied the badge on his chest and appraised him. Though the Marshal was a man of the law, his dark eyes, hair, and mustache made him appear more like what Scripture called the man of lawlessness—the devil. She shook away the thought and shifted her gaze to the boy, assessing his wariness. She approached him with a gentle smile, hoping to ease his fear. "I only want to talk to the boy— give him a chance to explain himself."

Mr. Jones closed the gap between them. "I don't think that's any business of yours." He narrowed his eyes.

Anna jumped back, the fire of whiskey spewing from his mouth. She had little interest in tangling with anyone whose mercurial moods had the potential to turn ugly.

"Why don't we let the marshal decide?" Anna met the lawman's eyes. "After all, isn't reporting a person's crime a matter of public interest?" Anna noted a few people had gathered at the bottom of the stairway, and she heard others congregating behind her outside the dance hall.

"Look, here—"

"The lady has a point, Marshal." Stefan's voice was low and steady. "The fellow deserves a fair hearing."

Anna warmed to hear Stefan defend the poor child.

"I think *I'd* like to hear what the boy has to say." Anna's gaze shifted to Pastor Thomas, ascending the stairs with Laurel trailing him.

The lawman surveyed his audience and then gave a half-hearted shrug. "Mr. Jones says he saw the Indian steal food from the kitchen."

Her compassion for the boy soared, especially in light of the dragon's contempt. Though he was only a couple of inches shorter than Anna, the lack of fat on his bones and his bedraggled state suggested neglect. How long had it been since he'd had a decent meal?

She stepped closer. "My name is Anna. What's your name?"

Suspicion crossed his eyes, and Anna decided on a more tender tact.

"I come from Ireland—a place across the ocean very far from here. When I was a child, we had a potato famine. My family nearly starved to death. I know what it means to be hungry. Are you hungry?"

The boy straightened his shoulders, his eyes defiant.

Anna tried again, searching his eyes with as much tenderness as she could communicate. "You're hungry, aren't you?"

He licked his lips and nodded.

At last, she'd made progress. "I can see you haven't had much to eat in recent days—"

"Look here, that's no excuse for stealing food, is it?" Mr. Jones blurted out.

"Be quiet." Stefan crossed his arms and gave the bloke a stern look. "Let's hear the boy out. Any objection, Mr. Tucker?" He shifted his gaze.

Clyde pursed his lips before responding. "I think I'd like to hear his response."

Irritation ignited the dragon's eyes. "This lying, thieving savage stole from me a while back." He got in the boy's face, poking a finger into his chest. "It was the only food I had, too, between here and Denver."

"When did you say that was, Mr. Jones?" Stefan probed.

"I ... a few weeks back." Mr. Jones stuttered, the question seeming to put him off-kilter. Then he straightened. "I can't remember exactly when it was—but it don't matter now, does it? He's a thief."

Anna watched the little man's greasy beard bob as he spoke. She likened him to Ireland's legendary leprechauns whose sketchy characters couldn't be trusted.

"Marshal, Mr. Jones has given us no proof." Stefan pointed. "The boy should be allowed to defend himself."

The lawman's mustache twitched, and Anna suspected he knew he was in a predicament. It wouldn't do to ignore the law in front of all these people. "He seems to respond to Miss Sullivan. Please proceed." He gave her a solemn nod.

"Names have a lot of meaning, don't you think?" Anna encouraged the boy. "I'm called Anna—a Christian name that comes from the Greek language, meaning 'full of grace.' My parents named me Anna because God had given them a baby girl. What about your name?"

He shifted his weight between his feet, his gaze bouncing between her and the lawman. Anna waited, hoping he'd respond.

"Dakota." He spoke at last. Anna clasped her hands. "It

means protector." He lowered his gaze. "I should have protected my family."

Stefan drew closer. "Where is your family now, Dakota?"

"My father was a brave warrior." He lifted his chin and became stone-faced. "He and my mother died at Summit Springs. I lived with my uncle until last summer. He died of despair."

Anna's compassion for the boy grew substantially stronger. She'd heard one man warn travelers on the train coming west about the battle at Summit Springs in 1869. According to him, the Calvary had gunned down the Cheyenne Dog Soldiers, leaving more than fifty of Dakota's kinsmen dead. But while it was supposed to have ended the five-year war between the Colorado Plains Indians and the U.S. Calvary, occasional skirmishes still happened.

"I'm so very sorry." Anna sympathized. "I know what it is to lose your parents. My mother died of a horrible illness when I was seventeen, and my father died of drink and despair—like your uncle. It's hard to watch your parents die."

"That still doesn't explain how he ended up at my inn." Clyde frowned. "Dakota?"

"For two moons, I stay in Denver." He shrugged. "Afterward, I follow the river."

Mr. Jones snorted. "Well, all this misfortune just makes me want to cry."

"I'm sure you're crying buckets full." Stefan's disgust came across loud and clear.

"Shows you what you know." Mr. Jones' voice dripped with disdain. "It's time to take this guttersnipe to the jailhouse, Marshal."

"Miss Sullivan—"

"Did you steal food from the kitchen because you were hungry?" Anna insisted, unwilling to be deterred from her task.

The boy hesitated, the fear reflected in his eyes. "It's okay, Dakota. I won't let anyone hurt you."

He licked his lips before answering. "No matter where I go, they do not listen to me. They say I must go away." His voice was solemn. "What should I do? I have to eat."

"There it is." Mr. Jones vented and pointed a finger. "He just admitted his crime, isn't that right?" He addressed the crowd, and a babble of voices agreed.

"And what would *you* do if you had no job, no money, and no place to stay, Mr. Jones?" Stefan spoke above the crowd.

"Well, isn't it lucky for me I don't work for the Singing Silver Mine anymore?" The man's lips curved into a malicious grin. Anna watched Stefan's nostrils flare, hands furling and unfurling as if he fought with himself to curb his anger. "I'd be begging on the streets just like Horace McKinley. Now, there's a man we should be helping, not this mongrel." He sneered, spitting and hissing like an angry cat.

"All right, Mr. Jones, you've said enough." Pastor Thomas stepped forward.

"So, you're an Indian lover, too, are you, *Pastor?*" The dragon shot at Pastor Thomas.

The preacher shook his head. "God does not distinguish between those who should or should not receive our charity. Is not God the Father to the fatherless in their affliction? Dakota deserves our sympathy as much as the folks in this town affected by the mine disaster."

"Doesn't the good book also say, 'Thou shalt not steal?'" Mr. Jones squinted.

"Seems like you should practice what you preach." Anna crossed her arms.

Mr. Jones laughed. "I would expect that from you, a bogtrotter from—where is it—Dingle?"

Anna gaped in horror as Stefan struck the hoist man with a

DONNA WICHELMAN

right hook to the jaw and knocked him against the corridor wall.

A dismayed roar went up from the crowd.

Mr. Jones pushed himself away and came at him with a fist. "You—"

"No!" Anna had no more shouted when Clyde stepped between the two men.

"I will have no fighting in this establishment." Clyde's head twisted back and forth between the two men until he got a nod from each. "We're supposed to be celebrating harvest with a ball, not a brawl." He turned to the lawman. "I've decided not to press charges, Marshal. This boy needs a meal and some good folks to feed him, not another excuse for anger and tomfoolery."

Mr. Jones got into the marshal's face. "Now, Marshal, that ain't what we agreed to—"

"He'll stay with us for the time being." Laurel rushed in, tossing a defiant glare at Mr. Jones. She stepped up to Dakota and put her hands on his shoulders.

Anna squared her shoulders as Pastor Thomas joined his wife. Perhaps this show of force would convince the Marshal to release the boy.

She turned her attention to Marshal Jacobs. He had crossed his arms, his mustache twitching back and forth. Waiting for his answer seemed to take eons.

At last, the marshal uncrossed his arms. "Pastor Thomas, Mrs. Thomas—I hope you know what you're taking on. These people can be brutal to the core. I expect being raised by the likes of the Cheyenne Dog Soldiers has corrupted the boy beyond rehabilitation. If I find he has violated the law in any way, I will put him behind bars and throw away the key. Is that clear?"

"I don't believe anyone is beyond hope, Marshal—even

242

you." Pastor Thomas dug his hands deep into his trouser pockets. "The love and forgiveness of Christ cover a multitude of sins."

Marshal Jacobs turned the boy around and removed his handcuffs. "You're a might better believer than I am, Pastor." He spun on his heel and stomped to the first floor. Mr. Jones hastened after him, protesting Dakota's release all the way out the door of the inn.

Clyde motioned for the crowd to disburse, ushering them back into the ballroom, leaving Anna with Stefan, Laurel, Pastor Thomas, and Dakota standing on the landing.

"You saved the day." Through tears of joy, Anna gazed at Laurel's hands, still on the boy's shoulders.

"No, my dear. *You* did." Laurel placed a palm to her cheek and smiled. "If you hadn't pressed for the truth, Dakota would be in jail."

"I think it's time we take Dakota home and give him a good meal." Pastor Thomas craned his neck forward to speak to the boy. "Would that be all right, Dakota?"

A grin broke on Dakota's lips. "I like deer meat and corn and squash. Apple pie too. And don't forget the chocolate."

They all laughed, and Pastor Thomas responded by encouraging them forward. "We'll see what we can arrange, Dakota." They left Anna and Stefan standing alone in an awkward silence.

Though he'd initially shown reluctance, she had to give Stefan credit for supporting her. The gesture endeared him to her all the more. "Thank you for coming to Dakota's defense and mine. You didn't have to."

"It was the right thing to do in the end."

"How's your hand?" She inclined her head. "You know, you needn't have—"

Stefan immediately placed a finger on her lips, peering into her eyes. "Elias deserved it." His eyes gleamed. "As I recall, you did promise a second dance before we were so rudely interrupted, and I intend to collect on your debt. Shall we?" He indicated toward the ballroom, and Anna had no choice but to comply.

Twenty-Five

A male pianist in coattails was playing the *Valses Sentimentales* by Franz Shubert when Stefan returned to the ballroom with Anna. Stefan knew the music well, his mother having forced him to play it for a piano competition as a young man. He had tired of it then, but tonight, he found the piece invigorating. It could only be the woman in his arms who sent his spirits soaring.

He led her onto the dance floor and swept her away in a lively rendition of the waltz. Exhilarated by the exuberant beat, Stefan whirled and twirled Anna about the floor, and all seemed right in his world. Indeed, he had not met another woman like her in all his encounters in Europe or America. She could have asked for his life, and he would have granted it.

The last time he had felt this alive was weeks before he departed for America in 1868. He and William had been anticipating the adventure of their lives. If only Charity had been as eager to embark on their adventure.

"You're far away, Stefan." Anna broke into his thoughts.

"Do you know you scare me, Anna Sullivan?" He spoke into her ear.

She drew back. "I don't know why I should—a bogtrotter like me."

Disgust exploded like dynamite in Stefan's head. He had detested the taunt. Anna deserved better. He squeezed her hand and dragged her roughly against him despite how his bruised knuckles throbbed. "I forbid you to use that term ever again."

Her eyes went suddenly bright. "My fingers, Stefan. You're hurting me."

He slackened his hold, not having meant to cause pain. "It's a hideous way to describe a decent human being."

"I thought you would despise me since I had made a spectacle of myself."

Stefan's mouth gaped. He stumbled, grumbling under his breath. Couldn't Anna see how much he admired her and respected her compassion? "Not in the least. I applaud your courage to fight for what you believe in."

"Even for an Indian boy?"

"Especially for an Indian boy. You persisted until you got to the bottom of his ill fortune. It's a rare person who will defend such a one scorned and rejected by society. Yet you did it to your detriment."

"No one else would. I couldn't stand by while Dakota was drawn and quartered by the likes of Elias Jones without a fair chance to be heard. That man makes my skin crawl."

Indeed, Jones was a snake. But there had been something else he'd said—a reference to a trip to Denver a few weeks back. It needled Stefan. He carried on for a while, but the music seemed more mechanical than they had experienced earlier. Anna also seemed to have distanced herself from him again.

"Tell me, what's going on in that complicated mind of yours?"

Anna pulled her head back, a too-quick smile on her face. "It's not important. We should enjoy the moment."

"But it must be for you to focus so diligently on it." Stefan coaxed gently, his heart beating faster, waiting for her reply, hoping he hadn't done something to destroy the trust they'd built earlier. "You can tell me anything."

He sensed her body go taut, but she didn't move away this time. "Mrs. Henley tells me you come from aristocracy."

Stefan went rigid. Why did Anna persist with the subject as if his wealth determined his regard for her? "Does it really matter? It has no bearing on my life three thousand miles away."

"It does to me."

Stefan wished they could talk about anything else. This time, he looked into her eyes. "Only because you insist on knowing. But it changes nothing."

He expelled a quick breath through his nostrils. "My parents come from wealthy families in their respective countries of Germany and England. My father comes from an intellectual class of people in Bavaria, but he is a renowned composer and violinist in his own right.

"My mother grew up in a family of privilege in Surrey. When she was sixteen, they introduced her to the Spanish diva Adelina Patti after she moved to Clapham and used London as her European base. Miss Patti became my mother's vocal teacher when she wasn't on tour and drew out the natural talent Mother possessed. Now my mother sings for The Royal Opera, where she met my father on a concert tour in England. They've always said it was love at first sight." He'd always envied the rare kind of love his parents had found.

"Hence the Singing Silver Mine." A wistful smile curved on

Anna's lips. "It's a fine thing you've done to honor your mother that way and even more reason to believe you're innocent of the charges against you."

"Indeed. It would be a slap in my mother's face, though uncivilized on any count."

"But your parents come with titles, yes?" Anna's brows furrowed. "Should I call you Baron von Maier?"

"Of course not." His irritation grew again. "Such titles are useless here."

"I was only pointing out—"

"That we come from different worlds. So, you've said." He wished he could get the ridiculous idea out of her head. "Is it impossible to believe I want to enjoy the company of the woman I have come to very much admire?"

A flash of pain crossed her eyes. "Where I come from, men of stature are expected to consort with women of equal standing. Perhaps they will trifle with women of low birth, but such dalliances are looked upon by their parents and peers as distractions. I do not want to be a mere distraction, Stefan."

"Perhaps these expectations exist in Europe. I pay no attention to them here." Why couldn't she accept that her former station in life in Ireland meant little to him—that she'd brought more meaning to his life than he had known in years —perhaps ever?

"Your first wife also came from aristocracy, did she not?"

The question stopped Stefan cold, though sweat beaded on his forehead. Perhaps the only way he could convince Anna of his sincerity—the only way she would understand his affections—was to talk about Charity's deadly deceit.

He released her. "Would you join me for a drink?" He didn't wait for an answer but cupped her elbow and propelled her toward the table set with bowls of punch and lemonade. He ladled himself two glasses of punch and downed them, allowing the liquid to burn his throat like swallowing the bitter pill of anguish he'd felt in the wake of his final weeks with Charity.

"Perhaps it's best if I—" Anna whirled to leave.

"I beg you, Anna, don't go." He grabbed her arm, leaving his glass on the table, and swore under his breath, recalling she repelled excessive drinking. "We need to talk." He showed her to the partially opened French doors that led out to a small balcony.

～

The moment Stefan ushered Anna onto the balcony, she detected another couple had already claimed the spot. But no more had they stepped outside than the girl rushed past them.

"Prudence ..." The boy followed her.

"Georgia's daughter." Alarm bells rang in Anna's head. "I should go after her."

Stefan reached to stop her. "Young love angst, I should expect. They'll work it out, Anna, as we must. Please."

Anna's gaze fixed on the door, still unsettled by what she'd witnessed between Mr. Rutherford and Prudence. Her first inclination was to go after Prudence. But perhaps Stefan was right, and all would turn out well. She remained with Stefan on the balcony, picking a spot near the wooden railing and peering into the night where the darkened mountains loomed in silent shadows. Her hands crossed to each shoulder to stave off the chilly night air.

What was there to work out? Anna had already loved a man once whose economic duty to family prevented them from ever marrying. Despite her developing affections, how could she allow love to flourish with another man who remained above her class and out of her reach? It would be heartache and misery all over again.

Stefan placed his coat over her shoulders. "You're shivering."

Anna wanted to return the coat, but the musky odor of his cologne enticed her to keep it where she could drink in the sweet smell one last time.

The lantern light filtering through the door illuminated Stefan's face as he leaned against the railing. "There are so many things to explain—things I rarely talk about ..." He rubbed his neck, pausing until Anna wondered if he would go on. At last, he spoke.

"After a whirlwind romance, my parents split their time between Germany and England to accommodate their travel schedules. But when the 1848 revolution failed, they fled—as many of the aristocratic and intellectual class did—and made their permanent home in England. I remember bits and pieces, but as a young boy, I couldn't understand what had caused the panic."

"Of course, you wouldn't." Anna had experienced her parents' distress as a youth but had no context to put it together. Only much later did she discover the details of the famine.

"Years later, my older sister Adelaide informed me my parents had kept their German citizenship, hoping a more democratic system of government might someday become a reality. That had not yet come to pass by the time I was old enough to attend university, but it still granted me the ability to attend the University of Freiburg, where I studied mining science."

Everything Stefan shared drew Anna's interest, but none changed the reality of what kept them apart. "Did they keep their titles?" Anna tried to catch his glance, but Stefan pinched the bridge of his nose, closing his eyes.

"Politically, my parents agreed with the revolutionaries who wanted to remove the monarchical system. But practically, their titles served them well, allowing them to enjoy the company of musicians and intellectuals. But that doesn't mean—"

"Then it seems we have nothing left to discuss." Anna removed his jacket, her heart squeezed by his admission. Stefan was from the aristocracy. She was not.

"Please, hear me out, Anna." He turned and repositioned the coat over her shoulders. "There is still much you don't know."

Anna put a small distance between them along the railing. Why did Stefan persist in this vain attempt to convince her their differences didn't matter? The more he enlightened her about his life, the clearer her vision became.

She drew Stefan's coat tighter around her as snow flurries swirled in the air. Her surroundings appeared like a small snow globe with glowing lanterns and lamp-lit windows illuminating their tiny world across town.

Anna picked out the Thomas house and warmed to their most recent demonstration of kindliness. She hoped Dakota would find love and comfort there. The Thomases were a beacon of light in a dark world—a world that continued to elude her.

"Go on."

"I met Charity in Peru, falling in love with her almost immediately." Stefan crossed his arms. "She was stunning— blonde and blue-eyed and full of spirit. She even forgave my faults, and God knows I have plenty. We married after only three months of courtship, and I believed ours would be the storybook marriage my parents had enjoyed."

So, Stefan *had* loved Charity passionately, but his tone didn't reflect it. What had happened to make him regret their union?

"But after I completed my internship, we returned to England in the spring of 1867 to join my parents in Surrey, and she became obsessed with London society. Her parents had known the royals—that's how her father got the commission in Peru—and once the Prince and Princess of Wales heard Charity was back from South America, we received numerous invitations to parties at Marlborough House."

Anna closed her eyes against the scene Stefan painted—a scene where he and Charity had hobnobbed with royalty. How could Anna ever imagine fitting in with such company?

"I became acquainted with William at one of those parties. We met several times to discuss the potential for rich ore deposits in Colorado and decided to explore the territory ourselves. The longer we remained, the more convinced we were. But when William and I returned to Britain, Charity worked her wiles to persuade me to stay in England."

"But you didn't."

A heavy sigh escaped his lips. "Charity knew when we left Peru, I would exploit any opportunity that came our way, whether in England or abroad. She'd even implied throughout our courtship that she was as driven by the adventure of travel as I was. The more William and I explored our options, the more I got caught up in moving to America."

"But Charity didn't concede to your plans?" Anna's mouth fell open. A sudden realization struck her with blunt force. Had Charity betrayed Stefan in some way?

"Not without a great deal of resistance. We fought incessantly. My father expressed concern. My mother suggested we put off coming to Colorado. Then, during one particularly nasty argument, Charity finally confessed she'd hated every moment she'd lived in Peru. She'd wanted nothing more than to return to England where she could enjoy the society of the royals again. That's when she launched her worst insult—the real reason she'd been attracted to me." His eyes focused in the distance.

"Stefan?"

Pained eyes peered at her. "I'll never forget the haughty look in Charity's eye. 'I would never have married you if I'd known you'd throw away your nobility.'"

"She wanted your title." Anna gasped, a hand flying to her mouth. The weight of truth fell hard and heavy on her heart. What treachery Stefan had endured—that Charity had married Stefan for his title and not for love as his parents had.

"God forgive me." Stefan's forehead dropped into his hand before he spoke again. "I lashed out in anger—said she could be a mining baroness in America if she wished, but we would be leaving in a fortnight. Then Ch-Charity ..." He choked.

"Yes?" A cold dread filled Anna's chest. She didn't want to know but couldn't stop Stefan from telling her the worst.

"Charity contracted typhus on the passage over and died." Torment smoldered in his eyes like a fiery furnace, and Anna groaned. "When they threw her body overboard, I couldn't breathe. It felt like someone had punched me in the stomach. I'd forced her to come to America against her will, and she'd paid for it with her life and the child she carried ..." His voice broke.

Stefan had had an unborn child—the story Laurel had alluded to months ago. "Ach, Stefan." She touched his arm, tears brimming her eyes with a desire to douse the burning anguish. "You couldn't have known Charity would die aboard ship."

"Paul Rutherford said as much. But at the time, I wanted to jump into the whitecaps alongside her. I very well might have if it hadn't been for William." He laid a hand over hers. "I've since learned to despise my title." His jaw clenched. "Which is why I've—"

The door onto the balcony burst open, crashing against the wood siding of the inn. Anna broke away from Stefan, and Prudence bolted across the space, hair mussed and tears streaking her face. "Miss Sullivan, I don't know where else to turn. I've just got to talk to you. I—" She froze, then gulped. "I'm sorry. I-I didn't mean to interrupt."

"Then perhaps you should think before barging in on a conversation." Stefan scolded. "Miss Sullivan and I were having—"

"It's all right, Prudence." Anna stepped between them, preventing Stefan from traumatizing the girl even more. "Mr. Maier and I were having a serious talk, but it can wait."

"Anna, I insist we complete—"

"And we will." Anna twisted around with an apologetic shake of her head. Couldn't Stefan see how she was conflicted? Of course, they needed to finish their discussion, especially now that she understood the hurt Stefan had suffered. But Prudence's pain was more urgent.

Stefan marched up to Anna. "Surely, she must see this is not the right time."

The terrified girl shifted her eyes back and forth between Anna and Stefan, her spine bent and chest caving. "I ... well, I ... Oh! I can never do anything right." She reeled and darted through the door.

Anna stared at him, nonplussed. "Well, that was a fine example of lending the poor soul an ear and a kind word." She handed Stefan his jacket as she passed him, then picked up her skirts and hastened after the girl.

"Anna." His footfalls trailed her through the ballroom, but

Anna refused to waste time by halting and having words. She would pursue Prudence into the street if she had to.

Anna scurried through the corridors to the stairway, where she caught sight of the blue taffeta skirt around the newel post at the bottom. She flew past several people, including Georgia and Margaret, acknowledging them with a nod and a halfhearted smile and apologizing once for bumping into Doc Floyd and spilling his drink.

By the time Anna reached the entrance, Prudence had fled through the feathery snow flurries. She stomped her foot. This was all Stefan's fault. If he hadn't frustrated the poor girl, Anna could have shouldered her concerns and then returned to Stefan to hear him out.

"It seems we have the opportunity to finish our conversation after all," Stefan announced behind her.

Anna whirled around to see his hands dug deep into his pockets. She might have forgiven him had it not been for the smirk on his face. "Not on my poor ma's grave." With her head held high, she spun on her heel and paraded the opposite way.

"You'll catch your death of cold," he called. "At least allow me to give you my coat and escort you home."

She spiraled a second time, indignant as a scornful cat on a Sunday. "Oh, you are a devil. I may come from humble means, but even I know it isn't etiquette for a man to escort a lady home from a ball. Go away with you. I can't talk to you right now." She waved her hand.

"Anna, be reasonable." He approached her. "We need to talk."

"Reasonable? Was it reasonable to dismiss the girl in her distress? We could have resumed our discourse once she'd calmed."

"Anna, I—"

"Please, Stefan. Just go. I need to think." She turned back for home, vexed, sensing his gaze followed her into the night.

Anna didn't care if she froze to death. There may have been a few moments when she had lowered her guard and allowed Stefan's tragic circumstances to gain her sympathy. But his insensitivity once more reminded her of their differing stations in life.

Oh, but how Anna would have liked to have retrieved her shawl from the footman and apologize to Stefan for spurning him. Too late. She'd already made her choice and would have to live with it.

A stiff breeze blew, sending leaves flying and snow flurries across her path, and she shivered down to her toes. Her dress flapped around her legs, whipping up remorse for her obstinance. "Ach, this temper 'tis a curse to be sure, Lord." She felt the cold blast at her back and detected the winds of change in the Rockies. Winter was settling in.

Twenty-Six

On Monday morning, Anna traipsed through two inches of fallen snow, leaving footprints up to the doorstep of Prudence Tucker's house. She gave the door a firm rap with her gloved hand and waited.

Prudence opened the door, her shoulders slumped and her countenance glum. It seemed she might burst into tears at any moment.

"May we talk?" Anna approached her with a firm but compassionate voice.

"Mother's at the inn cleaning and expects me to have done my chores before she gets home." Prudence hung on the door.

"Your mum's worried about you." Anna would not allow Prudence to daunt her and extended her foot, pushing herself inside.

Prudence gave in and let Anna into the small foyer. "I'm sorry to have interrupted your conversation with Mr. Maier. He seemed awfully mad at me."

"Don't you worry about Mr. Maier. He and I will take care of our business." Anna removed and placed her hat on a nearby table. She turned to Prudence. "I want to know what happened *before* you interrupted Mr. Maier and me on Saturday night."

Prudence lowered her head, her hands clasped behind her back.

Anna placed a hand on Prudence's shoulder and moved them to the divan in the living room, giving her no choice. "Come sit."

Prudence complied but placed herself as far away from Anna as possible, digging deep into the sofa.

Anna frowned and weighed what she would say next. "Ian Rutherford's a dashing young man, isn't he?"

"Ian Rutherford is a dirty, rotten scoundrel." Prudence blurted out and leaped to her feet.

It was as Anna had suspected, based on Laurel's reaction to the young man at the Harvest Ball. Anna joined Prudence, standing. "That's quite a harsh accusation."

"Not harsh enough." Prudence paced, then stopped before Anna. "But it wasn't only him. He did the dirty work, all right, but Elizabeth Henley and Frank Avery also had their part in it."

"Frank Avery's the boy Elizabeth was dancing with, right?"

"You remember how I was all disparaging of myself before the ball."

Anna nodded.

"I lost weight, like you suggested, which I guess Elizabeth noticed, too, because she approached me a few days before the ball all friendly—said I looked prettified and wanted to be friends."

"And you wanted to believe her, right? To finally feel accepted." Anna understood the temptation to fit in.

Prudence wetted her lips. "She said she had read *Pride and Prejudice* and wanted to learn more about the classics. Two days later, I received an invitation for tea. I almost pinched myself when I walked through her doors. The Henleys must have oodles of money."

"More than most around here, I would say." Anna knew the attraction of wealth and the disdain of it. Ach, the love of money was the root of all evil. Hadn't that exhortation been expressed in plenty a sermon? "I can see how you might have enjoyed the honor."

"She even made some special teacakes just for me." Prudence's eyes briefly sparkled. "We talked about all sorts of things. She even asked a thing or two about my wanting to be a writer—said she didn't have the right kind of imagination for it."

"I doubt that very much." The brattish girl with her winsome wiles and cunning chicanery had more imagination than anyone gave her credit for.

"Eventually, we got around to talking about boys. She became all conspiratorial-like, inviting me into her secrets and asking me not to tell the boys she liked the bookish stuff—said it would ruin her reputation. We had a good laugh over that, and it seemed we'd become bosom friends. Then, she divulged she liked Frank Avery and, very secretive-like, said she knew I was sweet on Ian Rutherford—said I could get Ian if I flirted with him more."

Anna hid a groan. She could see right through Elizabeth's ploy, but Prudence had been too naïve and eager to believe her. "And did you?"

"It wasn't like I did anything wrong." Prudence crossed her arms. "There are boundaries I won't cross."

"Of course, you didn't. But I think you were conflicted. Am I right?" Anna waited a moment before Prudence uncrossed her arms.

"When Ian asked to escort me to the ball, it didn't seem so wrong." She averted her eyes.

"Compromise in the beginning never does." Anna pressed her lips.

"I feel so humiliated." Prudence gulped. "Ian thought all my flirting meant he could take advantage. When I refused, he said Elizabeth was right about me all along."

"Oh, Prudence, I wish you could see how I see you sitting before me right now." Anna gazed softly into her eyes. "You don't need to have the perfect body or a handsome boyfriend or even bushels-full of money to make you significant. Sure, they're nice if they come our way, but if we see them in their proper perspective, they won't puff us up and turn us into cruel people."

Prudence bit her lip. "I guess I *did* let all the flattery go to my head."

"Mark my words." Anna stepped closer. "Someday, the right man will come along who will respect you for who you are. And he won't be asking you to compromise your morals or accept anything less than what you're worthy of. He'll treat you like a princess, even if you live like a pauper."

"I don't know how to act toward them now." Prudence's shoulders slumped.

Anna lifted Prudence's chin. "You hold your head high and continue to be the genuine girl you've always been. Pray for them, love them, maybe even invite Elizabeth to your house for tea—a real tea. At least give it some thought."

Prudence dipped her chin, then lifted it again. "I will, Miss Sullivan."

Anna observed the piano from the corner of her eyes and widened them. "And now you're organizing the madrigal choir for the Christmas Festival."

"Oh, yes. I love having you in the madrigal choir, Miss Sullivan." Prudence's eyes glistened.

Anna relaxed, smiling. "Music is in the Irish blood, you

know. Besides, the weekly practices give me a break from my sewing." She grabbed her hat and placed it on her head.

"Why don't you invite Elizabeth to sing in the choir? Show her you're willing to let bygones be bygones. Holding a grudge always hurts you more than it does the other person." It would also play into Elizabeth's vanity, but what difference did it make if Prudence was still the show's director?

Prudence hugged Anna at the door. "I won't forget what you said, Miss Sullivan."

Anna put on her gloves and walked out the door. If only she knew how to mend her bridge with Stefan.

Twenty-Seven

Anna sat with Laurel in the wooden pew while Pastor Thomas delivered his Thanksgiving message. He reminded the assembly that the day was set aside to give national thanks to God for providing freedom and liberty in this great land and as a day of personal thanks for God's amazing grace. Then, he ended the service with John Newton's hymn, "Amazing Grace".

Anna rose and joined Laurel, ambling the central aisle of the simple church. "You will still be joining us for dinner, won't you?" Laurel asked as they approached the vestibule.

"Of course. I wouldn't miss it, though if you saw the chaos in my little cottage, you'd understand the temptation to beg my absence. At least I have no worries about paying my rent."

"Your aunt would be proud."

"It must be a boon for your ego." Georgia's voice came from behind.

Anna craned her neck. "That it is, but sometimes I'm daunted by it."

"You'll be fine. The good Lord—" Georgia's eyes nearly popped out of their sockets. "Will that girl never learn?"

Anna followed Georgia's gaze to where Prudence talked in animated conversation with Dakota, Elizabeth Henley, and Ian Rutherford, laughing as though she enjoyed the camaraderie.

Georgia started forward in a huff, but Anna held her back. "Perhaps you shouldn't interfere. You can't be making begrudgery out of past—"

"Did you know she invited Elizabeth to sing with the madrigal choir?" Georgia frowned.

"Good, she took my advice." Anna pulled her shoulders back.

"Your advice?" Georgia glared. "I asked you to help her, not give her to the wolves."

"I seem to recall a sermon in which Pastor Thomas encouraged us to love our enemies, bless those who do evil unto us, and as far as possible, be at peace with all people."

"My husband did say that." Laurel twisted her lips in wry humor.

"Yes, but ..." Georgia pinched her lips together

"But what?" Anna's eyes widened. "It applies to everyone except ourselves? Trust the generous spirit of your daughter, Georgia, and trust God."

"Anna makes a good point." Laurel studied the girl.

"Hm. We'll see." Georgia let out a quick breath. "But next time Prudence gets the doldrums, I'm sending her to *your* house." She gave Anna a little poke and walked away.

Anna hoped Georgia wouldn't stay annoyed with her for too long.

"I'm sure she's already over it ..."

Anna heard nothing else Laurel said, distracted by Stefan walking by, engaged in an intense discussion with Pastor Thomas. He hadn't even acknowledged her, pushing the double wooden doors open to exit the church. A new set of emotions came to life, and Anna's shoulders drooped in misery.

"Perhaps it's time you take your own advice." Laurel inclined her head, her voice soft.

"Ach, there's no sense crying over spilt milk." Anna squared her shoulders. "But I am looking forward to roast turkey, mashers, and all the pies and trimmings."

"As am I." Laurel linked arms with Anna and led her out the door. "You can help me put the meal on."

Anna smiled, but inwardly, a pang of regret knotted her stomach for Stefan's absence at the Thanksgiving table. Did he feel equally sorry? She would probably never know. She had pushed him away.

The sweet-savory aromas of roasted turkey and dressing filled the Thomas house by mid-afternoon. Anna mashed potatoes at a center table with the potato masher and added milk and seasonings while Laurel hummed a hymn, preparing the gravy on a burner of the cast iron oven. Anna glanced at her friend from underneath half-closed eyelids. She seemed overly cheery as if she was furtively hiding something.

The kitchen was ample and homey for a Victorian home in Georgetown with its dark beaded wood-finished wainscoting, and it contained many modern conveniences such as a potato peeler and an icebox. A sizeable freestanding cabinet and one smaller one had been placed along the walls for storage, and several shelves displayed dishes, coffee pots, and tea kettles. Pots and pans hung from metal hooks, and a copper sink had been set into the counter in the corner. Anna wasn't jealous of her best friend but wished she might someday have a kitchen half the size.

Muffled voices came from the front of the house. Anna raised her head and glanced at Laurel. "You didn't tell me you had invited other guests."

"Didn't I?" Laurel appeared to freeze in place, then placed her spoon on the table and turned off the burner. "Now, don't get upset with me." She put up her hands. "I—"

"The most tempting smells are emanating from this room, Laurel." Stefan nonchalantly entered. Pastor Thomas and a cleaned-up, obviously well-fed Dakota followed him.

Anna stared at Laurel. No wonder her friend had appeared to be hiding something all day. Anna gave her a stern look.

"Welcome, Stefan." Laurel ignored Anna and greeted Stefan with a cordial smile. "We're almost ready for dinner. Clinton, will you carve the turkey?"

Stefan stood behind Anna, his arm reaching around her to dip a finger into the potatoes.

"Oh, no you don't." Anna lightly slapped his wrist but not before Stefan swiped a finger full of the white fluffy mixture, placed it in his mouth, and groaned with satisfaction.

"Don't you know it's a man's prerogative to taste what he's about to consume to ensure it's well-prepared?" He grinned.

"And don't you know it's not polite to stick your fingers into food others will be eating?"

"Ah, there is the rub." Stefan feigned resignation. "The dilemma of every male to appease the females in his life."

Chuckles came from the other males in the room. "What have I told you, my dear wife?" Pastor Thomas said, depositing one of the pieces of turkey he'd cut into his mouth and chewing with a smug smile.

Dakota also snatched a large piece of turkey from the

serving plate. "Stefan did say it was every male's prerogative." He bit off a chunk.

"Now I know how Captain Bligh felt when his crew mutinied on the Bounty." Laurel rolled her eyes in facetious surrender. "But, so as not to incite another uprise, you all can take a dish to the dining room table." She handed Dakota a plate of green beans and a bowl of cranberry sauce and gave Stefan a bowl of candied sweet potatoes. Her husband took the plate of turkey and a basket of bread, and they filed out of the kitchen, leaving Anna and Laurel to pick up the mashed potatoes and gravy.

"I should be quite vexed with you." Anna scolded her friend in hushed tones.

Laurel met Anna's gaze. "But you're not really, are you?"

Anna pressed her lips, exhaling through her nostrils. "No, but you deceived me."

"I didn't *exactly* deceive you. I just omitted to tell you." Laurel hedged, then clucked her tongue. "Oh, don't be annoyed with me, Anna. I hoped with Stefan here, the two of you could patch up your differences."

"Well, what's done is done." Anna ceded. "I can put away a disagreeable temperament for now and enjoy a meal of delicious food and good spirits."

"I knew you could." Laurel smiled broadly and led Anna into the dining room. The men waited before the table set with her most formal floral dinnerware and candles lighting the table.

"A sight to behold." Anna's eyes filled with moisture. "I thank my God every time I remember you." Her gaze met Laurel's. Indeed, God had blessed her with such a friend.

After Pastor Thomas prayed, they passed the food, filling their plates to the brim. For the next hour, everyone talked, eating and drinking and making merry.

From time to time, Anna looked up and savored the moment, amazed by how God had supplied the empty places in her life when she'd first come to Colorado. Throughout her tragic beginnings here in Georgetown, God's provision had been evident in the people he'd brought into her life—especially Laurel and Pastor Thomas and Clyde and Georgia Tucker. She'd also established a reputation for dressmaking extending across Clear Creek County. This week, requests had come in faster than she could fill them. Everyone wanted winter and Christmas garb for family gatherings and church festivities. How could she not be grateful? And Stefan? A stab of pain entered her heart. Yes, she could even be thankful for him.

At last, Anna sat back, her stomach satiated. "I don't think there's even a mite's room for another morsel."

Stefan wiped his mouth with a linen napkin. "My sincere compliments to chefs. I don't think I've enjoyed a meal more."

Laurel rose, and everyone slid back their chairs. "Clinton and Dakota, you're with me for clean-up duty." She picked up several dishes. "You two," she pointed to Anna and Stefan with an elbow, "can head into the parlor. We'll bring the pie and coffee as soon as the dishes are done." Clinton and Dakota followed her to the kitchen, leaving the dining room table barren.

An awkward silence permeated the room. "Shall we?" Stefan suggested. Anna bowed her head, then led the way to the parlor. They'd been here before. But perhaps they could remain cordial this time and carry on a reasonable conversation without her emotions getting in the way.

"You haven't mentioned the mine or the lawsuit." Anna stood near the fireplace with its roaring fire.

Stefan shrugged and pocketed his hands. "I didn't want to ruin the pleasantries of the day. It seemed inappropriate."

"You may be right." Anna dipped her chin, then tilted her head. "But how are you getting on?"

"Honestly?" When she nodded, he clenched his jaw. "My life has been in a bit of shambles." He unpocketed his hands. "Töpfer won't let up and ..." He gazed into her eyes. "I need to make amends for a wrong I've committed."

"Stefan, you don't owe—"

"The night of the Harvest Ball, I hoped to convince you I wasn't the cad you suspected of me. But instead, my boorish attitude pushed you farther away. It was beneath me."

Anna stepped toward him. "What are you saying, Stefan?"

"I wanted to make you understand at the Harvest Ball." Stefan covered his mouth, then continued. "After Charity and our child perished at sea, I went on a rampage to assuage my guilt. Some men would sink into despair. I blazoned the trail to carve out a legacy men would envy."

"Your mining empire."

"Which is about to topple in some twisted poetic justice." A wry laugh escaped his lips. "Until now, I've stampeded anyone who got in the way of building my empire. I've been arrogant, taking my wealth for granted, believing I was invincible. Greed consumed me. I became a slave to its allure, strategizing and trampling upon men's livelihoods, assuming I was doing something good for the community when, all the while, I was taking something from it.

"Then you rode into my world on that stagecoach, and you were like a fresh spring rain washing away the muddied waters of my soul. You tried to speak truth into my life, but I treated you with the same conceit that has become my habit. It became eminently plain to me on the night of the Harvest Ball that I'd been a fool. I deserved your disdain for dismissing that poor girl the same way. But I was too proud to see it. I can now only ask hers and your forgiveness."

Anna studied Stefan, the weight of remorse evident by how his shoulders curved over his chest and his desire to undo the past. She wished she could alleviate his pain but was uncertain how anything she could say would change the past. What had Cecelia said at their first Christmas Festival planning meeting? *I reckon we all got shackles we need to get freed from to get by in this life.* It appeared Stefan had taken the first step toward freedom. What about her?

A soft smile curved on Anna's lips. "I forgive you, Stefan." She spoke in a soothing tone. "Those days could not have been easy. But God will make something good from the ashes."

Stefan's shoulders relaxed. "Thank you. Your forgiveness means a lot." He stepped toward her. "I hope we can—"

"Your coffee and pie are served." Laurel walked into the parlor holding a silver tea service and put it on the credenza, followed by her husband and Dakota. They held plates filled with slices of both pies and handed them out.

Anna accepted her plate and a cup of coffee, her heart warmed by the company of friends and grateful she and Stefan had resolved their quarrel. She had no idea of what he had been about to say, but at least now they could indeed be friends, even if their differing stations in life would preclude a more intimate attachment. She would be satisfied with that, supporting him through these dark times.

Twenty-Eight

Anna had been so busy sewing gowns and garments the week following Thanksgiving that it flashed by in a flurry. She'd barely had a chance to catch her breath when Laurel stopped by on Friday to collect her for a meeting with the Christmas festival committee.

Laurel made a three-hundred-and-sixty-degree turn. "I can see what you mean by all the work. It's a wonderful problem to have, but ..."

"I'm in a whirlwind, working my fingers to the bone." Anna blew back flying wisps of hair that had fallen into her face.

"There must be a solution." Laurel frowned.

"Unless you have a hankering to pick up a needle ..."

"Oh, no, not me." Laurel put up both hands. "My gifts are elsewhere. You're the accomplished seamstress."

"Ach, a blessing and a curse."

"If you want to bow out of our meeting—"

"Absolutely not." Anna pushed her shoulders back. "I won't abandon the poor people of this town."

"If you're certain." Laurel bit her lip.

"Organizing the Christmas Festival comes first, and I'm determined to see it through." Anna donned her coat, pushed her hair underneath her hat, and picked up her leather satchel. "I'm ready." She whisked them out the door and turned the corner onto Rose Street.

"Look." Laurel's eyes sparkled once they had reached the business district and led Anna to a window display at the leather shop.

Anna's excitement bubbled up. "Virginia has done a grand job on the flyers, hasn't she?" Masterfully drawn, the festival flyers featured a decked-out Victorian Christmas tree and carolers and announced the Christmas Festival as a celebratory fundraiser.

Most homes and businesses had adorned their premises with lavish greenery and silver and gold accents and red bows, much like the Victorian fashion established by Queen Victoria and Prince Albert. Displays of decorated trees were indoors and out, and the Irish tradition of putting a candle in the window and hanging a ring of holly on the door had sprung up overnight. Everywhere Anna looked, Georgetown had blossomed with Christmas cheer.

She pulled the door open at McClellan Hall, allowing Laurel to go ahead of her.

"Hold the door." Margaret Cody ran up from behind, huffing and puffing. "I'm glad I'm not the only one late."

"Well, they can't start without the essential people, now, can they?" Anna said in good humor. They ascended the steep stairway to the second-floor hall, where the other ladies on the Christmas Festival Committee, or "The Committee" as Virginia had dubbed it, waited for them.

Today was The Committee's last meeting before the festival in two weeks. "Let's get started, shall we?" Anna called on each to report their progress.

With her husband's political influence, Virginia had secured a commitment from *The Colorado Miner* and *The Rocky Mountain News* to provide free advertising and editorials that covered Clear Creek, Denver, and Gilpin Counties over the weeks leading up to the festival.

Georgia had persuaded eateries in Clear Creek County to provide traditional Christmas fare at cost and donate the net proceeds. Cecelia also planned to bake up a storm, making the various confections she'd learned in her early enslavement days.

Laurel and Prudence had procured several groups to perform traditional Christmas music throughout the day along the main avenue and inside the McClellan Hall ballroom to enhance the festive spirit. The musical groups included Prudence's madrigal singers, a chamber orchestra, and a community band. A group of Irish miners had also been so enthused to hear one of their own conceived the festival that they organized a boys' choir.

Craftsmen and women enjoyed sixty-five percent off at Margaret's dry goods store on all merchandise used for making items available for sale at the festival. She'd also solicited clothing donations from people willing to part with their gently used items—an idea that prompted Anna to donate her aunt and uncle's clothes for the cause.

"As a reminder," Anna checked her agenda, "we come together the day before the event to set up the craft and food rooms."

"And remember," Margaret said, "The crafters will be here at three to set up their wares."

"Other questions before we adjourn?" Anna hoped they'd wrap up quickly so she could return to her sewing. She dismissed them when no one spoke up, and the chairs scraped back.

"Maybe people will demand we do it *every* year." Georgia donned her coat. "And we've got Anna to thank for being the brains behind it."

Anna's heart warmed to Georgia. She was glad their minor tiff had blown over. "It's far from a one-woman show, Georgia, but I'm pleased it's coming together."

"It just shows how a talented group of women like us can make a difference in this town if we put our minds to it." Margaret Cody made for the door.

"Here-here." Laurel made a strong-arm gesture, and everyone laughed.

"Hold up, Margaret. I need to pick up some things from the store." Georgia followed her.

"And I have a dinner to prepare for Charles—a meeting with members of the business community, including the city council and *your* Stefan Maier," Virginia stated poignantly.

"I wouldn't exactly call him *my* Stefan Maier," Anna blurted, tittering.

"I don't know about that." Virginia picked up her gloves and flapped them into her palm. "You both made a pretty good show at the Harvest Ball. It's still the talk about town, you know."

Anna's cheeks went hot. She disliked gossip, especially when she was the topic. "I suppose nothing goes without notice in a small town, does it? We only shared two dances, I assure you, Virginia."

"Whatever you say, dear." Virginia put on her gloves. "And it was three, which is two more than the requisite one required of a man and the ladies in attendance."

"The second one didn't count." Anna insisted. "We were interrupted by the scrap with Elias Jones."

"Whatever you say, dear." Virginia walked out the double doors, waving without looking back. "Tallyho."

Anna felt Cecelia's eyes on her after Virginia left. "What?"

Cecelia scrunched her nose. "Now, just who you think you're fooling, girl?"

"I don't know what you mean." Anna shuffled the papers in front of her. A stab of regret pricked her heart. Yes, she and Stefan had resolved their quarrel, but she couldn't see a way forward for them beyond friendship.

"Uh-huh." Cecelia sounded unconvinced. "Virginia's not the only person who observed you and Mr. Maier at the ball. From my place in the orchestra, I'd say what I observed was a right bit more than just friendly."

Anna squirmed like a cat that had been caged under Cecelia's scrutiny. She tilted her head and looked to Laurel for help.

"Don't ask me. We left early, if you remember." Laurel threw her hands into the air.

Anna jammed papers into her pouch. "Honestly, Cecelia. Even if there was something—which there isn't—Mr. Maier has more to do these days than attend to me. Besides, nothing could ever come of it, he being a man of the world and me being a poor peasant from Dingle."

"You know what the Bible says, 'Pride goes before destruction, and a haughty spirit before a fall.'"

"Hm," Anna smirked. "Maybe I should quote you the next time Mr. Maier gets on his high horse." Indeed, while she had absolved Stefan of his conduct at the ball, could a leopard change his spots that easily?

"He wasn't who I was referring to." Cecelia chuckled. "Take care of yourself, chile."

Anna closed her pouch, aware of Laurel's eyes fixed on her after everyone was gone. She didn't want to talk about Stefan, but escaping her friend's perceptive gaze was impossible. It unsettled her how much Laurel could read her.

Anna peered up. "You might as well say it." So much for leaving the meeting on time.

"All right." Laurel countered, tilting her head. "Are you going to spend the rest of your life running away from love?"

"I'm not running away from love." Anna dismissed the notion. "You saw my cottage. I'm too busy to give it a second thought."

"'There are many devices in a man's heart; nevertheless, the counsel of the Lord, that shall stand.'" Laurel put her shoulders back.

"Well, what does that mean?" Anna snapped. She shouldered her bag and moved to the other side of the table. If Anna had been a bird, she'd have flown past the stairs to the front door and outside into the wider world.

"I admit Stefan Maier can be insensitive—"

"An understatement, if there was one." Anna crossed her arms.

"Tragedy has softened him. Surely, you can see that." Laurel's voice went soft. "I've never seen him so dispirited. The innuendos and accusations have beaten him down. I don't know if he'll recover." Laurel bit her bottom lip.

Yes, Anna had heard the thickness in Stefan's voice the night of the Harvest Ball—the guilt and betrayal by the woman who should have stayed by his side—and the remorse for the conduct he confessed on Thanksgiving.

"I do care." She did, in her way. "I don't want to see Stefan suffer for a crime he didn't commit. But that doesn't mean I'm the right woman for him."

"Maybe you're the one to challenge him, bring out his better side."

Anna rubbed her temple. "It sounds like an awful lot of work."

"Perhaps, but worth it." Laurel offered a gentle smile. "If

you hadn't insisted the Marshal get to the bottom of Dakota's actions, Stefan might not have come to his defense. You must see he's the kind of man who'd throw himself wholly into making the woman he loves happy."

Anna had already resigned herself to accepting things the way they were.

"You don't know—"

"I know enough." Anna's cheeks burned with the searing pain of shame she'd felt the day Ina O'Connor had said she could never be one of them. Anna brushed the unbidden tears away. "I've known the scorn, experienced the humiliation, suffered others' smug stance of superiority. All the while, I died a little each time, as if they were digging my grave and pushing me into it."

Laurel peered at her with something akin to sorrow and surrender. She joined Anna on the other side of the table. "Of course, you're jaded by a family who should have embraced you and didn't. But I implore you. If Cecelia can forgive those who enslaved her and sold her family away from her and still embrace life to its fullest, you can too."

"I *am* embracing life here, Laurel. The Christmas Festival should be evidence of that. But I also know my place, and it isn't among the privileged class."

"Stefan may not acquiesce to the standards of social propriety as much as you believe." Laurel seemed to choose her words carefully, her shoulders slumping.

Anna slowly shook her head. "Perhaps now he thinks he wouldn't, but a day might come." Wasn't that what she'd told Seamus before she left for America? "If my sewing business continues to grow, I should be able to save enough money to rent a larger house and devote one part of it to tailoring."

"You *have* corralled quite a clientele." Laurel hung her head, fingering the table.

Observing Laurel's pensive posture, Anna regretted their disagreement. She disliked how it left her feeling empty. She lay a hand on Laurel's arm. "I will think about what you've said."

Laurel leaned in. "I want so much more for you. *Caitlin* would want so much more."

Anna linked arms with Laurel and led her to the foyer. "I believe Auntie is smiling down at us right now, glad we have become the best of friends."

"Have you considered what you will do with the property your aunt and uncle bought?" Laurel withdrew from Anna and faced her.

"I've been too preoccupied to think about it." Anna hesitated. "In the beginning, I dismissed it as beyond my reach and having little bearing on my circumstance."

Laurel averted her eyes, wrinkling her brow. She redirected her gaze at Anna. "But now you've made Georgetown your home, what will you do with it?"

"I know nothing about building a house or even where to begin."

"Perhaps you wouldn't have to." Laurel fingered her lip. "You could sell the land and invest in a house—perhaps on the upper side of town. Clinton says owning is a much better investment than renting."

"Owning?" Anna had never considered it.

"I understand a lovely home has gone up for sale on Barton Hill near Stefan's house."

A house on Barton Hill? Anna felt a chill drafting through the wooden double doors. The notion catapulted her back to her childhood when her parents had rented cottages on small farm acreages to make a living. "Da couldn't pay the rent when the potato blight hit, and the English landowner evicted him. We would have starved if it hadn't been for the workhouse."

She'd been too young to remember those days, possessing only vague, watery impressions of hunger that never ceased to gnaw at her stomach and a dank, dingy workhouse her parents had called the pathway to the dead. As it was, her older brother Ryan died of dysentery in the wretched conditions. The resounding consequences had left Da impoverished in mind and spirit and Ma picking up the pieces of a broken and fettered man.

"It would be a big step and a huge leap of faith." But the possibility left Anna's mind reeling. "Many devices in a man's heart, did you say?"

Yet, what were the purposes of the Lord? Anna had yet to grasp what He wanted for her future. In less than three months, she'd become a part of this community and earned enough income to consider a mortgage. But where did she go from here? Could it be God *was* guiding her path toward Stefan? Her breath hitched.

"Are you all right?" Laurel knitted her brow.

"I-yes." Anna flashed a brief smile, then dismissed the idea as the craziest she'd ever conjured. She pushed the door into the frigid air and drew her cloak against the cold. "Best to head home before the snow flies." She waved Laurel off.

Still, where could the notion have come from? Anna didn't know but wasn't prepared to analyze it today. Shaking off the idea, she marched forward to her cottage.

Twenty-Nine

Stefan traipsed through an inch of snow from his home to Hale Street, dreading tonight's gathering at Mayor Henley's house. Still, he was unyielding. Even the shadow of the man following him in the half-moon's light would not daunt his resolve.

How moronic did Mr. Jones think Stefan was? The feeble-minded fool had been following him since shortly after the mine disaster—no doubt Töpfer's design. Anyone with half a brain would have noticed his insidious presence. Stealth was not his forte.

Stefan continued forward, feigning a blind eye, passing several houses that belonged to the professional class of Georgetown in a four-block area that had come to be known as Barton Hill. Stefan knew at least two of their occupants would be at the Henleys' and expected the mood of the meeting to echo the heaviness of the steps he trod. Most blamed him for the town's economic decline, though the fault was not his.

As he approached the Henleys' generously sized gothic revival home, he observed light flickering behind the curtains and considered the numerous occasions he'd spent there. Most were lavish social events he'd enjoyed, laden with food, drink, and frivolity. Frequently, a string quartet provided music for dancing and entertainment.

But this night would be different. He had been summoned to answer their questions, and the conversation would take on a more critical tone. There would be no music to moderate it.

He climbed several stone steps to a walkway swept of snow, strode to the front porch, and knocked at the door.

"Good evening, Mr. Maier. Do come in." Mrs. Henley greeted him with a genteel smile. His eyes swept over her as he entered, noting blonde curls affixed with jeweled hairpins piled atop her head. The luscious sheen of her green, bustled dress enhanced a refined figure of grace.

"You look lovely, as always, Mrs. Henley." He gave her an honest compliment as he entered the broad hallway and removed his hat.

"Thank you, Mr. Maier." She bowed and closed the door behind him. He handed her his hat, and she indicated a gloved hand. "Please join the gentlemen in the parlor."

He nodded his thanks and walked through the French doors.

In times past, Stefan had imagined Charity hosting dinner engagements like this one, but his vision of what he desired in a woman had changed. Perhaps it was due to the precarious state of his finances. Maybe he'd discovered something of more excellent value than money, titles, or status could buy. If Anna Sullivan only knew what she'd done to him—making him aware that wealth was a means to serve the welfare of a community and not an end unto itself—then perhaps she could give credence to a courtship leading to marriage.

Stefan admired the parlor of rich woods, cross-beamed ceilings, and Victorian elegance. Several men in business attire gathered in front of a wood-surround fireplace—men who had the power to determine the direction of his future, men whose rigid postures and dour faces reflected in the mirror told Stefan all he needed to know.

Most of the men held high esteem in the community— Clyde Tucker, John Sieger, Paul Rutherford, and Mayor Charles Henley, a man he respected for his fair and pragmatic approach. Only Jerome Chaffee was not a resident of Georgetown, but his mining interest in Clear Creek County gave him a reason to be here. They knew each other well and were on a first-name basis among themselves. All, except perhaps Clyde, parlayed their positions for political aspirations, and all knew their political futures depended upon Georgetown's prosperity.

Mayor Henley whispered in Jerome's ear, then broke ranks to greet Stefan. "Welcome to our little soiree." Charles extended a hand. "Please join us." The man's smile hadn't reached his eyes—something Stefan should have expected, but that hurt nonetheless.

He accepted a glass of red wine from a manservant, sipped the fine French Bordeaux, and joined the gathering in front of the crackling fire.

"Are you looking forward to the Christmas Festival in two weeks as much as the rest of Georgetown?" Jerome studied Stefan from across the rim of his etched glass.

"I should think it's a welcome event by the community— imparts the Christmas spirit of love, fellowship, and good cheer." Stefan infused warmth in his tone.

"Here, here." The men resounded—all except Stefan's business partner in banking. Sieger had been distant of late— downright austere anytime they met to discuss business.

"But will it do what the organizers hope? We have at least four families in danger of foreclosure." Sieger seemed determined as ever to incite a debate. "What will you say when the festival doesn't raise enough cash to help them stay afloat?"

"I suppose next you'll be saying, 'Bah Humbug!'" Clyde smirked.

"I'm a realist." Sieger scowled like a lion, ready to pounce. "A town can't survive long when men are out of work. They will go elsewhere."

"And I have more confidence in these surrounding counties to show an abundance of Christian love and charity than you give them credit for." Clyde shot back.

"They wouldn't have to if the Singing Silver Mine hadn't ceased operations. Whose fault is that?" Sieger's eyes flinted hard as steel, his words slinging with such brutal force they struck Stefan like a rock.

"And who is the rapscallion who has convinced you I neglected to put employees' safety first?" Stefan snapped like a tree limb broken in two by a violent snowstorm. The man was supposed to be his friend and business associate in banking— that implied trust, not betrayal.

"Please, we're civilized men here." Jerome held up his hand. "Surely we can discuss these things more calmly and—"

"Are you saying you weren't negligent?" Contempt flowed from Sieger's mouth in flagrant disregard for Jerome's advice.

"I'm saying someone who wanted to implicate William or me caused the hoist cable to break. Any idea who that might be?" Stefan raised his glass with such force that a few drops of wine swished out, and the manservant rushed forward to clean it up.

Mayor Henley stepped forward, his eyes protruding. "That's an outrageous charge, Stefan—just as audacious as others suggesting you were lax in your regular equipment checks. Do you have proof?"

"No." Stefan backed off. He knew how lame his response sounded. All the legal wrangling and bad weather had kept him from proceeding with his investigation. "But I have a hunch—someone whose offers to buy me out I declined before the accident. I suspect he decided to force me out."

"But why haven't you opened the gates again?" Sieger put his empty glass on the table with a critical eye toward Stefan. "You could have installed the cable long before now."

Stefan's throat tightened. "These things take time, and currently, I don't have the men to make the repairs." Not that he couldn't have repaired the equipment himself long ago now that he'd procured the cable. But he still needed to inspect the shaft before removing the much-needed evidence. His gaze shifted back to Sieger. "And, as my business partner very well knows, I've been preoccupied defending myself of litigation proceeding from the Mother Lode Mine—"

"Töpfer's mine?" Clyde knitted his brow.

"His claim is adjacent to mine." Stefan's jaw went taut again, rising resentment threatening to reverse his resolve to hold anger at bay. "A Clear Creek County judge has placed an injunction against the Singing Silver Mine until it can be determined who owns the claim on that part of the mountain. Mr. Willard has filed a counterstatement to request a change of venue, hoping a more impartial judge will remove the injunction. I've kept the road open and plan to put men back to work as soon as the judge rules in our favor. But it's out of my hands until then." Stefan clenched his jaw. The repercussions were unthinkable.

"I suppose Georg chose not to attend the meeting tonight, knowing all this." Mayor Henley stared vacantly. "Gave some fallacious excuse."

"He's a sniveling coward." Stefan glared, unable to keep the

283

piercing edge out of his tone. In truth, he was glad he didn't have to hear Töpfer spout more lies.

"Perhaps he's only taking advantage of the new laws many other shrewd mine owners have done over the last months—like yourself, Stefan." Jerome asserted.

"Yes, but to whose detriment?" Stefan's chin rose though he inwardly squirmed. "I won't deny I've expanded my holdings, but at least I've helped build this community. Töpfer is only after personal gain."

"I'm afraid we'll be hearing more and more litigation flying about between owners and their claims." Mayor Henley rocked back and forth on his heels. "Since extra lateral rights took effect as part of the National Mining Law earlier this year, there have been reverberations across this land."

"Extra lateral rights?" Clyde furrowed his brow. "I heard about it before leaving my legal practice but never studied all the implications."

"I'm not sure there's a lawyer alive who understands all the legal ramifications." Paul swung his glass in the air. "It's a convoluted set of conditions to help decide who owns a claim."

"It gives owners the exclusive right to mine a vein if the apex or highest point occurs near the surface on their property, even though the veins extend under the surface outside the claim," Jerome said. "An owner can claim the vein even if it extends beyond his property's sidelines. But if the vein stops and starts somewhere else on your neighbor's property, the owner has no right to the second half unless he purchases his neighbor's claim outright."

"Sounds reasonable." Clyde frowned.

"The problem is," Paul shifted his weight, "silver veins don't work the way the law presumes. Just like the veins and arteries in your body, they go every which way—converging, diverging, and running everywhere and anywhere." His voice rose. "And surface in multiple claims, which in these mountains might end up higher than the first claim."

"It's a living nightmare." Stefan sneered. "An impossible task. Anyone who's ever worked a mine knows you're never sure what you've got until you get there." Stefan's vein had started higher and ran deeper than Töpfer would admit and was one of the richest in the county.

"*Pfff.*" Clyde's eyes bulged. "I see what you mean."

"What's more," Stefan added with chagrin, "since it's so difficult to prove, Georg can tie up any work on the mine for years to come. He thinks he's hurting me, but it's the working man he's really hurting and the well-being of this community." Stefan glared at Sieger. "So, you tell me who tampered with my cable and to what end."

Sieger averted his eyes. His hollowed cheeks made him appear gaunt. At one time, Stefan would have relished the small victory. Instead, regret settled in his chest. Sieger didn't know the real man behind Georg Töpfer. But what had it cost him? They would never repair the damage done to their friendship.

"It'd be hard to prove, as you said." Mayor Henley tilted his head and frowned.

"When does William return?" Paul lifted his gaze to Stefan's.

The question startled Stefan. "He should be back after Christmas. Why do you ask?"

"I was just thinking—" A knock at the parlor threshold hindered Paul's response.

"Dinner is served in the dining room, gentlemen." Mrs. Henly walked in. "I've tried to hold off our cook for the last fifteen minutes, but she's fit to be tied—says she will not have good food go to waste and even threatened to abandon her post. And you know how hard it is to acquire a good cook." She directed a deliberate gaze at her husband.

"Oh, dear, we cannot have that." Mayor Henley let out a woeful sigh. "Well, gentlemen, it seems we may have another civil war in my own home unless we comply." The men chuckled, and Mayor Henley addressed his wife. "You may tell the cook we'll be there straight away." Mrs. Henley nodded and left the room, leaving her husband to usher the men into the dining room.

Mayor Henley stopped Stefan at the end of the line. "Perhaps there's another way to come at this thing—beat Georg at his own game."

"If you can come up with one, I'd like to hear it." Stefan was skeptical.

"We'll have to resume our conversation later." Mayor Henley's hand was on his shoulder. "I doubt all is lost yet. Time to bring on a little levity to our evening, Mm-hmm?" He moved them along.

Stefan followed him to the table, praying the mayor was right, and the melody of his Singing Silver Mine would have a chance to hit its high notes for years to come.

As Mayor Henley promised, the discourse during the meal carried on in higher spirits. Stefan was glad for the reprieve as he cut his roast. "I'm sure everyone around this table voted for the bond issue last April." He couldn't imagine anyone not having voted for the two hundred dollars in bonds to help the Colorado Central Railroad continue its progress westward. "Advancement of the railroad west can only bring more prosperity to the mountains."

"Every merchant and minter between here and Denver I've

talked to—" Paul allowed the manservant to refill his glass before continuing "—hopes the Colorado Central will complete the narrow-gauge line from Golden. It seems a winning proposition for all of us."

"Some didn't vote for the bonds, though." Mayor Henley tapped the table. "They couldn't see the point of spending their hard-earned dollars on it."

"A short-sighted view in my book." Clyde leaned his elbows on the table. "The tourist dollars would more than cover the cost of the bonds. I'd have been crazy *not* to vote for them in the hotel business."

"An unfortunate reality exists, my friends." Jerome played with the end of his napkin. "Both tourism and statehood are in jeopardy if Henry Teller has anything to do with it."

"Why is that?" Stefan paused, baffled by the statesman's opposition. "Wouldn't everyone benefit if Colorado belonged to the Union?"

"Mr. Teller wants to see the Territory of Colorado excel, all right, but not until conditions are ripe for his interests." A vinegary smirk rose on Jerome's lips. "He continues to argue against statehood in Congress—political posturing mostly—to advance Golden as the state capital and gain supporters for his bid for Senate. And though we can be grateful Andrew Johnson is no longer president of the United States, there are those from the South who still sit on Congress and promote his anti-civil rights policies—policies that contradict the very foundation of colored suffrage we support here."

"Mr. Teller plays right into their hands by arguing against statehood." The mayor suspended his eating utensils midair.

"That is a fact." Jerome pressed his lips together. "Politics makes strange bedfellows."

"And greed spreads like cancer everywhere you look."

Politics wasn't the only thing on Stefan's mind. Look what greed had done to him.

"Not everywhere, Stefan." Mayor Henley leaned forward. "There are some very generous people in this town, as Clyde so aptly pointed out a while ago."

"Take Miss Sullivan, for example." Clyde laid his utensils on the table and leaned forward, directing his gaze at Stefan. "She hadn't been here a month when she suggested a Christmas Festival to help the hurting families in this town. Now, I mean no disrespect to you, but she's been a Godsend."

Stefan couldn't argue with Clyde's comment. He owed a debt of gratitude to the woman who had given life to the event. Her passion for lost souls and those in need had done more to engender his affections for her than anything else.

Stefan played with his food. Of course, Clyde wasn't trying to lay blame. Still, the mine's shutdown had hurt people in Georgetown.

"Don't be jaded, my old friend," Paul said between bites. "Your Miss Sullivan made quite a magnanimous gesture."

Stefan jerked his head up. "I don't think she belongs to anyone, least of all me." Though he wished she did. The light Anna had shed on his life revealed the very thing he lacked. But while she had forgiven him on Thanksgiving for his actions at the ball, Stefan feared he could not win her back.

"Come now, Stefan." Paul set his glass on the table. "The whole town is talking about how you and the Irish woman seemed quite enamored with each other at the ball. What was it? Three dances?"

"I don't see how three dances can be construed as *enamored*. Besides, one could say we only danced two waltzes, perfectly acceptable by the etiquette required." His irritation grew. Gossip ran rampant in this small mountain town. "Surely we have much better things to talk about."

"I couldn't agree with you more." Sieger's voice dripped with sarcasm. "Besides, there are bigger fish than you in this town."

Stefan cast steely eyes at Sieger, and the man met his gaze —shooting arrows of superiority at him. Stefan clenched his jaw, staring him down, fighting the urge to take the bait.

Tension in the room became as striking as a dissonant chord on a pianoforte.

"Come, gentlemen." Mayor Henley rose, breaking the silence. "Let us adjourn to the parlor. We still have much to discuss."

Stefan quit the contest, wiping his lips with his napkin and throwing it onto the table, utterly finished with the man he once called a friend.

Thirty

Anna's eyes popped open at dawn's first light, her mind running at full speed. It was December twenty-first. The morning of the Christmas Festival had arrived. Though the committee had decorated McClellan Hall the day before, there were still a million things to do. Time to rise and meet the committee at eight o'clock before the festival officially opened at ten. She braved the chill in the air, threw off her blankets, and readied herself for the day.

At half past seven, Anna made a final assessment of her appearance in the mirror. She'd donned the forest green, woolen bustled skirt and bodice she'd made just for the event and covered them with a matching cloak and bonnet with fur surrounding the edges. Then, she'd adorned the outfit with a white muffler and a woolen plaid scarf to add flair. Now, staring in the mirror, her breath caught. She couldn't believe how lovely the entire effect was, nor that the person she saw standing there was her.

She turned to make her way outside the cottage. Pulling the door shut behind her, the bells and holly Margaret had brought her jingled, and she tromped up Rose Street, humming *The First Noel*.

Despite the cold and the inch of fresh snow on the ground, the Christmas greenery of holly and berries hanging on many houses and street lamps put her in a celebratory spirit. She relished the trimmings the town had adopted in her honor. It brought a bit of her homeland to the community.

Anna climbed the steps to the upper room at McClellan Hall but stopped halfway. Was that chatter coming from the hall? Besides the committee, who had come to the Opera House so early?

"Isn't it wonderful?" Georgia met her at the entrance. "It's as if the good Lord has lit a fire under everyone."

"I—yes, but I didn't expect all these people so early." Anna's eyes went wide with wonder at the flurry of activity. Her heart grew ten times bigger as she wandered into a room filled with crafters and carolers who had descended on the venue.

"They came to pray with us." Laurel's eyes sparkled. She grabbed Anna's hand and joined the committee at the center of the grand hall. "Gather around everyone."

Tears welled in Anna's eyes as she fixed them on the men and women who had sacrificed their income to support the fundraiser. She raised prayerful hands to her lips, nodding at each one—her friends from the madrigal choir—Pastor Thomas, Prudence Tucker, Elizabeth Henley, Jake Sieger, Owen McCabe, and Calvin James. Then she mouthed a *thank you* to the vendors—Henry Lyons from Lyons Leather Shop with his saddles, buggy whips, belts, and men's and ladies' boots and shoes; Lucy McCabe with her homemade jams, honey, and breads; Amelia Johnson, who made jewelry out of her home; Cordelia Sumners of Hats and Bonnets and Things; Tilly Anderson from Gilpin County, who contributed winter woolens from her dry goods store; and Sam Rogers with numerous pieces of quality furniture from his woodworking shop.

At last, Anna found Rebecca McKinley—the woman whose husband had snubbed her the week after she'd come to Georgetown. "Hello, Miss Sullivan." Mrs. McKinley's eyes shone. "Mr. McKinley would be here if he could, but he's minding the wee ones. He wanted you to know we're grateful for what you're doing for us."

Anna's tears spilled over and cascaded her cheeks. The woman's presence overwhelmed her with gratitude. "But, shouldn't you be the recipient of all our efforts?" She brushed the moisture from her cheeks.

Mrs. McKinley looked at Margaret, then back at Anna. "Mrs. Cody provided the materials without charge so I could make the ornaments and wreaths. I thought it only right everyone should enjoy a bit of the Christmas cheer we celebrate in our native countries."

Anna wrapped her arms around Mrs. McKinley, compelled by the woman's humility and unexpected kindness. They embraced, and then the woman backed away to join the others.

"It's a tribute to the Lord's abundant blessings, is it not?" Laurel whispered to Anna.

Pastor Thomas stepped into the circle and led them in a prayer for God's abundant provision in the town's time of need. Anna prayed silently alongside him, moved by the tremendous outpouring of love and charity and hopeful that justice would come to Stefan so the miners could return to work.

After the prayer ended, Georgia gave a quick rundown of the various food and drink booths inside McClellan Hall and outdoors along the street. Drinks included hot chocolate, coffee, tea, and traditional eggnog. Varieties of bread encompassed German Stollens, apple strudels, cinnamon buns, and gingerbread. Traditional confections made by Cecelia and other sweets from around the world baked by Delmonico Bakery incorporated yule cakes, shortbreads, and butter biscuits.

"And best of all," Georgia finished, "Barton House, Ennis House, Yates House, and Peck House in Empire have offered traditional dinner fare for those traveling from afar and spending the night."

"'Tis a fine blessing, to be sure." Anna's eyes glistened, marveling.

After madrigal choir practice, she returned to the crafters' room and surveyed the tables, tugging on the strap of her bonnet. All seemed ready to open, but would the people come? She bit her lip. How could she encourage the crafters?

"A happy and prosperous Christmas to you, Anna."

Anna jumped, her pulse racing faster than a horse in a derby. Oh, how she relished that deep, resonant baritone voice. It was a voice that made her heart sing with a melody that spoke to her soul.

"Isn't that what the Irish say to each other at Christmas?" Stefan's eyes twinkled as he gazed into hers.

"Indeed, they do." She returned the smile, genuinely pleased to hear Stefan's greeting from her homeland. Ach, but how the quiver chasing through her body betrayed her affections. "And a happy and prosperous Christmas to you." She bowed.

He scanned the room with its decorated tree in the corner and garland hanging along the walls. "A fine room, it is."

She looked about the room proudly. "It's a tribute to all the ladies who put it together."

He remained silent for a time, long enough to make her

nervous. She studied him. "Can I do anything to help you? You're welcome to view the crafters' tables, though I can understand if you're concerned about what people might say."

He inhaled deeply before answering. "I can't very well go around hiding from people, Anna." He waved his hand. "Besides, I couldn't miss this glorious event for which you *and* your committee have toiled. I commend you for all you've done." His gaze settled on hers—those piercing and penetrating blue eyes—probing, proclaiming, provocative eyes—searching for the answers to something she was still afraid to acknowledge.

She put some distance between them and turned. "But your ancestors come from a place where Christmas Markets have been commonplace for centuries. I'm fairly certain we don't compare to the dazzling celebrations known in Germany."

"Perhaps not on such a grand scale." He followed her. "But then, as you said, Germans have been putting them on for centuries." He glanced about the room. "This a wonderful start."

"'Tis a start anyway."

Stefan opened his mouth as if he wished to say something. Then he closed it again and scratched his cheek. "Let me be the first to contribute to the cause." He moved on to Rebecca McKinley's table with his hands folded behind his back.

"Ach, what am I now supposed to make of that?" Anna fiddled with the straps on her bonnet. At least he had come to support the cause even at significant risk to himself for making a public showing. She had to admire his stand.

A smile curved on her lips. What's more, Stefan greeted her with an Irish blessing. Indeed, his effort counted for something.

That's it! She bounced on her toes. An Irish blessing!

Whether Stefan knew it or not, he had given her the words she would use to encourage the crafters.

She worked her way around the tables, starting at the opposite end from Stefan and wishing each crafter a happy and prosperous Christmas. As she toured the room, the steady flow of people coming in and buying items at the tables boosted her morale even more. She couldn't have asked for a better turnout and thanked them for supporting the cause.

As she approached the last table, Anna stopped. She wanted to offer a different blessing to honor Mrs. McKinley—a thanksgiving for her kindliness and support of others like herself affected by the mine disaster. It had to be something she'd recognize as meant only for her.

"Such a grand display, Mrs. McKinley," Anna said, then suddenly knew the blessing she would offer. "'May the blessings of Christmas be with you, may the Christ child light your way, may God's holy angels guide you and keep you safe each day.'"

The woman's eyes misted. "Oh, thank you, Miss Sullivan. It means a lot to receive such a blessing from you."

"'Twas the last Christmas blessing Ma gave me before she died." Anna's eyes softened. "It's held a special place in my heart. I hope in the days to come, you and your family will know the light and provision of God's love and joy again in your home."

"You're very kind." The woman lowered her gaze, then looked up again. "So far, everyone has been quite generous. Even Mr. Maier came by and bought a wreath."

Anna grinned. "Ach, I'd say that was very—"

"Pardon me, Miss. Could I see ..." A young woman interrupted them, needing help with one of the ornaments at the table, and Anna bid a quiet nod, leaving her to help the customer.

Stefan bought a wreath. Anna wandered stupefied. Would wonders never cease?

Down the hall, on the other side of the stairway, Anna slipped into another room where Virginia and Margaret instructed mothers with children to make Christmas ornaments. The children's eyes glowed with rapt attention as they made angels and embroidered red velvet Christmas trees.

"There you are." Laurel rushed up behind her with her winter cloak wrapped around her. "We need to hop to it if we don't want to be late for our first madrigal performance."

"Ach, thanks for reminding me." Anna joined her on a dash down the stairs and out the McClellan House door.

Outside, Anna drew the straps of her green woolen cloak tighter about her. Though the sun shone on virginal snow, making it sparkle like twinkling stars, the air was nippy. A glance at the snow-laden mountains almost made her believe she had stepped into a fairy-tale story, complete with people bundled in their woolen hats and coats, wandering the festooned avenue of the commercial district, and visiting the outside merchants' booths.

Laurel linked arms with her, treading the snow-packed street to where the rest of the madrigal choir waited in front of William Cushman's First National Bank Building. "I had to reprimand Dakota for snatching shortbread from the Delmonico Bakery table. I've grown very fond of the boy, but he still has some nasty habits to break."

"It's a trial, to be sure." Anna watched the boys' choir disburse with Dakota running alongside Ian Rutherford as they darted passed them on the street laughing. "But Dakota's already come so far under your guidance. Don't despair. He'll surprise you."

"I hope you're right." Laurel shimmied between two people from Anna.

"I was ready to send the posse after you." Pastor Thomas teased his wife.

"Don't ask." She pressed her lips together.

Prudence put a pitch pipe to her mouth, giving them their starting note, and Anna lifted her voice with the other eight men and women, singing "God Rest Ye Merry Gentlemen." The carol's harmonious melody in a minor key drew a small crowd.

After they'd sung their last chord, Anna stepped to the middle of the half-circle. She'd encouraged Cecelia to sing the next song since it was a negro spiritual, but Cecelia had refused, saying her voice no longer had the strength it once had.

Standing tall and brimming with joy, Anna addressed the assembly. "My good friends, it's a privilege for us to sing this next song. Many of y-you—" She stumbled, her gaze falling on Stefan and Mr. Rutherford in the gathering. He smiled at her, and they seemed alone in the universe.

Someone coughed nearby, and she jerked her attention back to the assembly. "Many of you know Miss Cecelia Richards—how much her presence has blessed our community. She's also been a great friend to me since I first arrived in Georgetown." Anna indicated the black woman in front of her. All eyes shifted in Cecelia's direction, and the woman grinned.

"Miss Richards and I have much in common, coming from lowly beginnings as we do. Yet, from these humble beginnings, our two cultures developed a tradition rich in music and song. This next song also expresses the humble beginnings of our dear Savior's birth. I hope you'll enjoy it."

Anna nodded at Prudence for her pitch. As they had practiced, Anna would sing the main lines of "Rise Up, Shepherd, and Follow," and the rest of the madrigal choir would respond with the refrain. Everyone together would sing the chorus.

Anna drew a breath. Then ...

There's a star in the East on Christmas morn.
Rise up, shepherd, and follow.
It will lead to the place where the Savior's born,
Rise up, shepherd, and follow.

Follow, follow,
Rise up, shepherd, and follow.
Follow the star of Bethlehem.
Rise up, shepherd, and follow.

Leave your sheep and leave your lambs ...

The words of the spiritual came slowly, striking, vibrant, the refrains full, compelling, resonant. Throughout the several verses, it seemed as if the madrigal group sang with one purpose, one voice, the harmonies rich and moving—a unified energy, like the melding of cultures and histories in this melting pot of a community.

A full ten seconds of silence followed the final note. The madrigal choir bowed, and the assembly gave generous applause.

Anna waved an arm toward Cecelia once more, and a grin wider than the thoroughfare sprang on Cecelia's lips as she clapped along with the crowd. Anna couldn't have been more delighted. She stepped back into the choir, finding Stefan's sparkling gaze on her and his applause equally eager. Her heart swelled even more.

Forty minutes and ten carols later, the choir finished their last song. The crowd gave them a rousing applause, then disbursed, leaving one man standing, his eyes solely on Anna.

Anna's mouth gaped, awed that Stefan had stayed for the duration, warmed that he still had eyes only for her. He sauntered forward and offered his arm.

Linking hers with his, she allowed him to take her for a carefree stroll back to Rose Street. "Didn't I see Mr. Rutherford with you earlier?"

"He's making certain Ian won't skip out on marching in the Santa Lucia Parade."

"I understand," Anna frowned, "though Laurel says he's behaving himself more these days. He and Dakota seem to have become good chums."

"Yes, though Paul hopes they don't play off each other's mischievous impulses."

"Em." Anna nodded as they walked in silence for a small distance.

"I can't remember when I've enjoyed a musical performance more." Stefan's voice broke the silence, his conviction surprising her. "I felt as if I were in London again at Christmas, listening to one of the professional madrigal groups sing on the street."

"I ... thank you, Stefan."

A sleigh filled with couples and children passed them, driven by one of Owen McCabe's grocery store clerks. The boys' choir was reconvening in front of his market.

"But, you know, we're just a small mountain town choir in the Territory of Colorado."

"Why do you do that?" Stefan's words jarred Anna with their blunt edge.

"Do what?"

"Always underestimate yourself."

"I don't."

"But you do." He halted them, unlinked their arms, and forced her to look at him. His face had tightened, and his eyes appeared troubled. "You won't see yourself as worthy of others' praise. Why have you given yourself over to such lies?" He held her gaze for several moments.

At last, she averted her eyes, unable to bear his scrutiny any longer, and moved them along again, each in their space. Though she didn't want to admit it, Stefan—the man who seemed the least sensitive of anyone in the beginning when he would have thrown her out of the cottage—had found her vulnerable spot. It was why she had understood Prudence so well.

She didn't believe she measured up and never considered herself deserving of anyone's praise. It had always been that way, comparing herself to Seamus's family and their expectations for marriageable material. While Ma had tried to counter their high and mighty ways with words of consolation and encouragement, Anna had always known her place. Even in Georgetown, she couldn't fathom how she could be in the same league with the Henleys—friends, yes, but in the same league?

Oh, she made a brave show of being the master of her life, deceiving everyone into believing she had everything under control. She'd even convinced Seamus she could get along without him, so he had let her board a boat for America. Ach, she had wanted Seamus to come after her, beg her to stay, stop the ship from sailing. But he hadn't. And so, she had come to America, her heart broken and her future uncertain.

In the depths of her soul, where it counted, she believed she was unworthy. She wasn't pretty enough, smart enough, good enough, talented enough, or rich enough to merit anyone's praise or admiration. Even her father had often chosen the bottle instead of his flesh and blood.

Stefan's expression softened. "Please believe me when I tell you the madrigal choir was impressive and your solo simply lovely. You might recall I've been around music in all its forms and in many places my whole life. Your madrigal choir's presentation could rival any of them. Prudence has done an excellent job of leading. And you ..." He groaned, struggling, it seemed, to get the words out. He reached up and fingered a loose curl. "You are the most inspiring woman I've ever known, Anna Katherine O'Sullivan—"

"But how did you—"

He placed fingers light as a feather over her mouth. "Yes, I know your full name."

"But how—"

"You've drawn me in by the kindness of your heart and your selfless concern for others. And you have the voice of an angel. Why would you ever think anything less of yourself?" His eyes bore into hers.

Anna shivered—partially from the cold—but mostly because she didn't know if she could believe him, though his eyes told her otherwise. Moisture brimmed her eyes. "Stefan, I—"

"Shhh." He put a finger to his mouth. "Don't spoil the moment." He put his hand under her elbow and led the way, giving her no choice but to accompany him.

They had walked a short distance when Stefan stopped to read the handmade sign on the cooking tent. "*Apfelstrudel.* I haven't had one since ... well, since I was last in Germany." He pointed with delight. "You must try some."

Anna giggled, for Stefan seemed as expectant as a young boy about to unwrap his favorite present from Saint Niklaus, as he called the German St. Nicholas.

After the clerk handed him two tin plates with slices of strudel and two sets of eating utensils, Stefan led Anna to a rustic wooden table and chairs. "Shall we give it a go?"

"It looks delicious." Anna cut into the sugar-coated, flaky crust and bit into the confection of raisins, cinnamon, and nutmeg-spiced apples. "'Tis a fine sweet, is it not?"

He smiled into her eyes as he bit into the confection and appeared to savor it as though he hadn't eaten for days. "Not quite like what I had growing up, but it will do. *Strudel* was saved only for special celebrations, but it was always something we looked forward to."

Except for the night of the Harvest Ball, Anna hadn't heard Stefan talk about his family. But telling this story of his childhood memories transformed him. It made him more enthusiastic, playful, and energetic. She liked this side of him very much and took another bite of her strudel.

Stefan chuckled. "You've got a bit of sugar here." He pointed at the corner of her mouth with his gloved little finger, his eyes focused on where he had indicated.

"Oh, dear." She swirled her tongue about the outside corner of her mouth.

Stefan laughed. "You've missed it. Here, let me." He removed his glove and rubbed her mouth with his thumb, his eyes never leaving her lips.

Anna closed her eyes, leaning into his touch. As sweet as the strudel had been, the feel of his caress on her lips evoked delicious sensations—sensations that chased through her body and made her tremble. When Stefan lifted his thumb a moment later, the warmth from his touch lingered.

Anna's eyes fluttered open and lit upon deep blue pools that seemed to speak into her soul. Her breath hitched. Could she believe the silent words imprinting on her heart? "Thank you for the strudel. You must finish my piece since you've missed it so much." She shoved the plate toward him.

Stefan studied her with great concentration, and the heat rose upon her neck and cheeks. A slow smile spread across his face. "I think I shall."

After returning the plates, he led Anna once again toward Rose Street. They turned left and joined the dozens of people lined up in anticipation of the Santa Lucia processional.

"I had an opportunity to be in Stockholm during one of Sweden's Santa Lucia celebrations." Stefan reflected, finding a view spot. "Did you know Santa Lucia is the patron saint of light?"

Anna shook her head. She'd only heard a vague reference to Santa Lucia somewhere in her past.

"The festival is mostly celebrated in Scandinavia and Italy and usually falls on December thirteenth. I can still remember the cathedral at night—a whole choir of girls dressed in white robes. They wore red sashes and wreaths of candles and lingonberry greens on their heads, walking the aisle and singing 'Santa Lucia.' Across the entire assembly, they lit candles to symbolize the Light of Christ coming into the world to chase the darkness away."

"Sounds magical. I should like to see it someday."

"Perhaps you shall." His eyes glowed with such intensity she couldn't break the lock on hers and didn't want to.

"This is where the two of you have landed." Laurel stood next to her husband.

Suddenly self-conscious, Anna put space between herself and Stefan. Had the Thomases observed the familiarity she'd exhibited with him just now?

"A fine day for a parade, wouldn't you say?" Pastor Thomas shook Stefan's hand.

"It most certainly is." Stefan flashed him an easy smile. How could he be so calm and relaxed?

"But I thought you had returned to the craft room." Anna hoped to divert attention from her rendezvous with Stefan.

"My husband reminded me Dakota is participating in the parade." Laurel placed a hand on her husband's arm, her eyes beaming.

"We've never missed our children's performances if we could manage it, have we?" He placed an inconspicuous hand over hers.

If either of the Thomases noticed Anna's discomfort, neither showed it. The couple's focus stayed on each other and their new ward. Anna bit her lip. Here she was, more concerned about her clumsy attempts to hide an innocent stroll than enjoying the company of friends. Yet the Thomases' love for each other and how they had accepted Dakota without reservation impressed Anna as right and good. Wasn't that extravagant love—love that knew no bounds nor considered any sacrifice too great?

"They're coming." One man shouted, and Anna noticed Mr. Rutherford in front.

The throng crowded in, and Anna lost her view and proximity to Stefan. She strained to glimpse the procession of youth dressed in traditional Swedish garb approaching them, singing the traditional "Santa Lucia" song.

The processional lasted only ten minutes, but when the participants arrived at the corner of Alpine and Rose, the younger children broke away, swinging baskets and handing out Swedish sweet cakes baked by Delmonico's Bakery. The Thomases joined Mr. Rutherford and their sons, leaving Anna with a profound sense of abandonment. Yet, just as she accepted one of the sweet cakes from a young girl, a hand cupped Anna's elbow, and a light shone into the dark place in her heart. She drew a deep breath and turned.

"Would you care to join me for a taste of Sweden?" Stefan held a braided sweet bread and flashed her a devil-may-care grin.

Anna's stomach quivered. She licked her lips. Oh, how this man affected her from the inside out. In Ireland, a comfortable, lifelong friendship with Seamus had grown into love—or she'd believed it had. But Seamus ultimately disappointed her, choosing his family over her. The sensations she felt with Stefan were new and different. They made her spellbound, floating on a cloud of make-believe after he'd praised her singing and kindly bought her a confection. He didn't seem to care she had no pedigree to recommend her and even said at the ball he despised those things. Could she trust her heart?

"Maier, you have gall." Elias Jones jumped out at Stefan in the street, sneering. "What business do you have showing yourself around here like you own the place?"

"Mr. Maier has as much right to be here as you do." Anna burst out, the irony of Mr. Jones' accusation hitting her. Stefan owned several properties in Clear Creek County, and she believed Elias lived in one of his rentals. That made his statement all the more preposterous. Still, the situation demanded decorum in the public eye—at least for Stefan's sake.

"We'll see about that when certain parties get through with him." He jeered.

"I don't want any trouble with you, Mr. Jones." Stefan gripped Anna's elbow. "Please, let us pass, and we'll forget this incident ever happened."

The Cornish man snorted. "Oh, you act so high and mighty. Think you're above the rest of us. Think you deserve to be bowed down to as if you were Prince Albert himself." The little man bellowed, his face contorted with disdain. "Well, you don't."

People walked by, noses pointed straight ahead as if deaf to the little man's rant.

Ach, tongues would be wagging later, Anna wagered. "Mr. Jones, this isn't the place."

"Oh, you'd like to shut me up, wouldn't you? Just like he's responsible for the mine being closed and all these people paying for it." Jones waved his hand.

Stefan removed his hand from Anna's elbow and stepped forward, getting into Jones's face. "Be quiet, you silly buffoon. You're making a spectacle. Now, I shall take this nice young lady—who doesn't deserve to be treated to your prattle—back to McClellan Hall, where she can continue directing this festival. Get out of our way." Stefan pushed him aside and linked arms with Anna. "Come on. Let's get you back before I do something I'll regret."

Anna glared at Jones, sending a silent message of disgust as they made their way to McClellan Hall. "What a nasty little man."

Stefan's demeanor remained sullen until they reached McClellan Hall. He opened the door and walked Anna inside to the bottom of the stairway. She regretted Jones had spoiled their last minutes together.

Anna turned to him. "Stefan, I—"

"Please, Anna." He reached for her hands. "I know this must seem sudden—arbitrary even, though I assure you it is neither sudden nor arbitrary. I implore you to search your heart. Can you see a future for us? I won't press you for an answer now, but I ask you to consider my proposal." His eyes lingered on hers a moment longer, then he spun on his heel and walked out the door, leaving her dazed.

Anna's heart pounded so hard she was sure it echoed in the

stairwell. What he asked of her—what he seemed to want from her—was impossible, wasn't it? Could she take the leap into those strong, wide-open arms, welcoming her into their embrace? How many times had she gone over it in her head? She couldn't bear it again if he rejected her in the end. She traipsed up the stairs, her heart tied in knots and her head swimming in circles.

Thirty-One

The afternoon of the Christmas Festival flew by. Anna felt like she was back on the express train from New York she'd ridden coming west, with little time to take in the scenery. Instead, she'd flitted here and there, helping in the ornament-making room, attending to the needs of the crafters, and singing in two more performances of the madrigal choir—all without stopping to take a breath.

At five o'clock, Anna bid the last customer farewell with a smile, then closed the door and leaned her back against it. Ach, she couldn't remember the last time she'd been so exhausted and ready to drop. Still, the committee had more work to do. Anna brushed back her curls, pushed away from the door, and stepped forward.

A light rap sounded behind her, and she spun back around. Her mouth dropped. Standing before her was the elusive woman and child she'd been searching for since October. The woman had become a slip of a thing, appearing wretched and cold and ready to crumple in her shabby coat and threadbare gloves.

"Nina." *Thanks be to God.* Anna steepled her fingers against her lips.

"I wonder, ma'am, if there might be leftover scraps and a warm blanket to spare."

"Please come in." Anna opened the door wider, resisting the urge to hug her. "I think we should be able to scrape together something for you and your boy."

The woman followed her into the hall, where Tilly Anderson approached them carrying a basket. "It was a wonderful day, Miss Sullivan. I barely have anything left of my winter woolens to take back to Gilpin County." She eyed Nina before setting the carrier on the floor. She opened the leather bag she'd shouldered, found an envelope, and handed it to Anna.

Anna peeked inside the envelope, eyes bulging. "So much."

"Even surprised me." Tilly picked up her basket. "If you do another festival next year, please give me a holler."

"Of course, thank you," Anna murmured, then called out before Tilly could leave.

"Yes?" Tilly turned around.

"I wonder if you might have something to spare for my friend. Nina's been on the streets with her son, you see, and—"

"Say nothing more." Tilly set the basket on the floor again and removed the linen cover. "I've still got a pair of mittens, a bit oversized but will do in a pinch, and a hat for the little one." She handed Nina the items. "And would you believe I still have one tartan blanket left?"

"I couldn't—"

"Of course, you can." Tilly placed the blanket into Nina's hands. "I'm sorry I don't have more."

"Thank you, ma'am." Nina pressed the woolens close to her body.

Anna thanked Tilly again, then turned to Nina, but she'd

already started out the door with her son. "Nina, please." Anna caught up with her. "I know someone who can help you and your son with a place to stay."

Nina shook her head. "But I don't—"

"She won't ask for money, I promise." Anna searched the room for Cecelia and found her with a broom, sweeping the floor. "Cecelia has a heart bigger than Brown Mountain and helps people like you down on their luck. Won't you at least let me introduce you?"

Nina reluctantly nodded.

Anna picked up Nina's son and led the woman across the hall. When they reached Cecelia, Anna explained the situation.

"I reckon you can stay with me a while." Cecelia held onto the broom. "It's not a big place, but it'll get you on your feet so you can take care of the little one." Cecelia placed a hand on the boy's face and smiled. "If you're willing to wait until we've cleaned up here …"

"It's a weight off my shoulder, ma'am." Nina offered a tenuous smile.

Anna showed Nina a chair where she could wait and handed the toddler back to his mother. "I'm glad you came to us, Nina."

When Anna returned to the crafters' stations, most of their tables had emptied of their wares, including Rebecca's wreaths and garlands. "You've done it, Rebecca—sold most of your Christmas decorations." Anna couldn't contain her enthusiasm.

"I didn't think anyone would want to buy *my* things." Rebecca's eyes dazzled.

"Of course, they loved your decorations." Anna smiled at her, even more impressed Stefan hadn't dismissed Rebecca's beautiful wreaths as mere homespun crafts. "They add the touch of holiday cheer to a place."

"Thank you, Miss Sullivan." A bright smile curved on Rebecca's lips. She picked up her crate and walked toward the door with a lightness in her step.

Anna smiled. God had indeed been good this day.

"We must do it again next year." Anna overheard Cordelia Sumners of Hats and Bonnets and Things. Laurel helped her pile six small empty crates together.

"Let's hope the miners will be working long before that." Laurel picked up three of them to help her out the door.

Cordelia's cheery disposition gladdened Anna's heart, but it gave her pause. Would they do the festival next year as Virginia and Georgia had suggested? She relished the notion of a yearly event but prayed the Singing Silver Mine would be back in operation long before Christmas next year. She didn't like to think about what would happen if Stefan lost the mine.

She closed her eyes. Her mind drifted to her stroll with Stefan—how he had reached for her loose curl, his words of admiration and praise, the adoration in his eyes, and his caresses.

"Anna." Virginia's insistent call snapped Anna out of her reverie. "Are you ready to help me count the money?"

"Y-yes, of course." She made a beeline for the table.

"Let's get to it, then, shall we?" Virginia pulled up two chairs.

Together, they counted the bills and coins and stacked them. Twenty minutes later, Anna jerked her head back. "This can't be right. Three thousand four hundred dollars? Count again."

Virginia counted aloud once more. This time, they added another ten dollars to the count.

Anna leaped up and whooped and hollered. "It's a miracle."

"What's all the commotion about?" Georgia and the other ladies rushed over.

"I knew the people of Clear Creek County would come through." Virginia placed the bills and coins into two envelopes. "More than thirty-four hundred dollars, ladies."

"And that doesn't even include the proceeds from the eating establishments." Georgia waved joyful fists.

"Hal-le-lujah!" Cecelia thrust her hands high into the air and twirled about, dancing and praising and singing, "Children, Go Where I Send Thee." Georgia joined Cecelia in the song, dancing together as if they were doing an Irish jig. Laurel, Margaret, and Virginia laughed and clapped along.

While everyone else frolicked, Anna remained in awe of what they had accomplished. Her eyes misted over in the wonder of it. She watched Cecelia bring Nina and the little toddler into their dancing frenzy and, for the first time, saw a grin as wide as the sky spring upon the homeless woman's face. Oh, how magnificent was the Lord to bring about the success of their efforts. Perhaps she wasn't destined to be the wife of a mining baron, but God had provided all they needed.

"Are you not going to celebrate with us?" Laurel's touch on Anna's shoulder startled her.

"I was just counting our blessings." She wouldn't confess her other preoccupations.

"It's appropriate." Laurel cast a gentle smile. Then, she leaned forward with big eyes. "But so is celebrating. Come on." She grabbed both of Anna's hands and gathered her into the circle. And for the next few minutes, Anna gave herself to the revelry.

∽

Stefan relaxed by the fire in the parlor and poured himself a glass of sherry from the decanter. He picked up *The Colorado Miner,* but after reading the same paragraph three times, he gave up and tossed the newspaper onto the nearby table. Anna Sullivan seemed to take up every nook and cranny of his thoughts. He couldn't deny his compulsion. Why did she continue to put up walls between them?

Earlier in the day, he thought they'd finally crossed a threshold past their material differences. He'd arrived at the opening of the Christmas Festival to prove his admiration for her efforts. Granted, she still seemed unable to accept his praises, but she'd seemed pleased he had wished her an Irish blessing—something he had learned from his housemaid.

He smiled. Anna Sullivan was one of the most adorable women he'd ever known—the way she tried to wipe the sugar off the corner of her mouth with her tongue when they'd eaten the *apfelstrudel.* He had shown great restraint, for if they had not been in the public square, he very well might have swept her off her feet like a western cowboy and kissed her with such ardent passion she'd have collapsed into his arms. And Anna had left no doubt of her affection for him. Her eyes had told him what he needed to know. Yet, she'd changed course after the parade. Why?

Fear. He'd seen it in her eyes. No matter how much he tried to convince her that their differing backgrounds didn't matter, she held on to a past that belied his words.

He recalled the accusations his former hoistman leveled at him in the street. Despite Anna's earnest denials, she had defended him, exhibiting her complete faith in him. Mr. Jones may have taken the opportunity to humiliate him, but it only made Stefan more determined to defeat Töpfer and win Anna's confidence.

The time had come for Stefan to descend into the shaft at

the Singing Silver Mine and gather the needed evidence to convict Töpfer. Even if he died trying, at least he would have made an effort to expose the dark shadow cast on all who crossed the man's path.

A loud rap on the front door brought Stefan to his feet. He glanced at the clock on the mantle. Who would call at this hour? He marched past the candlelit sconces in the wood-paneled foyer and opened the door.

"I've thought about nothing else for a week now." Paul Rutherford removed his hat and strode past Stefan.

"Good evening to you as well, Paul." Stefan closed the door after his friend and showed him into the parlor. "Couldn't this have waited until—"

Paul spun around. "You skirted around Sieger's questions about the hoist cable."

"What are you—"

"At the meeting with Mayor Henley, you came up with some flimsy excuses about litigation and lack of monetary and human resources. But that isn't the truth, is it?"

"Paul, I don't—"

"And don't tell me you don't know what I'm talking about."

Stefan placed a palm under his bearded chin, waiting for Paul to finish.

His friend fingered his hat. "I've known you for years, and I'm aware of your financial resources. You're very good at innovating when you need to. You would *not* have allowed a few hesitant investors to stop you from getting your mine back in working order."

Stefan let out a brief laugh. "If you know me so well, you tell *me* what I'm doing."

"It's obvious. You've already tried once to descend into the mine. I was there, remember?" Paul pointed with his hat. "And you're waiting for William to help you."

Stefan drove his hands deep into trouser pockets, meandered about the room, and then came face to face with Paul. "You're not wrong, but William doesn't return for weeks."

"And ...?"

"And what?"

"You're still trying to put me off. I can see it."

Stefan narrowed his eyes. Did he dare divulge what he had in mind? Paul would most likely try to talk him out of it. But since he seemed determined to drag the truth out of him, what was the use in denying it? "I can't wait another few weeks. I have to go back into the mine now."

"Alone? Are you crazy, man?" Paul moved closer, his eyes wide and disturbed. "It's been three months. Who knows how the earth has shifted in that shaft? And now, with all this weather closing in, it's a harebrained idea."

"You tell me how else I can substantiate the truth." There was no other way, even if it cost Stefan his last breath.

Paul rolled his hat through nimble fingers. "I couldn't help but notice how you and Miss Sullivan feasted your eyes on one another earlier today. How would she feel knowing you contemplated risking your life this way?"

The question knocked Stefan back. He'd been so obsessed with discovering the truth he hadn't considered Anna's feelings. He didn't want to cause her more pain. Still ...

"Don't you see?" Stefan shook his head, the letter he would write Anna already forming in his head. "It's for Anna that I'm doing this and everyone else in Clear Creek County. An egomaniac is running amuck among us. Töpfer cannot be allowed to get away with murder. Who knows where his savage tendencies will strike next? You? Robert Old? Hamill?"

Stefan set his chin. "Anna knows what kind of man Töpfer is. She experienced the collateral damage he left behind and organized the festival to rescue the innocent bystanders."

Paul rhythmically tapped his hat, eyeing Stefan with tightened rigidity, lips flattened into a straight line. In one swift movement, Paul flapped his hat against his thigh. "That's it, then. I'm coming with you. I won't let you descend into that infernal pit without backup." After a moment, Stefan laughed, and Paul glared at him. "I can't fathom what you find so humorous."

"You called the mine shaft an infernal pit. To be fair, it's not that hot at the bottom—ninety degrees at most. Besides, you can't watch my every move—too much debris in the way."

"Be that as it may," Paul directed a solemn gaze at him. "I'll be there to pull you out if something happens."

Stefan studied his friend's determined posture. "All right. Monday morning, seven o'clock sharp."

"I'll be here." Paul placed his hat on his head, and Stefan led him to the door.

"Don't be late," Stefan demanded as Paul walked away into the night.

Stefan sucked air between his teeth and closed the door. God willing, by Monday, they'd all be free of Töpfer's tyranny in this town. The alternative was unthinkable.

Thirty-Two

Congratulations for the festival's success came from every street corner and congregant at church on Sunday morning, warming Anna's heart. She had not only secured her reputation as a seamstress but as a member of the community. She couldn't have been more pleased.

Still, Stefan's proposal to consider a courtship occupied Anna's thoughts more than anything else. She debated with herself and prayed for wisdom. The devastating heartbreak she'd born in Ireland losing Seamus gave her reason to shut the door on any future with Stefan. But she couldn't deny her affections, which demanded she throw reason to the wind.

Early Monday morning, Anna's questions invaded her dreams. She tossed and turned in erratic sleep as Seamus and Stefan vied for her affections until her eyes popped open, and she sprang into a full sitting position. What had the dream meant? Was the Almighty telling her the past was dead and gone, and Stefan was now her present?

Anna glanced at the clock. Seven-fifteen. She had to find Stefan.

By ten past eight, Anna had washed, slipped into a day bodice and bustled skirt, donned her cloak, hat, and gloves, and stepped out of her cottage into the nippy air. Overhead, the blue skies promised a sunny day. She made straight for the upper end of town without pause.

Fifteen minutes later, Anna found Sarah pacing the front porch. The girl flapped a folded sheet of paper against her palm and perused the street in agitation. "Oh, Miss Sullivan. I'm so glad to see you."

"What's happened?" Anna frowned, searching the girl's frightened eyes.

"I probably shouldn't be telling you this." She tilted her head. "I just don't know what else to do."

"It's all right, Sarah." Anna softened her tone. "I promise."

Sarah nodded. "When Mr. Maier didn't come for breakfast, I checked his room, but he'd already gone. It's happened before, so I didn't worry. But a short while ago, I found this note on the parlor table." She handed the note to Anna. "I'm afraid Mr. Maier has done something very foolish."

Anna scanned the note.

Miss O'Donnell,

> *If I am not back by noon, find Marshal Jacobs and tell him*
> *Mr. Rutherford and I have gone to the Singing Silver Mine.*
> *He will know to come looking for us. I don't expect anything*
> *of dire consequence, but if it occurs, please ensure Miss*
> *Sullivan receives the letter on my bureau. I count on your*
> *discretion. Thank you for your ever-faithful service.*

Sincere regards, Stefan Maier

"Ach." Anna exhaled a quick breath, flattening her lips. She didn't want to alarm the girl, but there was no time to waste. Anna had to catch up with Stefan before he did something they would all regret. "I need a horse. Is Mr. Maier's groomsman about?"

"I don't think so, ma'am." Sarah wrung her hands. "Mr. Maier gave him the day off."

"Then I will prepare one of the horses for myself." Anna returned the note to Sarah, picked up her skirts, and walked backward. "Find the marshal now and inform him of the letter. Tell him it's urgent, and he must go to the mine immediately."

"Yes, Miss Sullivan. But ..." Sarah twirled a lock of hair that had fallen out of her cap. "What if I can't find the marshal right away?"

Anna stopped and gazed intently into the girl's eyes. "It may be as Mr. Maier said, and there's nothing to fret over. Do your best." She whirled, picked up her skirts, and darted to the stables.

Inside, she found the two Haflinger horses Stefan had used the first time she'd come to the house. "You're sure a beauty." She spoke softly to one filly, petting her. "I hope we can be friends because Stefan needs you." The horse leaned into her and gave a friendly snort, which Anna interpreted as consent.

Anna located the tack room and quickly readied the horse with bridle, saddle, and reins, then led the horse to the courtyard. The horse bowed her head and whinnied. "I know —not a proper skirt for gallivanting about the countryside, but it'll have to do." Anna placed her toe into the stirrup and mounted the horse in one swift movement.

"*Tsk-Tsk.*" Anna reined the horse right, then applied pressure to the horse's sides, taking off in full gallop toward the trail that wound up to the Singing Silver Mine.

Elias liked the money he made for doing nothing. At least, that's what most days consisted of, and that was what he looked forward to today—not much of anything.

He took his usual spot against a hitching post behind the mansion-turned-Phelps House, where he'd been staying for several weeks to get a clear view of Maier's estate across the road. It wasn't nearly the elegant inn Barton House was, but then again, Töpfer had reminded him this was not a luxury holiday. As was his daily habit, Elias had already saddled his horse in case Maier headed out. But Elias didn't expect it.

He put up his collar and blew on his hands. It was cold out here this morning in the shade. Of course, it was only eight o'clock, two days before Christmas in Georgetown. Blue skies overhead, though. It'd probably warm up nicely by midday.

If anyone had asked him, he might have told them following Stefan Maier wasn't worth his time. But no one asked. They only gave him orders: keep an eye out, provide reports, watch for the occasional disturbance, and inform the powers that be if anything interesting happened. It irritated him to no end. But as long as the money kept coming, he would keep his mouth shut. Besides, it was easier than his work at the mine.

Elias wasn't sure what constituted "interesting," but he kept Sigmund Dreher informed of Maier's day-to-day activities. The man carried out a reasonably consistent schedule with variations due only to whatever enterprise he conducted outside his house that day. Since the banquet in Denver, Maier stayed mainly around Georgetown, occupied by his business concerns at lawyers' offices, banks, lunch appointments with mining associates and smelters, and a hoity-toity meeting—presumably with the town council—at the Henley home two weeks ago.

Maier had ventured to the Singing Silver Mine three times since the cave-in. The first happened after the O'Hallisey funeral, which Elias had dubbed "interesting" since the man seemed so doggedly determined to get there on horseback. Elias followed him only so far and turned around to report it. Dreher thanked him with a wad of bills and sent him away to blow the bucks on booze.

Two more times, Maier had taken his carriage to the mine and brought back wooden boxes. Elias speculated on the content, but Dreher had sneered, saying Maier's empire was crumbling the same way the shaft walls had collapsed. He had snorted over that one, knowing why the walls had given way.

Yes, indeed, things didn't appear to be going well for Maier at all.

Elias combed his pocket for a toothpick and couldn't lay hands on one. He swore under his breath. He had nothing to get the debris out of his teeth from the steak and eggs he'd had for breakfast. Why was he freezing his derrière off anyway? He should have taken the day off. Maier wouldn't do anything these two days before Christmas, no sirree. At least not for another couple of hours. It wouldn't hurt if he went back into the hotel, found himself a toothpick, and warmed himself by the fire for a bit.

Twenty minutes later, Elias returned to his station by the hitching post. He crossed his arms and scanned the environs. Maybe when this job was over, he'd make his way to California. People said it was a mighty fine country and a whole lot warmer.

Elias glanced at Maier's house, expecting more of the same monotonous grind, then did a double-take. What was that

Sullivan woman doing outside Maier's house at half past eight?

He watched the maid, agitated-like, jerking about like a wound-up doll. After the women talked a bit, the maid handed Miss Sullivan a piece of paper, which she promptly read. All the while, Maier didn't make an appearance. Something was wrong.

Miss Sullivan returned the paper to the maid, then hastened to the stables. Several minutes later, she appeared again with one of Maier's fancy imported horses. No way. The Irish woman was going to ride the horse western style in her bustled skirt.

Elias ran into the hotel stables, grabbed the reins of his horse, and led him outside just in time to observe the Sullivan woman get onto the horse. Elias mounted his steed and waited by the stable doors until she made her move.

She reined the horse onto Hale Street. Elias followed a fair distance behind. The horse gained speed and galloped up the slope to the main road leading to Silver Plume. They were heading up to the Singing Silver Mine, sure as Elias's name was James Elias Jones.

Elias followed the girl for another five minutes, but by then, she had urged the horse into a full gallop. It was time to turn around. No doubt about it. Maier and his friends were up to something a bit more than interesting this morning. Time he told the boss to raise a little dust.

Thirty-Three

S tefan galloped onto the Singing Silver Mine property alongside Paul just after sunrise and jumped off his horse into an inch of snow. After tethering Sally to the hitching post next to the vertical wood-plank shaft house, he hustled Paul to the front entrance, his breath steaming from his nose and mouth in the cold mountain air.

A pin-prick of guilt needled Stefan. He never meant to involve Paul in his mess. Stefan appreciated his friend's desire to ensure his safety while uncovering the evidence against Töpfer. Still, the responsibility had always been Stefan's alone. The last thing he wanted was another innocent death on his hands.

Stefan unlocked the door and strode into the main room of the shaft house. The place was as cold as an icebox.

"Do you mind if we fire up the stove?" Paul rubbed his hands and headed to the stove on the other side of the room.

"Suit yourself." Stefan had expected the air to be nippy at this hour, but if they wanted to avoid Elias's prying eyes, they had to make it here early.

He surveyed the vast space inside the shaft house. Nothing had changed since he'd come to collect crates of documents in November. It seemed even God had forsaken the mine, leaving it an empty shell. Stefan inhaled, his chest filling with air. His Singing Silver Mine *would* sing again.

He studied the triangular-shaped hoist system. On the day of the disaster, he'd brought in William Chelsea, his foreman Horace McKinley, and Elias Jones to discuss how they'd retrieve the men. He hadn't let himself dwell on how many would come out alive. The goal had been to get as many out of there alive as possible. That's when they rigged a hook and eye system to send a rescue team into the shaft, but the process would be painfully slow—time the men below couldn't afford.

Stefan hung his head, letting out a groan. The grief was as heavy on his heart today as it had been the day of the disaster. He would not wait another moment to get the answers he sought. In October, the goal had been to secure the men. Today, he would secure the evidence he needed to prove what really happened that day.

Paul finished stoking the stove and returned to the hoist drum near Stefan. "What's the plan?"

"I'm going to do just what we started before Töpfer interrupted us two months ago." Stefan met Paul's eyes. "I'll harness myself onto the end of the cable. You'll operate the hoist controls."

"I'd feel better if we did a security check on those timbers before I send you down." Paul placed his hands on his hips.

"We don't have time." Stefan shed his coat and gloves and examined the boiler system to ensure he found no defects in the pipes since they had to divert the steam to the pistons that drove the drum. "I've known for months Elias Jones has been keeping a tail on my every move."

"Seriously?" Paul scoffed.

"I've been switching up my daily routine just to keep him off guard. I'm sure he knows by now I'm not at home and has informed Töpfer."

"What I wouldn't do to that scumbag." Paul let out a quick disgusted snort. "And he's a fellow countryman no less."

"That'll have to wait for later, I'm afraid, old boy." Stefan laid a hand on Paul's shoulder. "We have two hours on Elias and Töpfer. That means we need to fire up the boiler now." He pointed at the boiler foundation. "It takes an hour to heat the icy water in the cylindrical shell and generate the power to run the hoist system. It's not ideal, but it's what we've got."

"Then let's get to it." Paul removed his layers as Stefan opened the firebox on the left side of the boiler shell and lit the furnace with coal. Once the fire ignited, Stefan secured the door. The hot flue gases would travel through the tubes and heat the water inside before escaping the smokestack.

The operation consisted of a steam boiler, a single cable drum flanked by two steam cylinders, a tall, wooden two-post headframe, and a steel-framed cage with flooring and hood that brought men and ore up and down into the belly of the earth.

Typically, the steam cylinders powered the cable drum through reduction gears—rubber rollers that pressed against the drum. The hoist operator controlled the brake, clutch, and throttle with levers and foot pedals at the rear. On that Monday in October, the single drum hoist had been laid waste by the cable snapping, breaking loose the cage at one end and causing the drum to dimple at the other. But that didn't make sense. What could cause the drum to dimple like that? The only way he'd know for sure was to descend to the bowels of the shaft.

Stefan glanced at the levers and foot pedal that Paul would use. The same controls Elias had used. He gritted his teeth.

"Time to gather the gear." He led Paul to the blacksmith shop and changing area at the back of the building.

"Several hooks and harnesses are on the workshop table over there." Stefan indicated one way and strode the other. "I'll collect the lamps over here."

Stefan gathered two oil wick lamps—one for backup—a canvas mining cap with leather brims, and a larger oil lamp to illuminate the bottom of the shaft. He also checked the reservoirs in the small kettle-shaped lamps to ensure a flame would ignite at the spout, then found Paul at the back wall.

"I figured you'd want to take a few items with you." Paul handed him a belt stocked with a knife, cable cutters, screwdrivers, a hammer, rope, and a pick.

"Just what every miner needs." Stefan smiled and slapped his back. "Give me five minutes to get into my work clothes."

Stefan dashed to the changing room, where he donned dungarees and work boots and selected a pair of gloves to keep his hands from chaffing on the cable in the descent. Several minutes later, he joined Paul near the hoist system.

"It's only been forty-five minutes," Stefan checked his watch, "but by the sound of the vibrations in the steam cylinders, the system may have enough pressure to power the drum. Be ready. Let's give it a go, shall we?"

"Nothing ventured, nothing gained." Paul waved a hand.

Stefan led Paul behind the drum and sat in the chair. He showed him how to work three levers and a foot pedal that controlled the brake, clutch, and throttle. "Lord, let her roll." He placed his hands on the controls. Nothing.

"What's wrong?" Paul crossed his arms.

"Steam engine's not ready yet." Stefan tried again. Nothing.

"How long?" Paul's hands went to his hips.

"Maybe another fifteen minutes." Stefan rose and went

around to the boiler. Flue gases emanated from the smokestack. It couldn't be long. He tromped back, waited, and prayed, for only God knew the stakes.

Ten minutes later, Stefan placed his hands on two of the three levers and a foot on the floor pedal and maneuvered them. This time, the drum rumbled as it slowly came to life, and the cable moved forward. His heart lurched with a mixture of dread and delight—delight that the system worked, dread of going into the bowels of the mine and what he would find.

He gave the controls over to Paul. "You think you got it?"

"Only one way to know for certain." Paul sat in the chair, then put his hands on the levers. The drum rolled, and the cable unraveled. "Easy as riding a horse." Paul whooped.

"Whoa," Stefan called to Paul. "Reverse the end of the cable to two feet above the shaft."

Paul jumped up and came around. "You sure you want to do this?" He helped Stefan slip on the harness and hook up the wire cable. "There's no shame if you want to back out."

"I can't back out." Stefan hooked his belt. "Too many people's lives hang on the truth."

"I knew you wouldn't." Paul tugged on the connections. "But it was worth a try."

Stefan dug into a dungaree pocket, brought out two tin whistles, and handed one to Paul. "We need a way to communicate."

"Doesn't seem very useful above the noise of the machines." Paul flipped the whistle.

"You should be able to hear it through the narrow shaft." The whistle had aided Stefan's men before.

They tested a system of signals—one long whistle blow for start, two short blows for stop, and the opening line to the hymn "Pass Me Not, O Gentle Savior" if either one experienced trouble.

"And remember," Stefan said. "I've hit bottom when the cable is one length around the drum. Send me the signal if you haven't heard from me in twenty minutes." The time it took to make the slow and arduous descent.

Stefan lit his headlamp, then placed himself on the edge of the hole under the headframe. He had no idea how long it would take to find the evidence he needed.

"Wait a minute." Paul walked away and came back with a sledgehammer in each hand, several pieces of rope thrown over his shoulder, and a hook. He set the hammer on the floor and held the other. "If something happens to the whistle, hit the cable as hard as possible to ensure the reverberations reach the surface. I'll do the same, letting you know I've received your message." He attached the hammer with the lengths of rope and hooked it onto the eye at the end of the cable. "Okay, I think that'll do it. Take care, my friend."

Stefan saluted Paul, then watched him walk back to the controls and sit on the chair.

"Take it slow and steady." Stefan gave Paul the command. A shiver coursed his spine as if the ghosts of the dead had just breezed past him. He shook away the eerie feeling and focused on his task. Would the evidence present itself, or would this foray into the shaft be all for naught? He prayed this descent would not be the death of him.

Please, Lord. Now that love had come his way again, Stefan wanted a second chance—that was if Anna would have him. A moment later, the drone of the drum commenced, and the cable unraveled. He walked off the edge of the floor, suspended in space, and plunged into the dark pit.

Thirty-Four

Anna rode onto the Singing Silver Mine property and spotted two horses hitched near the shaft house. Leaning forward, she squeezed the horse's flank and sprinted straight ahead. "Whoa." She reined in and leaped to the ground beside the other two horses, the hum of machinery evident through the clapboard walls. Anna tied the horse and dashed around to the front entrance, the roaring noise of the machinery growing louder as she pushed open the door.

Spying Mr. Rutherford behind the boiler, she removed her gloves and headed for the hoist system, her gaze following the cable descending from the top of the headframe into the shaft. Alarm bells rang in her head. "Stop!" She strode straight for Mr. Rutherford.

He stared, his mouth slackening. "What are *you* doing here?" His hands loosened their grip on the levers, then tightened again. He sat taller. "A mine is no place for a woman."

"Neither is an Irish workhouse," she shot back, "but there

have been plenty of them working there over the years to keep a roof over their heads and food in their bellies."

"This isn't Ireland, Miss Sullivan." He bandied back, peering past her to the cable and moving one of the levers.

"No, but you'd be surprised what a woman can do under the right circumstances."

Anna eyed the drum. It appeared mostly depleted of its cable, and her stomach went taut. "You mustn't let Stefan go to the bottom." Her words ushered forth in haste. Paul needed to understand. "He's in danger."

"Stefan knew what he was doing when he entered the mine." Paul pulled another lever. "He gave explicit instructions, and I won't go against them."

"I admire your loyalty, Mr. Rutherford, but you don't know—"

"It's too late. Stefan's already at the bottom." Paul moved one of the levers, and the drum came to a standstill. He rose and walked around her to the shaft. Anna had no choice but to follow after him. "He'll give a signal when he's ready." He held onto one of the headframe posts, peering into the hole.

"You must get him up now." She demanded, hitching a thumb over her shoulder. "There's no time."

He looked up at her with raised brows.

"Please, Mr. Rutherford." She was desperate. "You've *got* to listen to me. I had a dream—"

"A dream." He unhooked himself from the post and turned away. "Seriously, Miss Sullivan, I can't imagine—"

"A premonition of sorts ... and Elias Jones followed me—"

"Elias Jones?" He jerked back around, frowning. "You're certain?"

She nodded. "Until I turned up the mountain, and then he headed back to town."

"To alert Töpfer, no doubt." Mr. Rutherford's eyes blazed.

He covered his mouth with a fisted hand, considering his choices.

Anna couldn't fathom what there was to contemplate. "You're wasting precious time—"

"All right. We'll bring Stefan up." He straightened and reached inside his coat pocket to bring out a tin whistle.

"I don't think now is the time—"

"Now is exactly the time, Miss Sullivan." He positioned his fingers on the whistle, then placed it into his mouth and blew the first eight notes to the tune "Pass Me Not, O Gentle Savior."

Anna threw up her hands. Perhaps playing the hymn was a cry for help from the Almighty, but this was not bringing Stefan back to the surface.

Mr. Rutherford stopped playing and then directed an ear into the shaft.

Anna grabbed hold of the headframe post and leaned into the shaft alongside him. Then she heard the faintest sound of the same tune whistled back at them from below. Her stomach fluttered.

"That's his cue." Mr. Rutherford ran back to the hoist platform and sat in the chair.

The drum came to life. Its monotonous vibrating thrum was music to Anna's ears. She backed away from the hole as the twisted metal wire cable appeared to spiral slowly upwards and out of the cavern. "How long?" She crossed her arms, tapping an elbow.

"Twenty minutes." He called back.

The laggard line moved too slowly for her liking. "Can you increase the speed?" When she didn't hear a reply, she looked up at Mr. Rutherford.

His steely gaze seemed concentrated on something or someone behind her.

She twisted. Georg Töpfer approached them with a

walking stick, and Elias Jones skulked slightly behind him. "Ach." She faced the ugly man and choked.

"What are you doing here, Töpfer?" Mr. Rutherford bellowed. "You've been served an injunction against your presence on his property."

"But I came all this way just to see how you're all fairing." Töpfer's fabricated smile ridiculed them both. "And it seems I'm not alone." He halted before Anna, his voice slimy as an Irish slug. He extended a hand, touching the hair beneath her bonnet. "To what do we owe the pleasure of having your company today, Miss Sullivan?"

"Believe me, I have no pleasure in it." She batted his hand away.

"Feisty thing, aren't you?" He chuckled, waving his hand. "In other circumstances, I might be inclined to explore that wild spirit. Unfortunately, I have no time for dallying with you today." He dropped his hand.

"Leave now, Töpfer, or I'll toss you out. You're in violation of ..." Mr. Rutherford's voice trailed away, and Anna followed his gaze to the entrance.

"Ah, Mr. Dreher." Töpfer's gruesome grin sickened her. "So good of you to make it here so quickly, and just in time, too, since that gentleman—" he pointed without looking, "—was just about to threaten me with bodily violence."

Anna tensed. The German strode forward like a professional soldier, his muscular build filling out his trousers, shirt, and leather vest. "Is that so?" Dreher joined Töpfer and Elias Jones, smirking like one of the devil's legions.

Dreher was at least a foot taller than her and gave off an air of invincibility with his chest out, shoulders back, and arms swinging at his side. He reminded her of Ireland's mythical underworld demons who warred against her people.

"Let me introduce you to Herr Sigmund Dreher." Töpfer

stretched an arm. "As you have probably already guessed, most men prefer not to wrangle with our friend."

"He's got a bit of an attitude, doesn't he?" Anna crossed her arms, feet planted wide apart. She could thrust out her chest with the best of them. So, what if her defensive posture angered Töpfer? The German braggart had riled her from the day she'd ridden into town. Besides, if she distracted him from Stefan's ascent, all the better.

"*Tsk, tsk, tsk.* Why so combative?" He walked two paces to look into the shaft. "Where is Maier anyway? We're only here to help."

A quick breath escaped Anna's lips. He was mocking them, toying with them. "You don't strike me as the helping type."

"Well, now you have hurt my feelings, Miss Sullivan." Töpfer pressed a hand against his chest. He turned toward Jones. "It's time we relieve Mr. Rutherford of his duties."

"Yes, Mr. Töpfer." Jones marched to the hoist platform.

"I don't think so." Mr. Rutherford leaped from the chair and ambushed him, and they scrambled on the floor of the shaft house.

Anna's gaze shifted to the cable spiraling upwards. Had Mr. Rutherford just left the hoist controls unattended with Stefan still ascending?

"Herr Dreher." Töpfer's tone exuded his exasperation at the futility of the fight.

Dreher grabbed Mr. Rutherford in a seemingly effortless move and threw him several feet away, where he landed with a hard thump, appearing lifeless on the floor.

Lord, help us! Anna groaned.

Jones brushed himself off and sat at the controls as Dreher rejoined Töpfer.

"I don't know what you see in your precious Mr. Maier."

Töpfer breathed down Anna's neck. His foul breath assaulted her nose. "But don't worry. I won't make him suffer long."

Anna whirled away in horrifying defeat. Devilment, that's what it was. *Lord.* Tears wet her cheeks.

When she woke from the dream that morning, Anna only wanted to tell Stefan she loved him and would marry him if he still wanted her. Instead, her foolish actions had led Töpfer right to Stefan.

Though Anna had been thinking of love, these men had been playing a deadly game. There was no doubt now. They had planned the disaster that killed her uncle and the other men. And if they had their way, they would kill Stefan, Mr. Rutherford, and her without remorse.

Anna couldn't allow Töpfer's plan to succeed. She would do anything to prevent harm to Stefan, even if it meant giving her life to stop the devil.

In her left peripheral vision, she detected movement and slowly turned. Mr. Rutherford shook his head, and she went utterly still.

He heaved a sledgehammer at Dreher, but the German sidestepped him. The hammer missed and landed several feet on the other side of the hole.

The German's nostrils flared. His muscles and veins strained against his skin. He turned on Mr. Rutherford, a resonant roar spewing from his vocal cords like the walrus that occasionally clamored on the Irish coastline.

Mr. Rutherford bounded for the other side of the room, and Dreher chased after him. The demon caught him from behind near the back door and twisted his arm behind his back.

"You haven't figured it out yet, have you?" The monster towered above him, speaking his German-intoned accent through clenched teeth. "I have killed men stronger and more skilled than you in battle." He scuffed him back toward Töpfer, meeting him halfway.

Töpfer got into Mr. Rutherford's face. "Did you *really* think you could escape?"

"That was no escape, Töpfer." Mr. Rutherford's eyes flinted. "If I could, I would tear you apart limb from limb."

While Töpfer remained distracted by the altercation with Mr. Rutherford, Anna shifted her position to the opposite side of the headframe and hid the sledgehammer under her skirts. From this angle, she peered askance at Jones behind the hoist controls, then stared. The man was unconscious and tied to the chair, his head slunk over. Mr. Rutherford must have been able to take him out before launching his attack against Dreher. Her breathing came fast and furious.

That Jones couldn't do any harm should have been good news. But Stefan's fate could be worse with no one controlling the hoist. Who would stop the drum when he came to the surface? Without a person to put the brakes on the cable, he would fly over the top of the headframe, then back to the hoist drum, where he'd be crushed and ground like mincemeat.

"You may believe you've won, Töpfer." Mr. Rutherford's righteous anger spewed, and Anna's eyes shifted to the three men. "But the war is not over yet."

"Take him back to the shaft." Töpfer ordered Dreher.

The German pushed Mr. Rutherford forward. "It will give me ever so much pleasure to observe your face as you watch your friend come to his end before you meet yours."

"You're a sick man, Dreher." Mr. Rutherford sneered, straining against the demon.

Dreher burst out in laughter—a jeering utterance as evil as the devil himself. They stopped several feet from the shaft. Had any of them noticed she'd moved?

"It's a shame you set your affections on a man with so little business acumen." Töpfer shook his head. "He should have accepted my offer to buy the mine when he had the chance."

"Mr. Maier is a million times more a man than you." She wouldn't allow this nauseating German to deride the man she loved. "At least he's earned his assets by hard work and toil. You've had to murder and steal to come by yours."

"Get off your high and mighty horse, Miss Sullivan." Töpfer sneered. "Maier has wrangled his share of capital from hard-working men."

Anna couldn't guess what wrangling Töpfer referred to. But even if Stefan had wrested men of their money, he could never be as deranged as this German.

"Ah, I see a headlamp shining from below now." Töpfer peered into the cavern and grinned. "Mr. Jones, prepare to apply the brakes." He waited for a reply, but none came. "Elias!" He walked a few paces toward the hoist platform and discovered what Anna already knew. He spun on his heel, scowling.

"What's the matter, Töpfer?" Mr. Rutherford smirked from his position between the two murderers. "Your lackey can't do your dirty work for you?"

Anna buckled, her heart racing, unable to appreciate the irony of his statement.

"Shut up." Dreher pushed him forward at an angle to the hole, forcing his head down.

A slow, maniacal burble erupted from Töpfer's mouth. "This is going to play out better than I'd hoped. And I have you to thank for it, Rutherford. Oh, yes. At least if Herr Dreher had released him over the shaft, you wouldn't have had to observe his mangled body below. But this ..." He waved, then peered into the shaft. "It couldn't have been more perfect."

Anna's fury flared with profound disgust, no longer caring

what happened to her. Stefan's life hung in the balance. She had to save him, but she'd have only one shot.

Stepping forward, Anna squatted, felt for the sledgehammer behind her skirts, and stood. Charged with a driving power she'd never known, Anna swung the instrument with the strength of David's slingshot to the head of Goliath, coming up just in time to watch the hammer hit Dreher's shoulder.

Dreher doubled over backward in writhing pain, springing Mr. Rutherford free. The ogre hit the ground with blunt force, his head smashing against the floor, knocking him out cold.

Mr. Rutherford grabbed Töpfer by the scruff of his collar before he could make a run for the door of the shaft house. "The controls, Miss Sullivan." He bellowed, struggling to hold on to the man and dragging him to the back of the room.

Anna dashed around the headframe to the hoist platform. Jones still sat on the seat, hunched over. She quickly untied the rope and pushed him off to the side. He grunted, but she ignored him and sat.

Looking at three levers and a foot pedal, Anna's pulse raced. Ach, how was she to know which of the levers to use? She inhaled and released her breath. *Please, Lord.* "I don't know how to work the controls," she yelled.

"It's easy."

Anna's head jerked up. Tears of joy moistened her eyes. Stefan had surfaced from the depths of the earth—a bit dustier for the wear—but alive and talking. Never had she seen such a glorious sight. She drew a breath. "And that would be ..."

"First, depress the foot pedal. It'll apply the brakes to the drum."

Anna pushed on the foot pedal. Slowly, the drum screeched to a complete halt. But when she looked at Stefan, he seemed too far above the ground floor. "What should I do now?"

"You're doing well." Stefan rotated slowly, his hands on the harness. "You'll have to reverse the drum. Take your foot off the brake. Then, very slowly, push the right throttle forward, but only a bit. Too much, and we'll have to go the other way again."

Anna lifted her foot from the pedal and inched the right throttle forward as slowly as she could manage.

"Stop!" Stefan commanded, and she immediately pulled back the right throttle and depressed the foot pedal. "Perfect. Now, bring the left throttle toward you as far as it will go."

Anna pulled the throttle forward. The machine idled, and she sat utterly frozen, staring at the levers within her grip, afraid to move.

"You did it, Anna." Stefan's congratulatory tone rang loud and clear. "You can take your hands off the levers now."

Anna let out a long, slow breath. Gingerly, she removed her hands from the levers and peered at Stefan. Pride beamed from his face, and she clasped her hands. *Praise be to God.* She stepped away from the hoist apparatus and hastened to the shaft where Stefan hung midair. Dreher still lay off to the side out cold, but for how long?

Mr. Rutherford joined Anna on the north side of the hole, breathing hard. "Töpfer's locked in the changing room, but we're not out of the woods yet, Stefan. You've got to swing yourself to the edge."

Stefan grabbed a knife from his toolbelt. "It'll be easier if I get rid of the sledgehammer." He slashed the rope, and the hammer fell into the recesses of the earth.

Anna gulped. That could have been Stefan if Töpfer had had his way.

Stefan threw the length of rope to his friend. "Pull me over."

Mr. Rutherford caught the rope and pulled Stefan to the floor next to the shaft. "Welcome back, my friend."

Stefan unhooked the harness and let the cable swing back over the shaft. He flashed a relieved smile. "It's good to be back and alive." He shook Mr. Rutherford's shoulders.

Anna waited for Stefan to see her. At last, he turned and walked several steps until he was only inches away from her and held her gaze. Anna caught her breath, for Stefan's eyes told her the profound emotion stirring in his heart. She hoped he could see the same depth of feeling mirrored in hers. "I came by your house this morning."

"You did? What was on your mind?"

"I'm done pondering."

"What took you so long?" Stefan swept her into his arms. Then, like a flint to stone, Stefan found her lips, and the sparks ignited a flame that sent shock waves to Anna's toes. Stefan must have felt the same electric pulse, for he deepened the kiss, but this time, it was deliciously sweet and tender and full of promise. And for the first time since she'd arrived in America, Anna knew without a doubt she had finally come home.

"E-hem."

A flush crept across Anna's face, and she disentangled herself from Stefan. "We were—"

"No need to explain." Mr. Rutherford grinned and twisted toward the door. "Marshal Jacobs and his deputy sheriff have arrived. His men are collecting Töpfer, Dreher, and Jones and taking them into custody. But he says he still needs a word with you."

Marshal Jacobs stepped forward and offered a hand to Stefan, then turned to Anna. "You sure do know how to raise Cain, Miss Sullivan." He jeered. "Looks like it was a mighty good thing your housemaid came for us. Though ..." He scanned the surroundings. "You all seem to have handled things pretty well on your own."

"Ach, Marshal Jacobs." Anna grinned. "We were never on our own. The Lord has been with us the whole time." But that was a story she would explain another time.

Marshal Jacobs coughed. "Yes, well, I'll need your statements as soon as you can get to the jailhouse."

"Of course." Stefan narrowed his eyes at Jones, now being handcuffed to the headframe by the deputy sheriff. "I think you will be very interested to hear my *full* statement."

Anna put a hand on Stefan's arm. "You found the evidence you needed, didn't you?"

"Stefan?" Paul probed his eyes.

Stefan's gaze trailed the other lawman, who now shoved Georg Töpfer toward the door of the shaft house. "Yes, I know exactly what happened and who's responsible."

Thirty-Five

A nna paused, gazing across the street to one of Georgetown's most illustrious estates, all aglow on this clear Christmas Eve. How was it that she, Anna Katherine O'Sullivan, would be among the honored guests at William Hamill's traditional Christmas Eve celebration? Where would Anna be without Stefan in her life? Had it only been three months ago she had wondered whether she would ever know happiness again?

Horses' hooves thudded through three inches of freshly fallen snow, diverting Anna's attention. She twisted as the lantern-lit Brougham carriage came closer and stopped. A driver dressed in a top hat and woolen cloak looked straight ahead as Virginia Henley stuck her head out the window. "Anna Sullivan, what are you doing out here? You'll catch your death of cold." Anna could vaguely make out Mayor Henley next to her on the seat.

"The Thomases offered me a ride." Anna grinned and held her hands up in the air. "I just couldn't resist taking advantage of the glorious skies."

"In all this snow? What about your gown? You'll ruin the bottom hem."

"I was hoping to get a view of the North Star, you see."

Elizabeth stuck her jewel-adorned head out the back window and craned her neck upwards. "And did you?"

"Nah. 'Tis a bit beyond the purview of these close mountains, but the walk was grand." Anna heard a disappointed grunt as the girl sat back again out of sight.

"Grand or not, you don't want to miss the festivities. Mr. Hamill is a stickler for punctuality, you know." Virginia's eyes bugged out.

"I promise I shall be joining you soon." Anna waved them away, and the carriage continued to the back of the house near the stables where several other guests had parked.

She tromped across the road and through the front gate of the property. Swept of snow, Anna made it easily on the walkway to the front door in her dress with its full train. She lifted a gloved hand to the door knocker, admiring the elaborate wreath made by Rebecca McKinley. A river of joy flowed through her veins as violin strings from the chamber orchestra inside grew to a crescendo through the cracks in the door.

"Good evening, Miss Sullivan." Sarah welcomed her into the foyer and took her cloak while garbled voices and laughter wafted in from the other side of the wall.

"But what are you doing here?" Anna gasped. "You haven't—"

"Oh, no, ma'am. I couldn't leave Mr. Maier now the two of you are courting."

Anna relaxed. "For a moment, I thought I'd have to have words with Mr. Hamill."

"No need, Miss Sullivan. Mr. Maier has only loaned me to the Hamills for the evening." She helped Anna remove her cloak. "But don't you look different tonight, Miss Sullivan—a proper elegant lady in your shimmering green gown."

"You are too kind." Anna straightened the reticule on her arm. So much had changed since their first meeting, allowing Anna to splurge on making a forest green gown of lustrous silk that shimmered in the light. The frock featured a square neckline trimmed in black ruffled lace, black lace overlays on the bodice and skirt, and a long curving train. Anna had completed the outfit with black lace gloves and a green and black feathered hat.

"Anna!" Stefan's voice reached her ears.

Sarah backed away as Anna's gaze shifted to Stefan, his eyes sparkling with light and love. She couldn't move, couldn't breathe, her stomach all aflutter, her eyes fixed on the one man who had become the center of her life. Oh, how exquisite he appeared in his formal black tail and white shirt.

He drew closer, his body taut, eyes searching hers. "I feared you might not come, that perhaps you had changed your mind after all. I'm afraid I've been a bit of a ..." He glanced at Sarah. "A bit of a loose cannon the whole day."

Anna drew in a sharp, quivering breath. Had she really caused this kind of stir in this man? She'd had similar fears—fears that had put her on edge, fears that she'd only imagined his affections, fears that he would not want a poor peasant girl from Dingle in the end. But, now, looking into those penetrating blue eyes, her concerns dropped away and were replaced by hope beyond all her wild imaginings. "I haven't changed my mind, Stefan."

Relief flooded his face, and a brilliant smile crossed his lips. He offered an arm. "I shall be pleased to escort the most enchanting woman I've ever known."

Anna linked her arm with his, and they walked toward the

parlor's threshold, feeling a lightness in her limbs. Would it always be like this—floating on air?

She scanned the small circles of refined people animated in conversation—some Anna knew, such as the Henleys, Tuckers, Thomases, McClellans, and Cecelia Richards. Some she had only heard others speak about—the Cushmans and the Chaffees. She had never even met the prominent Hamills, though she had seen them from afar at the Harvest Ball.

A manservant handed out glasses of wine, and another offered *hors d'oeuvres* from a silver tray. An abundance of greenery, candles, and bows in colors of red and silver and gold spread Christmas cheer throughout the room. At the center, an unlit tree graced a fireplace, its crackling fire warming the room.

"Are you feeling unwell?" Stefan asked.

"I ... no ..." Anna licked her lips. She gazed up at him, observing the love and concern in his eyes, and a sudden peace overcame her. "I had a moment of anxiety, being on your arm and uncertain what your friends would think." Her voice softened. "But I can see now that I was being foolish. I'm most happy to be here with you, Stefan."

A generous smile curved his lips. "Come, I want to introduce you to friends who will be important to our future." He led her to the circle where the Mayor and Virginia Henley enjoyed the company of the Hamills and the Cushmans.

"Mr. Maier, welcome." Mr. Hamill shook his hand and turned to Anna. "I hear you are a real heroine, Miss Sullivan." He bowed before her. She'd heard Hamill was handsome with a dark mustache and magnetic smile, but he was downright debonair.

Heat rose to Anna's cheeks. "You are very kind, sir."

"Not at all." Priscilla Hamill said with a brilliant smile. "We're all grateful to you for saving Mr. Maier and Mr.

Rutherford from that horrible Mr. Töpfer and his goons. Now, the town can get back to business as usual."

Anna met her elegant hostess's bright eyes and knew Stefan's circle of friends had accepted her.

"Mr. William and Mrs. Anna Cushman, may I present Miss Anna Sullivan." Stefan bowed his head toward the other couple

"Isn't it lovely we share the same name?" Mrs. Cushman's eyes danced. She offered a gloved hand. "I'm so happy to meet you. We Annas must stick together, don't you think?"

"I would like that." Anna shook her hand, glancing at Stefan for approval, and he nodded.

"You should know—" Virginia wore a satisfied smile, her chin tilting at an angle, "that Mrs. Cushman has the distinction of having been one of Mary Todd Lincoln's bridesmaids."

"*The* Lincoln?" Once again, Anna couldn't fathom how she should be privileged to stand in such high company.

"Well, it was a long time ago." Mrs. Cushman stated as a matter of fact. "Poor, Mary. She hasn't been well since Abraham died. It's all so sad." Her brow wrinkled.

"Merry Christmas, my friend." Mr. Rutherford had come up from behind and slapped Stefan's shoulder. His son accompanied him with a polite smile. "And to you, Miss Sullivan." He came around to join the group.

Anna welcomed the interruption. "A happy and prosperous Christmas to you, Mr. Rutherford, Ian." They'd become great friends since they collaborated to save Stefan's life.

"We have much to celebrate tonight, don't we?" Mr. Rutherford snatched an *hors d'oeuvre* from the offered tray and accepted a glass of Champagne from the other server. He flapped his hand, giving his son approval to join Elizabeth and Prudence in another corner.

"I understand the three of you had a rather harrowing ordeal." Mr. Cushman rocked on his heels.

"Yes, tell us what transpired at the Singing Silver Mine, Mr. Maier. Put to rest all the talk going around town." Virginia waved her half-empty glass.

"All right." Stefan set his glass on the marble-top table, and Mr. Hamill signaled the chamber musicians to desist their playing. "For almost three months, it was a nightmare trying to assemble the pieces …" Guests gathered around Stefan as he poured out a tale that seemed impossible from its inception, a story of Töpfer's treachery and deceit. Anna and Mr. Rutherford filled in the details of the horror they confronted at the surface while Stefan still hung in the belly of the mine.

"But how did the man orchestrate it all?" Mrs. Chaffee asked.

"An excellent question." Stefan rubbed his forehead. "Mr. Töpfer hired Sigmund Dreher to mastermind the plan. He knew the family in Germany and Dreher's mercenary past. If all had gone as he envisioned, Dreher would have done the job and left the country, and no one would have been the wiser."

"Which was?" Mayor Henley asked.

"Dreher assumed Elias Jones knew everything about the hoist system, including what would strain the equipment, and he was right. Without much prodding and a promise of future financial gain, Elias agreed to help him. He conceived the plan to place so much pressure on the wire cable that it would kink and eventually snap."

"What could do that?" Mrs. Cushman's face contorted.

"It was quite ingenious, really. Elias knew I shut down the mine on Sundays and assumed nobody would be around. He also had access to a key to the shaft house.

"Once he and his cohorts got inside, they overloaded the cage with equipment, rocks, and debris. They repeated the operation, starting and stopping, and the sudden release of tension until the cable would rebound and fatigue. Essentially, the wire rope would birdcage." Stefan formed the shape with his hands. "Individual wires within the wire rope would lose their ability to bend as they crossed the pulley and become vulnerable to breakage."

"But Jones would have had to repeat the operation countless times." Mr. Hamill frowned.

"You must remember. Elias had piled an overwhelming amount of weight onto the cage. He couldn't give an exact number, but he said he inspected the rope with each drop to find stress points."

Anna's stomach turned. That anyone could conceive such a villainous act—putting men's lives at risk and destroying their livelihoods for personal gain—could only come from the devil himself.

"I still don't understand how someone didn't see it on Monday morning or even how Elias could know when the cable would break." Mr. Cushman furrowed his brow.

"That's where they were most clever." Stefan spewed a wry laugh. "I usually do my thorough, hands-on inspections on Fridays. We all have to, as Mr. Hamill knows. The Friday before the disaster, I went out of town on business, something Elias would have known. I also trusted him to do the weekly inspections and tell me if he suspected a problem. But, their most ingenious plan was how they controlled when it would break.

"I found remnants of a temporary platform they'd rigged underneath the cage. They piled rock and debris on the platform, so the weight was overloaded even before the men entered the cage on Monday morning. They wouldn't have had enough light at the bottom to notice and probably would have figured any discrepancy in step height was a minor glitch in the hoist. By the time the third group stepped onto the cage, Elias only had to cause a sudden release of tension. By then, it was—" Stefan choked. His hand covered his mouth.

Tears stung Anna's eyes. She linked arms with him, and he patted her hand.

She studied their friends' sympathetic faces and braved a smile. "Mr. and Mrs. Hamill and good friends, these have not been easy weeks." Tears stung her eyes, and she took a moment to compose herself. "Yet, despite the pain and loss we have suffered as a community, God has seen fit to clear Mr. Maier of the charges and deliver the right men to justice."

Clapping resounded across the room. "Here, here."

"Tonight, we are all together this Christmas Eve. Should we not find comfort and joy in the company of those remaining and celebrate the Christ Child's birth?"

A murmur of yeses and nods surged throughout the room.

"Miss Sullivan speaks rightly." Stefan gave her a wan smile.

"Shall we gather in the dining room to commence with the wassail toasts?" Mr. Hamill led them to a table with an ornate silver punch bowl filled with wassail.

"Just think," Stefan whispered in Anna's ear as Mrs. Hamill distributed the cups. "It will be your job to hand out the wassail in our home next year."

Anna looked at him, her stomach churning. "But I—"

"This will be your job as mistress of Maier House for many years to come if you will have me." He spoke softly, all the love beaming in his eyes.

Anna's heart swelled, and she nodded through tears of joy and happiness.

"I've asked Mr. Maier to lead us in the wassail toast this year." Mr. Hamill indicated with his glass. "After all, if it hadn't been for his daring efforts and Miss Sullivan's brave assistance, we might all still wonder what would become of this great community."

"Here, here." Praise resounded among the friends.

"I want to thank Mr. Hamill for allowing me this opportunity. I hope you will indulge me this year. I want to change our traditional wassail by offering an English blessing." Stefan lifted his glass. "From the words of Bob Cratchit in Charles Dickens's *A Christmas Carol*, 'A Merry Christmas to us all, my dears. God bless us!'" He swept his arm up for everyone to answer.

"God bless us, everyone." The assembled elevated their glasses.

"Let us continue in the parlor for the Christmas tree lighting ceremony." Mr. Hamill led the way, showing Anna and Stefan to two chairs near the Christmas tree. He waited until the musicians were ready, then rose to light the candles.

Anna's heart grew with each candle Mr. Hamill lit. Stefan squeezed her hand. Had it only been yesterday their lives had seemed on the edge of the abyss? Never had she believed in her wildest dreams she would sit in the warmth of a home like this with a man like Stefan at her side, enjoying the company of such dear and esteemed people on Christmas Eve.

The musicians struck up "O, Come All Ye Faithful," and the guests erupted in song. When they had sung the final verse, Anna knew what she must sing.

"If it would be appropriate." She uttered to Stefan in a low voice.

He leaned into Mr. Hamill's ear, and the man whispered back.

Stefan rose, his eyes beaming. "My friends, if you attended the Christmas Festival and heard the gifted voices of our madrigal choir, you will also have had the privilege of hearing

Miss Sullivan sing. She has consented now to sing an ancient Irish Christmas carol."

Anna rose and faced her friends, lifting her eyes heavenward and giving thanks to the Lord for all his loving kindnesses.

Good people all, this Christmas time,
Consider well and bear in mind
What our good God for us has done
In sending his beloved son
With Mary holy, we should pray,
To God with love this Christmas Day
In Bethlehem upon that morn,
There was a blessed Messiah born
The night before that happy tide
The noble Virgin and her guide
Were long time seeking up and down
To find a lodging in the town
But mark right well what came to pass
From every door repelled, alas
As was foretold, their refuge all
Was but a humble ox's stall
Near Bethlehem, did shepherds keep
Their flocks of lambs and feeding sheep
To whom God's angel did appear
Which put the shepherds in great fear
Arise and go, the angels said
To Bethlehem, be not afraid
For there, you'll find, this happy morn
A princely babe, sweet Jesus, born
With thankful heart and joyful mind
The shepherds went the babe to find
And as God's angel had foretold

They did our Saviour Christ behold
Within a manger, he was laid
And by his side, a virgin maid
Attending on the Lord of Life
Who came on earth to end all strife
There were three wise men from afar
Directed by a glorious star
And on they wandered night and day
Until they came where Jesus lay
And when they came unto that place
Where our beloved Messiah lay
They humbly cast them at his feet
With gifts of gold and incense sweet.
Wexford Carol, 12th Century

Epilogue

February 1873

Anna recalled the first day she rode through Clear Creek County on the stagecoach, apprehensive about the days ahead. Nothing about these Rocky Mountains had been what she had expected. Indeed, at first sight, the watercolor she'd received from her aunt had depicted a place far more attractive than the harsh reality of it. An irrational fear of the close mountains had cast a shadow over her anticipation of life here. When she'd lost her uncle in the mine disaster, she couldn't fathom why the Almighty would have sent her to this God-forsaken place.

She now knew Laurel had been right all along. Men and women might plan and scheme, but it would always be the purposes of the Lord that would be established.

It had taken her some time and a change of perspective to approach the world with a little more latitude. It had been hard to cast off the prejudices of poverty and predilection without lingering bitterness or regret. But this was a new world where anything was possible.

She turned to see Stefan grinning, and her heart warmed. It was good to see him happy again. All would be well with the Singing Silver Mine, and they were about to embark on their new lives together as man and wife.

"Are you ready to go home, Mrs. Maier?" Stefan held out his hand for her to enter their carriage.

"More than ready." She took hold of his hand and smiled, hoping he could see all the love she felt for him radiating in her eyes. Indeed, the sun shone on Georgetown after all, and though the streets may not have been paved with gold, she'd done precisely what Ma had desired for her—to make better than egg and butter money. "Let's go home."

Historical Notes

Though I conjured Anna Katherine O'Sullivan in my mind while standing on a crest overlooking the Atlantic Ocean on the Dingle Peninsula, women like her existed all over Ireland, especially in the Dingle, considered one of the poorest districts in County Kerry during the nineteenth century.

Between 1837 and 1841, the population of Ireland grew from 6.8 million to 8.4 million as potato cultivation replaced a cereal and dairy-based diet. By 1845, a third of the agricultural land grew potatoes. Living conditions for the population became increasingly difficult with oppressive rents and poor housing. Then, the potato famine struck that same year. Mortality rates sharply rose as reports came in daily of someone who had died of starvation.

Ireland was under British rule, and many blamed the British government, which passed the Corn Laws and other policies that unjustly affected poor farmers. Britain enacted the Poor Law Act in 1838 to help alleviate poverty by legislating the building of workhouses throughout Ireland, but the act gave rise to the overpopulated workhouse system. They needed to construct more workhouses to handle the population, especially when the potato famine struck. Unfortunately, death and disease were as much a fact of life at the workhouse as the famine throughout Ireland between 1845 and 1852.

In the decades following the end of the famine, the peasantry who had survived remained poor. Since the 1700s, only a few wealthy families, called strong farmers for the substantial size of their land holdings, possessed land. These strong farmers generally leased less than five-acre plots to tenants in small cottages. If the tenants couldn't pay the rent, like Anna's Da, they were evicted and often ended up in the workhouse.

Despite the passage of education laws that allowed every child in Ireland to get an education until the eighth form, many Irish discovered that they could only obtain a higher standard of living by emigrating to America or Australia. Women from the peasantry, in particular, had no dowry to marry into wealthier families and couldn't find husbands to marry.

Thus, many immigrants—men and women—found themselves in New York or Boston looking for work. But because there were so many of them and prejudice ran high, signs saying "No Irish Need Apply" were found in various communities. It was no wonder many Irish immigrants traveled west to the Rocky Mountains, where the mining industry grew by leaps and bounds in places like the Territory of Colorado—a not-yet officially sanctioned state by the U.S. government.

Rumors of gold and silver in the Rocky Mountains surfaced long before Europeans arrived in the Territory of Colorado. At that time, the Native American tribes of Utes, Arapahoes, and Cheyennes inhabited the area.

Then, in 1850, a party of Georgians headed west during the California gold rush and found a meager supply of gold on Ralston Creek near present-day Golden. But it wasn't until William Green Russell organized an expedition in 1858 and camped along the confluence of the Cherry Creek and South Platte River (now the heart of downtown Denver) that they found profitable deposits. They established a small settlement named Auraria that later became Denver.

George Jackson was among the party and understood that gold on the plains flowed down from the mountains. He ventured into the Clear Creek drainage, where the valley opened up at Floyd Hill. Following the path to present-day Idaho Springs, he discovered his first gold on January 7, 1859. Rumor spread, and prospectors flocked to the mountains, where they found significant amounts of placer gold (mostly along rivers and creeks). But gold discoveries also sparked fierce competition for claims and available resources, and prospectors moved west.

Two brothers with Russell's party, George and David Griffith, felt discouraged by the number of prospectors and headed to Clear Creek Gorge. Still deterred by the competition, they moved up the valley to the confluence of Main and South Clear Creeks. They had learned by experience in California to look for hardrock veins called lodes on the sides of the valley. They were not disappointed; though they also found a silver vein, they initially ignored it.

Prospectors descended on the area and formed their corporations by day. By night, they retired to their camps, which eventually evolved into settlements. The one near the West and Main Forks of Clear Creek became George's Town.

All seemed to point to a thriving community until the gold bubble burst in 1864, when the constant need for more investment capital never paid off in revenues. George Griffiths packed it in and moved to Mexico. Many other investors pulled out.

In the fall of 1864, three prospectors—Robert Steele, James Huff, and Robert Taylor—discovered an extremely rich silver lode called the Gus Belmont Lode eight miles south of Georgetown on Mount McClellan at 13,200 feet. They headed to Central City to have their samples assayed, discovering a preliminary value of two to five hundred dollars per ton. The silver boom was on.

By the summer of 1865, prospectors from the east flocked to the region, and by September 1866, Clear Creek County was declared "indisputably" rich in ores by Central City's *Weekly Miners' Register*. Georgetown flourished. The town built a post office, and William Barton—a Bostonian—started construction on a two-story hotel. New clapboard buildings, housing banks, and business enterprises sprung up in a growing business district.

The thriving community also needed the infrastructure required, and very quickly, eastern missionaries created churches, lawyers established law offices, and Georgetown's first newspaper, the *Colorado Miner,* ran its first edition in May 1867. On January 28, 1868, the Territory of Colorado legislature declared Georgetown an official town.

Easterners weren't the only ones who came to invest in the mines. Attempting to raise capital to build smelting plants, mine owners also pursued investment from abroad. Robert Orchard Old—a native Englishman who had moved to America—was one man who banked on the silver industry. In 1868, he formed a joint-stock company—the British and Colorado Mining Bureau—with its main offices in London and branches in Colorado. The company shipped ores to England for smelting. Then, when the British saw how productive the mines were, they'd open smelting works in Colorado. His bureau remained prosperous until 1873.

According to historian Christine Bradley in *The Rise of the Silver Queen,* "The town's early rustic appearance [in 1872] gave way to fine homes, level sidewalks, a few trees, and elegant fences ... The streets of Georgetown were packed with new arrivals from every point of the globe ..." including Cornish, Welsh, and German miners, Italian retailers, Irish workmen, and the Frenchman Louis DePuy, who turned a small bakery into the elegant and now historic Hotel de Paris. It was also a town where formerly enslaved people could earn a living and invest in mines. All these elements coincided to create international flare and intrigue as people descended upon Georgetown to make their mark in the mining community."

Colorado became a state on August 1, 1876, and in August 1877, the first train arrived at the Georgetown depot. The Georgetown Loop still takes tourists today on a mile-long portion of track. Georgetown continued to be a bustling Victorian-era mining community until 1893, when the United States Federal Government devalued silver.

OTHER INTERESTING HISTORICAL NOTES

THE BARTON HOUSE

According to a *History of Clear Creek and Boulder Valleys in Colorado,* published in 1880, the Barton House was one of Colorado's most well-known, beloved, and lavish hotels for its comfort, elegance, and modern accommodations. The owner, Mr. William E. Barton, had a reputation for exceptional hospitality. The first house his father built in 1866 burned in early 1871 and was rebuilt and opened in April of the same year.

He operated the house through the summer but missed Boston so much that he sold the house to H.C. Chopin. Mr. Barton returned to Georgetown with his wife in 1876 and repurchased the property. At the time of publication, Mr. Barton still owned and operated the house, which was "beautifully situated on a high elevation on the base of Leavenworth Mountain" … consisting of "two elegant buildings." Clyde and Georgia Tucker were loosely based on Mr. Barton and his wife.

HOT SODA SPRINGS

The Ute and Arapahoe nations first used Hot Soda Springs in present-day Idaho Springs, Soda Creek being the dividing line between the two tribes. Miners later used the hot springs for washing. The property was purchased by Dr. E.M. Cumming in 1863, and he built a wood frame bathhouse and charged for the baths. The property changed hands in 1866 when Harrison Montague tore down the wooden structure and built two large bathhouses known as Ocean and Mammoth swimming baths. Early records show that five thousand people visited the baths yearly and claimed them to have healing powers. The baths still exist today as the Indian Springs Resort and have been modified and updated as a tourist resort. The hot springs would have been where Sigmund Dreher and Elias Jones met to scheme their dirty work.

THE PELICAN-DIVES FEUD

The feud between Stefan Maier and Georg Töpfer is also loosely based on a true account of a dispute that started in 1873 between the Pelican Mine—owners Eli Streeter and Thomas and John McCunniff—and the Dives claim owned by John McMurdy, having purchased part interest from Thomas Burr and a deed from William Hamill. Unfortunately, the Pelican and Dives claims overlapped, and litigation ensued.

At the forefront of the Pelican-Dives case was the apex law or "extralateral rights," one part of the 1872 National Mining Law. According to Christine Bradley in *The Rise of the Silver Queen,* "The right allowed the owners of a claim the exclusive right to mine a vein if the apex, or highest point, occurred within their property. The owner could follow the vein's downward course beyond the property's sidelines but not beyond the end lines unless [they] purchased the neighboring claims ... In reality, such veins seldom existed in the mining world. Veins and ore pockets went [everywhere] and often surfaced in other claims." Fierce feuding between the owners continued into the 1880s, resulting in hundreds of thousands of dollars in litigation fees and one murder. Ultimately, Pelican and Dives merged into one company under William Hamill's direction.

WILLIAM A. HAMILL AND CHRISTMAS AT THE HAMILL HOUSE

Among the many figures in Georgetown's history, William A. Hamill stands out as one of the most important. As a mining mogul, he was one of the wealthiest men in Clear Creek County, making money through land speculation and buying and selling mines in Georgetown and Silver Plume. Mr. Hamill also invested in newspapers, wagon roads, and railroads. He served as a state Senator in the first Colorado State Legislature, Chairman of the Central Committee of the Colorado Republican Party, and State Railroad Commissioner.

William and Priscilla Hamill had five children whose family fortunes were affected by the devaluation of silver in 1893. Mr. and Mrs. Hamill moved to Denver after that. Several of

Hamill's descendants still keep in touch with Historic Georgetown, Inc. (HGI). The most well-known of his descendants is Mark Hamill of Star Wars fame.

Historic Georgetown, Inc. is a not-for-profit corporation that encourages the "preservation of historic buildings, objects, sites, and areas related to the history of Georgetown."* They've worked hard to keep the Victorian character, apparent by its charming houses and community atmosphere.

HGI has lovingly restored the Hamill House. In *A Song of Deliverance,* I took some fictional license since Joseph Watson originally built the house in 1867 as a modest Gothic Revival home. It was only in 1874 that his brother-in-law, William A. Hamill, bought and expanded the house into a lavish mountain estate.

The Hamills were well known for entertaining and enjoyed inviting people to their traditional Christmas celebrations. Historic Georgetown, Inc. holds *Christmas at the Hamill House* each year. I can attest to a delightful evening treated to the yule log procession, a special reading of *T'was the Night Before Christmas*, the lighting of the Christmas tree, as well as an appearance of Saint Nicholas, and Christmas carols sung around the tree by the Silver Plume Singers. HGI also serves traditional Wassail as the Hamills would have done in the 1870s and '80s. Those in attendance are welcome to dress in Victorian costume with bustled dresses and ascot ties to help set the mood.

---

* See https://www.historicgeorgetown.org/about-hgi/

WILLIAM H. CUSHMAN AND JEROME B. CHAFFEE

Two other men who figured prominently in Georgetown were William H. Cushman and Jerome B. Chaffee. Both were friends of the Hamills.

William Cushman founded the First National Bank of Georgetown, which had historic ties to Abraham Lincoln. Cushman built several buildings that still exist today along 6th Street (aka Alpine Street). His wife was Anna C. Cushman, nee Anna Caesaria Rodney, daughter of Caeser A. Rodney, a U.S. Senator and Attorney General. Anna Cushman was a bridesmaid for Mary Todd Lincoln in her 1842 wedding to the future president.

A native of New York, Jerome Chaffee moved to Colorado in 1860 to invest in mining. He helped found Denver, Colorado, and the First National Bank of Denver in 1865. Though he never lived in Georgetown, his mining interests kept him involved in local concerns. He was also heavily invested in the politics of the Territory of Colorado, serving in its first legislature as speaker and later as a territorial delegate to the United States Congress. After Colorado became a state in 1876, Chaffee was elected to the U.S. Senate. His sole surviving child, Fannie Josephine, married Ulysses S. Grant, Jr., a son of the U.S. President.

THE GEORGETOWN CHRISTMAS MARKET

In case you wondered, Georgetown does have an annual Christmas Market. But the Market only began in 1960, making 2024 the sixty-fourth annual year since Historic Georgetown, Inc. produced it. I love the event so much, however, that I believed it would be just the kind of thing that Anna would invent to help the families of Georgetown recover from the mining disaster.

Each year, for the first two weekends in December, Georgetown dresses up the town to resemble a Victorian village covered by fresh fallen snow in the streets with a traditional holiday atmosphere. You'll find horse-drawn wagon rides, Saint Nicholas in his traditional dress, a Santa Lucia procession, a madrigal choir singing in the streets, outdoor food booths featuring homemade treats such as Apfelstrüdel, and shops with arts and crafts and other fun gifts.

CECELIA ROBERTS AND FORMER ENSLAVED AFRICAN AMERICAN CLARA BROWN

One of the most beloved personages in Clear Creek County was a formerly enslaved African American woman, whom people affectionately called Aunt Clara for her generosity and philanthropy. Though not technically a Georgetown resident, Clara Brown first settled in Denver, then moved to the mining town of Central City twenty miles northeast of Georgetown. She eventually invested in real estate and mining properties. After learning about Ms. Brown, I wanted to create someone similar to Cecelia Richards with a few tweaks.

Born into slavery in 1800, Clara spent her early years in Virginia and was sold several times to the highest bidder. A Virginian tobacco farmer, Ambrose Smith, bought her, and she moved with him to Kentucky. At age eighteen, she married Richard, and they had four children. But when Smith died, her husband and four children were tragically sold off to different people across the country. Clara vowed she would never stop looking for them.

Clara worked twenty years for her last owner, hat maker

George Brown, until he died in 1856. His will stipulated that Clara be freed and given money to begin a new life. Touched by his generosity, Clara began to search for her family. But three years later, heartbroken and running out of cash, she gave up.

Convincing a group of gold prospectors to take her west on a wagon train as a cook, Clara came to Colorado in 1859 and worked in Denver as a baker. She also helped two Methodist missionaries set up a non-denominational Sunday School. Eventually, she followed the steady stream of people heading to the mountains to make their fortune in gold and silver.

Clara settled in Central City, where she set up a laundry, offered her services as a cook and midwife, and began saving money. By the end of the Civil War, her income had grown enough to support herself, give to local charities, take in sick and injured miners, and invest in mining properties and real estate. She also set up a non-denominational Sunday School and gave money and time to four churches, holding services in her home and hosting missionary circuit riders.

Clara finally heard credible information in 1882 that her daughter Eliza lived in Council Bluffs, Iowa. By then, her funds had been spent down or extorted by unethical men in real estate, and friends helped her get to Iowa. Once in Iowa, she discovered that Eliza had been living there for some time, and mother and daughter were finally reunited. Newspapers all over the country carried their endearing story.

Clara brought Eliza back to Colorado, where they lived until Clara died in 1885. The Central City Opera House honored this extraordinary woman in 2003 with an opera called *Gabrielle's Daughter,* which they still perform today.

Discussion Questions

1. When Anna Sullivan gets the first glimpses of her new home in the Territory of Colorado, nothing is what she expected it to be—from the grand peaks of the Rocky Mountains to the minuscule size of Georgetown to Uncle Liam's not meeting her at the stagecoach stop. Then, the unthinkable happens when Uncle Liam dies in the mine disaster. What is your first reaction to difficult trials and circumstances when they don't work out as expected? Anger/Frustration? Resignation? Prayer? Read: Psalm 55:22, Psalm 121:3-5, Isaiah 40:30-31, Romans 15:13, Philippians 4:6-7

2. While Anna waits with all the miners' families for word about Uncle Liam's fate, Laurel encourages her. But at the end of Chapter Three, when Liam is among the dead, she cries out in despair of being alone. In Chapter Four, she expresses her feelings. "Was it too much to ask for a life of love, joy, and contentment? Would she always be relegated to this lonely, utter despair?" Was Anna really alone? Have you ever felt alone

in your circumstances? Health issues? Grieving loss of a family member or divorce?
Read: Joshua 1:9, Psalm 23, Isaiah 41:10, John 16:33, Romans 8:28, 35-39

3. In Chapter Five, Laurel sympathizes with Anna's unexpected circumstances and encourages Anna to trust God's providential plan. But Anna scoffs, saying it was a poor plan from where she sat. Have you ever blamed God or accused him of creating poor plans for your life? What is God's answer to your feelings about Him?
Read: Job 38:1-4, 42:1-6, Jeremiah 29:11-12, Romans 8:28, 2 Peter 3:9

4. We learn about Stefan Maier's strengths and weaknesses as he responds to the mine disaster. Our first real glimpse of Stefan's need to see the truth about his life is in Chapter Six when Pastor Thomas challenges his perspective: "You cannot expect God will grant you peace of mind as long as your heart in this matter is corrupted by greed." What do you think Pastor Thomas meant by that statement? Are you willing to root out sin's harmful effects on yourself and others?
Read: Psalm 51: 1-12, Romans 6:12-14, 23, Colossians 3:1-17, 1 John 1:7-9

5. When the ladies come together to form the Christmas festival committee, Cecelia tells her story of enslavement to freedom, finishing with the words, "I don't look down on anyone as if they don't deserve a kindness. I reckon we all got shackles we need to get freed from to get by in this life." What does Cecelia mean by shackles? What shackles have you had to get rid of in your life?

Read; Deuteronomy 5:6-7, Mark 8:14-21, Galatians 5:1 - 3, Hebrews 12:1-3

6. At the beginning of the book, Anna believes forces beyond her control have determined her life. One is the Irish system of land-holding that favored the moneyed class. Social class differences in nineteenth-century Ireland made it nearly impossible for Anna to marry well and find acceptance among her higher-class peers, making her believe class differences would always dictate her admission into social circles. How did Anna's beliefs affect her perspective of the world? How did her perspective jeopardize her relationship with Stefan? Do class differences still exist today? What does God think in James 2:1, 9?

7. Both Anna and Prudence Tucker experienced bullying by their peers. Instead of class differences, Prudence suffered because she was smart and maintained a moral code. In Chapter Twenty-Six, how did Anna suggest Prudence should treat those who persecuted her? Did Anna always follow her own advice? Have you ever been bullied? Did it make you bitter? Have you forgiven those who bullied you? What does the Bible say about loving your enemies and forgiving those who've hurt you?
Read: Romans 12:9-21, Luke 23:34

8. In Chapter Eighteen, when Stefan realizes he's about to lose the Singing Silver Mine and potentially his entire mining empire, Pastor Thomas's words from earlier in the book come back to haunt him. How does Stefan respond to his responsibility for what's happened? Why? What is his motivation? Who does Pastor Thomas compare Stefan to in Chapter Twenty-One?

Read: Romans 7:24 and Romans 5:8

9. Anna and Stefan's attraction for one another grows during the Harvest Ball. Yet, while Stefan wants nothing to do with the trouble between a starving Native American boy and Elias Jones, he's drawn by Anna's compassion toward Dakota. But later, during the dance, when Prudence disturbs Anna and Stefan's intense conversation about his past, and he has an opportunity to show compassion toward Prudence, he disappoints Anna. How should Anna and Stefan have handled their differences at the ball? What do you think about how Anna and Stefan resolved their quarrel on Thanksgiving?

10. We've explored several themes in A Song of Deliverance: love, forgiveness, repentance, kindness, compassion, and impartiality. Can you name others that you've thought of?

Acknowledgments

Every author knows that their books would never have come together without the help of friends, family, advisers, and others on the way to publication. I want to express my gratitude to the following people and organizations.

As always, I want to thank my Lord and Savior, Jesus Christ, for providing me with unfailing inspiration, especially when the words won't come but then arise at a most unexpected moment.

I can't express enough thanks to my husband, Jim, whose love and support throughout the ups and downs of my career have been inestimable. He's truly my backbone.

Thank yous go to Candee Fick, my story editor in the book's early stages. She is not only a great storyteller in her own right but also provided much guidance in helping me develop an appreciation for deep point of view. Thanks also to Amanda Cabot, whose opinion I value for her honesty, even when it was hard to hear. My gratitude goes to other members of Front Range Christian Fiction Writers who critiqued pages at different times: Audra Harders, Brad Leach, Carol Alford, Gretchen Carlson, Jane Choate, Jill Phipps, Jim Franckum, Karen Fischer, Leslie Ann Sartor, LoisAnn Armstrong, Marilyn Leach, Megan Menard, and Sheri Carmon. All of them are incredibly talented writers from whom I've learned a great deal.

I also thank Historic Georgetown, Inc. and Clear Creek

County historian Christine A. Bradley for her solid work in *The Rise of the Silver Queen*. I appreciate my friend Cindy Bell going along with my whims to go back to Georgetown to do more research and nudging me to talk to Christine in person about Georgetown's history.

I also thank my beta readers for their feedback on the flow of *A Song of Deliverance:* Jane Choate, Audra Harders, Wendy Debbas, Becky Jones, Michelle Jones, Cindy Stewart, and Gretchen Carlson.

Appreciation also goes to Linda Fulkerson, Owner/Publisher of Scrivenings Press, for taking a chance on me in her lineup of authors and acquisitions editor Carrie Schmidt—the brains behind *Reading is My Superpower*. Carrie's suggestions to strengthen the novel were spot on and added an element to the book it needed.

Many thanks also to members of our Bible Study group and church who've prayed for me over the years. I firmly believe prayer is the solid foundation girding everything in my life.

Finally, there have been many others in ACFW and elsewhere along the way whose help and advice have been invaluable. God's blessings to all of you.

About Donna Wichelman

Donna Wichelman's passion for writing began in elementary school, writing for the school newspaper. Later, she honed her skills at the United World College of the Atlantic in Wales, Great Britain—an international high school, where she focused on English Literature and discovered her love of the classics by authors such as Jane Austen, Charles Dickens, and William Shakespeare.

One of her most extraordinary adventures occurred researching Emily Brontë's *Wuthering Heights* while at the UWC of the Atlantic and visiting the Brontë parsonage in Haworth, England. While walking the moors on a drizzly day, she came upon an older man with a cap and a cane whose ancestors knew the Brontës. He delighted her with his stories and captivated her imagination with his words. A copy of Emily's poem *No Coward Soul is Mine* sits framed on her desk.

Donna received her master's degree in Mass

Communication/Journalism at San Jose State University in 1987, and she worked in public relations and communications until she turned to writing freelance full-time.

Her essays, articles, and short stories have appeared in various inspirational publications, including *Focus on the Family Magazine, Standard Publishing* for Adult Sunday School papers, and LIVE Magazine. Two of her devotionals also appeared in *A Cup of Comfort Devotional for Mothers and Daughters*.

In 2015, she indie-published *Light Out of Darkness*, a contemporary Christian suspense novel revolving around the unique story of faith and courage in the pre-reformation Christians of the French and Italian Alps known as the Waldensians. The sequel, *Undaunted Valor*, weaves Waldensian history around a contemporary story of intrigue and suspense.

Donna and her husband of forty years participate in ministry at their local church. They love spending time with their grandchildren, and bike, kayak, and travel whenever possible.

You May Also Like ...

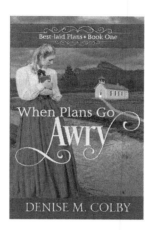

When Plans Go Awry—by Denise M. Colby

Best-laid Plans—Book One

Olivia Carmichael escapes her past to be the next schoolmarm in the small ranching community of Washton, California. Her plan? Live a quiet spinster life, alone, never to depend on anyone ever again.

Luke Taylor selected a mail-order bride, a necessity to help raise his two younger sisters and the only way he knew to protect his heart. His plans don't include being responsible for the beautiful new schoolmarm, who threatens his resolve between his need to stay away and his need to be near to make sure she stays safe.

Along the way, neither feel much in control of their circumstances. Olivia's carefully laid-out plans are challenged at every turn, and Luke's mail-order bride is not what he expected. Will Luke and Olivia learn to trust God's plan for their lives?

Get your copy here:

https://scrivenings.link/whenplansgoawry

Treasure and Trouble—by Betty Woods

Troubles of the Heart—Book One

Eugenia Hampton wants to be loved for who she is, not what she has. Her parents intend to see her married and cared for, but she's determined not to be a mere parlor decoration to show off some man's achievements. She wants a love match or no match.

Paul Stuart is tired of clashing with people over his abolitionist views. Especially with his father who is the overseer for Eugenia's father. He's saving money to move from Tennessee and buy a farm in Illinois where he can live in peace with people who accept him and his ideas.

Paul rescues Eugenia after her horse throws her. They form a secret, forbidden friendship based on their common family problems. Neither of them expects their relationship to grow into love. When Eugenia's father selects a non-Christian man for her husband, she must choose between her known and comfortable life of luxury or a lifetime of love with Paul where little else will be certain.

Get your copy here:

https://scrivenings.link/treasureandtrouble

Scrivenings
PRESS
Quench your thirst for story.
www.ScriveningsPress.com

Stay up-to-date on your favorite books and authors with our free e-newsletters.

ScriveningsPress.com